Seer Stone

Seer Stone

Donna Banta

MORMON ALUMNI
ASSOCIATION
Gone for Good

MORMON ALUMNI
ASSOCIATION
Gone for Good

MORMON ALUMNI ASSOCIATION, LLC

mormonalumniassociation.org

SEER STONE

ISBN

978-0-9900170-4-2

Contact the author at donna.banta@gmail.com

Acknowledgements

I would like to thank Johnny Townsend, Mark Piper, Ruth Wildes Schuler, Jon Shearer, Monya Baker, Marion Deeds, Margaret Speaker-Yuan, Terry Connelly, Jennifer Gowans-Vandenberg, and C.L. Hanson for their invaluable help.

For Mark Steven

Part One

The Perfect Man for the Job

"The tragic reality is that there have been occasions when Church leaders, teachers, and writers have not told the truth they knew about difficulties of the Mormon past but have offered to the Saints a mixture of platitudes, half-truths, omissions, and plausible denials."

D. Michael Quinn, "On Being a Mormon Historian," lecture before the Student History Association, Brigham Young University, Fall, 1981

Ten miles northeast of Parowan, Utah
March 2010

They want to forget what happened here, but I will not let them. Decade upon decade I have paced this creaking house, from the labyrinthine upstairs to the cobweb-laced parlor to the seedy great room to the vacant, cavernous kitchen that was once so warm and vibrant. My moans echo the halls. My ranting fills the emptiness. I whisper prayers in the darkness. And sometimes I roar.

They come to trespass, but I chase them off. I stand on the threshold and send them roaring, even into madness.

They want to forget what happened here. I will not let them. I will not leave until what was stolen is returned, and the inheritance recovered.

R omano crossed the black marble foyer of the upscale townhouse, the click of her leather flats muffled by paper booties. New construction. She could still smell the paint. She began on the ground floor. A sparsely furnished living room, an empty area probably intended for a dining room table, and an antiseptic kitchen. She opened the door to the garage to see a silver late-model Mercedes C300. Romano stepped in just far enough to lay her gloved hand on the hood. It was cold.

She closed the door, backtracked through the kitchen and living area, and climbed the stairs, one hand on the railing, her auburn ponytail tucked under a surgical cap, blank wall looming at her side. Officer Davis stood beside the door, securing the scene. She nodded to him and then to his partner, Sparks. She lifted the police tape an inch and peered into the room.

The victim lay sprawled on his right side on the bedroom carpet. Male Caucasian, around six feet tall, with fair, thinning hair, and dressed in a white button-down shirt, navy slacks, and black socks. A gold wedding band. No watch. The bullet had entered through his left temple and then blown out the right side of his cranium. Just beyond him an open gunmetal gray safe stood about three feet in height. It now served as a receptacle for the victim's skull and brain matter.

Romano looked over at Davis. He was as handsome as ever with his smooth dark skin and doleful brown eyes. A bit jumpy, though.

"Who's the vic?" she asked.

"Robert McKay Christiansen," Davis answered. "Medical doctor, age fifty-four."

Romano sensed even greater uneasiness in Davis's reply. Couldn't be that the crime scene had gotten to him. He'd seen plenty of those. She figured it must be her presence. He was likely still embarrassed about their uncomfortable confrontation last month. That would be when he abruptly broke off their almost two-year relationship because he just wasn't ready for "the next step." He couldn't commit. How original.

But that was history. Today they were professionals at a crime scene. "Did the deceased live here alone?" she asked.

"Yeah. He leased this place in January," said Davis. "He and his wife had separated."

"Who called the police?" Romano asked.

Davis again. "One of the nurses on his team. He hadn't shown up for surgery at the hospital. When she couldn't reach him on his emergency line, she called us."

"A welfare check, then. How did you access the premises?"

Now Sparks. "That low window in the dining area was unlocked."

Romano checked her watch. Nine thirty-four. "What time was his surgery?"

Davis's face clouded. He looked at Sparks. "Dunno," Sparks mumbled. Davis shrugged. "EMT's ballparked death about two hours ago. They just left."

"Passed them on the way in," Romano replied, still studying the scene. There was an unmade king-sized bed that looked slept in on one side, next to it a nightstand that held a cheap reading lamp and an expensive smartphone. A gold watch, a ring carrying keys and a car remote, some spare change, and a black leather billfold were bunched into a small circle atop a plain oak dresser.

"Happen to notice the make of that watch?" she asked.

"Rolex," Davis replied. "Looked like the genuine article."

"So presumably the killer wanted whatever was in the safe but passed on the nine-thousand-dollar watch," Romano observed.

"And the cell," Sparks added.

Romano craned her neck under the tape. Another plain cabinet housed a flat-screen TV. The closet door was open, revealing four crisp dress shirts sheathed in cleaners' plastic. Beneath them a pair of wingtips and some running shoes. Efficient and impersonal. Like a three-diamond motel room. Romano padded across the hall in her booties. The room opposite was just as spartan: a desk, a chair and another flat screen, this one attached to a computer. In her brief walk through, nothing in the downstairs living and kitchen area had earned Romano's notice. In fact, except for the carnage inside and around the safe, there wasn't a trace of blood anywhere, or dirt, or even shoeprints in the carpet. The place barely looked lived in, much less like the scene of a possible struggle.

She turned back to the officers. "Any theories?"

"Well, it's definitely not a suicide," Davis said, his voice still uneasy.

Romano smiled tightly. "Yes, I think we can assume that he didn't blow his brains out and then dispose of the gun." She glanced over at the victim and then back at Davis. "Also the casing."

Davis's face fell and he looked at his feet, just as he had during last month's uncomfortable confrontation. "I was being facetious."

"Forensics," a familiar voice shouted.

"Up here, Gatz," Romano called. Gatz and his partner, Mosely, climbed the stairs, both of them decked out in Tyvek suits.

"Whoa, Nellie," Mosely said when he saw the corpse. "That blood's mighty fresh."

Romano glanced at the gold watch on the nightstand. "Looks like he was getting ready for work."

"He's still in his stocking feet," Gatz observed as he crossed under the tape and aimed his camera at the victim.

"I want his mobile and his computer when you're through," Romano said. "And the car, too. It's in the garage."

"Sure thing, Lieutenant," said Gatz.

"Thanks, gentlemen. These are close quarters. We'll leave them to you."

Romano descended the stairs with Davis and Sparks following behind. She went through the front door, thanked the officer positioned outside, and then steadied herself on the porch railing with one hand, slipping off her booties with the other. After that, the surgical cap.

"Do you have contact info for the wife and the nurse who reported him missing?" she asked Davis as she peeled off the nitrile gloves.

"I do." He pulled out his notepad, tore off a page, and handed it to her. "There's something else I need to tell you."

"Oh yeah? You got some more brilliant theories like that suicide scenario?"

Davis blinked and Sparks smirked.

Romano immediately regretted her question. She was a professional, damn it. "What do you need to tell me, Officer Davis?"

"Christiansen was a Mormon."

"How do you know he was Mormon? Did you see some evidence of it in his house?"

Davis nodded. "I saw one of those passes to get into the Mormon temple on his kitchen counter."

"Good observation," Romano conceded.

A hint of that grin grazed his lips. She looked away, wondering briefly if he was dating anyone.

"Also, I'd seen him before, when you and Ryan were working that other case involving the Mormons…you know, the double murder."

She turned back to him.

"Christiansen was at that Mormon wedding reception, the one for Congressman Newsome's daughter."

Romano remembered the case and the reception but not Christiansen. However, she did recall those cute little outfits she'd sprung for back then. Solely for Davis's benefit. Now *she* was embarrassed. Romano buttoned her mouse gray suit coat and slipped the paper with the contact information into her brown leather messenger bag. She bid the officers goodbye and then ducked under the police tape and headed to her car, mentally chiding herself again for the cheap shot at Davis just now. Ryan had never spoken to her so unprofessionally. But then Ryan had never been her lover. She could at least give herself credit for that.

Somehow that didn't make her feel more professional.

When Matt Ryan retired last year, Romano knew she'd have to work hard to fill his shoes. She was younger and far less experienced. She sensed that some men in the department suspected she was promoted only because she was a woman—Davis among them, probably. Maybe Ryan, too. But she'd aced the lieutenant's exam and worked hard over the past year. She'd *earned* that promotion.

Nevertheless, at this moment she found herself asking: What would Ryan do?

A quarter past five in the afternoon and I was just now sitting down to read my morning paper. Not that I didn't already know the lead story. News of the Christiansen murder had been all over the radio. I opened to the headline: *Local Heart Surgeon Slain*. Everything beneath that was a blur. I sighed and reached inside my shirt pocket for my half glasses. A few months ago I'd resigned myself to the fact that I couldn't read a damned thing without them. But they'd yet to become a habit.

Glasses perched on my nose, I studied the picture of the once happy family. The caption identified the late Bob Christiansen, his now estranged wife, Annie, and his son, Sean, who was currently serving an LDS mission in Japan. Annie Christiansen. I'd met her three years ago at the Swizzle Stick. Copper hair, forest green eyes, and very married. Though not anymore, evidently.

The sound of crunching plastic startled me away from my *Abbottsville Gazette*. My namesake, two-year-old Ryan Zimmerman, had just hurled the choo-choo train I'd bought him across my living room. His bright blue eyes danced as he pointed at the wreckage.

I nodded back at him. "Good arm there, sport."

When I set up my private investigation firm last year, the first thing I did was convert my daughter's old bedroom into an office for my assistant. The second thing I did was hire Carrie Zimmerman to be that assistant. One of the many plusses to this arrangement was that Mrs. Z sometimes brought little Ryan to work with her. Bored with the hand-me-down amusements his mother brought for him, the kid had so far broken a pair of my reading glasses, lost my TV remote, and reupholstered my furniture with toilet paper. Tuesday I made a trip to the toy store, in part because I loved the little goofball, and in part because I was curious to see how long any child-oriented invention would hold his attention. Looked like the train was the first to lose his interest.

Little Ryan ambled around the maze of new merchandise he'd strewn across my living room floor. He snatched up his Tonka truck, rolled it across my coffee table and growled out the sound of an engine. I reached over and patted his peach-fuzzed head.

Mrs. Z emerged from the office carrying a manila folder. Style had become her new modus operandi. Today she wore a black silk top, cream-colored slacks, and ankle-high black leather boots. She stopped at the edge of the living room and stared at us. "Ryan, what on earth are you doing?"

One of the minuses to this arrangement was that it wasn't always clear which one of us Mrs. Z was addressing.

She took the truck away from her son and set it on the floor. "You shouldn't be playing on the furniture." Then to me, "And you should be putting together that report for Ms. Molino."

I gazed up at her over the top of my glasses. Two years ago, Mrs. Z had been the beleaguered, heavily pregnant Mormon housewife who'd helped me catch the guilty man trying to frame her husband for murder. Now she was my on-the-ball, svelte, lapsed Mormon assistant who was still helping me, only getting paid to do it.

"Right now I'm busy being this 'lil goofball's nanny," I told her.

"More like his partner in crime."

"That too," I admitted. "But I need the break. I spent half of last night and all of today chronicling the painfully predictable activities of Mr. Molino and a gentlelady who calls herself Mizz Delight."

"Ms. Molino has called twice today. She's very anxious to hear about your discovery." Mrs. Z handed me the folder and pen. "Checks for you to endorse."

"Thanks." I took the folder from her with my left hand and held up today's headline with my right. "Got any inside scoop on this?"

She sighed. "What a terrible thing. Unfortunately, I haven't a clue. Paul and I don't hear much since we quit going to church, and the Christiansens weren't in our ward. But my guess is the Mormons have Annie Christiansen high on their list of suspects."

"Oh yeah, how so?" I unclipped the pen she'd attached to the folder and opened it to find three checks. Two more were probably in the mail, making for a pretty good take by the end of the month. So far, the work hadn't been interesting, but at least it paid the bills.

"Annie's an ex-Mormon. That makes her capable of all sorts of crimes."

"Aha. Does that mean you're a suspect as well?"

"Could be."

I turned over the first check. "Got an alibi?"

"Just you."

"Pretty flimsy then." I shook my head as I signed. "Poor Romano."

"She's got her work cut out for her."

My mobile pulsed inside my pants pocket. I handed back the folder and then pulled out my phone. *Romano* flashed across its screen. "Speak of the devil." I hit accept. "Lieutenant Romano."

"Ryan, how's it going?"

"Can't complain. Know who popped the Mormon doctor yet?"

"Nope. I was hoping you could help me out on that."

"How so?"

The landline rang. Mrs. Z picked up little Ryan and hurried to the office to catch it.

"I was going over your notes on the Bishop Loomis case," she said.

"That was three years ago."

"Right. But it's still in your unsolved case file."

I took off my readers, returned them to my pocket, and then rubbed my eyes. "Thanks for reminding me."

"It says here that you met the vic's wife, Annie Christiansen, at The Swizzle Stick on January 23, 2007."

"Yes, I met Mrs. Christiansen at or around that time. She was with a couple of other former Mormons. One of them, Mark Crawford, has become a good friend. The other gentleman, I can't quite recall—"

"Steven Kelly."

"If you say so."

"What was your impression of Annie Christiansen?"

Hmm, how should I put it? Stunning? Gorgeous? "I thought she was helpful. I remember her explaining the Mormon female dynamic to me."

"Did she say anything about her family?"

"I believe she said that her son was dating one of our suspects in the Loomis case at the time. April Newsome, remember? Daughter of that dick, Dennis Newsome."

She chuckled. "Now, now. Mr. Newsome is our esteemed congressman."

"The only estimable thing about that arrangement is that he spends most of his time in Washington. I may actually vote to keep him there another two years."

"I know about your animosity toward the congressman, Ryan. And the former connection between April Newsome and Mrs. Christiansen's son is in your notes. I'm looking for something you didn't write down, perhaps because it didn't pertain to the case. Something about her husband, maybe."

"OK, let me think." I rubbed my eyes again and then pinched the bridge of my nose. "I remember a huge diamond on her left hand. I remember her saying that her husband was still an active church member. Oh, and I remember that toward the end of the conversation she left abruptly to go home to him."

"Like she felt guilty? Like he would be mad?"

"I didn't read that much into it. Only that she'd stayed longer than she'd told him she would."

"Did he even know where she was? He was this stalwart Mormon, and she is very attractive. Would she admit to him that she'd been out drinking with three other men?"

"She barely did any drinking. Not even half a glass of wine. As for the male companionship, Mark Crawford is gay, this Mr. Kelly had all the markings of a happily married family man, and I have to believe you don't think that I posed a threat to their marriage."

"According to her, they were definitely getting a divorce. But the doctor was still wearing his wedding band. Also, most of his belongings were at his former home, where Mrs. Christiansen resides. The doctor only had a few things at his townhouse. Some new clothes, a computer, and a safe that had been emptied, presumably by his killer."

I shrugged. "There are two sides to every divorce. Where are you going with this, Romano?"

"Well, she's the wife. Naturally, I needed to contact her. I tried her all day yesterday. No luck. I finally reached her at home this afternoon. She'd just come back after a few nights in San Francisco. She wasn't forthcoming about where she had been staying and claimed her mobile was dead. I was the first to tell her about her estranged husband's murder."

"I confess I'm not good about charging my phone. Half the time Mrs. Z plugs it in for me. And the murder just happened yesterday when she was out of town."

"Yes, but she was in San Francisco not Shanghai. It was all over the news."

"Maybe she wasn't listening to the news. We all need a break from it now and then."

"Maybe. Anyhow, she seemed genuinely upset at the news of her husband's murder, but not surprised. Then she let slip that while she was away her art studio and bedroom had been ransacked."

"Only the studio and bedroom?"

"That's how it looked to us. Crime lab guys found several clean prints, but all belonged to either Mrs. or Dr. Christiansen. She was nervous as hell the entire time we were there and insisted nothing had been stolen."

"Sounds like the intruder was after something specific. Maybe he or she didn't find it."

"True, and there was plenty there to steal. Silver, jewelry and gemstones, electronics, a handgun, registered to Dr. Christiansen, and not recently fired. No clips. The killer appeared to be after something at the murder scene, too. Only the doctor's place was as clean as a whistle, like a professional job. No visible clues. Just the vic, in front of his empty home safe, brains blown out, apparently at close range."

"A hired hit, maybe?" I yawned. "One intended to make a statement."

"That was my impression, yes. But then Mrs. Christiansen's studio and bedroom were just a mess, only there was no sign of a break-in, no broken lock or window."

"A professional can get in and out without a trace *and* make a mess without leaving any prints."

"True," she admitted, and then paused. I could tell she was considering what I'd just said—in fact, I could almost hear her mental gears clicking through the phone line. I envied her. It had been two years since I'd had a case I could really sink my teeth into.

"Mrs. Christiansen seemed to know more than she was letting on," she said finally. "I even wondered if she might have staged it herself. It's this bad vibe I got from her."

"Staging the break-in? That's quite a leap."

"It's been done before."

"Yes. But there's usually an obvious motive, like a false insurance claim. You just said Mrs. Christiansen didn't report anything missing." I stretched my legs and free arm to their fullest extent, like a cat. "That being said, sometimes I get vibes when I'm on a case, too. My general rule is to pay attention to them."

"Thanks, Ryan. I appreciate your willingness to let me pick your brain now and then."

"My pleasure. Makes me feel useful again."

"Seeing my Aunt Angie tonight?"

Because I was dating her paternal aunt, I allowed Romano one question about my social life per our occasional conversations. "She's fixing me dinner."

"Saw that necklace you gave her."

"Good luck with the case, Lieutenant."

"Bye, Ryan."

I pocketed my telephone and looked up to see Mrs. Z approaching, a sleepy-eyed little Ryan resting on her hip.

"Packing it in for today?" I asked her.

"In a minute. That was Annie Christiansen on the phone just now."

"You're kidding, right?"

"She wants to hire you."

Now I was the one getting the bad vibe. "To do what?"

"Didn't say, only that you're the perfect man for the job. She wants to see you. Tonight, if possible."

Annie Christiansen wants to see me. Annie with the soft voice, forest green eyes...and dead husband. I handed Mrs. Z my phone. "Would you please add her number to my contacts?"

"What is this job that I'm supposed to be perfect for?" I wondered aloud as I steered my Honda Accord into the lot at Angie's place.

Exhaustion took hold of me. I'd had maybe two hours of shut-eye over the past twenty-four, and that had been on and off outside the local Sheraton where Mr. Molino and Mizz Delight had holed up until checkout time. Still, I wasn't sure I would rest until I knew what Mrs. Christiansen wanted. I took out my phone and toyed with the notion of calling her. Instinct told me it was a bad idea, that I should stay away from her and the Mormons altogether. My mobile writhed in my hand and "Alice" lit up the screen. I hit accept.

"Hi, sweetheart."

"*Hi*, Dad."

I waited for her to go on. Something had to be up or she wouldn't be calling on a weeknight.

"I have some news."

"Did you get the internship at the design firm?"

"No. Well, I haven't heard back on that yet. But this is even better."

"What, then?"

"I'm getting married."

I shut my eyes. "I suppose you mean to Dirk?"

After a prolonged pause she replied. "We've been living together for almost three years, Dad. Of course it's *Dirk*."

"Right. I knew that. What I meant was…congratulations. When do you and Dirk plan to get married?"

"Maybe as soon as next month. It depends on how quickly we can pull things together. Also on you, of course."

"Me?" I asked, still processing. My only child was getting married. I figured I would probably have to attend. "As you know I don't lead much of a social life. Just let me know when and I'll be there."

"You don't want to be in on the plans?"

"Should I be?"

"You're the father of the bride, Dad. You're supposed to pay."

I'm supposed to pay. The words lingered in the air, as though in a thought bubble.

"Don't worry, we'll keep the cost down. The City Hall is free."

Free. So far so good.

"Then a smallish dinner reception at our favorite restaurant in Burbank, with an open bar, of course. Like you, I don't have that many friends. But Dirk has some good buddies, also family."

An open bar for Dirk and his good buddies—on me. "So, ballpark estimate on the headcount?"

"We're thinking thirty-five tops, plus anyone on your end. You'll bring Angie, of course."

Angie? To my daughter's wedding? "That wouldn't be appropriate."

"Not appropriate? Dad, you've been dating for two years."

Still struggling to grasp the situation, I momentarily lost myself in the mental multiplication of Dirk's thirty or so pals times the conservative estimate of six cocktails per person. "Are you two set on this joint in Burbank?"

"It's our favorite, Daddy."

My heart stirred at the sound of her calling me Daddy. "Sure, honey, it's your decision. I'm just wondering, with such a big crowd and all, if maybe a different venue makes more sense. One of those all-you-can-eat buffets, maybe? With the unlimited soft drink refills?"

Another prolonged pause. "I know this is a lot for you to absorb," she said finally. "We'll talk more later. But Daddy?"

"Yes?"

"I'm really happy."

Again, my heart stirred. "I'm happy for you, sweetheart."

"So what are you doing tonight?"

"Dinner at Angie's. I just pulled up to her condo."

"Tell her right away so she can keep her calendar open."

"Be safe, Alice," I replied, and then signed off.

I checked my watch. Six fifteen. I was already late for dinner. I put my phone back and pulled down the visor to look in the mirror. My baby blues were bloodshot and rimmed with dark circles. I found my drops in the glove box. Several blinks later I checked the mirror again. No improvement. Sighing, I got out of the car, tucked my sagging blue dress shirt back into the waistband of my tan khakis, pulled my tweed sports coat off the back seat, and slipped it on.

As I walked to Angie's building, I reflected on my daughter's news. Alice was marrying Dirk. Dirk the actor. Dirk who launched his career last year with a supporting role in the low budget flop, *Bunz*. I guess I shouldn't complain. Despite poor results at the box office, the film had managed to get him into SAG. And, despite the overall bad reviews, Dirk had garnered some grudging nods from the critics. He even had a part lined up in a new sitcom set to air on some cable channel not included in my subscription. What the hell, maybe I could get him to chip in on the tip for the bar tab.

While he wasn't my first choice for a son-in-law, I had to admit that Dirk loved my daughter. Truth be told, I wasn't all that surprised by Alice's news. I'd anticipated, and at times dreaded, this announcement for months. What hadn't occurred to me was that I might bring Angie along. That threw me for a loop. It seemed premature to invite Angie to something as intimate as my only daughter's wedding. But then, was I going to feel guilty if I didn't? Hard to say.

I put on my readers, scanned the list by the intercom, and pushed the button next to *A. Romano*.

"Is this the police?" she purred.

I smiled and rolled my eyes. "Yes, ma'am."

"Do you intend to search me?"

"Absolutely."

"But officer, what if I'm not decent?"

I glanced over my shoulder and then answered, "Makes my job easier then, doesn't it? By the way, your neighbor's standing next to me. Should I bring her up, too?"

The buzzer rang. I opened the heavy glass door, strode through the lobby to the elevator, and rode it to the seventh floor. Angie was leaning against the inside of her doorframe, arms folded across her chest and smiling. The peach-colored dress complemented her dark eyes and hair, and the tiny pearl drop I'd given her dangled above her neckline. I slung my arm around her waist, pulled her inside, and closed the door behind us.

"One of these days your next-door neighbor *will* hear you talking dirty to me through the intercom."

"No way would you let that happen." Angie wrapped her arms around my neck. "*You'd* be even more embarrassed."

"Oh, yeah?" I kissed her, my exhaustion melting away. It wasn't until several lingering seconds later, when we finally parted, that the delicious aroma from her kitchen invaded my senses. She saw the recognition on my face.

"Osso buco," she explained. "My grandma's recipe."

"I've died and gone to heaven."

"Well, you certainly look the dead part. Sit down, Matt, take off your coat." She slipped off my tweed jacket and pointed me to a beige upholstered armchair. The dining room table was set for two with a candle at its center. A bottle of red wine was open and breathing. She draped my folded sports coat over the back of the sofa, poured some wine, and brought the glass to me.

"Cabernet Sauvignon. It has antioxidants," she said. "Better for you than scotch."

I smiled up at her. "You take care of me."

"Somebody has to." She kissed the top of my head. "Dinner in a few and no, I don't need help."

Angie disappeared into the kitchen. Ordinarily I would protest her refusal to let me help, but tonight I was too tired to muster the objection. I stretched out in the chair and sipped the wine. It was tasty but didn't hit the spot the way a good scotch from my favorite bartender would right now. I shut my eyes and revisited that night at The Swizzle Stick. Annie Christiansen had run a slim finger around the rim of her wine glass. A bazillion carat diamond sparkled on her left hand.

I shook the image from my thoughts, opened my eyes, and gazed out the living room window. The sun was setting over downtown. If I pushed forward a little in my chair, I'd be in a position to see the police headquarters where I used to work. But I lacked the motivation. Downtown Abbottsville. It wasn't my view of choice. A couple of years ago I'd been all set to move back to San Francisco. Then I walked into an elevator at Abbottsville Hospital and met Angie Romano.

"Dinnertime," she said.

Angie was lighting the candle on the table. Its warm glow reflected against her soft cheeks and lovely wide-set eyes. She blew out the match and looked my way. "Coming?"

"Sure," I replied, my gaze still fixed on her. "I was just enjoying the view."

She grinned. "How about enjoying the meal before it gets cold?"

Wine glass in hand, I sat down and then waited for her to begin before taking a bite of veal shank.

"Angie, this is amazing," I said, once I'd swallowed.

She looked on as I took my second, then third bite. "When did you eat last, Matt?"

I stopped to think as I chewed. "This morning sometime. A couple of peanut butter cups."

"How nourishing. Were you on a stake out?"

"I was following a married businessman and his nubile paramour."

She sipped her wine. "You do have interesting work."

Actually, I didn't, and decided to change the subject. "How was your shift today?"

"Two babies, both healthy, both firstborns."

"I'll bet their moms were grateful to have the most talented nurse practitioner on the staff at their sides."

"I think they were more grateful for the painkillers. So, what did you think of his nubile paramour?"

"Class with a capital K." I poured more wine in our glasses and then casually inquired, "Say, do you know anything about that Dr. Christiansen who was murdered?"

She shook her head and swallowed. "Only that my niece is investigating the case. Also that he was a committed family man."

"Family man? He was getting a divorce."

"I was surprised to see that in the paper this morning." Angie used her knife to slice another piece of her veal off the bone. "But then I rarely saw him. He was a heart surgeon; they don't drop by to visit the babies all that often. Why do you ask?"

"Just curious."

We ate in silence for a stretch. My mind returned to that night at The Swizzle Stick. Annie's hand had felt soft and cool when I'd shaken it goodbye. My eyes had followed after her all the way to the door.

"Penny for your thoughts," Angie said, startling me back to reality.

I coughed and cleared my throat. "You'd be wasting your money."

"Not sure about that. Judging from your expression, I'd guess your mind's still on a certain Mizz Delight."

"I've already thought of her more than I care to." I laughed as I used my napkin to wipe my mouth.

She giggled. "Was she dressed attractively?"

"I'd describe it as obviously."

"Sounds better than the late-late show."

"It's not, I assure you." I set down my fork. "Delicious meal, Angie.

Sorry I'm not better company."

"You're fine." She took our empty plates to the kitchen. "Would you like dessert? I have chocolate ice cream."

"Thanks, but no. Any more and I'll drop off to sleep here at the table." I poured the rest of the wine into her glass, picked it up along with my own empty one, and followed after her.

"You cooked, I clean up." I set the glasses on the counter.

"I just have to rinse the dishes and put them in the machine."

"Meaning even I can handle it." I opened the dishwasher and nodded at her glass. "Finish your wine."

"Yes, sir." She picked up her drink and went to blow out the candle on the table. Then she came back and leaned against the refrigerator, swirling the wine in her glass. "Can you stay tonight?"

I shut off the water and looked over at her. "I gotta work."

Her face fell. "You worked last night."

"I know. I'm sorry, Angie."

She frowned.

"I need to have a report on the investigation first thing tomorrow. Also, I've got a call back to a potential new client."

"Oh yeah? Who's the new client?"

I turned away, busying myself with loading the last of the dishes into the machine. "I'm not sure I'm going to take on the case yet…but I promise I'll make it up to you. This weekend maybe?"

She smiled sadly. "So we're back to the weekend."

Ten fifteen and I was finally driving away from Angie's place, having sat through all of *The Blind Side* with her after dinner. Sullen, and clear across the sofa from me, she obviously wasn't in the mood for fooling around. She'd wanted me to stay over. She always wanted me to stay over. In fact, if Angie had her way, I'd be staying over every night and living out of half of her closet. But I wasn't ready to take that step.

Hell, I wasn't even willing to invite Angie to Alice's wedding, and not without reason. If I took a date to my kid's wedding, pretty soon people would be asking when the two of us were getting married. That wasn't a step; that was a leap.

When I was young, I was dying to take the leap, having proposed to my wife three months after we'd met. We were together for eighteen years until she died. Maybe that was the problem. I was never going to get over her.

I slowed to a stop at a red light. Like the good cop I would always be, I took in my surroundings. The sidewalks were empty, and I was the only driver sitting in the three northbound lanes. I obediently waited, tapping out an impatient beat on the steering wheel. Not a single car crossed the intersection. Downtown Abbottsville after dark. In San Francisco the party would just be starting.

The light turned and I hit the gas, my frustration gathering as I drove. Annie Christiansen had wanted me to call her back tonight. Now it was probably too late. As much as I'd wanted to, I'd have felt guilty about calling her from Angie's place. For that matter, I'd felt guilty for *thinking* about her at Angie's place. Fact was I didn't even want Angie to know Annie had called me. Much less Romano. Meaning I probably shouldn't call her back at all.

What I should do was outline the Molino report for Mrs. Z to compose and email tomorrow. If I set my mind to it I could have it done in an hour. That was, if I didn't go home. At home I'd be asleep on my sofa inside of ten minutes. What I needed was a well-lit diner and a pot of coffee. As luck would have it, the local Denny's was in the next block. I slowed at the sight of the iconic red and yellow logo, began to turn into the lot, and then hesitated—just long enough for the image of the scotch bottle to yank me down the road to The Swizzle Stick.

Hank the Regular waved at me from his stool. "Hey, Ryan. The old ball and chain give you a night off?"

"She's not a ball and chain." I slapped him on the back and then found my spot at the end of the bar.

Gus plunked a scotch down in front of me. "Nice of you to drop by."

"It's not like I've abandoned the place."

Gus scowled, shook his head, and went back to drying glasses behind the bar. I sipped my scotch, pausing to enjoy its progression down my throat. Definitely my beverage of choice. I sipped again, and then took out my pen and the pad with my notes on the Molino case. My thoughts returned to Mrs. Christiansen. The booth where we'd met was only a couple of yards away. Forest green eyes.

I glanced at the clock on the wall. Ten thirty. It occurred to me that she might still be awake. Given the events of the past twenty-four, she'd likely be up all night. I threw back more of the scotch, pulled my mobile out of my coat pocket and scrolled my contacts. They were all a blur. I exhaled in disgust, reached for my readers, and then froze.

No need to call. She was standing right beside me. Same copper hair, same green eyes, only this time with glints of turquoise. At first I thought it was my mind playing tricks on me. It was late, I was exhausted, and the scotch had gone straight to my head. But then she spoke.

"Lieutenant Ryan, I was hoping I'd find you here." A voice that could melt butter.

"Mrs. Christiansen," I breathed.

"Please call me Annie." She nodded at the stool next to me. "Mind if I sit down?"

"Of course not, Annie. And I'm not Lieutenant anymore. Just Ryan. Or Matt."

She smiled. Moist pink lips and small glistening teeth. "Ryan, then. It suits you."

Annie lowered her slim frame onto the seat and set a small black leather purse on the bar. She wore tight blue jeans and a loose-fitting white cotton blouse that tucked neatly into her waistband. The blouse was open at the neck, revealing a silver chain that ran down the length of her pale, lightly freckled throat, over her delicate and well-defined collarbone, and then disappeared into the folds of white cotton. I fought the urge to envision its ultimate destination.

"Like a drink, miss?" Gus asked.

"Yes, please. A glass of chardonnay."

"Put it on my tab, Gus, and bring me another too, will you?"

"On the way," he replied.

"Thank you, Ryan," Annie said.

"My pleasure."

"I called your office today and left a message with Carrie Zimmerman. Did you get it?"

I nodded yes and then drained the rest of my scotch. Gus poured me a refill and set a chardonnay in front of Annie. She picked it up and drank deeply, leaving less in her glass after one sip than she had after an entire evening three years ago. Her face was ashen, her eyes nervous, and her mane of copper-colored curls appeared to have been combed with her fingers. Romano had described her earlier as shaken up. She still was. Years of experience had taught me to distinguish real versus fake distress. This was the real thing. She'd just seen a ghost.

"Mrs. Z said you want to hire me."

"I do. You're the perfect man for the job."

"And what job might that be?"

She ran a finger around the edge of her glass. No diamond this time. "I want you to find who killed my husband."

"Police will do that for you for free."

"No." She shook her head. "They think I killed him. But I didn't, Ryan. Honest to god. I could never..." Her voice trailed off and she took on an expression so confused that I found myself suddenly tempted to take her in my arms and hold her.

I sipped my scotch instead. "Any idea who did?"

"Yes. And I'm afraid he might be after me now."

"Who's after you?"

"I don't know his name. He knocked on my door last Friday night and asked to see Bob. Something about an inheritance."

"An inheritance? What did he mean by that?"

"No idea. I told him that Bob had moved out. He asked where he'd moved. I lied and said I didn't know. He tipped his hat and thanked me. Very polite. In fact, he seemed harmless at the time."

"He was wearing a hat?"

"A cowboy hat, yeah. Also boots, jeans, and a western shirt. He was tall and skinny and I'm guessing in his mid-forties."

"Caucasian?"

"Yes, with blue eyes. Whatever hair he had was covered by the hat. He drove off in a big black pickup with Utah plates." She reached inside her purse for a slip of paper and smoothed it out flat on the bar. "This was the license number."

I glanced at the page, only a blur without my readers. "OK, I could track that down, to whoever owns the vehicle, that is. But why am I the perfect man for this job?"

"I feel good about you." She returned the paper to her purse. "I think you get me."

"Why do you—"

"The minute the guy left I called Bob," Annie interrupted. "He flipped out."

"Flipped out? How come?"

"Because he knew the guy and thought he was a creep."

"He knew him? Why was a successful doctor associating with creeps?"

"Part of his hobby, not his profession. He collected Mormon memorabilia. Some of the people he bought the stuff from were a little weird. In fact, *he* was getting to be a little weird. That's one of the reasons I kicked him out."

I swallowed more of my scotch. "What kind of memorabilia?"

She let loose a sigh and picked up her glass. "Letters, old journals, out-of-print Books of Mormon, antiques that once belonged to Brigham Young and the like."

"Any of it valuable?"

"Not to me, certainly."

"So you didn't keep any of it?"

"Oh, no. I made him take it all with him when he left. I wanted him to take everything, but he dug in his heels and refused to pack his clothes. He still thought we could patch things up. I knew that would never happen, but I caved and said he could come back for his clothes." She rolled her eyes. "That was four months ago."

"What did you mean when you said Bob was acting a little weird?"

"He was always online on this Mormon chat forum, getting worked up over this and that. Also he started hoarding historical stuff and hiding it all over the house. I'd open my drawer and there'd be some moldy old letters tucked in between my t-shirts. Drove me crazy. I had left Mormonism behind. Meanwhile, he'd become obsessed with it. The marriage was over."

I watched her sip her wine. The silver chain shimmered against her creamy, slim throat. I couldn't help but sympathize with her ex. She'd be damned hard for any man to leave. "So, what did Bob tell you about the guy in the cowboy hat?"

"He told me to never open the door to him again. Made me promise to load up the handgun he'd left behind for my protection. I had no intention of doing so, but for the sake of appeasing him, I said that I would."

"Did the cowboy hat return?"

"Not that night, and I was awake most of it worried that he would. The next morning I called one of my colleagues at Grafton College—um, I teach art there."

"Yes, I remember."

"Really?" She eyed me curiously, her gaze so intense it compelled me to look away.

"I was on a case. I took good notes." Out the corner of my eye I could see she was still watching me, wineglass in hand. A couple of long seconds later she took a sip.

"Anyhow." Annie set down her glass. "My colleague has a loft in San Francisco. She let me escape there for a few days. Took my phone but forgot the charger. I came home today to find my bedroom and studio turned upside down. Then I learned that my soon-to-be ex-husband was dead."

Swirling my drink, I sorted through the events in my mind. "So you last heard from Bob on Friday night?"

"That was the last time I spoke to him. He called me twice on Tuesday night but my phone was dead." Annie reached inside her bag and produced a cell phone. "He left me this message."

After a bit of scrolling, she punched a button on the screen and held the phone to my ear. I leaned against it to listen, feeling the tip of her soft finger on my temple, and catching a whiff of jasmine from her skin. "Annie, please call, I need to talk to you right away," a male voice, presumably the doctor's, barked in my ear. I leaned away and she returned the phone to her purse.

"This was Tuesday, the night before he was murdered?"

"Yes. He left the message at eight forty-five. But I didn't listen to it until today, when I finally plugged my phone in. My missed calls show that he tried me again twenty minutes later but didn't leave a message."

"Any other missed calls or messages when you got back?"

"Lieutenant Romano had called twice and left one message. A couple of missed calls from colleagues and an 800 number."

"Anything stolen from your house?"

She shook her head and then reached inside her handbag, pulled out a wrinkled wad of paper, and smoothed it out on the bar. "Someone threw this through my front window an hour ago. It was wrapped around a rock."

I put on my readers and peered down at the message.

Where's the inheritance?

"Times New Roman, bold type, italics, fourteen-point font." I fingered the paper. "Feels like twenty-pound stock. Could be from anywhere, including my office." I returned my readers to my pocket. "See anyone outside your window?"

Annie shook her head. "I was in the back of the house when it happened, cleaning up the mess," she explained, and then finished the last of her wine.

"Like another?"

Her hands still trembling, she set down her empty glass. "Yes, please."

I motioned first to Gus and then to the crinkled paper. "I take it you haven't shown this to the police?"

"No. They—that Lieutenant Romano—she thinks I'm guilty."

"The spouse of the victim usually makes the list of suspects."

Gus returned with both the wine and scotch bottle. He poured chardonnay almost to the rim of Annie's glass.

I glanced at my drink, still one sip left. Better to take it slow. "I'm good for now, Gus."

He nodded and walked away.

"Why do you believe Romano thinks you're guilty?"

"It's this feeling I have." Annie took a sip and then combed her fingers through her thick, curly hair. "Also the questions she asked me. Did I know I was still the beneficiary of his life insurance? Did I know the combination to his safe? I didn't even know he *had* a safe."

"And the insurance?"

"He never said and I never asked." She picked up her glass and then set it down without drinking. "But it doesn't surprise me that he hasn't changed things. I wanted the divorce and he didn't. Like I said, he hadn't even come back for his clothes."

"So you don't trust Romano, but you do trust me?"

"Yes, I feel good about you. Ever since that first time we met. Of course, I was married at the time."

"Yes, I remember."

"I'm not married anymore."

I met her eyes. "As of yesterday."

She frowned. "It's been over for a long time."

I finished my scotch, noticing that her glass was already half empty. I turned to signal Gus for the check. He had his back to us.

"You're not married, are you, Ryan?"

"Does that matter?" I asked.

Her lips parted but she didn't speak. Instead she gazed back at me with a disconcerting intensity. It was almost as if she could see right through me.

I reached in my pocket for my wallet. "No, I'm not married. But I'm in a relationship."

"Really?" She seemed genuinely surprised.

Exhaling, I estimated the tab plus tip and pulled some bills from my wallet. "Yes, really."

Annie ran a finger around the rim of her glass. "Most people who are in relationships aren't out drinking alone at this hour."

"You want to investigate *my* life, hire a different detective." I slapped the bills on the counter.

She shrugged and threw back the rest of her wine.

"I'm sorry," I began and then stopped, refusing to be drawn in. Then, looking into her lovely eyes, I realized that, like it or not, I already was. "I'll need to see where your intruder was searching."

Annie led the way in her white Volvo station wagon, its rear com-partment stuffed with easels and canvasses. I followed behind her in my Honda, still apprehensive about taking this case. Investigating the murder could put me at odds with Romano, and I liked having her on my side. Moreover, my physical attraction to this potential client could hardly be helpful. Nevertheless, I was inexplicably drawn to her, for reasons beyond her looks. Also, this was shaping up to be an intriguing potential case. For the first time in two years I felt excited about going to work.

We traveled down quiet, leafy streets lined with properties that increased in value as we progressed. Her house was a sprawling midcentury nestled in the middle of a tree-lined block. Its only light glowing from somewhere deep inside. She opened the garage door remotely and drove inside. I pulled into the drive behind her and climbed out of the car. She motioned me in through the garage.

"Let me go first," I said. "Make sure it's safe."

"You don't need to do that." Annie hit the button on the wall and sent the big garage door sliding to a close. Then she opened the door into the house and stood still for a second, her green eyes glowing in the dim light. "It's OK for now but we need to make it quick," she said.

She strode in ahead of me, flipping on light switches as she walked. We entered through an efficient laundry room and then passed into the kitchen. Stainless steel appliances, black granite countertops and oak cabinets. She dropped her handbag onto a round wooden kitchen table.

"Whoever broke in didn't spend much time in here," Annie said, and then, pointing to the refrigerator added, "Only the freezer door was ajar. I guess because people sometimes hide valuables in the freezer."

"Did you?" I asked.

"Just an occasional Dove Bar." She showed me to the dining room and twisted a knob on the wall. A delicate crystal chandelier shone from dim to bright over a solid mahogany table. Annie pointed to the buffet against the wall. "Didn't bother with my grandmother's silver, either."

"Metals are selling pretty high these days." I followed after her to the living room. The furnishings looked modern and expensive. Likewise the art on the walls. I was about to ask if the paintings were her own work when I saw the broken glass strewn across the polished wood floor, and beyond it the missile itself. I knelt down to inspect it. A smooth gray stone that could have been snatched off any number of landscapes in the neighborhood. Still squatting, I looked through the window to imagine the rock's trajectory. The street was too far away for it to have been a drive-by. Whoever had done this had to have approached on foot, probably flinging it from the middle of the walk.

A car engine ignited, headlights flashed through the front window, and tires peeled over the pavement. I jumped up and bolted out the front door to see a large, dark pick-up turn the corner at the end of the block. I couldn't make out the license plate. Pulling out my Maglite, I strode up the sidewalk, shining its beam along the curb until I spotted tire marks in front of the house next door. The treads looked large enough to fit a truck tire. I paused and studied the neighbor's house. Another ranch style with an expansive porch and a large double door. Except for the porch light, the place was dark, suggesting the occupants were either asleep or not at home. I looked up and then down the block. The silence was deafening. A person walking to his car would have generated noise—heels on pavement, the beep of a remote lock, a car door slamming. Any or all would have caught our attention on so still a night. We'd heard nothing. Had somebody been parked and sitting in his car when we'd pulled up? If that was so, I hadn't noticed. And I was pretty good at noticing things like that.

I turned back toward Annie's place to see her standing inside the door-frame, her arms hugging her chest like she was cold. "That didn't sound like anyone from the neighborhood," she said.

"You know the folks next door?" I asked as I closed and locked the door behind us.

"Yeah. They're a nice retired couple."

I peered out the front window. The spot where I suspected the car had been parked was just out of view. "Well, whoever it was is gone."

"For now, anyway."

Sensing her anxiousness, I turned my attention back to the glass on the carpet. "Where were you when the rock came through the window, Annie?"

"In my studio cleaning up. That's where most of the mess is—also in the master bedroom where Bob's stuff is stored."

"Let's go see."

She led me to a room at the end of the hall and switched on the light. More modern, expensive furniture, only this time in complete disarray. The contents of two tall dressers had been dumped onto the king-sized bed, heaping it with a mound of men's and women's disheveled clothing and upended empty drawers. The handgun the doctor had left behind for her was atop a trinket-strewn nightstand. All this mess in her bedroom, and she'd been busy cleaning her studio?

"Don't you plan on sleeping here tonight?" I asked.

"I never sleep in here anymore. I'm down the hall in what used to be the guestroom."

I nodded, taking in the mound of clothing on the closet floor. This wasn't a burglary; it was a search. And whoever broke in apparently didn't even care about hiding that fact.

"Where's your studio?"

"In here."

We passed through some French doors to a room that had obviously once been a patio. The floor was concrete, and windows covered three of the walls. The fourth, the one that housed the door we'd just come through, was still composed of the home's stucco exterior. The room was stuffed with easels, canvasses, paints and palettes, not exactly neat, but certainly put back together after the break-in.

"Most of the mess was around my jeweler's bench," Annie said, anticipating my question. "He'd dumped out the drawers."

She pointed to a high desk attended by a tall stool and a small torch attached to a fuel tank. A series of narrow drawers ran up its right side. I opened the top one. It held files, tweezers, and other tiny tools. Some larger pliers and a wad of steel wool filled the second. Then the third was jammed with gemstones divided into small Ziploc bags.

"You found these valuable stones just dumped out on the floor?" I asked.

"Yes. Also the gold and silver sheets and tubing from the bottom two drawers."

Stepping away from the desk, I peered out the window into the darkness. "I take it this is your backyard?"

Annie flipped a switch on the wall and the exterior lights revealed more concrete patio, and then a broad lawn that sloped downward and ended at a row of trees.

I ran a hand over my head and let it rest on the back of my neck. "There's no fence around this property?"

"No. We've never had a dog, and it's pretty safe here, up until now, that is."

Looking back at the jeweler's bench, I returned to the spot where Annie would have been working. From that vantage point a break in the trees afforded me a view of the street corner. "And these outdoor lights, were they turned off when you were back here straightening up?"

"Yes, I don't like having them on, they're a distraction." She flipped the switch, at once again eclipsing the backyard. "Why do you ask?"

"Just curious." It occurred to me that whoever had thrown the rock might have first spotted Annie from the street corner. Or perhaps he'd even come as close as the backyard. She couldn't have seen him from inside this brightly lit studio. "Do you recall hearing any noise before the front window broke?"

"No," she replied, fear seeping into her voice.

Some headlights appeared at the corner. A large dark vehicle idled several seconds at the intersection and then slowly turned right onto the cross street.

She stared back at me, her eyes widening. "Ryan, I'm beginning to feel like I should get out of here. That we both should."

"You're right," I said. "You can't stay here."

"Where can I go? I've already returned the keys to the loft. It's too late to collect them from my colleague now."

I blinked and looked out the window. In the darkness, all I could see was her reflection in the glass. Copper curls and small shoulders. If I took her home, I'd have to sleep on the sofa. Me on the sofa, and Annie in the bed ... Annie in *my* bed.

"Ryan, you really are the perfect man for the job."

I looked away from the window and back at her. Forest green eyes.

"OK, Annie. Go pack some things and I'll patch up your window. We'll leave your car here and I'll drive you to the Abbottsville Sheraton. You'll be safe there. I know the night manager."

H e was standing in the middle of my kitchen floor, gripping the thing with jelly-covered hands and shaking it up and down.

Having just come from the bathroom, I gasped, and then crept cautiously toward him. "OK, buddy, stand still, and whatever you do, *don't drop it.*"

"Bounce!" Little Ryan burst into giggles and launched my laptop into the air.

I reached down and made the save inches before it would have smacked the linoleum. Exhaling, I tucked the slim, silver Notebook under my arm and then took Ryan by the hand. "How 'bout we find some real toys to play with?"

He wriggled out of my grip and scampered toward the living room. I heaved another sigh and took the computer to the counter to wipe off the jelly. As I dampened a paper towel, I saw that this morning's cereal bowl was no longer in the sink, likewise my coffee cup and last night's scotch tumbler. Also, the porcelain was sparkling white and there was cleanser residue around the drain. I frowned. Mrs. Z again. I cleaned the jelly smudges off my laptop, tucked it back under my arm, and then went to the office. Mrs. Z smiled up at me from behind her desk. Her pale blonde hair was curled under pageboy style and her snug pink knit top flattered her slender frame.

"Is he being good for you?" she asked.

"He's always good."

Her smile faded. "What's he doing now?"

"Playing in the living room. Leave him be. He's fine."

"You know I don't expect you to watch him for me."

"You know I don't expect you to clean the kitchen for me," I told her.

"I don't do it for you, I do it for *me.*"

"Same goes for me and little Ryan," I said, truthfully. Although the kitchen was another matter. It was one of the disadvantages of working out of my home. I tried to keep all of my mess contained in my bedroom, but it had a way of seeping into the rest of the house. "I guess I should hire someone to clean up around here."

Her smile returned. "You mean like at a real office?"

Nodding, I dropped into the fake leather easy chair and squared the computer on the desk's edge. "I emailed you my outline of the Molino case."

"Yes, I saw. I'll get it out ASAP. So you're serious about taking on Mrs. Christiansen as a client?"

"Yes. Problem?"

Mrs. Z smirked. "You may reconsider when you hear what I've learned so far."

"Were you able to trace the license plate of that Utah truck?"

"Yup." She tore a page from her notepad and handed it my way.

I read aloud. "D. Wendell Flake, on Old Highway 91 outside of Mona, Utah."

"I also found Dr. Christiansen in an LDS chat room." She pointed at my laptop. "Check your email. I sent you a link just now."

I opened up my computer and blinked at the fuzzy icons on the screen. Mrs. Z was fishing a pair of my readers out of her drawer when a crash sounded from the direction of the living room.

"Oh my gosh, I hope that wasn't the lamp." She jumped from her chair, tossed me my glasses, and rushed from the room.

"Relax," I called after her. "It was the Tonka truck."

A couple of seconds later she returned. "You were right," she told me. "It was just the truck."

"Yup. I've got his sounds down. It's the detective in me." Glasses now perched on my nose, I scrolled my inbox to the message from Mrs. Z.

"This is the last day, Ryan, I swear," she promised as she settled behind her desk. "I've got a new babysitter lined up for next week."

"Sure you can swing that on your salary?" I knew that she already paid for pre-school for her youngest daughter.

"It will be tight until September. Then all three girls will be in public school. Also, Paul can help out. He works at home two days a week."

"That's good," I replied, although I couldn't help but worry that Mr. Z, a busy CPA, might grow tired of working with little Ryan underfoot while his wife left home to earn a pittance from me. "Hopefully by then I can afford to give you a raise."

"All part of my plan. Did you get my email?"

"I did," I said, and returned my attention to the laptop. The body of her message contained only a hyperlink. I clicked on it. *Real Mormon History* appeared across the top of my screen. Beneath it, someone who called himself Truth Seeker wrote: *Does anyone have any information about the original family that lived in old Hatcher Farm outside of Parowan?* "What am I looking at?" I asked her.

Mrs. Z pushed away from her desk and rolled her chair over next to mine. "It's the bulletin board for this Mormon history site I just happen to know about. All I had to do was go back one week and I found him."

"Where does it say this was one week ago?"

She pointed to the screen. "The date is at the bottom of every post."

"You're saying this Truth Seeker person was Dr. Christiansen?"

"No." She reached across my lap, tilted the computer toward her and used the arrow key to scroll down the screen. "Truth Seeker asked the question, then midway down the thread, Bob Christiansen weighed in."

She turned the computer my way again. Before me on the screen was a post from "Mormon Doc": *The Hatcher Farm originally belonged to Zedekiah Hatcher, patriarch of a large polygamous family during the mid-nineteenth century. It is some ten miles northeast of Parowan, Utah. He received revelation through a seer stone, which I now have in my collection.* Attached to the post was a picture of a small round brown stone with two tiny side-by-side holes pierced in its center. Its diameter, handwritten along the edge of the photo, was 30 millimeters, roughly the size of a half-dollar.

I looked back at her. "What the heck's a seer stone?"

"A magic rock. Joseph Smith used one to write the Book of Mormon. He put it in the bottom of his hat and looked inside to see visions."

"Why the hat?"

"Kept out the light."

"Aha! And there were other Mormons besides Joseph who used these rocks?"

"Oh, sure. I grew up in Parowan. It was like the seer stone capitol of Utah for a while. People used them to find missing children, tell the future, decide which crops to plant and when. I remember seeing my Great-Grandpa Tanner with his. He had visions all the time. Claimed the stone told him to marry my great-grandma."

"That was a good thing."

Mrs. Z smiled and rolled her eyes. "Not sure she thought so. Right after he died, she pitched the thing into the canyon."

Intrigued, I straightened in my chair. "Had you heard of this Hatcher Stone?"

"Not until today."

I returned my attention to the post about the stone. "How do you know this Mormon Doc was Doctor Christiansen?"

"At first I only suspected it. Then I called the guy who owns the website. He checked his stats and was able to trace the poster's IP address…"

Taking off my glasses, I squeezed the bridge of my nose and blocked out the rest of her explanation. The technobabble was obscuring the material point. "OK, but wait," I said, returning the glasses to my face. "You called this website owner, and he just offered up this information? Why on earth would he do that?"

"He's my favorite cousin."

The words—*he's my favorite cousin*—repeated over again in my mind. Then the room fell silent around me, save for some faint but persistent tapping in the distance.

"What's he banging on now?" Mrs. Z started to rise from her chair.

"Don't get up. It's his wood hammer. He's pounding another square peg into a round hole."

She sat back down and I refocused on the screen. Mormon Doc's admission had prompted a slew of responses, most of them requesting personal phone or email exchanges. And now we had an insider who could track them for us. I looked at her over the top of my readers, incredulous. "Who is this cousin and where does he live?"

"Name's Jesse Pratt. He lives in Parowan. Half the people in Parowan are my cousins. But Jesse's the one I'm closest to."

"How amazingly fortunate."

"Really? And how is that?"

"Because you and your cousin, Jesse, can lend great insight into this investigation."

Mrs. Z frowned. "The best insight I can give you is to drop this case."

"What are you talking about?"

"Jesse located all the people who responded to Mormon Doc on the thread. They're all in Utah."

"He can place their locations?"

"Oh, yeah." She reached over and scrolled a few posts down the thread. "This guy, the one who calls himself Marshmallow Man, is the scary one."

I adjusted my glasses and then focused on his post—merely a brief request for a private correspondence and an email address. "He's scary because?"

"Jesse tracked him to a house in Mona, Utah."

"Where our Mr. Flake lives?"

"Most likely it's him, yes, and most likely he's the guy in the cowboy hat you told me about. The one who paid Mrs. Christiansen a visit. I found his driver's license online; she can ID the picture. And Mona property records show he's the sole owner of a house on Highway 91. I looked up its street view on Google Maps. It's on a huge parcel of land."

"So he's rich."

"Not necessarily. Land in plyg country doesn't sell for what it would here."

"Excuse me? Plig?"

"I mean he's probably a polygamist. Mona is in Juab County, that's smack dab in the middle of it. My advice would be to raise heaven and earth to find that stone and hand it over to him. Either that or troll the banks of Lake Grafton until you come up with one that looks just like it."

I took in her solemn expression. Little Ryan's hammer still pounded in the living room. "Aren't you being a little alarmist?"

"Ryan, I grew up around these people. I know them. He's a patriarch, out in the middle of nowhere, presiding over his own little fiefdom. My guess is he wants to be a prophet. But he can't do it without this rock." She reached over and squeezed my wrist, surprising me with a rare physical gesture. "Believe me, Ryan, he will do whatever it takes. He's on a mission from God."

"Like the Blues Brothers." I shot her a smile.

She didn't return it.

I stood and set my laptop on the desk. Stuffing my hands in my pockets, I paced across the room and then turned to face her. "You think he'd kill for this seer stone?"

Carrie arched her brows. "Could be he already has."

Had to admit, she had a point. "Have you printed out his picture for Mrs. Christiansen to ID?"

She rolled her chair back around to her desk. "It's next on my list...*if* you still plan on taking her on as a client, that is."

"You want a raise, we've got to have clients."

"Well then, she first has to sign a contract *and* send us a substantial retainer."

"OK. Handle it via email. She has internet at the Sheraton."

"Speaking of which, is her room coming out of that retainer?"

"Sure," I mumbled and glanced over the top of my glasses to the window.

My backyard flowerbed, I noticed, was now filled with new plantings about to bud. More of Mrs. Z's handiwork. She probably got tired of looking out at my old weed-patch. For *her,* not me. The newly organized flowerbed posed a stark contrast to the mess the intruder had left at Annie's house. I could imagine our Mr. Flake guilty of that. But the homicide?

"Doesn't make sense," I ventured. "According to Romano, Christiansen's murder scene was as clean as a whistle. Like a professional job."

"So?"

"Could a hick from Utah—" I began, and then caught myself.

Mrs. Z smiled. "Don't underestimate us Utah hicks, Ryan."

"Indeed I won't."

Another crash in the living room. Mrs. Z jumped from behind the desk and rushed after it.

I dropped back into the fake leather chair, took off my readers, and rubbed my eyes.

That had been the lamp.

It took five minutes to clean up the shattered mess, and an additional twenty to convince Mrs. Z that my late wife's grandmother's art deco floor lamp was really a reproduction I'd picked up at a garage sale.

Her mind at least partially at rest, Mrs. Z printed out the pictures of D. Wendell Flake and the Hatcher Stone for me. Then, with a chastised little Ryan banished to the corner beside her desk, she returned her attention to the computer screen. "I'll see if Jesse can help me ID the others who inquired about the stone."

"Good idea. See what else you can find out about Flake, too. Is he really a polygamist? What line of work is he in?"

"Sure thing."

As I turned to leave, my daughter's copy of the classic, *The Runaway Bunny,* caught my eye from its spot on the bookshelf. I took it down and handed it to little Ryan. He accepted it mournfully. I patted his peach-fuzz head.

"OK, Mrs. Z, I'm off. Call if you need me."

"You want me to call, you'd better take your phone," she replied, her eyes glued to the screen. Then before I had a chance to ask, she added, "Kitchen counter, should be all charged up by now."

"Good thinking," I shouted as I unplugged the mobile. The screen lit up to show that it was indeed fully charged. Also that I had two text messages. I put on my readers. One was from Angie, the other from Annie. It occurred to me that my girlfriend and my client had practically the same name. The notion that I might confuse them when talking to one or the other struck me with dread.

The first text, from Angie, had come in at eight forty: "Missed you this morning." I glanced at the clock on the coffee maker. Ten thirty. Too late to catch her before her shift. I made a mental note to call later, then scrolled to the second one. It had just come in. From Annie Christiansen: "Check out time is 12:00, not sure what to do next." I texted back: "Stay put, I'm on my way."

I hopped in the car and headed downtown to the Sheraton, making good time in the late morning traffic. It was a bright, cool spring day, and last night's misgivings seemed to evaporate in the sunshine.

Mrs. Z had done a crackerjack job of tracking down Flake and the seer stone. But there were still unanswered questions.

For example, why the glaring difference between the murder and burglary scenes? And why were there no unfamiliar prints at the burglary? Sure, a professional could get in and out without a trace, but then why leave behind such a mess? Had it been done intentionally? Also why the cryptic note about the inheritance? If Flake really wanted this stone, wouldn't he have asked for it specifically and arranged a delivery point? Was it Flake who sped away from Annie's house last night? The loose ends continued to gnaw at me, so much so that when I approached the hotel at ten forty-five, I took an extra spin around the block to process more of my thoughts.

Stepping out of the elevator, I strolled the thickly carpeted corridor to room 605, knocked on the door, and smiled in the direction of the peephole. A few seconds later I heard the rattle of the chain lock, the turn of the knob, and Annie's invitation to come in. She looked pale, pretty, and considerably more composed this morning, with her hair in neatly combed curls and her make-up carefully applied. She wore a powder blue long-sleeved light wool dress with a wide scoop neckline. The silver chain shimmered along her throat and then disappeared underneath the fuzzy, blue fabric.

"I just approved and returned your contract to Carrie Zimmerman. Also a retainer via PayPal." She turned and led me into her room. "You're not cheap."

"Nope." We passed by a long bathroom vanity. Her black leather handbag lay partly open atop the counter, and a small rectangle of soap sat next to the sink.

"I made coffee. Would you like some?" she asked.

"Thank you, yes."

"Black, right?"

"Sure." A shiver tickled my spine. Annie seemed to know a lot about me—how I took my coffee, how I wasn't married, how I wasn't ready to commit to my girlfriend. Last night's misgivings began to resurface. Maybe meeting in her hotel room wasn't such a great idea.

I found some relief when I saw that her overnight bag was packed and sitting on a foldout luggage stand and that she had gone to the trouble to loosely remake the bed. I walked toward the table-for-two against the window. Behind it, the view of downtown included my girlfriend's condominium complex. If I'd wanted to, I could probably have calculated which windows belonged to her. Instead I took a seat in the chair facing the opposite direction.

Annie brought two ceramic mugs to the table and sat across from me. "Sorry it's just hotel coffee."

"Looks great." I took a sip. It wasn't too horrible, on par with my local gas station anyway. "Get some rest last night?"

She nodded, her eyes surveying the room. "I felt safe here."

"Good. Hopefully you'll be even safer tonight." I went to my coat for the copy of Flake's picture, unfolded it on the table, and fished my readers from my shirt pocket.

"That's him," she said, before I had the chance to ask. "He's the one who came to my house Friday night."

"You're sure?"

"Positive. Who is he?"

Returning my glasses to my pocket, I explained, "Name's D. Wendell Flake. He lives outside of Mona, Utah."

Annie grimaced and then took a drink of coffee. "Mona? I wonder if he's a polygamist."

"We're looking into that."

"Do you think this Flake character killed Bob?" she asked, wrapping both hands around her cup. Her fingers were long and slim and lightly freckled. No rings.

"He's certainly a suspect."

Annie slid her chair away from the table and crossed her legs, hiking her skirt partway up her thigh. I noticed a small mole above her right knee.

"I've no idea what that inheritance could be. But whoever threw that rock wants to hurt me."

"Why do you say that?"

As she sipped her coffee, the wide neckline of her wool dress slipped over her shoulder, there was no sign of a lingerie strap. "Just a hunch."

"Annie, I need more than your hunches to go on. Have you had contact with anyone else who might have been doing business with your husband?"

She shook her head slowly. "No. At least not that I know of."

"It's possible a suspect will show up at his funeral. Have you made any arrangements yet?"

"I'm having his remains shipped back home to his hometown in Colorado," she said. "Bob's mom and sister will hold a Mormon service for him there."

"Oh," I mumbled, confused. I picked up my cup, but instead of drinking, blurted out, "You didn't want a service here, for your son and your acquaintances? His patients?"

She paused to comb her fingers through her hair. I noticed she wasn't wearing earrings, only the long chain that disappeared into her neckline. Strange for a woman who had a jewelry-making studio in her home.

"Our son, Sean, is in Japan serving an LDS mission."

"Yes, I know," I replied, my cup still stalled halfway to my mouth. "But I assumed he'd be coming home for the funeral."

She smiled sadly and gazed out the window. "You assumed wrong. He's not allowed to come home."

"That seems harsh," I said, although she didn't appear to hear me.

"Bob must have communicated with Mr. Flake on the internet," she said, turning back to me. "Is there a way we could get ahold of his computer?"

I sighed. "Possibly, if my former partner, Romano, agrees to share information with me. But Mrs. Z did the next best thing. She found some communication between Bob and Flake on a website." I patted my coat to find the pocket where I'd left the picture. "Have you ever heard of a seer stone?"

"Joseph Smith used one to translate the Book of Mormon."

"Well, apparently Smith wasn't the only Mormon who used a seer stone. There were others, including this polygamist named Zedekiah Hatcher. He lived outside of Parowan, Utah in the 1800's." Still searching my pockets, I began to wonder if I'd left the copy of the photo in the car, when I saw that it had, in fact, adhered to the underside of the picture of Flake. I passed it to her.

Annie's eyes widened.

"Evidently your husband acquired this so-called Hatcher Stone. He posted this picture of it online. We've deduced that this is what Mr. Flake meant by his *inheritance*."

"Oh my god," she breathed.

"Have you seen it before?"

"Yes."

"Have any idea where it might be now?"

"Sure do," she replied and then pulled the long, thin silver chain out from underneath her neckline to reveal a glossy green and brown pendant with two tiny side-by-side holes at its center.

Blinking rapidly, I reached for my readers. "Are you telling me *that's* the Hatcher stone?"

"Evidently." She held it away from her neck for me to see. "How was I supposed to know that on top of all those old letters and journals, Bob was hiding magic rocks around the house?"

I took the pendant in my hand and ran my thumb around the edge of its silver bezel and then across the rock's shiny surface. It was green and brown with flecks of gold, and still warm from her body.

"It was in a drawer in my jeweler's bench, along with some other stones," she explained. "Just a plain brown rock with tiny little holes, but it intrigued me somehow. So, I threw it in my polishing tumbler and this amazing color appeared. It was so beautiful that I just had to set it."

I took off my readers, let go of the stone, and watched it drop softly in place on the outside of her dress.

"I've worn it ever since. Funny, but I feel like it's been protecting me." She carefully tucked the seer stone back underneath the blue wool. "Maybe it *is* magic." She shook her head almost imperceptibly. "Gosh…how crazy would that be?"

"Pretty damned crazy," I replied. "In fact—" I froze at the ringing of the room landline. I stared at the phone and then back at Annie. "You tell anyone where you were?"

"Of course not."

I stood and picked it up on the nightstand. "Hello?"

There was a short pause, a click, and then a dial tone. I glanced out at the view of downtown. Dozens of windows looked into ours, in Annie's condominium tower alone. In *Angie's* condominium. I dialed the hotel desk.

"Front desk, this is Peter," a cheerful voice sang.

"Peter, this is Matt Ryan in 605. Did you just transfer a call to my room?"

"Yes, sir, I did."

"Do you have any idea who it was? We lost connection."

"He didn't say."

"It was a man, then."

"Yes. Um, he spoke with a slight twang."

"Did he ask for me by name or room number?"

"By name. Of course, we don't give out room numbers."

I shut my eyes. Why the hell did I reserve the room on my card? "Right. Thank you, Peter."

"Mr. Ryan?" Peter said as I was separating the phone from my ear.
"Yes?"

"Whoever it was first asked for Ann Christiansen. Then for Ann Snow. Then he asked for Matthew Ryan."

"Thanks, Peter. Listen, I'd like to check out now, can you take care of that for me?"

"Absolutely. I'll charge the card you gave us. Just leave the key in the room and you're good to go."

Dropping the receiver in its cradle, I looked over at Annie and asked, "What's your maiden name?"

"Snow. Why?"

"Never underestimate a hick from Utah," I said, mostly to myself, then, "We need to leave."

"Don't worry," I said as we rode the elevator down. "He was probably calling through a list of hotels until he found us. We'll be gone before he gets here."

Annie gazed back at me, her demeanor cool and collected, perhaps thanks to the stone. Its magic had no such effect on me. I scanned the lot as we approached my car. A man in a business suit stood on the curb. His hair was white blonde and his eyes were hidden behind mirrored aviators. I kept watch on him while we buckled our seatbelts and then on the rearview mirror as we turned onto the expressway. No sign of a black pickup or any other suspicious vehicles. Satisfied that we weren't being followed, I recalled Mrs. Z's words this morning. *He's a patriarch, out in the middle of nowhere, presiding over his own little fiefdom. Now he wants to be a prophet. But he can't do it without this rock.*

"Is there any way you could turn that stone back to its original appearance?" I asked.

She pulled the green and brown swirled pendant up and held it in the palm of her hand. "It would be easier to find another brown rock and doctor it to look like the original."

"You could do that?"

"Sure. At home in my studio."

I checked the rearview mirror again. No apparent sign of a tail. "I'd rather not go back there just yet. Is there another place you could use?"

"The classroom at the college."

Probably too obvious as well. The last thing I wanted was for this Flake character, or whoever it was, to suspect we might be making a reproduction. I was about to explain this when she interrupted my thoughts with, "Or my colleague's loft in San Francisco. I could bring my tools."

"Sounds good. Why don't you arrange to collect the key from her?"

While Annie called her colleague on her mobile, I wondered where we might find a replacement for the seer stone. I thought back to the picture Dr.

Christiansen had put up on the internet. The Hatcher Stone was just a small riverbed rock with holes in it. We could probably find something comparable to it in shape and color at a landscape supply store.

Annie returned her phone to her handbag. "She's leaving the key in my box at the college. I can pick up some tools there while I'm at it."

"Good deal."

The yellow light wouldn't hold this time and I was forced to stop at the intersection. Above us, a shiny new billboard called for called for Congressman Newsome's reelection. Underneath the cheesy smile it read, *Faith – Family – Fiscal Responsibility*. My mobile pulsed. I took it out of my inside coat pocket. Angie. I cringed for a second and let her go to voicemail. Then the light turned, and I hit the gas.

Annie combed her fingers through her hair. "I love going to the City. When Sean left for his mission, I was keen on moving there. Bob, on the other hand, began begging me to move to Parowan. That's when I finally sent him packing."

A muted alarm sounded in my brain. "Why Parowan?"

"He'd just come home from visiting this abandoned farmhouse there. Belonged to an old Mormon family that was somehow related to me."

"The Hatcher family?"

She shook her head. "Don't think so. My Mormon ancestors were named Snow."

"Why didn't he move to Parowan himself after you split up?"

"He claimed he couldn't live there without me. Something about my family connection."

"Really? And you don't know what this connection is?"

"I'm sorry, Ryan. At the time I did my best to tune him out."

I parked in front of the Fine Arts Building at Grafton College, undid my seatbelt, and opened the car door.

Annie grabbed my arm. "Wait."

I pulled the door closed. "You don't want to go in yet?"

"Yes, but you don't need to." She checked her watch. "Class is about to let out. It'll be crowded, and I'll only be two shakes."

"What if it's not safe?"

"Nothing's going to happen to me with all those people around. Besides, we've got a first-rate security guard. Name's Toots."

"Be careful," I said and watched her hurry inside, at the same time trying to picture Toots. I figured him a chronic grumbler. I would be if people called me Toots.

My mobile pulsed again. To my relief it was Mrs. Z. "What's up?"

"Looks like our Mr. Flake is a polygamist who recently split from a large Southern Utah affiliation." A crash sounded through the phone line. "Shoot. Can you hold a minute?"

Smiling, I lowered the mobile from my ear. A man who resembled the business suit in the hotel parking lot stepped out of the building to make a call. I studied him for a second. He had darker hair than the guy at the hotel. Also red-tinted Oakleys rather than aviators, and no necktie. Still, the similarity made me anxious. My eyes stayed on him as he finished his call and went inside.

"Don't worry, he didn't break another lamp," Mrs. Z said.

I returned the phone to my ear. "You were saying…about Mr. Flake?"

"Right, so he'd just left his congregation. That could be one reason he wants the stone. You know, for personal revelation."

"Or running his own fiefdom."

"Exactly, also according to some of his previous posts on the Real Mormon History board, Flake is somehow related to the Hatcher clan."

"Hence, it's his inheritance."

"Maybe. Also he grows sugar beets and makes homemade marshmallows."

"Aha. That would explain the handle, Marshmallow Man."

"You got it," Mrs. Z said, and then in a muffled voice to Little Ryan, "No! Naughty boy."

"Aw, don't call him that," I told her.

"From what little I've been able to read today," she resumed, "the original owner of the stone, Zedekiah Hatcher, ran a wildly successful farm around ten miles outside of Parowan. Maybe Flake thinks this stone can help him do the same."

"Right," I replied, scanning the windows of the Fine Arts building. Nothing suspicious. Still, I wished Annie would hurry so we could be on our way. "Do you have an exact location for the old Hatcher farm?"

"I got a picture off of Zillow. It's been on the market for over a year now."

"Hmm, kind of thought it might be," I replied. "Will you do me a favor and check to see if this Hatcher property has any connection to a family called Snow?"

"I'll do my best. How come, Ryan?"

"Right now it's just a hunch. Got anything else for me?"

"A little. There were two others seriously interested in purchasing the stone. One, who called himself G. Hatcher, appears to be a Gordon Hatcher, a wealthy building contractor with homes in both Salt Lake and Park City. Also he's a member of the Twelfth Quorum of the Seventy, meaning he's an LDS bigshot."

"And his name actually is Hatcher? Maybe he's the one after his inheritance."

"Well, he does claim to be Zedekiah's relation. But it's doubtful he believes the stone will make him a prophet. Leaders of the mainstream church reject all the hocus pocus stuff from their past, and this Mr. Hatcher appears to be on his way up the ecclesiastical ladder. More likely he's just a collector."

"And who is our other potential buyer?"

"Calls himself Stripling Warrior."

"Stripping Warrior?"

"*Stripling* Warrior, Ryan. It's from the Book of Mormon."

I sighed. "OK."

"So far most of his posts have come from what is probably his home in Orem, Utah."

"Do you have some kind contact for him?"

"Sure. He posted an email where Dr. Christiansen could contact him. They all did."

"Well, that's a huge start."

"Also, Alice called."

"Really? She called the office?"

"Yes. She wanted us both to know that the premiere of Dirk's new cable show airs this Monday at 8 p.m."

"Oh, right. I'll make a note of that." I signed off and pocketed the phone.

Annie was walking out of the building, key in one hand, a small plastic toolbox in the other.

Minutes later we were entering the freeway. I merged over a lane and set my cruise control for sixty-five. Relieved we were finally on our way, I tried to return to the subject at hand. "Bob purchased the Hatcher Stone before you separated, right?"

She shrugged. "I guess so."

"Otherwise he wouldn't have hidden it in your jeweler's bench."

"OK, makes sense."

"So, before you split up, he'd purchased this magic stone from Parowan and was contemplating a move to an old farmhouse there. That seems like too much of a coincidence." A slow truck transferred into my lane, causing me to hit the brake and then maneuver around it.

"Not necessarily. I imagine a lot of his collectibles came from Southern Utah. It's nut country down there. The only connection I see is that one of those nuts probably killed Bob." She yawned and tilted her seat back a notch. "Stop worrying, Ryan. You're going to catch the creep. I can feel it."

I glanced over at her, noticing that the outside breeze had toyed with her copper curls, playfully arranging them around her creamy freckled cheeks. Looking away, I took a second to reset the cruise control and then, eyes on the road, kept to myself for the next several miles.

"So, Ryan," she said, breaking the silence. "You know all about my failed marriage. Tell me about your relationship."

I frowned. "Her name is Angie and we've been together two years."

"Do you live together?"

"Not yet. We're going slow."

"That sounds…sensible."

"You're not paying me to fix my relationship."

She raised an eyebrow. "So it needs fixing, then?"

"*No*," I snapped, and then switched to a recap of my conversation with Mrs. Z.

"I've never heard of any Hatchers in my family, but I suppose it's possible," she ventured once I'd finished. "But do we absolutely need to know if I'm related?"

"I'd like to know, yeah. A family relation mattered to Bob. Flake, too. And to the mystery person who flung that message about the inheritance through your window."

She straightened her seatback to its original position. "So, I'll make a reproduction of the stone and then what?" Her neckline slipped, revealing her bare shoulder. I looked back at the road.

"Better make three reproductions."

"Why so many?"

"So I can contact the three interested parties and offer to negotiate on your behalf."

"We're going to sell them all fake stones?"

"We're going to give them the fakes. You don't want money. You just want to rid yourself of your estranged husband's weird collection."

Annie scoffed. "You've got that right."

A text came in on my mobile. I pulled it from my jacket pocket. Angie. I squinted to read without my glasses. Something about dinner.

"Are you going to break the law and return that text while driving?" Annie asked.

"Nope."

"If it's important," Annie went on, "we could get off at the next exit and you could text back."

When I didn't respond she added, "I could go for a little walk so you could have some privacy."

After a mile of utter silence she gave up the subject and asked, "OK, so we meet these guys, give them the stones, and then what?"

"I'll meet them."

"You don't want me along?"

I stole a look in her direction. In this light, her eyes had taken on a gentle mossy hue.

"That's my job," I said. "Your job is to make those duplicate stones."

We stopped at a landscape store I knew in Oakland. It sold decorative rock in bulk, the smallest increment being five pounds. While Annie sifted through a crate of round brown stones, I put on my glasses and read Angie's text.

Dinner at 6 tonight?

I checked my watch. Already three o'clock. Sighing, I typed my response with my index finger. Never understood how the kids could do it with their thumbs.

Sorry Ange. Got to work late tonight.

I hit send and then stared lamely at the phone, feeling guilty. Then, just as I was about to return the thing in my pocket, she texted back.

It's never too late to come by.

Still staring at the screen, annoyance seeped in to replace my guilt. Was she sitting by the phone? Had to be to reply so quickly. At three p.m. she might be on a break. That could explain it. Still, I felt cornered. I stuffed the phone in my jacket pocket, put the readers in my coat, and strode over to Annie. My mobile pulsed an incoming text. I decided to deal with it later.

"Finding some good candidates?" I asked.

"I think so. They're all a little thicker than the original, but I can grind them down."

"They may not know that. The pictures Mrs. Z found online didn't show the thickness, only the width."

"Good point." She tossed the brown stone atop the others in her metal basket. "This should do me."

The salesclerk packed our selection into a plastic bag and then ran my credit card for the payment.

"Did you get a chance to return that text?" Annie asked me as I held the car door for her.

I remained mute as she slid into the passenger seat. When I climbed in the driver's side, she repeated the question. I took the time to buckle my seatbelt, start the ignition, and check the rearview mirror before finally breaking the silence.

"How are you going to alter the stones' appearances?" I asked.

She rolled her eyes, presumably at the change of subject. But then she spent the remainder of the ten-minute ride answering my question. I admired how animated she became as she discussed her craft, also the graceful way her slim hands moved to accompany her description. Sadly, as we entered the western span of the Bay Bridge, I had to interrupt to ask where we were going.

"The Marina," she replied.

"Whoa, you have a wealthy colleague."

"Family money."

"Which street?"

"The place is on Bay. But first we need to make a stop on Chestnut."

"What for?"

"Provisions. The fridge in the loft is empty and we *will* need to eat."

Provisions. For a meal together. I hadn't counted on that. But then, I did need to eat, and there was no way I could get back to Angie's in time. Her text, *It's never too late to come by,* flashed in my brain. My hands tightened on the steering wheel. Why not stay in the city for dinner?

"I'm a whiz with pasta," I told her.

She grinned. "A man who can boil water. That's new territory for me."

I slowed as we exited the freeway at Ninth, my smile broadening at the notion of actually cooking the meal. I hadn't done that since my daughter left home. My wife used to let me cook. But with Angie, dinner was always ready, and I was always late. I felt my hands tightening on the wheel again. Indeed, why the hell *not* stay in the city for dinner?

After a couple of times around the block, I found a metered spot on Chestnut. I got out of the car and searched my pockets for change. Only two cents.

Annie closed the car door behind her. "I'm pretty sure I have some."

She unzipped her purse, pulled out her wallet, and accidentally knocked her cellphone out as well. It landed face down on the pavement. I reached for it, but she beat me to it, her head almost butting mine in the process.

"Such a klutz," she said, laughing as she dropped the phone in her purse and then emptied a collection of coins into my hand.

I fed the meter. "Fifteen minutes."

We strode past upscale clothing shops, design stores, and posh restaurants. When we got to the neighborhood market we parted ways, each with our own baskets. I was mulling over what kind of pasta to prepare when I passed the meat counter. A glance at their house-made sausage screamed Bolognese. I had the butcher wrap me some links, also some ground veal and sirloin. Mindful of the ticking time on the meter, I grabbed a can of San Marzano tomatoes, a box of spaghetti, some good olive oil, a baguette, and a bottle of sangiovese. Then I headed for the produce aisle for garlic and herbs. Annie was already there, picking out apples. Her basket looked jam-packed. Milk, granola, coffee, ice cream, and sundry other things underneath.

"Hopefully you won't need all that," I told her. "I want to wrap this as soon as possible so you can go home."

She smiled brightly and placed one and then another apple into her basket. "This is just for tonight and tomorrow morning."

When we got to the checkout, I learned that the sundry other things in Annie's basket amounted to a bottle of single-malt scotch. Rather than protest, I stoically put it and the rest of our purchases on my card. After all, why the hell shouldn't I enjoy a drink in the city? The Swizzle Stick could spare me for another evening. And there wasn't any scotch at Angie's place. Nothing but that cabernet with its damned antioxidants. At the end of the day, all I wanted was a good scotch. Preferably a single malt. I glanced back at the bottle.

The address on Bay was only a few blocks away, but it took us almost thirty minutes to find street parking. By the time we got out of the car the wind had picked up, blowing chill gusts off the water. Annie folded her arms tightly across her chest. Instinctively, I slipped off my sports coat, wrapped it around her shoulders and then, stepping around to face her, gazed into her beautiful green eyes. In that moment I realized that, however unintentionally, in my mind, this was turning into a date. I wondered how she saw it.

"Such a gentleman," Annie said softly.

I opened the back of the car and she reached in and retrieved her overnight bag, her hand brushing against mine in the process. I grabbed the groceries and we walked briskly down the blustery Marina block to the arched entrance.

Reaching for the door, I was relieved to find it securely locked. Good solid deadbolt. There was an intercom next to it. Each tenant had a button, like at Angie's place. I squinted to scan the list of occupants. A blur without my readers, and then eclipsed when Annie stepped in front of the intercom and unlocked the front door.

It was a prewar building with an elaborate art deco lobby. There was a crescent of brass numbers above the elevator with an ornate arrow that indicated the car was on *2*. Annie hit the button and the motor engaged. The arrow moved from *2* to *1* to *L* and then the doors slid open and we rode in silent anticipation to the ninth floor. I glanced over at her and then at my feet, shy all of a sudden, like a kid. But when we entered the apartment, my shyness gave way to amazement. "Wow," I whispered.

"You like it?"

It was a corner unit that took in the Marin Headlands, the Golden Gate Bridge, and a quadrant of the glittering San Francisco Bay spanning clear to Alcatraz. "You do have friends in high places."

Annie nodded and then pointed to a spot behind me. "Why don't you set those bags in the kitchen?"

The kitchen was a skinny galley number with state-of-the art appliances and a collection of pots and pans that dangled over a butcher-block island. I set the grocery bags on the island and turned to take in the rest of my surroundings. A small dining table was positioned next to the western window looking out at the bridge. A boxy beige sofa and two matching side chairs were grouped in front of the north-facing window. To the left of them in the corner, a quilt-covered queen-sized bed was partially hidden behind a wooden Oriental screen. There were two doors along the apartment's eastern wall. One, I presumed, was the bathroom, the other probably a closet. In between them stood a small mahogany writing table adorned with only a reading lamp and a plain leather desk pad. I was struck by how unlived-in the place looked. Very strange for such fantastic digs—but then, lucky for her, I supposed, at least for now.

"Nobody knows you're here, right?"

Annie dropped her overnight bag onto the bed, spread my jacket on top of it, and set the toolbox on the desk. "Just my colleague."

"This colleague of yours, does she know not to tell anyone you're here?"

"She does, and she's got her nose in research for the next couple of weeks."

For convenience's sake I'd slipped the bag of stones inside one of the grocery sacks. I carried them to the desk.

"Here you go," I told her. "Let's get started so we can throw this creep off your trail."

"Great. Give me a minute."

Her purse in hand, she disappeared behind the door on the left. A second later I heard the water running. I went back to the kitchen and unpacked the rest of the groceries, positioning the bottle of single malt in a place of prominence on the kitchen island. I checked the time on the oven clock. Four forty-five. I waited while it turned to four forty-six. Then I looked at the scotch bottle. What the hell, it was after five in Utah.

I went to the cupboard for a glass. Eight tall ones for water, eight matching shorter versions for juice. I took down one of the shorter numbers and splashed in some amber liquid. Just then Annie came out of the bathroom, tossed her purse on the bed, and picked up my jacket, folding it neatly over her arm. Her unruly mass of hair was now pulled into a ponytail.

"Thanks for loaning me your coat."

"My pleasure. Can I pour you a drink?" I asked.

"Not until I'm through using the equipment. But I would like some music."

Annie opened the closet next to the desk. On its floor stood a no-frills wine rack housing six bottles, some empty wood hangers dangled along a clothing rod, and a slim black CD player sat on the shelf above. She put my coat on a hanger and then, with one push of the button, sent French sidewalk café music wafting through the speakers lodged in the corners of the ceiling. She looked to me for approval.

I smiled. "*C'est magnifique.*"

Seemingly satisfied with my response, she grabbed one of the empty paper grocery bags, folded it into a neat rectangle atop the desk, and used it as a surface to sort through her cache of stones. Meanwhile, I unwrapped the meat, cracked open the olive oil, grabbed a pan from a rack over the island and within minutes was sizzling up a storm in the skillet, on my way to a serious batch of Bolognese.

"Smells good," Annie called.

She took a pair of safety glasses out of her toolbox and put them on top of her hair like a headband. Then, after attaching a tiny grinding bit to a small electric drill, she lowered the glasses onto her nose and began grinding the edge of one of the stones. Her neckline slipped over her shoulder. I paused to sip my scotch, humming along with the Parisian accordion. I decided that there was nothing sexier than a redhead in a clingy wool dress and plastic safety glasses wielding a power tool. It also helped that the sun was now sinking beneath the Golden Gate Bridge and bathing her in a golden-pink light. She stopped for a second to switch on the desk lamp. Then she looked over at me and smiled, just slightly, like the Mona Lisa.

I switched on the kitchen lights, tasted the sauce, added more oregano, tasted again, and tossed in some extra pepper. Then I stepped back to let the meaty concoction simmer. I sipped my scotch and looked out at the spectacular sunset, French music swirling around in my brain. Out the corner of my eye I saw Annie coming my way. She slipped behind me and, placing her hands on either side of my waist, crabbed past me into the kitchen.

"What do you need?" I asked.

"Water." She found a pie pan in the drawer beneath the oven, took it to the sink, and filled it halfway. "The stones are pretty dried out. I don't want them to shatter when I drill holes into them."

"Good thinking."

I watched her swish back to her work, feeling especially happy about our in tandem efforts. Seconds later the high-pitched whir of her drill competed with the accordion. I splashed more scotch in my glass, sipped, and tested the sauce again. Just right. Satisfied, I took my drink to the window. The sun had slipped below the horizon, and a clear waning moon had appeared in its place. The desk lamp spot-lit Annie's face as she finished drilling her last stone. She removed her safety glasses, returned her tools to her kit, and killed the light.

"Join me for a drink?" I asked her.

"Sure," she replied as she set out the three new seer stones on the island. "There should still be an open bottle of white wine in the fridge."

"Coming up." I took down one of the short glasses from the cupboard, found the wine, and filled the glass just over half-full.

She thanked me and sipped slowly, studying the three rocks. "What do you think?"

I glanced down at them. A proper examination would require the readers I'd left in my coat. "Look like genuine, authentic seer stones to me," I said, and then reached up to the rack above the island for a pot to boil the spaghetti.

She took another drink, her body swaying gently to the music. "I thought I might have to file them a little, but I think they're good to go. Just hope these guys aren't so in tune with the Spirit that they can tell they're fakes." She laughed.

I chuckled along, for her sake, but in truth this was no laughing matter. With Annie's life possibly in danger, we had to make this work. I filled the pot with water, splashed in some olive oil, and set it over a high flame. Then I pulled out my phone and squinted at my contact list until I found Mrs. Z's mobile. She picked up on the second ring.

"Hi, Ryan." A boisterous din clamored in the background.

"Sounds like you made it home."

"I did. Do you need me to run back to the office?"

"Oh, no. But could you do one more thing for me when you get the chance?"

"Sure."

"You can access my email from your home computer, right?"

"Yeah."

"Great. Compose an email saying I represent Mrs. Christiansen and that she is in possession of the Hatcher Stone and is willing to part with it for free. Then send it out individually to each of the interested parties."

"She has the stone?"

"In a way, yes."

"What if all three of them take the bait?"

"We're prepared for that."

"OK, if you say so. Anything else?" A girl screamed *Mom*. Mrs. Z shushed her.

"No, that's it for now. But I may need a thing or two over the weekend. Will you—"

"I'll be around."

I grinned. "You're the best."

Still smiling, I pocketed the phone and looked at Annie. "Don't let me forget to take those rocks with me tonight."

She rested her drink on the island and gathered up the stones. "I'll put them in your coat pocket now."

While Annie went to the closet, I took the opportunity to add a tiny splash of excellent single-malt to my glass. It was going down very well. *No more tonight,* I told myself as I twisted the cap back on the bottle.

"That amazing aroma has made me so hungry," she said as she came back to the kitchen.

"Once the water boils, we're on the home stretch."

"I'll set the table," Annie said.

"Good thinking."

Indeed, it was, I reflected. When a woman cooks, she multitasks. She sets the table. She times the vegetables. When a man cooks, he throws the food in the pot, stands back, drinks his scotch, and then when it's ready, he finally realizes that he might also want a fork, and perhaps a plate. I watched appreciatively as Annie covered the small table with a blue linen cloth. Then I enjoyed another pleasant sensation as she slipped behind me for some dishes in the cupboard. It occurred to me that I could have picked up the makings for a salad.

"Maybe I should slice the bread," I ventured.

"I've got that covered," she replied, pulling a small wooden board from a drawer. "It's time for you to start the pasta."

"Oh!" I exclaimed, upon seeing that the water had come to a full rolling boil.

"Then you can open that bottle of red wine you picked out," she added. "There's a corkscrew in with the silverware."

Nodding, I put the spaghetti into the pot, turned down the heat, and found the corkscrew. It was red with a liquor store logo stamped on its side. I opened the bottle of sangiovese while Annie lit the candle on the perfectly set little table. The accordion continued to play. We were still in France.

Minutes later we were seated across from each other and toasting.

"Delicious," she moaned upon taking her first bite.

"Glad you like it." I sipped my wine. Not a bad choice if I did say so myself. The sauce had turned out damned well too. I reminded myself to cook more often; and then, looking out at the twinkling towers on the Golden Gate Bridge, I also resolved to come to San Francisco regularly.

I twirled pasta around my fork. "Sure is an amazing view."

Annie looked past me out the front window. "I hadn't noticed this until now, but is that a lighthouse blinking on Alcatraz?"

"Yup. First one built on the West Coast."

"No kidding? How do you know that?"

"Not sure where I learned it," I said as I refilled our wine glasses. "I was on the San Francisco force for over a decade. Picked up a lot of trivia. Either that or I learned it from my wife. She grew up here. Could have given tours."

"Could have? She's not here anymore?"

"She died ten years ago."

Setting down her wine glass, Annie paused to study me. "I'm sorry," she said finally.

"Thank you."

"No other woman since then?"

I swallowed and dabbed at my mouth with my napkin. "Just Angie."

"You really loved your wife."

"I did, yes. But why do you say that?"

"Your expression right now. Also the fact that you've gone ten years without anyone."

"Except for Angie," I added.

"Who isn't exactly filling your wife's shoes."

Smiling, I took my time to chew and swallow. "So, Mrs. Christiansen, do you think you've made some passable replicas of the Hatcher Stone?"

She glared at me for a second and then giggled. "Ryan, you are changing the subject on me again."

"Yes, I am."

"OK, fair enough." Annie pointed her fork in my direction. "But don't start calling me Mrs. Christiansen. That's below the belt."

"Deal." I helped myself to a slice of bread. "Do you have a good replica?"

She drew the real seer stone out from under her dress and held it in the palm of her hand. "It's a little hard to tell since I've altered the appearance of the original so much. But I think so."

I leaned forward to study the shiny green and brown orb. Even without my readers, the tiny gold flecks were remarkably well defined, and seemed to radiate their own light. "The thing does seem to have a special spirit about it."

Slipping the stone back inside her neckline, she asked, "Do you believe in the supernatural, Ryan?"

"Not really." I twirled more pasta around my fork and then paused before putting it in my mouth. "Although, when I was a cop here in the city, we used psychics sometimes. They were actually pretty helpful."

She nodded and we both fell silent while the charming café accordion filled the void.

"Have you been to France, Annie?"

"Yes. I was there three years ago. In Brittany with Bob."

"I seem to remember having some delicious oysters from Brittany when my wife and I were in Paris years ago." I poured more wine for both of us. The bottle was emptying at an alarming pace.

"Paris. I've always wanted to study there. Had a program all picked out. Bob, of course, vetoed the idea. But you took your wife?"

I grinned. "It was crazy. We were fresh out of school, had no money, but on a whim, I bought tickets to Paris for her birthday. Maybe one of the silliest things I've ever done."

Annie leaned back in her chair and swirled her wine, the lights on the Bay twinkling behind her. "You regret it?"

I gazed into her liquid green eyes. "No," I replied softly.

Annie smiled and shook her head. "Bob would never have done that. Everything had to be carefully planned and paid for in advance. And he was always on his best Mormon behavior. He was royally pissed at me for drinking wine in Brittany." She took a long sip and then abruptly set down her glass. "That reminds me. There's a wonderful cabernet franc we should try next. Let's open it and let it breathe."

I laughed out loud at the suggestion. "Not for me. I have to drive."

Annie swirled her sangiovese. "OK, but don't run off. The night's still young. Only eight o'clock. We'll have coffee and dessert later."

I glanced at my watch. The watch Angie had given me. It was a gift for the one-year anniversary of our first date. Not a Rolex, but not cheap either. And she'd taken care to choose one with a big dial I could read without my glasses. All I'd given her was flowers. But only because I happened to see them by the checkout at Safeway. And thank god I'd seen them. Because I'd had no idea it was the anniversary of our first date. For that matter, I still couldn't remember which day it was. Sometime in June.

"You have somewhere you have to be?" Annie asked.

I glanced back at my watch. It kept good time. Right now, it said five minutes after eight. I looked out at the glittering bay and then into Annie's soft green eyes. "Nope," I replied, doing my best to sound casual. "I can hang around."

She smiled and then sipped her sangiovese. I emptied the rest of the bottle into both of our glasses.

Eight o'clock turned to nine and then to ten, as we went from sangiovese to a bit of tawny port to vanilla ice cream drizzled with some raspberry syrup, that—upon closer examination—turned out to be raspberry liqueur. We talked about my job, her art, my daughter, her son, our shared disenchantment with religion and our joint love of both San Francisco and Paris. I found myself opening up for the first time in years—ten years to be precise. With Annie I felt young and crazy again. So crazy I might even buy tickets to Paris.

But when I looked to see that the watch that Angie had given me read ten thirty, I felt my age creep up on me. "Annie, I'd better have that coffee now and be on my way."

"OK."

She went to the kitchen and scooped fresh grounds into the bottom of a small French press, set some water to boil, and then excused herself to the bathroom. I pushed back from the table and shut my eyes, enjoying the pairing of a pleasant buzz alongside the French music.

When Annie returned, she poured boiling water into the glass carafe, took a mug from the cupboard, and came back to the table. I noticed her hair was freshly combed and that she'd applied a new coat of lipstick. Smiling, she pressed the plunger to the bottom of the carafe and poured my coffee into a charming blue and white flowered mug. Yet another seamlessly elegant presentation.

I took a sip. It was remarkably rich and smooth. "You're not having any?"

"No," she replied. "It will just keep me up."

Nodding, I took another sip. I noticed that some of the raspberry liqueur still lingered in the corner of her mouth.

"You know, Ryan, you could crash here tonight."

I coughed mid-swallow. "No, Annie, that wouldn't be appropriate."

"You could have the sofa."

My eyes traveled back to that sweet, glistening spot at the corner of her mouth. "Annie, I'm afraid I'd be too tempted to—"

"Come to bed with me?"

"Yes," I replied and then stood up matter-of-factly.

"I want you to come to bed with me," Annie whispered. She reached up and fingered the silver chain along her neck. It still plunged into her blue woolen neckline.

Shaking my head, I went to the closet for my coat. The three fake seer stones rattled inside the pocket as I slipped it on.

"Are you leaving because of Angie?"

"I'm leaving because you're my client. Even if Angie wasn't in the picture, it would be inappropriate for me to be involved with a client."

A wan smile crossed her face. My response, it seemed, had pleased her. She stood and walked toward me. The closer she came, the more I wanted to take her in my arms and kiss her. I backed away and placed a hand on the doorknob.

"What about when I'm no longer your client?" she asked.

"Cross that bridge when we come to it." I let myself out and shut the door behind me.

Halfway down the hall the alcohol hit me. I never should have had that port, not to mention the goddamned ninety proof raspberry sauce. Stumbling forward, I told myself a brisk walk in the fresh air might do the trick. But when I got to the elevator and saw my fuzzy reflection in the metal door, I realized that crashing on Annie's couch was now the only responsible option. I went back to her door and knocked.

She answered right away, as if she'd been standing there waiting. Only the lights were dimmer now. I started to speak but she hushed me with a soft finger to my lips. I stepped inside and closed the door. She was so close I could feel her breath on my face. Her hair curled around her cheeks, the silver chain still glistened along her throat, and her neckline had slipped off both of her shoulders. She reached up and caressed my cheek.

After that things started to blur.

I remember tasting the raspberry sauce on her lips and tongue. I remember her dress was exceptionally soft. Almost as soft as her skin. I remember running my hands over her curves, feeling wool and then skin and then wool again. Then only skin. I remember later we were somehow on the bed. I remember we made love with an intensity and passion I hadn't felt in years. And as I fell to sleep, I remember seeing her pale body wrapped in the white linen sheet, her copper curls sprawled across the pillow, and the seer stone around her neck glowing like an other-worldly orb.

The next day I awoke feeling happy. Gloriously happy. Christmas morning happy. I rolled over to see Annie in bed beside me, sound asleep. I fingered a lock of her hair that had strayed to my pillow. It hadn't been a dream. She was really there.

The digital clock on the nightstand switched to eight twenty-six. I rolled out of bed, quietly collected my clothes, and crept into the bathroom. The tiny facility was equipped with what looked like the original sink and a brand new shower. I stepped into the stall and turned on the faucet. In seconds hot water was streaming through the large saucer-shaped showerhead. There was a bar of Dial Soap and a bottle of Head and Shoulders on a metal caddy. Funny, I was expecting something different. Crabtree and Evelyn maybe. No matter, I made use of what was there. Then I toweled off, dressed in yesterday's clothes, found some toothpaste on the shelf and used it and my finger to wash my teeth. When I came out of the bath the digital clock had turned to eight forty-five, and Annie was drowsily sitting up, still wrapped in the bed sheet. First thing in the morning and she looked gorgeous.

"Morning, sleepyhead." I sat down on the bed and kissed her, imagining the raspberry liqueur lingering on her lips.

"Morning, Ryan," she murmured, and kissed me again.

I ran my fingers through her soft curls. "I thought I'd walk up to Chestnut Street and get us some coffee at that little shop we went by yesterday."

She yawned and stretched her arms out in front of her. "We have coffee here, Ryan."

"I know. But I want to get out and walk. Clear my head and refocus on the case." I stroked her cheek. "You did hire me to solve a case."

"Refocus here," she replied, a trace of early morning snappishness in her voice. Then in a gentler tone she added, "I can fix us something."

"I really do want to get out for a moment. Can I borrow the key so I can get back in the building?" When she didn't answer, I asked, "Or should I ring the intercom?"

"No, take the key," she said, smiling. "What happened to my..."

"Your purse?" I had a vague memory of it falling off the bed last night. "Here it is."

I bent down and scooped it off the floor. Annie snatched it away from me and unzipped the bag part way, felt around, and then came up with a small leather and chrome keychain. Generic. Like everything else in this place. I stuffed it in my pants pocket and went to the closet for my coat. Found it instead on the floor by the front door.

"Any requests?" I asked cheerfully as I slipped on my jacket and brushed the dust from the sleeves. The fake seer stones still weighed down my pocket.

"A latte, I guess," she replied.

"You got it."

Outside the air was cool and the streets empty. Saturday morning. People were enjoying their day to sleep in. I turned onto Chestnut. In my current state of euphoria everything looked brilliant. The MUNI bus was especially shiny. The mailboxes glowed. The man at the newsstand smiled as if he knew me. And the tiny coffee shop, with the antique grinder in the window, was as charming as anything I'd seen in Paris. I ordered a latte, a black coffee, and a couple of chocolate croissants. Then I pulled out my phone and put on my readers. The texts from Angie appeared on my screen, inducing a passing shudder of reality. I switched to my email. All three of the interested parties had responded to my query about the stone. The barista called my name. I pocketed my phone and glasses, collected my order, and strode back through the Marina, taking my time, laid back and confident, like this was my neighborhood and I was on my way home. Home to Annie.

When I got there, she was in the kitchen wiping down the counter. The bed was made, last night's dishes were cleared, and she had put on blue jeans and a loose, V-necked turquoise top that flashed a tease of midriff. Her copper curls were pulled into a ponytail and the thin silver chain still glistened along her throat. I set the coffee on the little table and then came up behind, reached inside the shirt to hug her around her bare waist, and kissed her neck.

She sighed. "You really are the perfect man for the job."

"Speaking of which, quick breakfast and then I've got to get to work."

"So soon?"

A sharp knock on the door interrupted my reply. We both stared in its direction.

"Any idea?" I whispered.

Annie's face paled and she shook her head no. "Maybe we shouldn't answer."

I crept over, peered through the peephole, blinked, and rested my head briefly against the door. Then I turned the knob and opened up to Detective Lieutenant Stella Romano.

Part Two

The Unusual Suspects

"The only men who become Gods, even the Sons of God, are those who enter into polygamy."

LDS Prophet Brigham Young, *Journal of Discourses,* v. 11, p. 269, August 19, 1866

T he stairs creak as I descend the porch. For decade upon decade the sun beats down upon this house, upon this land, and upon me. In the brightness everything dulls. The yellow house bleaches to gray. The flowering, fruitful fields turn to dust. Even my passion, once a firestorm, fades to patience. All I have left is patience.

I pace the weed-filled, rocky land and relive the annual sowing, as I have every spring since it was all taken away. Imagining the sacred stone in hand, I close my eyes and envision the outcome. Then, through inspiration, I select the best seeds, plan the rotation of the crops, and preside over my family as we plant, tend, and bring forth the most bounteous harvest in the county.

Only months ago, I felt the stone's sacred presence return. My heart leapt. After decades of waiting, I was to be set free! But alas, it was not in the possession of a rightful heir. My heart sank again, and then patience prevailed.

Everything must be restored by way of the proper authority. Only then will the truth be revealed, the bounty return, and this house come to life once more. The time is near. I can feel it. Today, as I walk back across the barren land, climb onto the creaking porch, and return to the cobweb-laced parlor, the beginning of a song stirs within me

R omano had just parked the car when he appeared in her rearview mirror. She almost didn't recognize him, what with the self-satisfied expression and the hint of swagger in his step. But it was Ryan all right, strolling toward her car, two coffees and a pastry bag in hand. He didn't even see her. Just walked right by and up to the building where Romano suspected Mrs. Christiansen was hiding out.

Romano grabbed her brown leather messenger bag off the passenger seat, got out of the car, started to call his name, but thought better of it. Instead, she slung the bag over her shoulder, waited for Ryan to let himself in, and then walked slowly to the entrance. Peering through the glass door, she watched the elevator close. She rang the super and announced herself as "Lieutenant Romano, the police detective from Abbottsville who called yesterday afternoon." He buzzed her inside. Then, standing in the center of the charming Arts and Crafts lobby, she watched the brass arrow slide all the way up to *9*. Seemed they were both headed for the same floor.

She cooled her heels in front of the elevator, asking herself what the hell he was doing here. The first thought made her stomach turn. Aunt Angie had phoned last night. Ryan had stood her up. Said he had to work. Didn't bother to call later. Romano fell back on her usual reassurances. He was a private investigator. He didn't work nine to five. But truth be told, Romano was starting to feel that Ryan had been acting an awful lot like Davis had before their break-up.

But would Ryan have spent the night here? With Mrs. Christiansen?

No, she told herself.

A former cop jumping into bed with the prime suspect in a murder case? Not plausible. And he wasn't a cheat. Romano remembered her lonely old partner who'd spent eight years pining over his dead wife before he'd even allowed himself to date.

The elevator door slid open, and she stepped inside, punching the ninth floor button with extra emphasis. Ryan had told Aunt Angie the truth. He was working. Mrs. Christiansen must be his client. Last night he'd been immersed in the case and, like the dolt he was, he'd forgotten to call. Romano's stomach started to settle. That was the Ryan she knew, loved, and sometimes wanted to strangle. She figured he'd been on the road to the City just ahead of her. Picked up breakfast to start the workday. Just like he'd sometimes done for her back when they were partners.

Romano stepped out of the elevator and paused as the door shut behind her. Ryan's involvement with Mrs. Christiansen, while surely professional, might still prove a disturbing development. She moved along the hallway, carefully, on the balls of her feet. Because he was her former partner and mentor, Romano wanted to believe that there were a few things Ryan didn't know about his new client. However, because she was a cop, she had to be sure that he didn't know them. Employing the element of surprise might help her gauge his reactions.

She stood at the door and listened hard. A faint muffle of voices, not far away. By the tax records, she knew the place was a studio. Four hundred square feet. So just about anywhere, other than inside the bathroom, would be nearby. Romano knocked sharply and then positioned herself in front of the peephole. Seconds later she saw the shadow of somebody on the other side. Most likely Ryan. A few seconds passed. Probably because he was surprised, shocked even. He needed to collect himself. Then the latch clicked, and he opened the door wide.

"Ryan." Romano feigned surprise. "What are you doing here?"

He stepped back to let her enter. His expression remained even, but Romano detected an underlying confusion.

"I'm conferring with my client," he said, motioning to the dining set where she was sitting.

Romano nodded at Mrs. Christiansen. She looked pale and frightened, but also carefully groomed. Her hair was combed and tied back, and she'd bothered to put on her makeup. Glancing around the apartment, Romano admired the high-end furnishings. An elegant but seldom-used pied-à-terre. Sort of what she'd expected. There was a tidy kitchen, a toolbox on the little desk, and a single suitcase alongside a woman's handbag atop the neatly made bed. The only sign of interaction between Ryan and his client was the coffee and pastry bag he'd brought with him just now. They sat on the dining table in front of Mrs. Christiansen. Clear across the room from the bed. Romano felt a tinge of guilt over her initial suspicion.

"Since when has Mrs. Christiansen been your client?"

"Officially since yesterday morning," Ryan replied. "But I technically began my investigation Thursday evening, a couple of hours after I spoke with you."

"Mind if I ask what she's hired you to do?"

"Find the person who killed her husband."

Romano smiled tightly. "Funny, that's my job too."

"Maybe we can help each other," Ryan suggested.

"I hope so," Romano replied, gearing up for the kicker. "I've called your client's mobile six times over the past twenty-four hours and have yet to hear back from her. You know anything about that, Ryan?"

He blinked three times in succession. Then he turned to his client. "Is that true, Mrs. Christiansen?"

For Ryan, that was as flummoxed a face as Romano had seen him make. His expression, combined with the inflection when he repeated Christiansen's name, confirmed her theory. His client had been holding out on him. She turned to Mrs. Christiansen, who clutched her paper coffee cup with both hands.

"Mrs. Christiansen," Ryan repeated, "is that true?"

"My mobile's been dead," Annie Christiansen replied.

"Do you have your mobile here with you?" Romano asked.

When his client didn't respond, Ryan interjected, "She had it with her yesterday, but I never heard it ring, and we were together most of the day."

Romano walked over to the dining table and peered down at Annie Christiansen. She had begun to slowly spin her paper cup on the table's surface.

"May I see your phone, Mrs. Christiansen?" she said.

Annie gazed up at Ryan. "Do I have to show her my phone?"

Ryan exhaled and pinched the bridge of his nose. He was about to reply when Romano beat him to it.

"No, Mrs. Christiansen, you don't need to show it to me. I was merely *asking* if you would."

Ryan let his hand fall from his face and started to speak. Once again, Romano beat him to it.

"Now, if I were to come back here with a search warrant, that would be different."

"Lieutenant," Ryan said, "as always, I am perfectly willing to cooperate with the police. I saw Mrs. Christiansen with a mobile phone that I presumed to be hers on two occasions yesterday. First, at around noon when she used it to make a call—which would indicate that at least at that time, the battery was still operable. Later in the day, I saw it fall out of her purse onto the sidewalk. But I never heard it ringing and had no idea you or anyone else was trying to reach her."

Romano looked down at Mrs. Christiansen. She was still spinning the coffee cup.

"She made a call? Do you know to whom?" Romano asked, her eyes still on Christiansen.

"Her colleague at Grafton College," Ryan explained. "The one who owns this apartment. She wanted to borrow her key."

"What?" Romano started to laugh, caught herself, and then, softening her tone, said, "Ryan, the owner of this apartment doesn't work for Grafton College. The owner of this apartment is Congressman Dennis Newsome."

Ryan gazed back at Romano, his face motionless, as though suspended in time. Then he turned slowly and fixed Mrs. Christiansen with an expression Romano didn't recognize. A jumble of emotions. Anger, disgust, betrayal and underneath it all, a rawness. He'd been cut to the quick. Annie Christiansen looked up for a second and then, straight back down at her feet.

Heaving a sigh, Ryan turned away from his client and stared out the window that faced the Golden Gate Bridge. "How'd you know to look here?" he asked Romano.

"Well, she'd claimed to be in the City earlier this week, at the time of her husband's death." Romano smiled. "She told me the same story about staying at the colleague's place."

Ryan shut his eyes for a couple of long seconds.

"I imagine you can deduce the rest," Romano went on. "I drove over to Grafton College and talked to the secretary in the Art Department. She didn't know of any colleagues with fancy City condos, but she did mention that Mrs. Christiansen had called last Tuesday, before Dr. Christiansen's death, to say she was extending her stay at a friend's place in the City. So I decided to try and trace her location via her mobile phone. Since she was the deceased's wife who'd seemed to have gone missing, it wasn't hard to convince a judge to subpoena her phone records."

"And calls from her mobile linked her to this apartment," Ryan concluded wearily, resignation settling in.

"To this building. But when I obtained the list of owners and tenants, the Mormon congressman's name naturally jumped out at me."

"Naturally," Ryan repeated.

"You didn't notice Newsome-Birnbaum LLC on the intercom outside?" Romano ventured.

Rather than answer, he issued a short, mirthless laugh. Then he buttoned his sport coat and brushed some dust off the sleeves. "I know you're anxious to speak with my client, but I'm about to take off and wondered if I might have a private word with her first."

Romano paused to consider this. Leaving them alone to potentially collude was a risk. But Ryan had always been an honest cop, and she needed his future cooperation. "OK. I'll wait in the hallway."

Out in the hall, Romano strolled in the direction of the elevator until she heard Ryan shut the door. Then she crept back on the balls of her feet and listened hard. Muffled voices, hers more elevated than his, but neither decipherable. Romano stayed at the door as long as she dared and then backed a few yards away. She wasn't sure what to make of her former partner's reaction. Clearly he was surprised by his client's sneaky behavior. But her connection to Newsome seemed to upset him as much as her evasion of the police. Sure, Ryan hated the guy. Also, Newsome had a reputation for being a womanizer, and Mrs. Christiansen's access to his place suggested a relationship between the two. An affair with a married congressman would be an imprudent move on Christiansen's part. But why would Ryan care? She was just a client, and cheating wives and husbands were his bread and butter nowadays.

Moreover, why hadn't Ryan noticed Newsome's name on the intercom? Pretty careless for such a good detective. Then she remembered.

Ryan had let himself into the building with a key. Her stomach began to turn again. When would Christiansen have given him her key?

Ryan emerged into the hallway, his business face intact. "She'll see you now."

Nodding, Romano started for the door.

"Oh, and Romano," Ryan said.

She turned to face him.

"We'll talk later?"

"We certainly will," she said, and watched Ryan's back as he walked to the elevator. It opened as soon as he hit the button.

The door to the apartment stood ajar. Romano tapped twice, then entered. Annie Christiansen was still sitting where she'd left her, dabbing her eyes with a coffee shop napkin. A key attached to a plain leather and chrome ring now lay beside the pastry bag on the dining table, presumably returned by Ryan. Perhaps this meant Mrs. Christiansen wouldn't be extending her stay here. Or that Ryan wouldn't be coming back.

"I'm sorry I didn't return your calls, Lieutenant," Mrs. Christiansen began. "But I'm willing to answer any of your questions now."

Mrs. Christiansen wiped her eyes again with the napkin. She looked shaken, just how Romano would expect a woman in her spot to look.

"I appreciate that, ma'am. But maybe you'd like to take a minute to collect yourself?"

"Thank you, Lieutenant. I would." Mrs. Christiansen got up from the table, went into the bathroom, and shut the door.

At the sound of running water, Romano dropped her brown messenger bag onto a dining chair and went to the kitchen. On the surface, it was spotless, the counters still damp from a recent wipe down. The dishwasher stood slightly open. Breaching protocol, she cracked it open further and peeked inside to see a load of dirty dishes. Two place settings, glasses, a skillet, a large pot, the parts to a French press coffee maker, a faint whiff of garlic. Romano glanced back at the cups from the local coffee shop. These dishes hadn't been used for breakfast. Yet they were still wet. She'd rinsed and loaded them this morning, perhaps because she'd been too preoccupied last night. Or maybe *they* had.

Romano's stomach soured as she crossed the room, the realization closing in on her. She wanted to deny it. For god's sake, the woman was a suspect in a murder case. And he was a professional who was dating her aunt. But when she rounded the foot of the bed, she spotted the damning evidence on the floor underneath the nightstand. She'd know it anywhere. After all, she'd helped pick it out. It was a fine timepiece that had cost Aunt Angie the better part of a paycheck. And it had a large dial that he could read without his glasses.

"You *idiot*."

R omano's words still echoed in my brain. *The owner of this apartment is Congressman Dennis Newsome.* I waited until my former partner was safely in the hall, and then carefully shut the door behind her. *Congressman Newsome's door.* Then I made a beeline for her handbag and snatched it off the bed. *Congressman Newsome's bed.* Shuddering, I drew a breath and then unzipped the bag, ripped out her phone, and tossed her purse back on the bed. The screen on her mobile lit up to read:

6 missed calls

3 voicemails

"Ryan, I'm sorry."

I pulled out my own phone, scanned my contacts, and hit dial. Annie's mobile writhed in my hand. I held it up for her to see.

"You didn't notice this? Vibrating in that tiny little bag?"

"Yes, but I didn't want to talk to her. Can't you see?"

I dropped the phone into her handbag, zipped it shut, and slipped my own mobile back in my pocket. Then I shut my eyes and massaged my temples, doing my best to clear my head and regain some semblance of objectivity. To— at least for the moment—push last night out of my mind.

Finally, I walked over to the dining table and stared down at her. "What I see is a woman who is trying to avoid the police."

"Because they think I'm guilty, I can feel it."

"Are you guilty?" I asked.

"No." She covered her face.

"You're guilty of lying to both me and the police about who owns this apartment." *Newsome's apartment.* "What else have you lied about?"

She looked up at me. "Nothing, Ryan, I swear. I couldn't tell you about Dennis Newsome. I was just so embarrassed. Also, he's married and running for reelection. He wanted our friendship kept secret, too."

"I can see how the truth might be inconvenient for both of you."

"It was a mistake, and it's been over for months now. At the time, I was planning to split with Bob, I needed legal advice, so I called Dennis. He's a lawyer, you know—"

The last thing I wanted was the details. "Did Bob know about your consultation with Congressman Newsome?"

"Of course not."

"You sure about that?"

"Yes. We were still living together. Bob was the jealous type."

"With good reason, apparently."

"Ryan, honestly, it was only a handful of times, always up here in the City. I just happened to hang onto his key and—"

"*Mrs. Christiansen,* your social life is none of my business, except as it relates to this case. Newsome is in the midst of a reelection campaign. If your husband threatened to expose the congressman's extramarital activities, that might be a motive for murder."

She buried her face in her hands again. "It was over as quickly as it started. It was nothing." Annie dropped her hands and stared up at me. "And it *is* your business. After last night everything is your business."

"Was that your agenda? To seduce me into whatever it is you're tangled up in?"

"What do you think? That I'm some sort of *temptress*? My son's serving a Mormon mission. I'm forty-eight years old, for crying out loud."

Her voice trailed away, and tears welled in her eyes. I stood watching her for several seconds. As angry as I was, there was part of me that still wanted to comfort her. That would be the part of me that she'd been playing for the past thirty-six hours. My inner putz. Jesus Christ, what had I gotten myself into?

First, I reached for my handkerchief. Then, reconsidering, I took a coffee shop napkin out of the croissant bag and handed that to her instead. "Dry your eyes. You're about to talk to the police."

I pulled the key to the apartment from my pocket and tossed it on the table. *Newsome's key.* Then I started for the door.

"Wait, Ryan, you're not leaving?" She stared back at me in horror. "What should I say to the police?"

Exhaling, I turned to her and said, "Mrs. Christiansen, you're paying me to find your husband's killer. If you want representation before talking to the police, you need to call a lawyer. *Hire* your friend, Newsome, again."

More tears formed in her eyes.

I let loose another sigh, and then in a slightly more conciliatory tone said, "When the lieutenant leaves, move to a hotel downtown. And change cabs on the way over to be safe. If Romano found you here, then somebody else might, too. An investigative reporter even, looking for a scoop on the congressman." Shaking my head, I marveled at the recklessness of this entire undertaking, starting with my own bad judgment.

She dabbed her eyes. "You're staying on my case, right?"

"We'll talk later." Turning to leave, I walked as far as the door and then added, "That is, if you answer my call."

Out in the hall, Romano waited a respectful distance from the door. Keeping my expression even, I promised to catch up with her soon. The elevator, mercifully, opened as soon as I pressed the button.

I blew through the lobby and out the entrance grateful that the neighborhood was still quiet, and I could make my shamefaced escape without notice. To think that less than half an hour ago I'd been strolling these streets with a goofy grin on my face, imagining that I was going *home* to my girlfriend. I ducked into my car, tore away from the curb and set my inner GPS for the Bay Bridge.

As I drove east from the Marina, I wondered if Romano's suspicions had been right all along. Maybe Annie had ransacked her own house. In fact, maybe she'd hurled that rock through her own window. Of course, she couldn't have been in the mysterious car that sped away from the curb, but she might have enlisted the help of a friend. Dennis Newsome's cheesy grin flashed in my brain. I shook him from my thoughts. This was all speculation. The point was Annie Christiansen no longer seemed the innocent victim I had taken her for.

Stopping at a red light in front of the Wharf, I waited while a procession of tourists crossed in front of my car. Two of them appeared to be smirking at me. Who could blame them?

Hell, Annie had lied from the get-go. Starting with telling me she'd returned the key to her female colleague. Probably because she hoped I would be fool enough to take her back to my place. It wasn't an altogether outrageous assumption. I was almost fool enough to take her back to my place.

Then there was that anonymous phone call to her hotel room—which might also have been arranged by Annie. Again, more speculation. Whether it was the work of her accomplice, the mysterious Mr. Flake, or another person entirely, was impossible to determine at this point. But whoever was behind it had gone out of his way to be obvious. As the good detective I usually was, I would never have called and then hung up on somebody I was shadowing. Much less peeled away from the curb in front of her house. Unless I wanted to draw attention to myself. Of course, at the time none of this occurred to me. Probably because I was distracted by my client's provocative neckline.

"I'm beginning to see a pattern here," I said aloud, just as I was curving around the Embarcadero past the massive sculpture, *Cupid's Span*. My face frozen in a scowl, I reminded myself that the artists, Claes Oldenburg and Coosje van Bruggen, created the steel and fiberglass bow and arrow as a tribute to San Francisco's reputation as the "Home Port of Eros."

Even the City's public art was mocking me.

Man, had I fucked up, and now it was all coming back to haunt me, and to the tune of a French accordion. Annie dropping her phone on Chestnut Street, and then snatching it up before I could see missed calls on the screen. The apartment that was supposedly owned by a female artist, only nothing hung on the walls. Sparse, expensive furnishings, high-end water and juice glasses in the cupboard, then a liquor store corkscrew and a cheap wine rack in the closet. No clothes on the rack.

Finally on the freeway, I sped past the sign that announced the last San Francisco exit. The French music, no longer charming, screamed in my brain like the calliope from a circus act.

You didn't have to be Kojak to build the profile. The owner was a professional man with expensive tastes. And he didn't drink. That cheap wine rack and corkscrew had to have been part of Annie's set-up. Because if the owner had been a drinker, there would have been a fancy wine refrigerator and a sleek little bar stocked with pricey liquor, along with the appropriate stem and glassware.

Traffic coming off the Bay Bridge slowed as drivers merged in different directions. I took a minute to find my lane and then, once in place on my eastbound artery, I accelerated through the light, late morning traffic, anxious to put the Home Port of Eros behind me.

Whoever this teetotaler was, I went on to reason, he rarely used the place anymore—hence the absence of clothes in the closet and perishables in his fridge. Perhaps he'd taken a leave of absence, or a temporary assignment elsewhere, say as a U.S. Congressman who now divided his time between Washington D.C. and his home district. But he held onto the place anyway, because he might need it again when he returned to his career. Also because it was a great little pad to escape to whenever he wanted to slip away for some nookie with a member of his constituency.

My knuckles whitened along the steering wheel and the accordion pounded in my brain. I turned on the radio and channel surfed until I landed on Led Zepplin's "Immigrant Song." I cranked up the volume. Robert Plant started singing in French. I shut him off.

Taking a couple of deep breaths, I relaxed my grip on the wheel. I needed to pull myself together, to gain some perspective. I'd been a crazy man ever since Annie had walked into the Swizzle Stick on Thursday. Honestly. Since when did I just jump into bed with a woman?

I checked the clock on my dash. Ten fifteen on Saturday morning and I had yet to call my girlfriend…my *friend*, Angie. That was the most we could ever be to one another. She deserved a man who would be faithful to her, and that wasn't me. Since when did that stop being me?

No matter. The problem was, how to break it? Not over the telephone, of course. But I did need to finally call her. I activated my hands-free. Three rings and she still hadn't picked up. Can't say I blamed her. I waited through the voicemail message and beep.

"Hi, Angie. I'm sorry I didn't get back to you yesterday. I really am. I'll try you again soon. Bye."

I disconnected the call, sighed, and then, surprisingly, felt relieved. At least I was on my way to my old self again. That would be the lonely, pathetic, cynic on the downside of middle age, whose only faithful companion was his job. Right now, my job was to find a murderer. Even if the murderer turned out to be my client.

The music in my head had finally subsided, only to be replaced by a throbbing pain. Then a rumble in my stomach reminded me of the croissant

I'd left behind. There was an IHOP a couple of exits up the road. I decided to make a pit stop.

I snagged a space near the diner's front door, groped my glove box until I found my travel-sized bottle of aspirin, and headed inside.

The hostess offered me my choice of seats. I picked a booth by the window. Seconds later a waitress arrived with a glass of water. She was a petite young Latina with a reserved manner and a voice that didn't aggravate my headache, perhaps because she'd caught sight of the aspirin bottle in my hand. Smiling gratefully up at her, I ordered scrambled eggs, hash browns, bacon, rye toast and "coffee, please, *lots* of coffee."

She left and I shook out four tablets and threw them back with the glass of water. Then my waitress returned with a large coffee carafe and a cup. Another grateful smile. I poured, sipped, and immediately felt my brain begin to focus.

I drifted back to the case. Painful as it was, I had to acknowledge that her relationship with Newsome might not be over. As a candidate for Congress, vulnerable to public scandal, he wouldn't have just forgotten that she still had his key. Surely he was aware that she had access to the loft and probably had someone who kept tabs on when she used it. And with whom, I reminded myself.

Whether she was his current or former mistress, letting Annie hole up in his flat during an election year was a huge risk. Why had he agreed to it? Was he worried she might expose their affair? Was he somehow involved in the doc-tor's murder? Was she? What if this seer stone was a diversion meant to distract me from a different motive closer to home? I now realized that both the rock through the window and the vehicle that peeled away from Annie's house could have been staged events. Maybe the break-in was, too. But why? To scare us? To throw suspicion on this Flake character?

The waitress arrived with my eggs. I peppered and salted and then eagerly dug in. Nothing like a diner breakfast.

But in spite of all of her deceptions, I couldn't believe Annie had shot her husband. Romano said the murder weapon had been a large gun, maybe a .357 Magnum. It would have taken both of her small hands to hold and fire something that size, plus it would probably have left a burn mark, and I didn't notice any. Moreover, my obvious prejudice aside, I had a hard time envisioning this lovely, artistic, gentle soul blowing a guy's brains out. She could have hired someone, of course. But why would Annie do that? The life insurance? The guy was rich. Wouldn't she have expected a fair divorce settlement? Maybe not if he'd discovered her affair with Newsome. Still, like she reminded me this morning, she had a son on a Mormon mission. Would she hire someone to blow his dad's brains into his empty safe? This wasn't just a hit. It was a statement.

Heaving a sigh of frustration, I noticed that my waitress had left the bill on the table. I pulled out my wallet, began to take out a couple of ones for the tip, stopped, reconsidered, and dropped a ten on the table instead. Then, as I headed for the cash register, I went to check the time on my watch.

Shit! I stared down at the pale circle on my tanned wrist. *Man, had I fucked up.*

My change from the IHOP cashier wadded in my fist, I beeped open the car, leaned against the driver's side and glared down at the pavement. *Goddammit, where the hell had I left that watch?*

I stuffed the change in my wallet and made a quick inventory of my coat and pants pockets. Not there. Then I got into the car and rested my forehead against the steering wheel, telling myself to calm down, think rationally. The last time I'd seen it on my wrist was at nine last night, right before my lame attempt to leave the apartment. *Newsome's apartment.* After that things were a blur. But logic—if it could be applied in this situation—told me that I hadn't removed it during the night. I'd been too preoccupied with taking off the essentials. It must have come off the next morning before my shower. So it was still in the bathroom, probably on the shelf or maybe on the back of the toilet tank. Either way, unless she'd used the facilities, Romano couldn't have seen it.

My mobile pulsed in my pocket. Hopefully Angie. I pulled it out. No luck. But second-best. Mrs. Z and a return to the case.

"Hi, Ryan. I've learned some interesting things about our Mr. Blair Thurgood."

"Who?" I asked.

"The guy from Orem who wants the stone. Also calls himself Stripling Warrior. Haven't you read your email?"

I rubbed both eyes with my thumb and index finger. "Not yet. I had some personal business to attend to this morning."

"Oh. Are you at home now?"

"No, but I will be in thirty minutes," I replied, and then, noticing the unusual lack of background pandemonium on her end, asked, "Where are you?"

"In the car. I was hoping I could use the computer at the office to do more research on the case."

"Great. When I get there, you can bring me up to speed."

"I'll put on a pot of coffee for you."

"You don't need to make my coffee," I said, but she had already hung up.

I spent the rest of the drive home contemplating why anyone would be so anxious to acquire this rock. It wasn't tied to somebody famous so it couldn't be very valuable. Of course, if the parties inquiring after it truly believed the thing was magic that would make it priceless, meaning I was potentially about to deal with three highly irrational individuals.

"Utter and complete kooks," I said aloud as I turned onto my street to see a large black pick-up with Utah plates parked in front of my house.

Jesus Christ. That polygamist Flake was inside with Mrs. Z. I parked next to her car in my drive and checked the glove box for my gun. *Damn.* I'd left it on the top shelf of the kitchen cupboard. Since going private I'd pretty much quit carrying. Hardly needed to for my caseload. I got out of the car and was creeping toward the side door when it flew open and Mrs. Z waved me inside.

I bounded up the step and followed her through the laundry room and into the kitchen. She pointed to the window over my sink.

"Mr. D. Wendell Flake, in the flesh."

"What's he doing here?" I asked. "Did you give him my address?"

"No, but it's in the book, and his email said he'd 'speak with you directly.' I guess a phone call wasn't direct enough for him."

Peering through my curtains, I spied a fair-skinned, fortyish, severely stoical looking man dressed in a cowboy hat, western shirt, and jeans. He sat ramrod erect on one of my porch chairs cradling a mug from my kitchen in his hands.

I looked back at Mrs. Z. "You just let him inside?"

Mrs. Z took down a mug from the cupboard, filled it with coffee from the fresh pot she'd promised, and handed it to me. "Don't worry, Ryan, I was wrong about him. He's not scary."

"He's not?"

She leaned against the counter and folded her arms across her chest. I noted that even on the weekend she looked polished, today in a black linen jacket over a white t-shirt and blue jeans. No more gingham-checked jumpers for this former Mormon woman.

"There are two types of creepy Mormon polygamists," she explained. "The scary kind and the wimpy kind."

"And you could tell just by looking at him that he was the wimpy variety?"

"Sure. Once I'd loaded up that gutless shotgun of yours and aimed it at the horny coot's chest."

The coffee mug slipped an inch or so and splashed scalding liquid on my fingers. I set it on the counter and reached for a towel. "You *loaded* my shotgun?"

"That one you keep locked in the hall closet."

"Yes, I know where I keep it, but—hey, what do you mean gutless? Is a twenty-gauge not adequate for your needs?"

"Not for shooting Mormon polygamists."

"Never tried that sport," I half laughed. "How'd you find the key to the closet?"

"It's in the drawer with the coffee filters." She rolled her eyes. "The handgun in your cupboard would have done better, only I've never used one. And I sure as heck wasn't going to aim something I didn't already know how to shoot."

"Good thinking," I replied, absorbing the absurdity of the situation. "But what exactly did you load my shotgun with? I don't have any shells."

"You do now." She smiled brightly. "When you told me we were going to be investigating Utah polygamists, I went straight to Walmart and stocked up. I got some clips for your handgun, too. You know, Ryan, if you're going to start taking on dangerous clients, you really ought to go back to carrying."

"Uh-huh." I took a sip of my coffee, noticing it had cooled to just the right temperature. I thanked her for brewing it. She didn't appear to hear me.

"Around ten minutes ago I heard this big engine roar up to the house. I looked outside and right off I knew it was him. Recognized the truck and the plates that I ran for you yesterday. I loaded the gun, walked out front, and aimed for his chest. His hands flew up in the air and he screamed, 'Don't shoot.' Then he started blubbering."

"What would you have done if he'd turned out to be the scary type of polygamist?"

"Lowered my aim to his crotch."

A mental picture flashed in my brain. Mrs. Z blowing off a Utah polygamist's nuts in the front yard of my suburban California tract home. Thank god I only kept a twenty gauge.

"Good thing he surrendered," I replied evenly.

"Whined like a baby. Sounded just like Great-Uncle Moroni when Great-Aunt Lavinia came after him with the pitchfork."

I took another sip of coffee. "Talk to him at all?"

"Nope. I thought it best to let him calm down. Besides, I knew you'd be here any minute and would like a fresh crack at him. But it might be a good idea if I sat in on the conversation. You may need a translator."

I looked through the window at Flake again. He seemed content at the moment, albeit with a subtle, dazed expression that, back in a simpler, more wholesome time, I would have merely passed off as stoned. He lifted the mug to his mouth.

"What's he drinking?" I asked.

"Coffee. He takes it with cream, no sugar."

"Coffee?" I turned to her in surprise. "Isn't he a Mormon?"

"He's also a polygamist. The plygs don't think they need to obey all the rules on account of the sacrifices they make living the higher law."

"Sacrifices like group sex with the wives?"

Mrs. Z gazed back at me, utterly nonplussed. "You catch on quick, Ryan."

I poured myself more coffee and headed out back, motioning her to follow. "Yep, I'm going to need a translator."

I saw what she meant. D. Wendell Flake was definitely not a scary variety polygamist. The meek tip of the hat was the first give-away, followed by the limp handshake. After that, the exceedingly tentative manner he handed over his cup when Mrs. Z offered him a refill, as though dangling a bit of raw meat in front of a snarling pit bull. Then there was that stoned expression of his, clearly the extension of a mind untethered from reality. The guy was weird, to be sure, but nowhere near the frightening creep that Dr. Christiansen warned Annie about.

"Forgive me for dropping in unannounced," Flake began as he watched Mrs. Z take his cup to the kitchen.

"No problem." I settled into a chair opposite him.

"Well, the *missus* sure had a problem with it."

"Excuse me? The missus?"

Flake motioned toward the house. "That Utah gal of yours."

"Mrs. Zimmerman is my assistant." I cleared my throat. "What makes you think she's from Utah?"

Despite the fact that my patio was shielded from the sun, Flake's eyes appeared to be dilating. "You mean she's not?"

"She is from there originally."

He raised an eyebrow, as if some fuzzy realization had settled upon him. "That Sister Christiansen of yours isn't from Utah."

"Mr. Flake, I am a private detective. Mrs. Christiansen is my client and Mrs. Zimmerman works here as my assistant during business hours."

"This here is Saturday," Flake observed.

I was forming a response when Mrs. Z walked back out with his coffee.

"Cream, no sugar," she said.

He took the mug and smiled up at her. "Thank you kindly."

She glared back at him. His face fell. He sipped his coffee and then fixed his clouded blue eyes on a spot beyond me.

"The Lord bade me to hie here," he said.

I looked over at Mrs. Z, who was now leaning against my round patio table with her arms folded across her chest.

"He means God told him to get here as quickly as possible," she explained. "There's a Mormon hymn, 'If I Could Hie to Kolob.'"

"What's a Kolob?" I wondered aloud.

"The planet God lives on," Mrs. Z explained.

"Aha!" Then turning to Flake, I asked, "God sent you to my place to claim the Hatcher Stone?"

"Yes, as I told Brother Christiansen, it was to be my inheritance."

"Sir, did you know that Brother...I mean Dr. Christiansen has been murdered?" I asked.

"I heard he'd hied to the next sphere, yes," Flake replied, his eyes still cast somewhere beyond, perhaps into that next sphere he referred to.

"Well, wherever the doctor went, he didn't hie there willingly. Somebody blew his brains out with a large caliber pistol."

Flake blinked and the corners of his mouth quivered.

When he didn't reply I went on to say, "We think somebody may have killed him in order to get the Hatcher Stone. Do you have any idea who might want to do that?"

Flake shook his head slowly. "It wouldn't do any good to kill for the stone. The Lord will only bestow it upon its rightful heir."

"Mr. Flake, why do you want the stone so much?" I asked.

"For heavenly assistance with my sugar beet crop. Also for the enhancement of conjugal relations with my wives."

Exchanging a droll look with Mrs. Z, I decided to change the subject. "I understand you make confections?"

He nodded. "Marshmallows are my specialty."

"In his heyday, Zedekiah Hatcher used the stone to maintain the most successful farm in Southern Utah," Mrs. Z explained, and then frowning, added, "What makes you think you're the rightful heir?"

"I'm a direct descendant of the family."

"How can you be a direct descendant?" she asked. "Your last name is Flake."

"I'm related through the maternal line," Flake replied.

"*Really?*" Mrs. Z pushed herself away from the table and placed a hand on her hip. I waited for her to ask another question, but she appeared to have fallen into her own thoughts.

Flake turned to me, his eyes actually seeming to focus. "Do you have the stone in your possession, sir?"

"I have what my client believes is the Hatcher Stone." I reached for one of the fakes inside my pocket. "Understand that we have no way of proving its authenticity. We assume it's real because it was found in Dr. Christiansen's former residence and because it resembles the picture he posted on the internet."

I handed him the stone. He set aside his coffee mug and took it gently in his hands. Then he looked back at me, his billiard ball pupils gleaming. "This is authentic."

"Then I hope it will help you with your business and other relations," I said, smiling.

He stroked the rock lovingly. "I haven't much money, but you can have what little I have on me."

"Mr. Flake, as I said in my email, my client has no desire to sell the stone. It's yours for free."

"In that case, I will ship you a deluxe case of my prizewinning marshmallows."

"Thank you. That's very generous." I glanced over at Mrs. Z. Her thoughts were still elsewhere. Then I turned back to Flake. "I wonder if you might answer a few questions."

"I'll do my best," he replied, still stroking the rock.

"My client, Mrs. Christiansen, claims you paid her a visit on Friday evening before last, is that true?"

"Yes, sir. I went there looking for her husband," Flake said, his eyes still on the stone. "Very nice lady. But she couldn't help me so I bid her goodbye."

"Did you meet with Dr. Christiansen before he died?"

"Finally, yes. It took some doing." He ran his finger clockwise and then counter-clockwise around the rim of the stone. "I left him phone messages throughout the weekend that he never returned. Then on Monday afternoon I went to his office, but his gal said he was making his rounds at the hospital."

I looked over at Mrs. Z. She'd gone back to leaning against my patio table.

"So, when did you finally catch up with the doctor?" I asked, turning back to Flake.

"Monday evening. I waited for him outside the hospital and followed him to that new townhouse of his. I spoke with him at his doorstep, just as I had with Sister Christiansen. Only he was real jumpy."

"Jumpy how?"

"Like he'd seen a ghost."

I flashbacked to Annie Christiansen at the Swizzle Stick on Thursday night. She'd also seen a ghost. "Go on."

"He told me he'd misplaced the Hatcher Stone, but was confident that he would track it down in the next day or two. Then he shut the door in my face and left me to wait on his porch. A minute later he came back out and handed me this big thick envelope. Said it had his receipt for the stone, some of its history, potential heirs, and other useful information I might need. I guess so I'd know his offer was legit. He told me to hang onto it as it could prove to be valuable."

"May I see this envelope?"

"I left it back at the motel for safe keeping."

"Which motel?"

"The Pine Cone. Do you know it?"

"I do indeed. Anything stand out to you? Among the information in the envelope, that is."

"No, sir. All that fine print gave me a headache, can't say I studied it much. I already believed Brother Christiansen. I'm very good at spotting a lie," Flake boasted as he slipped the fake into his pants pocket.

"Fine quality to possess," I observed.

Flake nodded stoically. "'Tis indeed."

"Last Thursday night somebody threw a rock through Mrs. Christiansen's window," I said. "Any idea who might have done that?"

"No," Flake said, his eyes clouding.

"Were you around her house at all on Thursday night?"

"No." Flake blinked and seemed to focus. "She's a real nice lady, and it wouldn't do any good to scare a nice lady like that. The Lord will only bestow His inheritance upon the rightful heirs."

Satisfied that I had successfully picked Mr. D. Wendell Flake's brain of all its useful information, I stood, thanked him for his time, and handed him my card. "I'd like to see that envelope, if you don't mind."

Flake nodded. "After this I'm going to check out of the motel, get some supplies for the trip home, and put some gas in my truck. I can stop here on my way out of town. That Utah gal of yours can make as many copies as she wants."

"Thank you."

We walked together to the front door where I received another limp handshake, another meek tip of the hat, and a business card that read, *D. Wendell Flake, The Marshmallow Man,* atop a county road address and a 435 area code number.

"Call the next time you're in Utah," he said in parting.

I waited while his truck roared away and then went to the kitchen to find Mrs. Z rinsing Flake's coffee mug in the sink.

"What'd you think?" I asked.

"I want to learn more about this Hatcher family."

"OK, you do that. Meanwhile, I'd better check my email."

"Oh, right." Mrs. Z snapped to. "I've already printed it out for you. Also my research so far."

I followed her into the office and, seeing the two bulging manila folders sitting side-by-side on her desk, settled into the fake leather easy chair, put on my readers, and cheerfully anticipated yet another of Mrs. Z's meticulous reports.

She handed me one of the folders and settled behind her desk. "Mr. Gordon Hatcher responded first. Just five minutes after I sent him the email last night."

I opened to a copy of a ten-year-old newspaper photo of Hatcher conversing with an elderly trio that the caption identified as the Mormon First Presidency. In what appeared to be his mid-thirties at the time, Hatcher was tall, medium build, with a thick head of brown hair. The caption also read: *Hatcher to assume a major role in downtown retail development.*

"You'll see in his email that he's very anxious to collect his ancestor's stone and will fly in at your convenience."

"So this guy's a Mormon big cheese," I surmised, still studying his picture.

"He's in the Twelfth Quorum of the Seventy," Mrs. Z said. "That's big, all right, but maybe not big enough for Hatcher. I'm guessing he's a GA wannabe." She tapped the eraser end of her pencil on her notebook.

I looked at her over the top of my readers. "What's that?"

"Sorry for the Mormonspeak. What I mean is he wants to be a General Authority or GA as we call them. The biggest of the big cheeses. So he devotes his time to brown-nosing the Brethren."

"The Brethren are also GA's?"

"Another term for the men who run the church, yeah." She pointed her pencil at the picture. "That retail development is a huge mall in downtown Salt Lake City that was bankrolled by the church. Hatcher is a contractor. My guess is he gave the Brethren a sweet deal on labor and materials. Also, while he claims to collect Mormon antiques, he actually donates most of his acquisitions to the church." Pointing again at the folder she'd given me, Mrs. Z added, "There's a piece in there about his gifts to the LDS History Museum."

I leafed through the pages. More articles about the Salt Lake mall and images of Hatcher schmoozing the so-called Brethren. Finally, a piece about the museum with a depiction of Hatcher aside a pioneer handcart. "So more brown nosing."

"Looks that way. My guess is that if Hatcher ever does become a prophet, it will be through the conventional chain of command, not some magic rock."

"OK. Tell me about this Stripling Warrior."

Her smile brightened. "That would be our Mr. Blair Thurgood, and he is turning out to be an interesting individual."

She got up from behind the desk and brought me the other folder. The first thing inside was a printout of an ad for *Thurgood Automotive*. It featured a squeaky-clean uniformed repairman leaning against a fender, a blue-collar version of Gordon Hatcher. I looked to Mrs. Z for a summary. She leaned back against the side of her desk, folded her arms across her chest, and crossed one ankle over the other.

"Mr. Thurgood responded fifteen minutes after I sent the email. He wrote that he couldn't travel to collect the stone, but that he was very interested and asked if you could mail it to him."

"A car repairman probably can't spring for a plane ticket."

"Also, his wife was recently fired from her position at BYU."

I looked at her over the top of my readers.

She smiled down at me. "This is where it gets interesting."

Closing the folder in my lap, I took off my glasses and returned them to my shirt pocket. "I'm listening."

"Up until recently, Thurgood's wife, Dr. Meredith Snow, was a popular professor of Agricultural Science at BYU. There's a photo of her in the file."

Annie's voice echoed in my brain. *My Mormon family's name was Snow.*

"Say," I interrupted, "did you ever find any connection between the Hatcher farm and a family named Snow?"

Her jaw slackened. "Oh my gosh, I totally forgot that you asked me to look into that. I'm so sorry, I'll—"

"Don't worry, it can wait." I raised a hand to wave off her apology. "Go on about Dr. Snow."

"Right." Mrs. Z drew a breath. "She's a member of Sisters for Equality, an organization calling for the ordination of women to the LDS priesthood."

Donning my readers again, I flipped through the file until I found an article with Snow's picture. The story, from October of last year, bore the headline, *Mormon Feminists Protest at LDS General Conference.* In the photo, Snow, a slender, neatly coiffed redhead, stood with seven other women beneath the spires of the LDS Temple in Salt Lake City. "Is her activism the reason she was fired from her job?"

"Sure. BYU is owned by the church, and LDS leaders do not tolerate public opposition to their views. Her local leaders have scheduled a court to excommunicate her."

I closed the folder and pocketed my readers. "Sound like nice guys. But what do you figure her husband's motivation might be?"

"Not sure yet. He's publicly stated that he does not support his wife's views on women assuming the Mormon priesthood." Mrs. Z pointed to the file in my lap. "Um, there are three articles, one from the *New York Times.* I printed them out. It's all there for—"

"I'm sure it is." Smiling, I stood and tucked the folders under one arm. "I will study it thoroughly. But it sounds like the first order of business is to contact these men and arrange to give them their genuine fake seer stones."

She made a face. "Is that your plan? To give Hatcher and Thurgood fakes?"

I reached inside my pocket for the two remaining stones and set them on the desk. "They're all fakes. Flake's too. Mrs. Christiansen made reproductions."

"I'm not so sure that's a good idea, Ryan." Mrs. Z said, pushing herself away from the front of the desk.

"How come?"

"You seem to have forgotten what a close-knit community the Mormons are. Play out this scheme of yours and within days—if not hours— word will leak that more than one person is in possession of the Hatcher Stone. Then your suspects are bound to smell a rat."

Jesus, was I ever off my game. "Hadn't thought of that."

Frustrated, I excused myself to my room, dropped into my easy chair, and opened the file to the *Times* article about Dr. Meredith Snow. Even through my readers, the print began to blur. Last night's binge was catching up with me. I tossed the files onto my bed, shed my clothes, and stepped into the shower in my master bath. Taking longer than usual, I let the hot water rain down on me, washing away Newsome's Dial Soap.

Feeling better, I toweled off, put on fresh clothes, and dialed Angie. Still no answer. I left another message and then stared down at the file folders on the edge of my bed. Now that I'd supposedly given the stone to Flake, how best to approach Hatcher and Thurgood? Thurgood would be relatively easy to track down in Orem. But Hatcher, being wealthy and more insulated, might be a little harder to reach if I couldn't offer some kind of incentive. I opened his file and, after a half-minute of hunting down my readers, found the email he'd sent last night.

> *Dear Mr. Ryan,*
> *I'm very interested in acquiring the Hatcher Stone from your client, Mrs. Christiansen. As a direct descendant of its original owner, I am an especially motivated buyer and can fly to CA as early as tomorrow. I look forward to your reply.*

Neat, to the point, and signed with an automatic signature that included his office and mobile number. Not much else I could read into his message. But, based on Mrs. Z's research, he was obviously a successful and influential man, probably in possession of an above average intellect. Mrs. Z was right. I couldn't pretend I hadn't already parted with the stone. But perhaps I could finesse the offer a bit. After all, I hadn't promised Flake that the stone I'd given him was authentic, only that it resembled the picture. Maybe I could pretend Christiansen had two stones that looked like the original. Only I'd left Flake with the impression that he had the only one. But hopefully he was removed enough from Salt Lake City, not to mention reality, to get wind of any scam. Hopefully.

Phone still in hand, I dialed Hatcher's mobile. He answered on the second ring in a deep, steady voice that exuded authority.

"Mr. Hatcher, this is Matt Ryan. I contacted you on behalf of my client, Mrs. Ann Christiansen."

"Yes, hello, thank you for responding to my email. I am very interested in acquiring the stone. I can be in California by late this afternoon. May I meet you then?"

"Yes. But there is something I must tell you first."

"What's that?"

"Mrs. Christiansen found two stones identical to an online photo of the Hatcher Stone."

"*Really?* How fascinating," he replied. "One of them must be a decoy."

"A decoy?"

"It wasn't unusual for decoys to be made of these so-called prophetic aids, to throw potential thieves off the track. Either way, both artifacts have historical value to a collector like myself. Also, as I said in my email, I happen to be a direct descendant of Zedekiah Hatcher."

His skepticism over the stone's powers seemed to confirm Mrs. Z's conclusions. "So-called, you say? There was another man here just moments ago who claimed he could tell which stone was authentic and took it with him."

Hatcher coughed and cleared his throat. "Who was this man? If he collects antiquities, perhaps I know him."

I chuckled softly. "I didn't take him for a collector, more like, well…he seemed to be a very spiritual person. He'd been in contact with Dr. Christiansen ahead of his death." I hesitated, wondering if I should even bring up the envelope that Christiansen had given Flake. While mysterious, its contents probably weren't proof of anything. Then again, it did add a hint of legitimacy to this scam I was trying to pull. "Apparently, Dr. Christiansen entrusted some documentation to this man before he died."

"Do you have a copy of this documentation?"

"No, but we can try to obtain one for you. Meanwhile, Mrs. Christiansen is willing to part with the duplicate stone for free, if you're still interested."

"I am, but as I said, I will have to travel to collect it. Can you guarantee that you will hold it for me until I get there?"

"Absolutely."

We arranged to meet him at four at a taqueria near the Abbottsville airport, rang off, and then found the email contact for Blair Thurgood. If he was truly unable to afford the travel, that would make him an unlikely suspect in a murder that took place here. Also, I knew where he worked and, if need be, I could find him. I checked my watch, cursed at my bare wrist, and then looked over at the clock on my nightstand. Twelve forty-five. A little over three hours to kill before I met Hatcher.

I decided my time might be best spent pursuing a suspect with a more compelling motive for murder—namely, the discovery of an affair with the victim's wife. My stomach souring, I realized that I was going to have to pay a call on Dennis Newsome.

I threw on my jacket and went to find Mrs. Z in the office. She was so focused on her computer screen that when I greeted her, she jumped.

"Didn't mean to startle you. I was just going to ask you to email Mr. Thurgood that the stone is no longer available."

"Will do."

"Also, can you find out if Congressman Newsome is in town?"

She made a face and then fiddled with her mouse and began typing. "I suppose his appearance schedule is on his website. But why exactly do you care about the whereabouts of the guy you like to call 'that *dick* Newsome?'"

"He may have a connection to the case. Remember how Mrs. Christiansen said she had a colleague with an apartment in the City?"

"She was there at the time of the murder."

"And she was there last night as well."

"Oh goody." Eyes still on her screen, Mrs. Z grinned as she clicked her mouse. "No more hotel bills."

I ran a hand over my head and let it come to rest on the back of my neck. "Actually, I told her to move to a hotel downtown for safety's sake."

"*Downtown*? As in downtown San Francisco?"

"For now, yes," I continued, "the apartment doesn't belong to a colleague. It belongs to Dennis Newsome."

"Really?" She squinted up at me. "Why would Mrs. Christiansen lie?"

I took care to keep my expression even. "Evidently she and Newsome started an affair right before she separated from her husband. She was embarrassed about it and didn't want to admit she still had a key to his place."

Mrs. Z let out a long sigh. "Mormons can be a sleazy bunch. Don't forget to pack your handgun."

"You want me to carry a concealed weapon?"

"You've a permit, don't you?"

"Yes, but now that I'm a civilian I'm limited in where I can carry. For instance, I'm banned from courthouses, schools, and businesses that sell alcohol."

"Uh-oh. That final restriction certainly presents a problem." She twisted the computer monitor for me to see.

I put on my readers and peered down at the screen. "What am I looking at?"

"The congressman's website. Last night Newsome was the after-dinner speaker at an Abbottsville Chamber of Commerce event. Would you like to listen to an excerpt?"

"I would *not*," I replied, removing my glasses.

"Tonight he debates Mrs. Kincaid at Grafton College. And tomorrow night he is speaking at a special meeting at the LDS Stake Center. The public is welcome." She smiled up at me.

"Any idea where he was at the time of the murder?"

Shaking her head, she frowned at the screen. "Doesn't say here. I'll have to do some more digging."

"OK, I'll be gone for the rest of the afternoon."

The fake stones were still on the desk where I'd left them. I slipped one of them in my jacket pocket and then looked at my wrist for the time. *Shit.*

"Where's your watch?" Mrs. Z asked.

"Misplaced it," I muttered.

"Got your phone?"

"Yes," I replied, patting my pocket.

"Is it charged?"

I sighed. "I'll plug it in the car charger."

"Sure you won't take your firearm?"

"I'm sure."

"Just so you know, both gun and ammo are in your kitchen cupboard."

"Thank you. That's comforting." I smirked. "Mr. Flake is on his way to collect his belongings and check out of the Pine Cone Motel. He should be by soon with an envelope he received from Dr. Christiansen. I'd like you to make copies of the contents."

"Sure thing."

"No need to load the shotgun." I winked. "Also, will you please call Mrs. Christiansen on her mobile and find out where she is staying?"

"Will do," she replied.

I smiled and then, turning to leave, added, "After that go home to your family. It's Saturday, for crying out loud. The rest can wait."

"You're working today."

"That's different," I called back to her as I opened the front door. "I don't have a life."

Immediately regretting my words, I braced myself for an inquiry about Angie. It never came. Instead, after a brief silence she simply said, "Be careful out there, Ryan."

I figured Newsome Campaign Headquarters would be the best place to start. I plugged my phone into the car charger and drove downtown. There was a spot right in front of the place. An oversized image of the prick's face smiled at me through the window. Turning away in disgust, I noted that my car was idling across from Angie's condo and just up the street from the police headquarters where her niece worked.

The clock on my dash read one o'clock, meaning that Angie, having spent her Saturday morning sleeping in, drinking coffee, and completing today's crossword, was now strolling the stalls at the farmer's market, probably wearing jeans and one of those turtlenecks she liked, and sipping a fruit smoothie. Romano, on the other hand, was certainly still at work, either in San Francisco, here in Abbottsville, or somewhere in between. But probably not in the office at her desk. I couldn't exactly place Romano, but I knew precisely where to find Angie. For some reason that depressed me.

The phone rang. Mrs. Z. I turned off the engine.

"I hope you're on your way home," I said, in lieu of a greeting.

"I'm still waiting on Flake."

"Huh, sort of thought he'd be there by now."

"Maybe he has a lot of packing to do."

"Figured a guy like him could fit everything he owns into a single backpack."

"I imagine he'll be here any minute. In the meantime, Mrs. Christiansen has checked into the St. Francis Hotel on Union Square."

One of the most romantic hotels in the City, I noted. "Great."

"She's booked the room on her own credit card as well as advanced us more money."

"Good. Although the credit card might be traced."

"Well, I doubt any of our suspects have that capability. Unless Flake figures out a way to use that fake stone you gave him."

I laughed mirthlessly. She was probably correct, but who knew what a nimble hacker could accomplish? Especially for the right price, something both Newsome and Hatcher could afford.

"I sent the email off to Thurgood like you asked," Mrs. Z added.

"Thank you."

"Also, on the morning of Dr. Christiansen's murder, Congressman Newsome was on the House floor debating an energy bill. I found him on CSPAN. Would you like to listen to his remarks?"

Rolling my eyes, I thanked Mrs. Z, got out of the car, and pocketed my phone. Since Newsome was the sort of man who would most likely contract out a killing, his whereabouts at the exact time of the crime didn't necessarily exonerate him. That being said, I always liked to know the answer before I asked the question. I made a mental note to save up for a raise for Mrs. Z, as well as a bonus for overtime.

The desk in the smallish front lobby of Newsome Campaign Headquarters was manned by a comely brunette who probably still needed to show ID when ordering a cocktail. In spite of the girl's obvious appeal, I figured the Congressman wasn't doing her. Too risky and too close to home. Better a more mature woman. Like a soon to be divorced, forty-something artist, I concluded, doing my best to keep my humiliation in check.

As luck would have it, Newsome happened to be on the premises, meeting with some advisors. Moments after the pretty brunette announced my arrival, he was out in the lobby pumping my hand hello.

"Mr. Ryan, I was sorry to hear that the Abbottsville police force lost one of its finest last year."

"Thank you," I replied, the disingenuousness in my voice rising to match his. Then, pulling my hand out of his grip, I added, "They're paying me a fair retirement."

"Which you now sweeten with some private detective work, I understand. Are you here to make a contribution to my campaign?"

I smirked.

"It's small business owners like you who benefit most from my responsible fiscal policies," he explained, cheesy grin intact.

"Actually, I was hoping you could help me with a case I'm working on."

"Is that so? Now I'm really curious." He motioned toward the door he had just come through.

I followed him into a large office that hummed with conversation and ringing telephones. Young people hovered over laptops lined up along four parallel worktables. Most of his staff was fair-haired, and none made eye contact with the candidate as we breezed past. Campaign posters covered the walls save for one large space occupied by some muted flat-screens streaming CNN, FOX News, and MSNBC. I spotted a couple of middle-aged thugs in expensive suits chatting up a female staffer. Maybe the advisors Newsome had just met with.

Newsome led me into what served as the break room. There was a low-end apartment complex fridge, a cheap microwave, and two vending machines, one for soft drinks, the other for snacks. No coffee pot. A campaign poster hung above the sink. Candidate Newsome and his family: his well-coiffed wife, corporate-suited son-in-law, and obviously pregnant daughter. I sighed inwardly. Another Newsome offspring waiting to be unleashed on the world.

The rest of the room was dominated by a chrome and plastic table very similar to the one in the break room at police headquarters where Romano and I had questioned him a couple of years ago.

He pulled his wallet out of his pocket. "Buy you a drink?"

"Thanks, I'll take a Sprite."

Newsome fed some bills into the slot, took one and then another green can from the bottom of the chute and brought them to the table. I popped mine open and took a sip. Very refreshing.

I watched Newsome do the same, noticing his custom-made suit, gold and black enamel cufflinks, and manicured fingers. The man certainly knew how to make a good appearance, and he was a charmer. No wonder the women loved him. A particular type of woman, I reminded myself before taking another drink of Sprite. Its refreshment level had now gone south. My anger gathering, I decided it best to start with a neutral subject.

"Ready for your debate with Mrs. Kincaid?"

He nodded enthusiastically as he finished swallowing. "She's a formidable opponent, but we're on the higher ground—on policy and, of course, morally."

I set down my Sprite and drew a breath. I couldn't even stomach small talk with this asshole. Better get to the point and fast. "I've been hired by Mrs. Annie Christiansen to find the person who killed her husband."

He raised both eyebrows. "She doesn't think the police will do that?"

"She's worried they're on the wrong track. Who do you think might have killed him?"

"Maybe one of those crackpots he bought his Mormon collectibles from."

"You knew about his collection?"

He shrugged. "Everyone who knew him knew about that. Word was some crank from Southern Utah was looking for him right before he died."

I nodded. "As a matter of fact, I just met the gentleman you're referring to."

"Find out what he was after?"

"Something called a seer stone. The doctor couldn't locate it. Then, after his death, Mrs. Christiansen discovered the artifact among her own possessions. I turned it over to the gentleman in question today."

Newsome's eyes darted up at me. They were crystal blue with a wolflike sharpness to them. "That should tell you something. The guy wanted this relic. Christiansen couldn't deliver it, so he killed him."

I paused to appreciate the irony. Newsome was playing out the stereotypical role of villain in a made-for-TV mystery: the guilty party who tries to throw the detective off his scent by helping him solve the case. "I think there might be some holes in your theory there, Congressman."

"Really? How so?"

"Well, in the first place, if the guy wanted this relic so bad why commit murder without recovering it?"

"Maybe he thought Christiansen had lied to him about having the stone, flew into a rage, and killed him."

I tried to imagine Flake flying into a rage. The notion caused me to stifle a snicker. "Possible, but not likely. The doctor supposedly gave this gentleman some sort of written documentation before he died."

Scowling, Newsome studied his can of Sprite, as though reading the fine print. "What is this documentation? Where is it?"

"Dunno. What and where do you think it might be?"

He sipped and then swallowed some of his drink. "I've no earthly idea. I wasn't even here. I heard about Dr. Christiansen's tragic death while I was still in Washington."

"Yes, you were debating an energy bill on the House floor."

"You bothered to check my whereabouts at the time of the murder?"

"As I would with any suspect."

"*I'm* a suspect?"

I picked my can up and swirled the contents. "Of course, a guy like you would most likely hire someone to commit a murder, so that shoots a hole in your alibi."

"Ryan, why, in heaven's name, would you think that I might be involved in the murder of a man I have, for many years, considered a close friend?"

"Because he found out you were fucking his wife." I downed the rest of my Sprite and lobbed the can free-throw style at a large gray trash receptacle. Score!

"That's outrageous," Newsome spat, his face reddening.

I smiled to myself. He was even more rattled than I'd hoped. "He threatened to blow the whistle on you. Upend your campaign."

A cheerful staffer loped through the door. When he saw Newsome his face fell. He went to the refrigerator, snatched out a lunch bag, mumbled "Excuse me, sir," and then high-tailed it out as quickly as his long legs could carry him. Unfortunately for me, the boy wasn't quick enough to keep Newsome from regaining his composure.

"Ryan, I assure you Mrs. Christiansen is nothing more than a friend." He straightened in his seat. "One I've rarely seen since she quit attending our church."

"So why does she have a key to your apartment in San Francisco?"

The asshole blinked.

"That romantic little place in the Marina with the great view and surround stereo. She says the two of you *rendezvoused* there on more than one occasion."

A bemused smile crossed his face. "Ryan, you sound unduly irritated. Also, you seem to know a lot about my apartment. Could it be that you've been spending time there? Enjoying my view and...listening to some romantic tunes, perhaps?"

My teeth clenched. I wondered how a swollen lip might flatter him in tonight's debate with Mrs. Kincaid. "You haven't told me why she has a key to your place."

"Nor do I need to. While I'm always happy to cooperate with the police, I feel no such compulsion when it comes to private detectives. But to satisfy your bizarre curiosity, I will tell you that a few months ago Mrs. Christiansen came to me for guidance on how to proceed with a divorce. She seemed vulnerable, almost desperate. Since I've no expertise in family law, I couldn't advise her. But seeing how distraught she was, I loaned her the use of my flat as a retreat. How she spent her time there, I don't know. Only that she wasn't with me."

Vulnerable. Desperate. The perfect victim for him to prey on. "She tells it differently."

"Then it's her word against mine." Newsome stood and buttoned his immaculate navy suitcoat. "And I'm a respected member of Congress and a happily married man."

Rather than respond, I directed all of my mental effort toward keeping myself from clocking the respected, happily married congressman right there in the shitty break room he provided for his staff.

"Now, if you'll excuse me, I must get back to my campaign." He turned and quit the room, leaving his Sprite can behind on the table for somebody else to dispose of.

Damn. I'd let him get the better of me. And the fucking French music had begun lilting in my ears again. After a couple of deep breaths, my brain silenced, and I collected myself.

When I paced back through the office, the candidate was nowhere to be seen, likewise his two advisors. But the room still hummed with the activity of his staffers, none of whom made eye contact with me as I passed their workstations. The fact that they responded to me in the same manner they had Newsome was unnerving. Did they think I was an asshole, too?

Nodding goodbye to the brunette at the front desk, I pushed through the front door, checked my watch, and scowled at the sight of my bare wrist. Then I looked up to see Lieutenant Stella Romano stepping out of her car. It was parked just behind mine.

"Well, fancy meeting you here." I smiled.

She gazed back at me with an unsettling expression. Not exactly hostile, but not exactly friendly either. "I take it you just paid a visit to your favorite congressman?"

I leaned against the trunk of my car and folded my arms across my chest. "'Fraid so." I smiled again.

The look on her face remained the same. "Do you mean to imply that the congressman wasn't very helpful to you, Ryan?"

"Is he ever?"

Full-blown hostility now flashed in her eyes. "I've a feeling that proving Mrs. Christiansen's innocence is going to be an insurmountable task. You may regret signing up for it."

My mobile pulsed in my pocket. I reached to answer, then, gauging the impatience in Romano's glare, let it go to voicemail. I hoped to god I wasn't ignoring Angie again. "I didn't sign up to prove anyone's innocence. I was hired to find a murderer."

"You sure about that?"

"What are you getting at?" I pushed away from the trunk of my car and straightened to my full height. "What did Mrs. Christiansen say to you this morning?"

She clicked her remote. Her car lock beeped its response. "You're on your own with Annie Christiansen, Ryan."

"Ho-kay. It's just that in the past we've always helped each other out." My mobile pulsed again. I fought the urge to pull it out of my coat pocket. "Say, Romano, if you see your aunt, will you please tell her that I've been trying to reach her?"

She coughed up a bitter laugh. "You're on your own with my aunt, too, Ryan."

I drew a blank.

"But that reminds me." Romano reached inside her handbag. "I thought you might be missing this."

My lips parted as she dangled it in front of me. When I finally reached out, she dropped the watch into the palm of my hand.

"Where'd you find it?" I mumbled.

"On the floor. Between the bed and the nightstand." She turned and disappeared into Newsome Campaign Headquarters.

For the next minute or so I stood by the car staring at the mound of shiny chrome still parked in my hand. Then I remembered the phone calls. I hopped in the front seat and donned my readers. To my immense relief, it hadn't been Angie. Instead it was my daughter, Alice, and she'd left two messages.

I scrolled down to the oldest and hit play:

"Daddy! Hi. Listen, I think I may have gotten you in a bit of hot water. I called Angie because I wanted the recipe for those pork chops she'd fixed when Dirk and I visited last month. Anyhow, we got to talking and—jokingly, of course—I asked if you'd recovered from the news I'd laid on you Thursday. She went all quiet, so I threw in, 'You know, me and Dirk. The wedding that my dad's paying for. You're coming with, right?' When she still didn't respond I went on to say—and I can't believe I went on to say this—'Dad must've mentioned it. He was just about to go to your house for dinner when I told him.' Oh god, I'm such a dope. But I can't believe you didn't tell her. Do you really not want her to come? How can you not bring the long-suffering, hard working woman who's been nice to your daughter, laughed at your jokes, cheered you up when you were down, cooked your meals, watched your diet, and who, you know, has spent many an *evening* with you for two whole—"

Her voice cut off. I slowly removed my hand from over my eyes, reached into the gap between the seat and the door to where my glasses had fallen, put them back on my face, and scrolled to the second message:

"Sorry, Daddy, I talked too long for your voicemail, I guess. Anyhow, I tried to make excuses for you, but they all sounded lame. Because, well, you don't really have a good excuse, do you? I think it was the shortest conversation we've ever had. Not to mention the most awkward. You really need to call her, Dad. Oh! And we're narrowing in on a date for the wedding. Dirk's just waiting to hear back from his old fraternity brothers. He wants them all there if possible. Love you! Bye."

I retreated into a stupor and remained there for an indefinite span. Finally, I came to enough to check my watch. Shit. It still wasn't on my wrist, nor was it in my hand. Had I lost it again? Or was it still not found? Maybe when I'd gotten here, I'd accidentally banged my head trying to get out the car door, blanked out, and then merely dreamt that Romano had discovered my watch underneath the random bed I'd had drunken sex in last night. Same went for my daughter's phone calls. Maybe I'd only fantasized that my girlfriend might now know that, after two years, I still wasn't ready to invite her to a family wedding. And the open bar I was supposed to stock for Dirk and his entire fraternity? Could it be that it also was a cruel invention of my deeply disturbed, self-loathing psyche? I looked down at my phone. Alice's messages were still in my voicemail. I was awake, all right. But the nightmare refused to end.

Sighing, I bent down and felt around the floor of the car for my watch. Turned out it had fallen atop my left shoe. I strapped it on my wrist. The time read ten minutes after two. Almost two hours to kill before my meeting with Hatcher. I considered paying Angie a call. After all, she was just across the street and most likely home from the farmers market. Only by now she was probably too sore to even buzz me into the building.

My phone pulsed. Mrs. Z.

"Hi, there. Hear from Flake yet?" I asked her.

"No, and I'm starting to worry. I even called the Pine Cone Motel but nobody answered."

"I'm only five minutes away. I'll head over there and see what's keeping him."

Pocketing my phone, I shifted into gear and gratefully sped away. I wasn't proud of myself for this, but truth be told, I was anxious to be anywhere other than the street where my soon to be ex-girlfriend lived. Even if anywhere was the shittiest motel in town.

Morty Jacobsen, the Pine Cone's front desk manager, had loosened up around me since I'd left the force. But he still kept me at arm's length. As chief concierge of the local "no-tell motel," his guests' privacy was always priority one. So I was relieved to find a new teenaged surrogate in Morty's place when I walked into the lobby. The kid was tall and gangly and dressed in shiny polyester pants, a thin, short-sleeved dress shirt and a clip-on tie. His bright orange hair was piled atop his head in a loose cone, perhaps deflated from its original faux-hawk; and his hands, the size of small chickens, were nervously shuffling through what appeared to be incoming mail on the front desk. The telephone rang and he jumped, sending a couple of envelopes sliding across the counter and onto the floor. For a second he wavered. Should he answer the phone or pick up the mail? Then he saw me and abandoned both options.

"Can-I-help-you-sir?" he blurted out, so rapid-fire it sounded like one long word.

"Friend of mine, a Mr. Flake, has been staying here. I wonder if you can tell me if he's checked out."

"Flake? That name sounds familiar." He reached beneath the counter, opened a drawer and then closed it. "Has he checked out? Oh yeah, the file." The kid reached for a tin file box and then looked up at me. His eyes were bright blue and pink around the rims like a rabbit's. "It's my first day alone on the job."

"No problem. Take your time." I bent down, picked up the mail he'd dropped, and set it on the counter.

"Mr. Flake has not checked out yet, sir."

"OK, I wonder if you'd ring his room." I pulled out my business card and handed it to him. "My name is Matt Ryan. He'll be happy to see me."

"Oh, Mr. Ryan. I remember now… shoot!" He handed back my card.

"That's why the name Flake sounded familiar. He came by the office about an hour ago. Had a package for me to mail and asked me to fax some papers to you. I already have your card ... somewhere." The kid fooled with more of the papers on his desk.

"Fax, really?" I wondered why the change of plans.

"Here it is." He set my card atop a pile of mail and then reached beneath the desk, produced a thick legal sized envelope, and placed it in front of me on the counter. I squinted to see Dr. Christiansen's return address printed in the top left corner. This had to be the documentation he'd promised. But why fax all of a sudden? Had he been spooked? "Did Mr. Flake seem nervous at all?"

"I didn't notice. There were a couple of check-ins, the mailman stopped by, and the phone just wouldn't stop ringing. Like I said, it's only my first day by myself."

"You said there was a package?"

"Yeah. Just a small padded envelope with a bunch of stamps on it. But it wasn't for you. It was going to Utah. The mailman just picked it up."

"Remember who it was addressed to?"

"Um, yeah. It... Oh, I'm sorry sir, I can't say. My boss, Mr. Jacobsen insists on confidentiality."

"Oh, yes, I know Morty."

He brightened. "You know Mr. Jacobsen, sir?"

"We go way back. What's your name, son?"

"Billy. Billy Macon."

"Nice to meet you, Billy. The next time I see Morty, I'll remark on your professionalism." I respectfully backed away from the counter a couple of steps.

"Gee, thank you, sir."

"Would you mind ringing Mr. Flake's room? Maybe he can tell me who the package is going to."

"Of course, sir."

Billy Macon used an old rotary landline to dial the room. The machine's volume was so high I could hear it ringing from where I stood. Flake had changed his plans, but why? Was he in too much of a hurry to come back by my office? If that was so, why hadn't he checked out yet? I had a bad feeling about this.

"Sir, he's not picking up. If you don't mind waiting, I'll go to his room. Maybe he left without checking out."

"Thank you, Billy. I'll stay right here."

Billy started for the door, stopped, backtracked to the desk, collected a key from behind the counter, and then headed again for the room. Once the kid was finally gone, I took Flake's envelope off the counter and slipped it into my inside coat pocket. Then I crossed the lobby and cracked open the front door just enough to see Billy mounting the stairs to the second floor. When I heard him reach the top, I stepped out a bit further and spied his feet loping along beneath the railing. He stopped at room 216.

I returned to the lobby and was cooling my heels when Billy's high-pitched scream sent me running for the door.

"Oh my god…oh my god," he moaned.

I took the stairs two at a time. When I got to him, he was preoccupied with heaving his lunch over the railing.

The door to Room 216 was partway open. I stood at the threshold, squinted in the dark, musty light, and then, covering my hand with my coat sleeve, yanked the cord to open the front curtain. Squinting again in the sudden brightness, it took a second for my eyes to adjust and then focus on Mr. D. Wendell Flake, slumped on the floor next to the bed, and shot through the temple with a large caliber gun.

Realizing time was limited, I took out my phone and snapped some pictures of the corpse from as many angles as my place on the perimeter would allow. Only forensics could say for sure, but the areas of dried blood on the victim's cheek and the surrounding carpet led me to conclude that Mr. Flake had hied to the next sphere some thirty minutes ago.

I turned to see Billy leaning against the railing. He had stopped throwing up but was still shaking so violently that the cheap ironwork rattled along with him.

"I can't believe he just blew his brains out like that," he stammered.

"This was no suicide."

He stared back at me, his pink-rimmed rabbit eyes bulging.

"If he had killed himself the gun would be beside his body."

"You mean somebody killed him?"

"'Fraid so, kid. Say, did anyone else come by today asking for Flake?"

"No-sir-nobody." One long word again, and, drawing a jagged breath, he added, "I didn't sign up for murder."

"Then you might want to consider another line of work."

"I have to call Mr. Jacobsen."

"You might want to ring the police as well." I slapped a steadying hand on his shoulder. "I'll walk you back to the office."

Billy pushed away from the rail and then staggered a step.

I caught him before he pitched forward. "Easy there, tiger."

"Mr. Jacobsen's not going to like this," Billy mumbled as I led him down the stairs.

When we reached the office door, I paused to calculate my strategy. "Listen, kid, the police will probably question you. OK if you mention me. I'll be talking to them myself. But I'd rather you didn't mention the fax or the package Flake had you send."

"Oh, no, sir. Mr. Jacobsen insists on complete confidentiality for his guests."

I opened the door for him. He passed through, covering his mouth to contain a residual dry heave.

As I let the office door swing closed behind Billy, I couldn't help but appreciate the irony. For once, Morty's infuriating noncompliance with the police was working to my advantage.

Reporting the murder was my legal and professional obligation. Also an act of good will, as I wanted the law on my side. Up until this afternoon, that was. Now that Romano had officially declared me "on my own," I no longer felt any good will, only the necessity to protect my license. Striding to the car, I dialed Romano and waited while my call went to voicemail. "Ryan here. I've just come from the Pine Cone Motel where there has been a recent murder, possibly connected to the Christiansen case. Kid at the desk discovered the victim. I'll be in later to make a statement."

I checked my watch. Almost three o'clock. One hour until my meeting with Hatcher. What I needed now was a reasonably private place to examine the contents of the envelope I'd nabbed from the motel counter. I climbed in my car and snaked through the neighborhood, making sure I wasn't being followed. Convinced that nobody was on my tail, I steered north toward the airport. Then, at the urging of my growling stomach, I settled on McDonald's where I ordered a Big Mac and a large coffee and found a quiet corner booth. The restaurant was empty save for a couple of boisterous children and a father who appeared unaccustomed to caring for them on his own.

A killer was out there somewhere, probably nearby, and probably still looking for the stone, its documentation, or both. I now regretted mentioning the existence of these so-called documents to anyone. Thanks to me, both Newsome and Hatcher were aware of them. That made me worry about Mrs. Z. I dialed her number.

"No point in waiting for Flake anymore," I told her.

"Why's that?"

Once I'd explained, she murmured, "Oh dear," and then, after a few seconds of silence, asked, "So he was shot in the temple like Dr. Christiansen?"

"Execution style. Just like the doctor."

"Oh my gosh, *that* can't be a coincidence."

I separated the phone from my ear for a second, taken aback by the excitement in her voice. "It's beginning to look like the work of a serial killer."

"Oh my gosh!" she repeated.

"Mrs. Z, I want you to go home to your family. In fact, take some time off. I'll solve this one and call you in on the next assignment."

"Are you kidding? I can't drop this case now."

"Weren't you the one who was arguing for me to do just that?"

"Ryan, I've been researching the Snow family like you asked. I haven't found a direct link to the Hatcher farm yet, but Snows were definitely in Southern Utah as early as the mid-1850's. I think I may be onto something."

"Whatever it is can wait. Two people have been murdered by some kook who's obsessed with this stone. I don't want the mother of my namesake to be next on the list."

"For heaven's sake, Ryan. I can take care of myself."

"How? With my gutless shotgun?"

"Maybe I should saw it off."

"Very funny. Please go home, OK?"

"All right, boss," she replied in a sweet, motherly tone that undermined any recognition of my authority.

Lacking the energy to argue, I bid her goodbye and cased the restaurant again. Still empty except for the staff and the overwhelmed dad and kids. I wolfed my sandwich and used the poor excuse for a napkin to wipe the grease from my hands. Then I donned my readers, took Dr. Christiansen's envelope from my pocket, and removed a tri-folded chunk of paper. When I opened it up, a smaller envelope dropped address-side down onto the table. When I picked it up it felt like photographs. I set the envelope aside and turned back to the stack of papers. On top was the picture of the Hatcher stone that Dr. Christiansen had shared on the internet. Then a real estate flyer for a farm in Parowan, Utah. The building in the photo looked stately but run down. "Own a piece of pioneer history!" the caption read.

Next came a scholarly article on seer stones entitled, "Romancing the Stone: the role of interpreters in early Mormon history." Five pages printed front and back and stapled together. It looked like something I might want Mrs. Z to tackle, if and when I let her back on the case. Underneath the article was a copy of a letter penned in faded, flowery handwriting I would need a magnifier to decipher, but the signature at the bottom read, Brigham Young. Then came another copy, this time of a list typed on an old manual typewriter. The heading read, "Heirs to the Hatcher Stone." Two-thirds of the way down the column of names I saw "Ann Elizabeth Snow, b. 1964" highlighted in yellow. After that there were some scanned pictures of what looked like the old farm in its heyday. One featured a stately gentleman arm and arm with a serene, delicately boned woman. "Francis Cannon Snow" was spelled out in pencil below. I wondered what his connection to the Hatcher family might be but fought the urge to mention the name to Mrs. Z. Better if she stayed out of this for now.

A gaggle of teenagers burst into the restaurant and blew my concentration. I checked my watch. Three-thirty. School was out and it was almost time for me to leave to meet Hatcher. I refolded the pages and then turned over the smaller envelope. At once I recognized the address stamped in the top left corner. Hollingsworth Detective Agency. That would be Fred Hollingsworth, my fancy competition across town. He had four employees and his own office in a strip mall. A shiver of dread traveled my spine. I had a

sinking feeling about what I was going to find inside. Still, I had to open it just
to be sure.

I was actually somewhat startled. Not only did Fred snap Annie and
Newsome in various states of PDA, kissing, snuggling, hand-holding, and, of
course, entering and exiting the San Francisco apartment building. But he had
also caught them en flagrante in the back of Newsome's SUV. I stared down
at the sight, the congressman's lily-white ass glaring back at me. My stomach
churned. Evidently, they'd been too impatient to make the trip to the condo.

Shaking my head, I slid the photos back into their envelope. Poor Dr.
Christiansen. He really didn't need to see that. The PDA was enough to prove
infidelity. Should have hired me instead. I would have spared him that indignity,
not to mention cut him a better hourly rate.

As I drove toward the airport, my disgust over the unseemly images of
Newsome with Annie gave way to a deeper concern. Why the hell were incrim-
inating photos of Newsome mixed in with documentation about the Hatcher
stone? I thought back to this morning's conversation with Mr. Flake. On the
Monday night before Dr. Christiansen died, Flake had followed him to his
townhouse. When he'd answered the door, the doctor had seemed jumpy. Like
he'd seen a ghost. Then he went back inside, leaving Flake on the porch. When
he came back to the door, he had the envelope. Had Christiansen forgotten
he'd left the pictures of Newsome and his wife inside? Or had he given Flake
the pictures on purpose? As a message, maybe? A warning? Maybe safe
keeping?

The taqueria by the airport had a tiny parking lot. I pulled in and was
just turning off my ignition when a black Lincoln Town Car slid up to the curb.
A tall, dignified man in a business suit climbed out of the backseat. He was a
standout against the smattering of other customers, most of them airport
ground crew coming off their shifts. I paused to take in his appearance. His
photo in the newspaper clipping Mrs. Z had found was a good ten years old.
Either the photographer had failed to capture his image or Hatcher had aged
exceptionally gracefully. His stride into the tiny establishment was confident
and peppy, he wore a genial expression, not unlike the one usually fixed on
Newsome's face, and his brown hair was impeccably coiffed, suggesting a stylist
was among his entourage. First glance, I didn't trust him.

I fumbled with my phone a second, trying to set it on "do not disturb"
without my glasses. I gave up and turned it off. Then I walked into the joint
and bought a Mexican Coke at the counter. Hatcher was sitting at one of the
few tables with neither food nor drink in front of him. This left me with another
impression. He was the sort of man who felt entitled to take up space at a
restaurant without ordering anything.

I walked over and extended my hand. "Matt Ryan."

He came to his feet. "Pleasure. I'm Gordon Hatcher, as you've obviously concluded."

"Took a wild guess." I helped myself to the chair across from his. "They make a mean burrito here, if you're interested."

Hatcher frowned and shook his head. "Too much grease," he explained, his voice loud enough to catch the ears of the counter staff.

I took a long pull on my Coke. Like with Newsome, I had no stomach for small talk with this guy. I set my drink on the table and reached inside my coat pocket. "Here's what you came for, then." I put the stone down smack dab in front of him, where his food should have been.

He leaned forward to examine it. Seemingly satisfied, he scooped the rock into his hand, and gazed over at me. His eyes, while not dilated, seemed to mimic Flake's in intensity. "This is it all right."

"You're sure it's not a decoy?" I took another pull on my Coke.

"Well, it makes no difference. As I told you on the phone, the decoy also has value."

I cast my gaze downward, focusing on the polished toe of Hatcher's black leather lace-up. "Some folks thought the real thing was a pretty powerful tool. Valuable enough to kill for, even."

"That's all history now."

"Is it?"

Mr. Hatcher slipped the stone into his coat pocket. "Are you a Mormon, Mr. Ryan?"

I shook my head. "Lapsed Catholic."

"Outsiders like to think we Mormons practice polygamy and blood atonement, put rocks into our hats to see the future. There might have been some of that back in the day. But it's been greatly exaggerated, and now it's long gone. We're just nice, normal, hard-working folks, like the rest of the world."

"Well, in my experience, the rest of the world is full of nasty, dysfunctional, hard-working nutjobs, like the one who killed Dr. Christiansen."

Hatcher nodded slowly. "Terrible thing. Will you please give his widow my condolences? Also, will you thank her for letting me have the stone?"

"Absolutely."

"On the phone you mentioned some written documentation. Information Dr. Christiansen gave to another party."

The envelope weighed inside my coat pocket. There could be a killer nearby who was after it. Hatcher didn't look like a killer, but he didn't look trustworthy, either. My mind flashed to the image of "Ann Elizabeth Snow, b. 1964" highlighted in yellow among the list of heirs. I decided on the fly not to share it with him. "Yeah, that would be the man we gave the other stone to. I asked him for copies of whatever he had but I've yet to hear back from him. I will let you know if and when I do, though."

Hatcher's smile remained genial, but disappointment showed in his eyes. "Thank you. I'd appreciate that. Did this man happen to say what sort of documentation he had?"

Again on the fly, I decided to use this as an opportunity for some of my own research. "No, but I wondered if it might be a genealogical record. He referred to the stone as his inheritance and claimed to have his own link to the family. Out of curiosity, did a family named Snow have any connection to your ancestor's stone or farm?"

"As far as I know, both belonged solely to Zedekiah Hatcher." His expression remained pleasant, but there was an edge to his voice. "Did the gentleman suggest otherwise?"

"Oh, no. Although a man named Francis Cannon Snow came up in conversation. Ever heard of him?"

Hatcher's eyes narrowed and the genial expression evaporated. He drew a breath and his face relaxed. "No. Can't say I have. In what context did his name come up?"

"He didn't elaborate." I smiled. "As I told you on the phone, this man was a very spiritual person. Also a bit unhinged, I'm afraid."

"I see. You do meet some characters in the antiquities business." Hatcher stood. "I hope you don't mind, but I'd best be on my way. My pilot expects high winds later this evening."

"Not at all." I rose and shook his hand. As we left, two guys holding fat burritos and a couple of beers hurried over to claim our table.

Outside the breeze had picked up and Hatcher's ride sat waiting for him at the curb. When he saw us, he started the engine. Hatcher reached for the door handle and then turned and, with that genial expression of his, asked, "Will you send me copies of the documentation when you receive it?"

Smiling back at him, I replied, "Anything he gives me I'll send on to you. But don't hold your breath. Like I said, he was a little unhinged."

Also, he was a little dead.

My body felt like it was midnight, but my watch said it was only four forty-five. At least that meant happy hour at the Swizzle Stick had started, and I sure as hell could use a drink. I climbed into my car and made a beeline for the bar.

On the way over I rewound the encounter with Hatcher. He appeared to be exactly who he said he was, a collector interested in his ancestor's magic stone. That was a good enough reason to fly all the way to California to collect the thing, especially since he had the convenience of a private jet. But it was hard to imagine him committing murder to acquire it. Nevertheless, I had a bad vibe about the guy. His little speech about the Mormons being "normal" sounded too much like the party line. And, judging by his reaction, I was willing to bet he knew the name Francis Cannon Snow.

Happy hour at the Swizzle Stick consisted of six geezers gathered around the corner table and three women at a booth showing each other pictures on their telephones, probably of their grandchildren. Hank the Regular was on his stool. I slapped him on the back as I passed by to my place at the end of the bar.

Gus sidled up and poured me my scotch. "Getting windy out there?"

"It's picking up, that's for sure."

"How's the ball and chain?"

"No more ball and chain, Gus." Then before he could ask, I added, "And I don't want to talk about it."

"OK, then I don't want to hear it." A wisp of a smile crossed his lips.

I tipped my glass toward him and he turned away and let me be. Exactly what I needed. Solitude. And a drink. My mind was spent, incapable of forming an intelligent thought, much less engaging in conversation. Thank god I didn't have a stake out tonight. Also, thank god for this quiet bar, my empty house, and my lonely, pathetic life.

"Ryan, I've been trying to reach you."

Her voice was familiar, but she sounded like she was underwater. "Mrs. Z. You didn't go home." I squinted up at her.

"Your phone's turned off."

I shook myself awake enough to find my phone and turn it back on. I squinted at the screen. Two missed calls from Mrs. Z and one from Mrs. Christiansen. None from Angie.

"For heaven's sake, it's barely five o'clock and you look hammered." She pointed at my glass. "How many of these have you had?"

"None. I just got here. I'm worn out is all. It's been a long day."

"Well, the day's not quite over."

Gus appeared and, in his most courtly voice, asked, "May I bring the lady a drink?"

Gesturing to the stool next to mine I asked, "What can I get you, Mrs. Z? Would you like a ginger ale?"

She climbed onto the seat and smiled sweetly back at me. Then, turning to Gus, asked, "May I have a Tanqueray martini, up and dirty, please?"

"You got it," he replied.

I blinked three times in succession. This had been one hell of a shocking day and, evidently it wasn't over yet. "How did you know I'd be here?" I asked her.

"I didn't. First I went to Denny's. When you weren't there, I figured it had to be either the bar or the McDonald's, and given you weren't carrying, I opted for the bar."

The sound of the martini shaker clattered in the background.

"Aha."

Gus delivered Mrs. Z's martini in a frosty glass. It had two olives. I half expected her to toss it back, but she took a tiny sip and then ate one of the olives.

"So what's the big emergency?" I asked.

"No emergency." She popped the second olive in her mouth and then dug through her handbag. "It's just that we're going to Utah first thing tomorrow and I wanted you to have time to pack." She handed me an envelope. "Flight information is in there. We leave at seven a.m. Mrs. Christiansen is covering the cost of our travel."

I gazed back at her, attempting to process the information.

"I'm sorry, Ryan. It was a decision I wouldn't ordinarily make for you, but your phone was off and seats on tomorrow's flights were filling up."

"Why…" I began, and then took a slow draw of scotch instead.

"Mrs. Christiansen called me. She tried you first, of course, but—"

"My phone was off," I said, my mind beginning to clear.

"Right. So she got a call from this guy named Buck Finlay who owns the old Hatcher farm in Parowan. Evidently Dr. Christiansen had expressed an interest in the property. Finlay learned of his death, so he called Mrs. Christiansen to see if *she* might be interested in purchasing the place. He invited her to Utah for a tour."

"And she wants me to check it out." I shrugged. "I guess that could be a lead."

"Oh, I'm sure it is, especially after what I've learned today." Mrs. Z dove back into her handbag, this time for some printed pages. She set them on the bar next to my scotch. "I found the link between the Snows and the Hatchers." She sipped more of her drink.

I immediately recognized the title, "Romancing the Stone." "Oh. I already have this," I told her and pulled out Dr. Christiansen's envelope.

"Oh my gosh, is that the documentation?" She grabbed the thing, yanked out the papers and laid them out on the bar. "How did you get it?"

I described how I'd lifted the envelope from the clerk at the Pine Cone Motel and then went on to explain my initial perusal of its contents.

When I finished, she picked up the findings from the Hollingsworth agency. "So this sleeve of pictures was mixed in with the historical stuff? That's so weird."

"Tell me about it."

"OK, but you haven't read the article about the stone yet?"

"Nope."

"Did you at least see who wrote it?"

I looked back at the article. "'Romancing the Stone: the role of inter-preters in early Mormon history' by Meredith Snow, PhD," I read aloud.

"That's the BYU professor I was telling you about, the one who was fired for advocating for women to have the priesthood."

"The one married to Blair Thurgood?"

"Exactly." Mrs. Z went back to rifling through the doctor's papers. Then, looking up briefly, she added, "Mr. Thurgood emailed you back earlier today. He said he urgently needs the stone and wants the name of the person you gave it to."

"Urgently?" I sipped my scotch.

"So he said." Mrs. Z began to page through Dr. Christiansen's documents, turning over the picture of the stone, the real estate flyer, the article by Dr. Snow, and then stopping to focus on the old letter signed by Brigham Young.

"Can you make out that handwriting?" I asked her.

"Oh, yeah. My family has one of these, actually. It's a letter from Brigham Young to Zedekiah Hatcher ordering him to move his family from the Salt Lake Valley to Parowan, Utah." She turned to the typewritten list of potential heirs to the Hatcher stone.

I sipped my scotch again. "See how Ann Elizabeth Snow is highlighted?"

"I do." Mrs. Z mumbled, and then flipped through the scanned photographs, stopping at the image of Francis Cannon Snow and wife. "Well, hello there, Francis," she said.

"Do you know that man, Francis Cannon Snow?"

Mrs. Z's eyes darted up at mine and she smiled sweetly, just as she had when I'd offered to buy her a ginger ale. Then she straightened on her barstool, took a sip of her martini and said, "Ryan, the man in that picture is Zedekiah Hatcher. The *woman* is Francis Cannon Snow."

"Oh. I just assumed from the spelling, I guess." I slurped my scotch. "Is that important?"

"It certainly is." She turned back to the list of potential heirs. "Did you happen to read any of the other names here?"

"No. I just noticed that Ann Snow was highlighted."

She passed it back to me. "See if you find anything unusual."

I set aside my scotch, put on my readers, and read aloud, "Rebekah Louisa Snow, Zilpha Lyman Snow, Marian Marie Snow, Georgina—" I took off my readers. "These are all women."

"You got it. Francis Cannon Snow was a prophetess, and her gifts were passed down through the female line." Mrs. Z took another sip of her martini.

"Well, I'll be damned. I imagine that made a lot of old patriarchs angry back then."

"Indeed it did." She sipped again. "It's making a lot of old patriarchs angry now, too."

"I'm listening."

Mrs. Z glanced at her watch and then shook her head. "Read Dr. Snow's article. I'll fill in the rest on the plane tomorrow. I need to go home, make dinner, and put my kids to bed. Also I need to pack." She threw back the rest of her drink and hopped off of her stool.

"Pack," I repeated. "Tell me. Exactly why are you coming to Utah with me?"

Mrs. Z hooked her handbag over her shoulder. "Do you know why Utah is the only state in the country that executes by firing squad?"

"No."

She smiled sweetly. "You're going to need a translator."

Part Three

The Heir and the Spares

"I condemn it (polygamy), yes, as a practice, because I think it is not doctrinal. It is not legal. And this church takes the position that we will abide by the law. We believe in being subject to kings, presidents, rulers, magistrates in honoring, obeying and sustaining the law."

LDS Prophet Gordon B. Hinckley, *Larry King Live,* August 9, 1998

Ten miles northeast of Parowan, Utah
March 2010

As I wander the upstairs rooms, yesteryear's screams echo off of the walls. The prophet's henchmen stormed the house that night, snatched us from our beds. The leader forced Zedekiah to kneel, and shot him through the temple, to make a statement, he claimed. Then the brethren set upon me. They threw me to the floor and took turns violating my flesh. When they were finally sated, the leader yanked me off of my back and commanded me also to kneel. He put a gun to my head and fired. Then they abducted the sister wives and left me here for dead. Soon to be forgotten. Or so they hoped.

My hand reaches to my temple, as if either exists. Real or imagined, I feel the crater in my skull. Taunts and jeers ricochet inside what was my cranium, the brethren exploding in laughter. To think that I, a woman, might possess the gift of prophecy. Let them laugh. The gift is real, and it is mine, as is this house. Many a patriarch has challenged me, some of them worthy adversaries. Those were the contests I relished. Sadly, my latest opponent owns an especially weak intellect and little fortitude. His feeble efforts fail to provide any diversion. Only the occasional amusement when he dares to trespass. But so fleeting. I rattle a window, and he runs screaming into the night.

Lacking a worthy adversary, I am left to divide the time between painful memory and debilitating ennui. Like Sisyphus, I tackle my boulder of tedium from dawn until dusk, repeating the process again and again. My solace is the belief that the sacred stone and its heir will one day return. I finally sense that day is nigh.

R omano rolled over and looked at her bedside clock. Sunday morning and she was awake before seven. This after crawling home last night just after eleven p.m. She turned onto her back and tried closing her eyes again. It was no use. These days any attempt to sleep late was interrupted by the reality of the empty space next to her. Romano sat up, yawned, and then dragged her-self to the bathroom.

As the shower stall clouded, her mind cleared. She'd done some of her best thinking in the shower…also some of her best foreplay.

Romano stepped out from under the stream. *Forget the past. You're on a case, damn it!* She grabbed the shampoo and worked her hair into a lather. Yesterday's events were still a jumble in her mind. Her first thoughts were of the murder at the Pine Cone Motel. After all, it was what had kept her up last night past her bedtime. The victim, D. Wendell Flake of Mona, Utah, was shot at close range through the temple, same M.O. as the Christiansen murder. Forensics reported that the victim was wearing Mormon underwear. Presumably for his protection, Romano observed darkly. Also, Flake and Dr. Christiansen had exchanged emails over the acquisition of a Mormon artifact.

She rinsed the shampoo from her hair, worked in some conditioner, and rinsed again.

Morty Jacobsen had been noncommunicative as usual. Same with the kid who discovered Mr. Flake's body. At least at first. But Romano sensed fear in the way Billy Macon's oversized hands fooled with the papers on the hotel desk. When his shuffling uncovered Matt Ryan's business card, she jumped to attention.

"Why do you have his card?" she'd asked him.

Dread flashed in Macon's red-rimmed eyes. "He…um, Mr. Flake wanted me to fax some papers to him."

"What papers?"

Macon's paws started dancing on the desk again. "There was an envelope. It was right here, but…it's *gone*." He looked up in horror. "Oh-my-gosh. Mr. Ryan must have taken it with him."

With that Billy Macon had cracked like a bad oyster. Ryan was there at the time of discovery. Saw the murder scene, probably snapped pictures of it— although the kid couldn't verify that because he'd been too busy vomiting his guts out over the railing—and maybe even lifted said evidence from the scene. Of course the latter couldn't be proven either, as Billy hadn't actually witnessed the theft, and the Pine Cone's lobby security cameras had coincidentally been on the fritz. A common occurrence at that establishment, as Ryan well knew. But Ryan also knew he was bound to report the murder, as evidenced by the voicemail Romano finally discovered on her phone late last night.

She sighed in resignation. Even though he was no longer her boss, it seemed that former police lieutenant Matt Ryan was still leading her investigation. Romano stepped out of the shower and wrapped herself in a towel.

She wiped away a circle of steam to examine her face in the mirror. Her eyes were bloodshot, and bags hung under them. Frowning back at herself, Romano realized she'd let emotion cloud her judgment. She was pissed at Ryan for cheating on her aunt. But that was personal. Professionally she was going to have to swallow her pride. At the very least so she could learn what was in that mysterious envelope the victim had left behind. Still wrapped in her towel, she went back to her bedroom, sat down on the edge of her bed, and stared at her clock. Ten after seven. Romano reached for her phone on the nightstand and then paused a second. Would he even be awake at this hour? Unless he'd taken on another potentially felonious but irresistibly sexy client, odds were he'd gone to bed alone last night. That would make him as pathetic as she was. Come to think of it, Aunt Angie might be better off without him. Romano hit the speed dial. Her call went straight to voicemail.

She exhaled and waited through the beep. "Ryan, it's me. Listen, I'm sorry I was so hard on you yesterday. I hope we can go back to helping each other. Give me a call, please."

Romano returned the phone to the nightstand. The towel parted to reveal her left thigh. She gave it a squeeze. Getting flabby. Since the break-up with Davis she'd traded out exercise for fast food. *Forget the past. You're on a case, damn it!*

Coming to her feet, she hastily made the bed, hardly a chore since only half of it was ever unmade. Then she unwrapped the towel and tossed it onto the spread. She rummaged through her lingerie drawer, found what appeared to be her last clean pair of panties, and went to her dirty-clothes basket for a bra. A survey of her closet revealed that it was past time for her to take her suits to the cleaners. Staring at the slim choice of options hanging on the rack, it occurred to her that slacks and a t-shirt might actually be the best choice for today's destination. She went to her dresser for a top and then back to the dirty clothes for pants. A search for clean socks seemed futile at this point. Instead she stepped barefoot into brown suede loafers and went to the bathroom where she combed out her wet hair and pulled it into a ponytail. The mirror above the sink was now clear. Her pupils were less bloodshot, but the bags still showed under her eyes. It had been over a month since she'd worn make-up.

Swept up in a surge of defiance, she grabbed the tube of foundation off the counter, squeezed out too much into her hand and smeared it across her cheeks and under her eyes. After that, she brushed on blush and added a shaky application of eyeliner. Determined to retake command of her personal life, she fetched her dirty-clothes basket, carried it to her tiny laundry closet, and set it on top of the washing machine. Back in the bedroom, she collected her purse and an armload of dry cleaning and took them to the car. It wasn't until she was a mile away from her place that she realized she had forgotten to load and start the washing machine. Also that the dry cleaners was closed on Sunday.

Romano parked in front of the place anyway and stared blankly at the hours posted in the shop window. Next door was her local Starbucks. Lucky coincidence since she'd also forgotten to eat breakfast. Of course, the principal items in her fridge at the moment were half a jar of mayonnaise, milk that had expired two weeks ago, and a box of yellowing baking soda. She flipped down the visor and checked the mirror. The sloppy application of eyeliner made her look like a raccoon. Closing her eyes, Romano took a minute to absorb the reality that her personal life had slid out of control.

All the more reason to focus on her work. Rooting her glove box for a pack of tissues, she checked the mirror again, this time to wipe the excess liner from below her eyes. Then she got out of the car and went for coffee. Funny how a skinny vanilla latte was sometimes all it took to alter a person's worldview.

When Romano parked in the lot beside the Mormon church building, she felt feisty and energized. Yesterday's conversation with Congressman Newsome had been unproductive. He'd been surly from the onset, probably because he'd just come from a meeting with Ryan. Then, when his receptionist interrupted them, he'd brusquely excused himself, only to come back and say that he had to leave immediately and would call her at his earliest convenience. Not long after that Romano had been called to the scene of a murder.

This seemed a little too coincidental. Had Newsome been interrupted for reasons connected to Flake's murder? Did he know Flake? Romano wanted to talk to the congressman about that. Moreover, she had discovered the Hollingsworth Agency's report on Newsome and Mrs. Christiansen in Dr. Christiansen's email. She definitely wanted to talk to him about that. Also, it pissed her off that Newsome had gone this long without calling her back. All things considered, it seemed like a good time to invade the congressman's comfort zone.

Clad in her wrinkled slacks and t-shirt, Romano immediately felt out of place among the church-attired Mormons filing into the building. She'd done this by design, of course but now wondered if she'd gone too casual. After all, she was on duty. Ironically, her unhinged personal life worked to her professional advantage. She grabbed a blazer from the dry-cleaning pile and slipped it on. Then, coffee cup in hand, she hooked her purse over her shoulder and strode toward the building.

An official looking gentleman in a navy-blue suit approached her seconds after she walked into the busy church foyer. "Pardon me, miss. Are you visiting with us this morning?"

Smiling brightly, Romano was glad to feel the room's attention focus on her. "No, sir. I'm looking for the Honorable Dennis Newsome."

"I see. Brother Newsome is speaking at this morning's service and will be available for questions afterward. We have roped off an area in the chapel specifically for members of the press, although we do request there be no beverages—"

"Oh, I'm not from the press." Romano reached into her bag and then held up her badge, drawing faint gasps from those around them. "I'm Lieutenant Romano from the Abbottsville Police Department. Can you tell me where I can find him?"

"I-I'm not sure." The official façade disappeared. "I'll have to ask the bishop. I'll be right back."

"OK, thanks."

Romano returned her badge to her handbag and walked to a window overlooking the parking lot. Sipping her latte, she noticed that two news vans had pulled up, also a black pickup. A couple of muscular men jumped out of the truck. Romano recognized them. They were at Newsome's campaign office yesterday.

"Good morning, lieutenant. I'm Edgar Bromley, bishop of the Fourth Ward." A gentleman announced, shattering her reverie. He was tall, genial, and appeared to be somewhere in his seventies.

She shook his extended hand. "Nice to meet you, bishop."

"Congressman Newsome is in my office." He motioned her ahead of him, opened the office door and then, when Newsome stood to greet her, discreetly closed the door behind them both.

After a perfunctory handshake, Newsome pointed her to a chair and then settled behind the bishop's desk. Romano ignored his directive and remained standing.

"Lieutenant, what the heck do you think you're doing?"

"Hopefully finishing our conversation."

"You could have done that without barging into my church and waving your badge around."

"Well, I had to identify myself in order to gain access. You're an important guy."

"Yes, I am, and my time is valuable."

"As is mine. You didn't call me back."

"That's it? I didn't call you?"

Romano took a step forward. "It's not nice to ignore the police, congressman."

"Oh, for crying out loud." He rolled his eyes "I'm not ignoring the police."

"Then we'll talk. Right now."

"I'm about to speak in church!"

"Either we talk now, or I'll arrange to have some uniformed officers escort you downtown directly after your speaking engagement."

Newsome jumped angrily to his feet in an obvious show of strength.

Romano didn't flinch. "I believe I noticed at least two TV news vans in the parking lot just now."

Newsome sank back into his chair. "You know, you may be an even bigger pain than your old partner, Ryan."

Romano smiled inwardly. Without intending to, the congressman had just paid her the best compliment of her professional life.

Matt Ryan, Private Investigator
Abbottsville, California
Sunday, March 28, 2010
5:45 a.m.

W henever I have the occasion to fly out of Abbottsville International Airport I am reminded of what a small burg I've relocated to. This morning was no exception. While SFO was no doubt a swarm of activity right now, Abbottsville had barely woken up. But sleepy airports have their perks. For example, cheap long-term parking that's within walking distance of the terminal. Carry-on strapped over my shoulder, I passed a short row of taxis, and then across the lanes of cars pulling up to the curb.

When I got to the sidewalk, Mr. Z's blue Toyota Camry rolled to a stop at my side. Mrs. Z smiled up at me through the passenger side window. I went to open her door and then paused respectfully when they leaned together for a kiss. He stroked her cheek as they parted. So much love packed into a simple gesture.

I opened her door and she climbed out, carry-on bag in tow. Then I stuck my head inside the car and reached across the passenger seat to shake Mr. Z's hand. "Thanks for lending me your wife for a couple of days. I'm afraid she's become indispensable to me, too."

His smile was as warm and steady as his handshake. "She loves working for you, Ryan. That makes me happy."

"I'll get her home to you ASAP."

I shut the car door and went to stand beside Mrs. Z. I wondered how happy her husband would be if he knew his wife was helping me track down a serial killer. As he drove away, I asked her, "Does Mr. Z know that Mr. Flake was murdered yesterday?"

She sighed and turned to walk inside. "I hid the paper from him this morning and kept the radio off in the car."

I offered to carry her bag. She refused but allowed me to motion her through the door ahead of me. We came to a stop at the TSA checkpoint. She set down her carry-on and slipped off her cream jacket to reveal a sleeveless navy top cut from the same fabric as her slacks.

"But he'll find out soon enough," she added.

Rolling my eyes, I took out my Ziploc bag of liquids. "One hint of danger and you're on the next flight home."

"Sure thing, boss."

The line through security was light but tedious, thanks to regional airport clumsiness. By the time we'd cleared the metal detectors, our flight to Salt Lake City was in the final stages of boarding. We hoofed the length of the terminal to our gate, a distance that seemed inordinately long for a regional airport. Caught up in the flurry of boarding, taxiing, taking off, and obligatory visits to the lavatory, it wasn't until we had been served our packaged trail mix and complimentary beverages that we finally relaxed. That would be halfway through our short flight, since our late booking had limited our seating options to the back row.

"First thing after we land, I need to buy a firearm," I said.

"Oh, no worries. My Uncle LaVar can loan us arms and ammunition."

"*Us?*"

"I meant *you*, of course."

"Right," I replied, already suspicious. "That's very kind of your uncle, but I would hate to risk leaving him defenseless."

"I…don't think that will be a problem."

Deciding to defer the decision, I asked, "When do we see the Hatcher Farm?"

"We have an appointment with Mr. Finlay tomorrow morning." Mrs. Z squinted. "It's at eleven o'clock." She emptied her bag of trail mix onto her napkin. "Did you get a chance to read Dr. Snow's article?"

"Did my best. I faded pretty fast last night." I sipped my coffee. It was already cold. "But I think I got the gist. Francis Cannon Snow was a prophetess who usurped her husband's authority and ran the household."

"And the most productive farm in Southern Utah at the time." Mrs. Z emptied the remains of her can of Bloody Mary mix into her plastic cup. What? No vodka?

"Until Brigham Young found out about her and the magic stone."

"Not the stone so much. In her article Dr. Snow points out that other Mormon women used seer stones for their own personal revelation. Brigham didn't mind that."

"Oh, really?"

She nodded. "In some ways Mormon women had more perks in the old days than they do now. For example, pioneer women were allowed to issue health blessings with consecrated oil, a practice that is restricted to men in the modern church."

"Interesting," I replied.

"Besides, Brigham didn't place much faith in seer stones and didn't use them himself. But Francis Snow had declared herself a prophetess. Brigham couldn't let that slide. It was a challenge to the patriarchy as well as to his personal authority. There was only room for one prophet."

"So he arranged for her ritualistic killing, as a statement."

"That's Dr. Snow's theory. Although there's no direct proof that Brigham ordered the attack on the farm. But he had visited Parowan right before the murders, and correspondence shows that he had become aware of Francis Snow's growing influence just ahead of that visit."

I took one last sip of cold coffee, solely for the jolt of caffeine. The stuff was too weak to provide one. "But Francis Snow had been in control of her farm for ten years. Why didn't he learn about her sooner?"

"Well, the Mormons have always been good at keeping secrets. Also the place was pretty remote. The only settlers were families ordered down there to expand the kingdom. The brethren in Salt Lake rarely paid them a visit."

I thought back to Dr. Christiansen's documentation. "There was that letter from Brigham ordering Hatcher to move his family to Parowan."

Mrs. Z nodded as she swallowed the last of her drink. "Right. Like I said, my family has one of those, too."

"Will I get to meet some of your family when we go down to visit the old farm?"

She smiled. "You won't be able to avoid it. Half the county is related to me."

Sudden pressure inside my ears signaled our flight's initial descent. "I suppose we should look up Dr. Snow and her husband, Blair Thurgood, as well. They live in Orem, correct?"

"We can try to see Dr. Snow today if you like."

"Oh, good. You have her contact information?"

"I took the liberty of calling her yesterday. I hope you don't mind. I couldn't reach you and—"

"You talked with her personally?"

"For about ten minutes, yes."

"What did you tell her?"

"Not much. That I'd read her article, that Dr. Christiansen had obtained the stone at some point, that he had been murdered in a similar manner, and that we were representing his widow. Also that her husband, Blair Thurgood, had expressed an interest in the stone."

I picked up my cup and swirled its stale contents. "Did she seem interested in the stone?"

Mrs. Z shrugged. "Well, it's hard to say without seeing her face, but she didn't sound interested. Although she was mildly surprised that her husband wanted it."

"Surprised, how? Angry? Confused?"

"More like amused." Mrs. Z crumpled her cocktail napkin and put it inside her empty cup. "She gets home from church at twelve-thirty today. We can drop by anytime after."

"After church?" I asked and then, sighing, added, "I forgot today is Sunday. Guess I'm pretty out of it."

The flight attendant came by to collect our trash. I added my half-cup of cold coffee to his sack.

Mrs. Z smiled and lightly patted my arm. "Yesterday was a long day."

"Indeed it was."

"There's something else I need to tell you."

I turned to her. "What's that?"

"Angie called the office yesterday afternoon."

"I've been trying to get ahold of her."

Mrs. Z's periwinkle eyes gazed gently back at me. "She mentioned that and asked me to tell you to stop calling her."

"She won't talk to me?"

Mrs. Z pursed her lips, "She said she'll call you when she's ready."

The pilot instructed the flight attendants to prepare for landing. I brought my seat upright with a jolt, and let loose a loud exhale.

She patted my arm again. "Sorry, Ryan."

As our aircraft plunged toward earth, I shut my eyes and mapped my own descent. As recently as last Thursday I had enjoyed the love a good woman. Now, only three days later, that same woman regarded me with such animosity that she'd cleared my belongings out of her home and stopped speaking to me. Talk about a free-fall. Did she know about my indiscretion with Annie Christiansen? Could Romano have told her? Instinct told me, no. Sure, Romano was sore at me, but I couldn't see her repeating something that would only cause her aunt unnecessary pain.

Besides, the problem was bigger than that. For two years Angie had been waiting for me to commit. Then yesterday she found out that I hadn't even bothered to tell her about Alice's wedding. It was finally time for her to face facts. I hadn't been worth waiting for. I thought of how Dirk, whom I'd long held in quiet contempt, had done right by my daughter and asked for her hand in marriage. At least Alice had found a good one.

The plane slammed down onto the runway, evoking gasps and nervous laughter from inside the cabin. I craned my neck around and caught the eye of the flight attendant seated in the galley.

"This is the first time the copilot has landed this model of aircraft. Might take her a while to get the hang of it." He winked. "Women drivers."

I smiled back at him and then faced forward and scowled. Could be that the pilot was simply unfamiliar with the aircraft. But in my current state of mind, I was more inclined to believe that having spotted my name on the passenger manifest, she decided to make a statement.

Even though it served a major metropolitan area, the Salt Lake International Airport maintained a regional atmosphere. Since we only had what we'd carried on, we were able to bypass baggage claim and make the short walk to the rental car desk. Mrs. Z seemed pleased when I told the representative that we would both be driving the vehicle. Then, upon arriving at our white Ford Taurus, she asked, "Mind if I drive the first shift? I know where we're going."

"Good call." I handed her the keys.

When we climbed in the car, the first thing we did was set our watches ahead one hour. Six minutes after ten a.m.

Mrs. Z started the ignition. "I don't know about you, but that packet of trail mix didn't exactly hit the spot."

"Not even nearby," I agreed.

"Want to grab some brunch? We've got time to kill before Dr. Snow's church lets out."

"Sounds good. Know a place?"

"You bet." She turned out of the rental car lot and sped toward the highway.

Recognizing Mrs. Z's competence behind the wheel, I tilted my seat back, relaxed, and made the most of being a passenger. Billboards flew by the window, advertising an odd mix of consumer options. Mormon missionary supplies, tattoo removal, breast enhancements, emergency provisions, recovery for porn addicts, quilting and scrapbook paraphernalia. I supposed this jumble of contradictions was somehow entwined in the Mormon lexicon.

Tract housing developments also zoomed past, their patchwork uniformity interrupted by exit ramps lined by chains and big boxes: Applebee's, Chili's, Target, Costco. White steeples popped up every mile or so, all of them identical to the one atop the LDS chapel in Abbottsville. Classic suburban sprawl with an LDS twist. Only here the man-made mediocrity was dwarfed by the stately peaks that graced the horizon. Soaring into the brilliant blue sky, the rugged pine-clad slopes were capped with a lacey veil of snow. A backdrop so magnificent it could only have been imagined by God.

"Beautiful," I murmured.

"The Wasatch Front is nice," Mrs. Z replied as she exited the freeway. "But wait until you see the mountains I grew up with."

"Looking forward to it."

We turned onto a street called West Temple. It was broad and straight and heavily commercial. When we came to an intersection, a directional sign pointed to the Salt Palace Convention Center.

"I take it we're near downtown?" I asked.

"Temple Square is just a few blocks ahead."

"Isn't that where the LDS Church has its headquarters?"

"The Church headquarters, the Tabernacle, and the Salt Lake Temple." She moved into the left-turn-only lane and sped to make the light. "But the pub is right here."

When we walked into the place, I immediately felt welcome. It had a cozy ambience, a friendly and attentive staff, a lively clientele, and an impressive beer list, all of which hinted at a robust nightlife. Located blocks away from Mormon ground zero, the place had the added appeal of a safe zone, especially on a Sunday. We ordered off the brunch menu. Huevos rancheros for Mrs. Z, a Denver omelet for me. Coffee for both of us.

While I greedily slurped my first decent cup of the day, Mrs. Z entertained me with some local history. When the early Mormon settlers arrived here there was only sagebrush, so they planted trees, mostly fruit and Lombardy poplars. Irrigation canals used to run through downtown Salt Lake City. The Beehive House, also on Temple Square, was where some of Brigham's wives lived.

The waitress arrived with our meals and I immediately dug in. It did not disappoint. "Best Denver omelet ever. And it's in Salt Lake City."

Mrs. Z grinned. "I know, right? Same here with the huevos rancheros."

For the next minute or two we did nothing but eat until Mrs. Z prudently suggested that we both slow down.

"Good idea." I set down my fork and sipped some coffee.

"Last night you said that Francis Snow still angered the current church patriarchy. Why is that?" I asked.

"Because the modern church leaders don't want stories about female prophets to circulate. They're every bit as opposed to the ordination of women as Brigham Young was."

"So, Dr. Snow is part of a movement to extend the Mormon priesthood to women, sort of following in her ancestor's footsteps?"

She swallowed some refried beans. "Exactly. The article we read was originally published through BYU Studies. But it's since been taken off their website."

"Thanks to pressure from LDS leaders, no doubt."

"Probably." Mrs. Z's phone sang from inside of her purse. She set down her fork, reached for it, and then smiled. "It's a text from home. Looks like Bailey helped Ryan clean up after breakfast."

She passed me her phone. I found my glasses and then grinned at the image of the Zimmerman's golden retriever licking sticky goo off my namesake's face. That reminded me. I hadn't taken my phone off of airplane mode. Passing the mobile back to Mrs. Z, I reached for my own and turned it on. When I saw a missed call from "Romano" on the screen my heart raced, then I realized the caller's first name was Stella, not Angie. She had left a message.

"I got a voicemail from Romano."

"Oh, yeah?"

I held the phone to my ear, sighed, and put it and my readers back in my pocket. "Says she wants us to work together."

"She's had a change of heart?"

"Could be."

The waitress walked up with the coffee pot and pointed to our cups. We both nodded eagerly.

"Or…maybe she realized you're ahead of her in the investigation," Mrs. Z suggested after she'd taken a sip.

"That's the direction I'm leaning." I went to take a bite and then realized I was no longer hungry. "When I first saw the name, I thought it was Angie, not Stella Romano."

Mrs. Z pushed aside her plate and drew her coffee cup in front of her. "I'm sorry, Ryan."

I waved a hand in front of my face. "You don't need to hear about my personal drama."

"Why not? You hear about mine. Of course, the principal players on my stage are children and pets. My whole life is a Disney movie. I could use a little intrigue."

"Yeah, well, the intrigue in my life belongs in one of those 'men behaving badly' flicks. Something my future son-in-law might star in. My daughter is getting married, by the way."

"I know, Alice invited us. She's so excited."

"She's inviting everyone," I mumbled, recalling the botched invitation to Angie.

"Ryan, what are you talking about?"

"Nothing." I closed my eyes and rubbed the bridge of my nose. "Angie was absolutely perfect for me, and I drove her away."

Our waitress reappeared to ask if we wanted to box our leftovers. I declined and asked for a couple of warm-ups and the check. She took our plates and then returned with the coffee pot and bill. Mrs. Z waited through this routine in silence, her kind eyes fixed on me. I might have been comforted if I didn't feel so undeserving of her sympathy, not to mention embarrassed about where this conversation was leading. Time for a new subject. Anything. "Say, you were going to tell me why Utah is the only state in the country that executes by firing squad."

Mrs. Z shook her head. "You didn't drive Angie away. She's just mad and needs time to get over it."

"She needs to get over me."

Mrs. Z picked up her cup and then set it back down. "Don't be ridiculous. She's crazy about you."

I nodded. "But I'm not about her. That's the problem. I want to be, but…" I sighed and sipped my coffee.

"But you don't love her," Mrs. Z said, finishing my sentence.

"It's ridiculous. She really is the perfect woman for me."

"Not if you don't love her." Mrs. Z stared into her cup, as if contemplating her next sentence. "Look, Ryan, I never had the pleasure of meeting your late wife. But I've heard a lot about her from you and especially from Alice."

"I really loved her. We both did."

"I know." She looked back at her cup and then drew a breath. "She was a nurse, correct? Just like Angie."

"That's true. She devoted her life to caring for others."

"You especially," Mrs. Z added. "She kept the dinner warm when you were late, watched your diet, always lent a listening ear. Also, just like Angie…am I right?"

I wrapped my hands around my mug and thought for a second. "You *are* right. Angie is exactly like my late wife."

"Not exactly, Ryan. Nobody can be exactly like her, not in your mind anyway."

I stared back at her and then mumbled, "Oh my god," as the realization settled upon me. "Are you saying I've been replacing my wife?"

Mrs. Z tilted her head to one side. "Ryan I'm not a psychologist. I'm just saying you might try something new. Someone outside your comfort zone. Could be a pleasant surprise." She held up her cup. "Two years ago, I had my first taste of coffee. Took one sip and threw it in the trash. Then, over time, I grew to like it. Now I can't imagine life without it."

"I'm replacing my wife." I moaned. "How cliché is that?"

"It's just a theory. I'm sorry if I—"

"Oh, no. It's a sound theory. And don't be sorry. If you hadn't said something, next thing you know I'm telling Kim Novak to put on that dress and pin her hair back."

"I think you're overdramatizing. Remember how I said that when my great-grandpa died, my great-grandma pitched his seer stone in the lake?" She pushed back from the table a couple of inches. "After the funeral Great-Grandma shared some wisdom with all of us girls in the family."

"Is that right?" Smiling wearily, I pulled my business Visa from my wallet and set it atop the check. Seconds later the waitress collected them.

"She said that if she had been young enough to remarry, she would never pick another man like Great-Grandpa. 'Husbands are like dogs,' she told us. 'You don't want to follow up with the same breed. After so many years with a retriever, it might be nice to have a lapdog.'"

"Aha. Wisdom indeed."

The waitress returned. I thanked her, donned my readers, calculated a twenty percent tip, and signed.

"If something ever happened to Paul, I would definitely go with a different breed," Mrs. Z went on.

"Oh yeah? What breed would that be?" I asked, pocketing my readers as I stood.

"I don't know. Maybe an Evel Knievel kind of guy."

"Evel Knievel." An image from this morning resurfaced in my brain: Mr. Z in his blue Toyota Camry creeping away from the terminal at five miles an hour. I burst out laughing. She did as well, and we kept it going all the way to the car.

"Not sure I'm comfortable with you driving after that revelation," I said as I held the door open for her.

Once we were out on the open road again, I thought to return Romano's call.

Staring out my passenger side window, I dialed, held the phone to my ear, and when my call went to voicemail said, "Ryan here. Tag, you're it." I turned to Mrs. Z. "Looks like she's hard at work on a Sunday."

"She's not the only one," Mrs. Z said.

She studied the road and I the scenery, taking in the grandeur of the mountains and the mediocrity at their feet. Walmart, Cracker Barrel, gaudy arcades advertising one-stop family fun, more cookie-cutter subdivisions. A minivan whizzed around us sporting a bumper sticker that read, "Get U.S. out of the U.N." Then, as the road curved around a massive granite peak, the suburban sprawl disappeared in the wake of some low-lying institutional-looking buildings.

"This bend in the road is called 'Point of the Mountain,'" Mrs. Z said, breaking the long stretch of silence.

"Is that a prison up ahead?"

"Utah State Prison. It's been home to Ted Bundy, Warren Jeffs, and Mark Hofmann. Hofmann is still there, I believe."

"Who's he?" I asked as the facility whizzed past my window.

Mrs. Z smiled. "He forged a bunch of Mormon historical documents and sold them to collectors. This was back in the 1980's. When one of his transactions got sticky, Hofmann killed a collector with a homemade bomb. He tried to do the same to the collector's business partner but accidentally killed the guy's wife instead."

"Jesus."

Smile intact, she added, "Collector's name was Steve Christensen."

My jaw dropped. "Any relation?"

She laughed. "No."

"So there are a bunch of forgers out there who con Mormon collectors with fake historical stuff?"

"Off the top of my head I only know of two." Mrs. Z slid her gaze in my direction. "Mark Hofmann and you."

"Great."

She returned her attention to the road, leaving me to consider the sad fate of this Hofmann character. If I didn't watch myself, I could end up his cellmate, I mused. Then, as we passed a sign announcing the city of Orem, the more logical scenario sunk in, me being blown to bits. "I'm starting to think you should go home tomorrow."

"Don't be silly." She flipped on the blinker and we exited the highway. "Uncle LaVar will supply us with all the protection we need."

I heaved a sigh. "Not necessary."

"Yes, it is, and, besides, you said you wanted to meet my relatives."

"Well, that's true."

We sped by more chains, more big boxes, and a shopping center called University Mall.

"Is the mall's name a reference to BYU?" I wondered aloud.

"Partly. BYU is just down the road in Provo. But Utah Valley University is here in Orem." She grinned. "The lesser institution."

"Why is that?"

"Worldliness, of course. It's not run by the LDS Church."

"Aha. Meaning it's not the place to find a superior mate."

"In fairness, there is some truth to that, at least in my case." She pulled to a stop at a large intersection. "I met Paul at BYU."

A young couple crossed the street in front of us, the man in a navy suit, white dress shirt, and red tie, the woman in a floral print dress and a lacy cardigan. Smiling, laughing, walking hand in hand, both of them toting leather-bound scriptures. Wholesome innocence personified. A decade ago, they might have been Mr. and Mrs. Z.

"But then, that's also where Annie met Bob Christiansen."

An image surfaced in my mind. Annie gazing up at me, her head on the pillow. Newsome's pillow. Mrs. Z thought I should hookup with someone outside my comfort zone. Annie was certainly that.

The light turned green and we drove toward the mountains, the retail collage giving way to tree-lined suburbia, with more churchgoers filing down the sidewalks, all dressed in a disturbingly similar manner. I noticed the streets were numbered rather than named.

"Eight-hundred East?" I read aloud as we turned the corner.

Mrs. Z nodded. "Brigham Young laid out his cities on numerical grids. Boring, I know, but it does make it easier to find things. Except..." She turned another corner.

"Except?"

"Except I've forgotten Dr. Snow's house number."

"Do you have the address written down somewhere?"

"Yeah. It's in my handbag. In the backseat, of course."

"No worries. I'll get it for you." I twisted around and made a grab for the strap but fell just short of it.

"We're on the right street," she said. "I know that much."

Unhooking my seatbelt, I turned back around, and grabbed it easily, just in time to see a black pickup careen around the corner, come within inches of our bumper, and then swerve past, drawing stares from the suits and floral prints. The name on the door read, *Thurgood Automotive.* I dropped the bag back onto the seat and refastened my seatbelt.

"Follow him," I said.

"You think that's Dr. Snow's husband?"

"Either that or one of his employees."

"A very angry employee."

The pickup pulled into the drive of a handsome gray brick ranch style home. A meandering bed of daffodils followed the path to the porch where two pansy-filled urns flanked either side of the front door. Mrs. Z slowed to a stop at the curb, rolled down our windows, and turned off the ignition.

A morbidly obese man lumbered out of the truck, started for the house, and then, upon seeing his truck roll back a foot, hoisted himself back in, presumably to set the brake. His vehicle now secure, the guy got out again, this time thinking to slam the door shut behind him. Decked out in a white shirt, tie, dress slacks, and a slightly shiny sport coat that could no longer be buttoned across his girth, he tromped across the daffodils and banged on the front door.

"That's Blair Thurgood, all right," Mrs. Z said.

"Really?" I squinted back at the jerk.

"Imagine him with more hair, less bulk, and wearing a freshly launder-ed repair shop uniform. Then he's the man in the ad."

I thought back to the picture Mrs. Z had printed out for me. "I guess so. But what would an educated woman like Dr. Snow see in a guy like him?"

Mrs. Z shrugged. "She had to marry someone, right? And he probably just charmed the dickens out of her at that BYU mix and mingle."

Thurgood banged on the door again, stormed halfway back up the walk and then swung around.

The door drew open and a slim, graceful woman appeared at the threshold. Her hair was deep auburn and her expression mild yet firm. She gazed at Thurgood and then beyond him to our car, her eyes briefly locking with mine. In that moment something stirred within me, an urge both powerful and protective. While not sexual, it nevertheless mirrored the sensation I'd felt when I first laid eyes on Annie.

Thurgood let loose a thunderous growl and then stormed toward his wife.

I instinctively reached for the car door, preparing to intervene. But when I went to pull the handle, Dr. Snow placed her hands on her hips and stared Thurgood down. He jolted to a stop and then bounced back a step, as though repelled by an opposing magnetic force.

Her gaze relaxing, Snow looked toward a commotion alongside her house. A large-boned, muscular brunette appeared, hefting a moving box across the lawn. She dropped it onto the front walk and the unsealed flaps flew open, revealing a mess of cords and cables.

"Noooo!" Thurgood lunged forward again. His wife repelled him with another mighty glare. He staggered backward and stared lamely at the box.

My curiosity piqued, I motioned to Mrs. Z. We climbed out of the car and crept across the street to just within earshot.

"Thanks, Lucinda," Dr. Snow said to the brunette.

"Oh, there's more," Lucinda replied as she stomped back around the house.

Dr. Snow remained on the porch, hands back on her hips, glaring

Thurgood down. "Yesterday I heard clicking on my landline. I knew you had to be behind it. It took Denise under a minute to find the bug. But Lucinda had to run to the hardware store for a bolt cutter large enough to break that padlock on your storage shed. Tell me, Blair, did you find my conversations...titillating?"

"Who gave you the right to touch my stuff?" he bellowed.

Dr. Snow arched an eyebrow and then looked our way. "Are you Carrie?"

"Yes, I talked with you yesterday, Dr. Snow," Mrs. Z responded as we advanced to the edge of the porch.

"Please, call me Meredith."

Thurgood swung around and glared at Mrs. Z. When he saw me, his eyes widened. "What's this? You have *men* signing up for your movement now?"

"We actually have quite a few men. But these people are here for a different reason," Dr. Snow explained.

"I'm Matt Ryan." I extended my hand to Thurgood. "We corresponded recently over my client's seer stone."

Thurgood scowled, ignoring my gesture. "You're not giving that stone to her, are you?" His gaze shifted back at Meredith.

"No." I withdrew my hand.

"Who then?" He squinted back at me, ferret like.

"I'm not at liberty to say."

"Thanks for nothing then." Thurgood picked up the box and carted it to his pickup.

I smiled hello to Meredith.

"Nice to meet you, Matt," she called.

"Most people call me Ryan."

Lucinda reappeared, lugging another box, this time with a computer monitor poking out the top.

"Please, come in, both of you."

We obliged, nodding in tandem to Lucinda. First came a sunny entryway. Then a small, elegant living room set off to the right. But my eyes were drawn forward to the kitchen, which was obviously the heart of the home. We followed after Meredith, inhaling the rich aroma of roasting meat. A pixie-like woman who looked to be about Alice's age was spreading a cloth on a long farm table. She looked up at us and smiled.

"Denise, this is Carrie and Ryan," Meredith explained. "They're here to discuss the article I wrote about my ancestor. You know, the piece that got me in all that trouble?"

"Nice to meet you," Denise said.

"Denise is an engineering major," Meredith added. "She's a big help around the house."

"I can imagine," I replied, noting it had taken her under a minute to find Thurgood's phone tap. I wondered what other ways her skills might have proven handy.

"You'd be surprised how many skill-sets we need to keep our co-op going."

I turned to see Meredith staring straight at me, as though addressing my unstated question. Her eyes were a swirl of blue and green.

"So your organization is more than just a movement for women to be ordained to the priesthood?" Mrs. Z asked.

"Oh, yes," Meredith replied. "We started out as a small support group. Helping each other with childcare and home repairs." She went to the sliding glass door and pointed into the backyard. "We put up vegetables and fruit that we grow in our own yards."

Mrs. Z and I looked to see a woman wheeling soil over to a large raised flowerbed. Behind her stood a substantial greenhouse. Beyond the greenhouse loomed the snow-capped mountains.

"That's Brenda," Meredith explained. "She's helping me prepare that bed for planting. It's that time of year when everyone is anxious to move the seedlings out of the greenhouse, but don't dare risk a frost."

I admired the impressive glass and aluminum structure. A blonde ponytail drifted by an open space in the window and then disappeared behind a giant palm frond.

"How many places should I set?" Denise asked as she pulled a stack of plates from the cupboard.

Meredith turned to us. "Will you stay for Sunday supper?"

"No, thank you," Mrs. Z and I replied, almost in unison.

"We just ate," she said.

"It smells wonderful, though," I added.

"Seven, Denise," Meredith said, "at least for now." Then to us, "Shall we go sit in the living room?"

While we settled onto the sofa, I saw Thurgood and Lucinda through the front window. She was walking away, and he was shouting after her. The door opened and she hurried inside and shut it behind her.

"Insufferable man," she said.

"Is that all of it?" Meredith asked.

"*No*," Lucinda groaned. "He's going to have to make another trip."

"Oh, good heavens." Meredith smiled after Lucinda as she trudged away.

I glanced out the window to see Thurgood tearing away from the curb. My mind jumped to another dark pickup that sped away from Annie Christiansen's house on Thursday night. Then, looking back at Meredith's tranquil expression, I couldn't help but return to my quandary over her bizarre domestic situation. What on earth had she seen in this asshole?

"We met at BYU," Meredith explained.

Startled, I blinked once and then again. It was the second time the woman had seemed to read my thoughts.

"At a mix and mingle?" Mrs. Z asked.

Meredith chuckled. "Family Home Evening group."

Mrs. Z nodded. I wasn't familiar with the term but figured it for some sort of church social activity.

"Back then we had some things in common. We were both outdoorsy people. He liked to build things; I liked to grow things. It seemed like a good match, especially since we were creeping into our mid-twenties. That's scary territory for Mormon singles. So we married and moved into a tiny apartment near campus. He worked and I stayed in school, expecting to drop out when I got pregnant. Only the pregnancy never happened. Didn't know why at the time. The doctor said we were both healthy." She rolled her eyes. "Now I realize that my eggs were rejecting his sperm."

She paused and we shared some strained laughter. Muted voices drifted in from the kitchen, also the rattle of pots and pans.

"Anyhow," Meredith continued, "I continued my studies and started teaching part-time. His business prospered and he expanded his shop. I earned my doctorate in Agricultural Science, landed a tenure track position at BYU, and we bought this house, mostly with my money. I started expanding my mind and finding my voice. Meanwhile, he fixed cars, tinkered with computers, and narrowed his own mind."

"So, now he's moving out?" I asked.

"Finally. I kicked him out of the house in January. He took his clothes and his guns but left a bunch of electronics locked up in the shed alongside the house. *Said* he'd come back for it all." She rolled her eyes again. "He came back, but not to collect his stuff. To spy on me, evidently. I warned him if he didn't clear his things out today, they'd go to the dump tomorrow."

I thought back to the detective Dr. Christiansen hired to spy on Annie, also to the belongings he left behind at her house. Belongings he also promised to come back for. "Mr. Thurgood owns guns?"

Meredith nodded and crossed her legs. Wide-leg black silk slacks and a beige blouse, a departure from the floral print skirts we'd seen on her neighbors.

"Yes, for hunting, I assumed. But when he moved out in January the sisters saw him carrying off what looked like an arsenal."

My gaze darted back to her face. "An arsenal? Was he a violent man?"

"You mean would he shoot somebody point blank through the temple?"

I blinked. Again with the mind reading. I began to feel like I was losing control of this interview. "Then you are aware that my client's husband, Dr. Christiansen, was murdered in the same manner as your ancestor, Francis

Cannon Snow?"

"Yes, Carrie told me, and no, I don't think Blair is capable of such a thing." She smiled. "He might shoot himself in the foot, though."

We laughed and the mood lightened.

"Meredith, I understand Mrs. Z also told you that Mr. Thurgood had contacted Dr. Christiansen about obtaining the Hatcher Stone."

Her turquoise eyes danced. "Yes, what kind of crazy idea—wait, did you just call her Mrs. Z?"

Mrs. Z smiled tightly. "That's what he calls me."

"Oh my heck," cried Meredith. "That's so retro. It's like that British adventure duo from the 1960's. What was—"

"*The Avengers*," Mrs. Z interjected. "Only, unlike Mrs. Peel, I don't get to carry a gun. Also, I refuse to wear tight leather trousers and spike heels."

Meredith let out a full-throated guffaw, collected herself, and then asked, "So Carrie, is this 'Mrs. Z' business his idea or yours?"

"Are you kidding? *His*. I can't tell you how many times I've invited him to call me by my first name. Finally gave up."

There was now no question that I'd lost control. "Well, you call me by my last name."

"Yes, but isn't Ryan what you like to be called?" Meredith asked.

"Absolutely," Mrs. Z answered for me. "Everyone calls him Ryan."

I nodded my agreement to Meredith and, veering us back on track, said, "You were saying...about your estranged husband and the Hatcher Stone."

"Oh, right." She drew a breath. "I was shocked when Carrie told me that he wanted it."

"He told us acquiring it was urgent," I added.

Meredith rolled her eyes. "When that man wants something it's always urgent. The stone was featured in the article I'd written. I imagine that's why it surfaced on Blair's radar. But it's a real stretch to think that he believed it was actually magic. Crazy as he's been lately, Blair's still too conventional for that."

"So there aren't many aspiring prophets milling around Utah anymore?" I asked.

"Sure there are. Only nowadays they're written off as cranks, at least in mainstream circles." Meredith chuckled. "But then, you don't need to venture far to float outside the mainstream, especially when you head south on I-15. Plenty of cranks around these parts, that's for sure."

My mind focused on the crank she'd kicked out of her own house, the gun and electronics hoarder she claimed wasn't capable of violence. I was about to press harder on the subject when Mrs. Z spoke up.

"I'm curious. As an agriculture professor, what prompted you to write a scholarly history paper for *BYU Studies*?" she asked.

"It started out as research," Meredith replied. "Francis Cannon Snow was one of the most successful farmers in the territory. But then my interest in her deepened. In part because she was my ancestor but also because our situations seemed parallel in some ways."

"Because of your current campaign to ordain women?" Mrs. Z asked.

"Mostly because we both started successful female co-ops. However, you make a good point. Francis Snow was murdered by a gang of local priesthood leaders. But sources claimed that Brigham Young was behind it. Now I'm set to be excommunicated by a group of local priesthood leaders. But I strongly suspect the authorities in Salt Lake City are behind it as well."

I leaned forward and rested an elbow on each knee. "So back in frontier times the Mormon leaders might kill to retain power, but now they just excommunicate?"

Meredith drew a breath. "I certainly hope that's all they do to me." She laughed.

Still leaning forward, I met her gaze. "Ma'am, I'm afraid another Mormon was murdered just yesterday, again by a gunshot to the temple. He was also trying to acquire the Hatcher Stone from Dr. Christiansen."

Her jaw slackened. "Who?"

Meredith remained stoic as I described the details. She seemed to be saddened but not surprised. When I finished she let loose a sigh. "You said this Mr. Flake lived in Mona. Was he a polygamist?"

"Yes."

"Like I said, head south on I-15 and you're going to find your share of cranks. It's still frontier times down there, not like in Salt Lake City."

I leaned back against the sofa. "Perhaps. But years of police work have taught me that there's a little bit of the frontier in even the most civilized of neighborhoods. You still need to be careful, Meredith."

"Don't worry about me, Ryan. The sisters have my back. It's you who needs to watch your own, especially if you're planning to poke around Mona." She chuckled. "It's ironic that there's all this competition over something that on its own has no value."

"Why do you say that?" Mrs. Z asked.

Meredith's turquoise eyes danced again. "Francis Snow didn't need a seer stone any more than Joseph Smith needed one. Perhaps they thought otherwise, but the truth was both had the gift. Whether you believe they were prophets of God or merely charismatic leaders, the magic came from within themselves, not from some object."

My mind shifted to the stone hanging from Annie's neck, its golden flecks shimmering even in the darkness. Whatever its value, it did have a special spirit about it.

"Do you believe in magic, Ryan?"

I looked up to meet Meredith's clear gaze. "I'm agnostic."

The sound of clinking glassware along with the smell of boiling potatoes signaled that Sunday supper was close to being served. I glanced at Mrs. Z, cuing our exit.

She caught my eye briefly and then turned to Meredith. "On the phone you said you were going to church today."

"That's right. I try to go most Sundays."

"Is that what you wore?" Mrs. Z gestured at her slacks.

"I started wearing pants to church about three years ago. The brethren thought it controversial at the time, now it's the least of their worries."

Mrs. Z grinned. "Do you intend to continue protesting the male-only priesthood?"

"Oh, yes. Our numbers are growing."

I slapped a hand on each knee and came to my feet. Meredith and Mrs. Z rose also. "Thank you so much for your time." I shook her hand. "May we call you again? I've a feeling we might need to."

"Of course." Meredith walked us to the door. "Even better, join our next protest in Salt Lake City."

"We'd love to," said Mrs. Z.

"We would indeed," I agreed. "But it may not work out."

She opened the door and Mrs. Z and I stepped out onto the porch. Then, leaning against her doorframe, Meredith folded her arms across her chest. "Not enlightened enough, Ryan?"

"Oh, I think I'm enlightened. It's just that our investigation may conflict with—"

"Why exactly is it that you call Carrie *Mrs. Z?*"

"Professional reasons, I guess."

Meredith looked back at me, confused.

"She's happily married to a terrific guy." I stuffed my hands in my pockets. "The last thing I want is for him to get the wrong impression."

"So it's out of respect for her husband?"

"Exactly," I replied.

"You may not be as enlightened as you think, Ryan." Meredith gently tapped a finger in my direction. "Join us next time. Could be eye-opening." She winked and shut the door.

"You really don't like being called Mrs. Z?" I asked as I yanked the seatbelt across my body.

"It's OK, Ryan." She started the ignition and pulled away from the curb. "I'm used to it."

"You know, you could have said something."

"I thought I had."

The weariness in her voice spurred my annoyance. For crying out loud, she'd only objected a couple of times. How was I supposed to know it was such a big deal to her?

I was about to pose the question when she said, "All the men at church insisted on calling me Sister Z."

I calculated the odds on my winning this contest. They were not good. "So…about Utah executing by firing squad—"

"Out of respect for Paul, of course," she added, ignoring me.

Pinching the bridge of my nose, I drew a deep breath, and, summoning my most tactful tone, began, "I know you've dealt with a lot of Mormon assholes—"

"I've dealt with a lot of assholes all right, but not all of them are Mormons."

I winced and she burst into laughter.

"I don't think you're an asshole. If I did, I wouldn't work for you."

"Thank you," I mumbled.

Mrs. Z pulled up to a stoplight and then shrugged. "An asshole would have suggested that the whole thing was my fault for not making a bigger deal out of it and then reminding him over and over again."

I coughed and then cleared my throat. "I appreciate that you shared your feelings with me."

"You're welcome," she replied.

I turned my attention to the scenery. We were on another residential street, this one lined with uniformed churchgoers walking home to smaller houses that were remarkably similar in design. Either the developer had offered few options, or the neighborhood had voted unanimously on the model, paint, and even the pinecone wreath for the door. Likewise, the landscaping copycatted down the block, with each dwelling boasting a moustache of hedge atop a long chin of newly mown grass. Clean, orderly, and creepy. Like the introduction to a *Twilight Zone* episode.

"Where the hell are we, Carrie?"

"On our way to my Uncle LaVar's. We're almost there."

"Is there some law that mandates a pinecone wreath on every door?"

She laughed. "The ladies probably all made them at a church craft night and now feel obligated to display the hideous things."

"Did they coordinate their paint and landscaping at craft night, too? Also their wardrobes?"

"Could be."

"Should I assume they're all packing your Uncle LaVar's heat as well?"

"Oh, no." The woman I must now call Carrie (because I'm not an asshole) parked at the curb. She turned to me in earnest. "In a way these houses are much like the Mormons themselves. Their facades are all alike. But step inside and there's no telling what you'll find."

"Do they know we're coming?" I asked as we strolled up the walk and past the copycatted hedge to the door.

"I talked to Uncle LaVar last night." Carrie paused before ringing the bell. "I should warn you that my uncle has some very strong opinions."

"OK," I replied in an offhand manner meant to reassure her. Although I suspected "strong" might be an understatement if she felt I needed warning.

Carrie pressed the button. It rang a Westminster chime, as the others on the block most likely did. The door swung open, and a merry, white-haired woman smiled back at us. Her floral print dress was strained at the waistline and fluffy pink slippers had replaced what probably had been some sensible, low-heeled church shoes.

"C'mon in, honey!"

Carrie stepped over the threshold and gave her a hug. Then she gestured toward me. "Aunt Jane, this is Ryan."

She shook my hand in a healthy grip that suggested some long days of physical labor. "You're that detective our niece loves working for."

I smiled, buoyed by the notion that Mrs. Z...*Carrie* apparently hadn't characterized me as an asshole to her relatives. Not so far, anyway. "Nice to meet you, ma'am."

Aunt Jane waved me inside. "Call me Jane, please. Nobody's sir or ma'am in this house."

The front room was an explosion of needlework. A patchwork quilt dominated one wall. Underneath it, a pink and purple crocheted throw covered the back of the sofa, lacy white doilies adorned its armrests, and another throw—this one solid purple—stretched across the seat cushions, obscuring whatever the couch's original upholstery might have been. Five handmade pillows, each embroidered in a different flowery motif, propped against the pink and purple backrest, presenting a formidable challenge to any average-sized person who might care to take a seat. Samplers crowded the surrounding walls, extolling homespun Mormon virtues: "Love at Home," "Families are Forever," "I am a Child of God." The one closest to where I stood read, "Be Ye Therefore Perfect," in careful silver cross-stitch. I put on my readers and leaned in for a quick study. Not a single flaw that I could see.

"You do nice work, Jane." I pocketed my readers.

"This is certainly amazing, Aunt Jane." Mrs. Z's eyes traveled the walls.

"Indeed it is," I replied, and then to myself: You meant *Carrie's* eyes, asshole.

"Just a hobby." Jane waved away our praise. "My doctor actually suggested it, as a stress reliever."

"I guess you've had a lot of stress lately?" Carrie asked.

"Oh, *no*," Jane sang, landing on a cheery note that rang slightly off key.

Again I took in our surroundings. The body of handicraft therapy in this room alone seemed substantial enough to diffuse a complete mental collapse. For the first time today, I craved a scotch. Unfortunately, the hand-stenciled clock on the wall told me it was only half-past three, and the closest drink was probably miles away.

Jane motioned to what appeared to be the room's single piece of available furniture, a worn easy chair flanked by a bursting at the seams sewing basket. Knitting needles threaded through baby blue yarn lay atop the doily-covered armrest. "This is my current project. I'm making covers for your Uncle LaVar's ammo boxes."

While I moaned my approval, Carrie said, "As a matter of fact, that's what we need to see Uncle LaVar about."

"Right." Jane's smile faded. "I'll take you to him."

We passed through a small, tidy kitchen with burnt orange appliances. The walls displayed more samplers, this time offering mealtime etiquette tips, such as "Wash Your Hands," and "Clean Your Plate." The smallness of the space combined with the largeness of the messaging gave the room a cloying feel, sort of like a wholesome, downhome brainwashing experiment. I diverted my gaze to the counter where bargain-brand cans of tuna, cream of chicken soup, and peas sat aside a Ziploc of dried egg noodles and a round cardboard container of powdered fruit punch.

Jane opened the back door. "Will you stay for Sunday supper?"

My stomach turned over.

"Thank you, Aunt Jane, but we can't," Carrie said. "It's a working trip."

"But it's still the Sabbath," Jane protested.

"Criminals never rest," I declared with a corny flourish and then froze, mortified that those words had escaped my mouth. Already the damned samplers had wormed their way into my psyche and overtaken my speech pattern. The woman I must now call Carrie sliced a look in my direction. I declined to meet her gaze.

"What Ryan means is that a case can go cold quickly," she explained as we followed Jane across the grass toward a medium sized shed at the edge of the lot. The backyard, I noticed, was not as carefully maintained as the front, perhaps because the tall fence kept it safe from the neighbors' prying eyes.

"Maybe it's just as well." Jane stopped in front of the door to the shed. "Your Uncle LaVar is in one of his moods."

"Oh yeah?" Carrie said. "What set him off this time?"

"Same as always. Opposition to his world view."

Carrie shot me another look, this one ominous. I winked back at her. Then Jane yanked the door open and called, "Your niece is here."

We stepped inside and Jane shut the door behind us. From where we stood the only sight was a long industrial shelf stocked with flats of canned goods, and the only sound was the crunch of Jane's slippers as she walked back across the yard. Her footsteps trailed off and the room fell silent.

"Uncle La—*Var*," Carrie called.

"Back here," an angry voice snapped. "You want to see me you have to get around all your aunt's crap."

We went to the end of the canned goods storage and then turned sideways and slid single-file through the opening between the wall and the shelf. More shelves loomed on either side of us, this time crammed with metallic barrels, shrink-wrapped stacks of MREs, flats of water bottles, and more canned goods. I noted that the peas and tuna fish were the same off-brand as the cans on the kitchen counter.

"*Un*-cle," Carrie called again.

"I'm still here," the voice snapped back. "Behind all of her crap. Daft woman thinks all we need is food during the apocalypse. Truth is we need weaponry, to defend ourselves against the unruly mobs."

We followed his voice to the end of the shelf-lined corridor and then entered into an open area squared off by heavy-duty padlocked cabinets. A sulking old man in a faded plaid shirt was sitting behind a large worktable. His gray hair was buzzed close to his scalp and his mouth was fixed in a frown. The parts of a dismantled AK-47 lay strewn in front of him. At his back, one of the cabinets stood open to reveal more assault rifles.

His eyes warmed when they caught sight of Carrie. She rushed over to hug him. He rose to awkwardly to receive her, but then bristled when she tried to kiss his cheek.

"That's enough of that," he growled.

"Oh, all right." Carrie withdrew her embrace and stepped aside. "This is Ryan, by the way."

Uncle LaVar made a show of straightening his untucked shirt and then hitching up his cargo shorts to reveal even more of the exposed Mormon underwear that dangled at his knee. Then he sat back down and gave me the once-over. "You the fella she works for?"

"We're actually more of a team," I replied.

"Aunt Jane says you're in a mood," said Carrie.

"Darned right I am. This morning I'm at the filling station and that commie kid is working the register. As usual he has on one of those radical t-shirts. Today it's *Save the Earth*." LaVar picked up his gun barrel and rubbed it with a stained kitchen towel. "Typical long-haired hippie. Wears a ponytail, just like a girl."

Carrie sighed. "So what did this kid do? To put you in this mood, that is?"

"Oh, I wouldn't give him the chance. Instead I march right in there, slap a hand down on the counter, and say, 'So, how do you like *your black president?*'"

"And what did he say?" I asked.

LaVar winced. "He makes this girlie little laugh and changes the subject, like the commie coward he is. Tries to sell me stuff, which is a waste of both our time since I'd already paid at the pump."

He threw the towel down on the table. "Love is Spoken Here" was embroidered along its edge, in script large enough for me to read without my glasses.

Carrie came behind and rubbed his shoulders. He appeared to grudgingly appreciate the gesture. "Why did you go to the counter, then?" she asked.

"Set him straight, obviously." LaVar wrenched his shoulders away from her grip. "Then I come home to read my paper, and see all hell's broken loose, this time in your neck of the woods."

"Now what?" she said.

LaVar picked up a paper from the seat of a nearby chair. "Says here that the pinko organization that calls itself Pacific Gas and Electric is preparing to spy on all you Californians. That is, if you don't wise up."

"How?" I asked.

Ignoring my question, Carrie took the paper out of his hand and gave it a quick once over. "Uncle LaVar, I thought you were going to quit reading this rag when you and Aunt Jane moved into town."

"What? And turn my back on the conspiracy?" LaVar grabbed the paper and looked at me. "Did you know that the PG&E will soon be violating its customers' rights with something they call the *Smart Meter*?"

I tilted my head back and then brought it slowly forward. "Oh, right. It's their new technology for reading—"

"New technology, my Aunt Fanny." LaVar's cheeks and ears were now bright pink and his forehead glistened with perspiration. "It's how they spy on you, measuring how much gas you use, how much electricity you use, what you use it for, and *who you use it with*."

Carrie came back over next to me, folded her arms across her chest, and looked down at her uncle. Her gaze was gentle but firm. "Uncle LaVar, instead of working yourself into a state every Sunday, why don't you go to church with Aunt Jane? I'll bet there are some real nice folks in your ward, some who even see things your way."

"They're OK, I guess." LaVar looked toward his lap, drew a deep breath, and ran the back of his hand across his brow. When he returned to meet Carrie's gaze, the color had left his cheeks and his forehead had lost its sheen. "Your mother, your uncles, your Aunt LaFawn, and I were raised in a good Mormon home. Lots of fine values in that religion, and I'm proud to be part of it. That's why I still wear the angel underwear." He cleared his throat. "Well, also because your Aunt Jane won't let me in the bedroom without it."

Carrie laughed softly. "So go to the Sunday meetings. Rejoice in the fine values of your community."

"Can't do it." He shook his head.

"Why on earth not?" she asked.

LaVar's eyes widened. "They preach some crazy things at that church."

When we told him we were going down to "plyg" country, LaVar's first instinct was to arm us with a grenade launcher. I did my best to tactfully decline, glibly speculating that my California gun permit probably didn't allow for large caliber projectiles or warheads. Rather than inspire the intended humor, it instead incited a tirade against the government, complete with reddening cheeks and ears, and more beading along his brow. Once his niece had again placated him, we bargained down to a Glock 22 for me and, against my objections, a shotgun for Carrie.

Ten minutes later we were walking back through the grass to the house, guns and ammo in tow.

"Now, that 10-gauge is going in the trunk and is only for dire, and I mean *dire* emergencies," I told her as we climbed onto the back porch.

"Absolutely, Ryan."

I held the door for her. "You have any idea how much recoil that thing packs?"

She stopped on the threshold and fixed me with a withering look. I immediately regretted the question.

Jane was back in her easy chair, at work on the baby blue ammo box covers. "I take it you're not just going hunting," she said once she spotted the Glock.

"No, we're on an investigation down in Parowan, with maybe a stop in Mona as well," said Carrie.

"Mona?" Jane yanked a length of yarn from her skein. "Haven't been there in ages."

"Do you or Uncle LaVar know anybody around those parts?" Carrie asked.

"One or two."

"How about a Mr. D. Wendell Flake?" I said.

"Dell Flake? Sure, we know him. He used to have a booth at the Cedar City farmer's market. Had the whole family working it. I got to be pretty friendly with his wife."

"Which wife?" I asked.

Jane chuckled, her knitting needles still at play. "His first wife, the legal one. She's the only one I know. 'Course, there aren't many folks around those parts who *don't* know Louisa Snow."

I did a double take. "Her name is Snow?"

"Technically her maiden name. But she still uses it. Goes by Weezie Snow."

"Interesting that she's kept her maiden name," said Carrie.

"Maybe she didn't want to be known as Snow-Flake," I ventured.

"Tell that to the folks down in Snowflake, Arizona," Jane said.

"That's right," Carrie said. "It's named after the Snow and Flake families who settled there."

Jane gazed beyond us. "Come to think of it, I've known several Snow women who've kept their names." She rested her knitting in her lap. "I should pay Weezie a visit. Mona's only about forty-five minutes south of us."

"You say she knows everyone around Mona?" I pressed.

"And parts far and wide. Weezie's a firecracker, not your average plyg wife. And Dell, he's just as sweet as can be. Crazy, mind you, but with a heart of gold. Sort of like my LaVar."

Carrie and I smiled sadly. Clearly Jane hadn't heard about the murder. I was weighing whether or not to mention it when Carrie made the decision for us.

"They're good people, then," she said.

"Salt of the earth." Jane picked up her knitting again. "But not without their enemies, I imagine."

"How so?" I asked.

"Plyg men don't like to see a woman wearing the pants, and Weezie definitely does." Jane pulled more yarn from her skein. "But they like it even less when a man encourages his woman to wear them, which is what Dell does. That didn't go over well in Parowan. Don't imagine it does in Mona either. You be careful down there, Carrie."

"We will." Carrie bent down to kiss her aunt's cheek. "Say, are the Flakes still living in a house on Highway 91?"

"I'm pretty sure that's where it is. But let me check." Jane set aside her knitting, pushed out of her chair and crossed the room to an antique secretary. She opened the drop-down writing surface and, after some hunting and scribbling, came back to Carrie with a pink notecard. "Here's the latest address and phone that I have. If you see them, will you tell Weezie I said hello?"

"OK if we head to the hotel now?" Carrie asked once she was strapped into the driver's seat.

"Sure. Not much more we can do today." I buckled myself in. "Is that address your aunt gave you the same as the one you tracked down for Flake earlier?"

Carrie started the ignition. "Looks like. I'll have to check my notes to be sure the house number is the same. Should I try to call when we get to the hotel, make sure she'll be around to see us tomorrow morning?"

I rubbed my eyes, considering the suggestion. "Let's not. People tend to be more forthcoming when they're caught off guard. Also it's a small town and everyone knows her. Shouldn't be too hard to chase her down."

As we drove back through the neighborhood, each house with its pinecone wreath, I couldn't help but reflect on the unique individuals we'd just met. Carrie's uncle and aunt were characters to be sure, but not without their charm. On the one hand, LaVar put on the "angel underwear" and slept beneath at least three hand-knitted blankets in a bed that was no doubt surrounded by cross-stitched inanities such as "Home Sweet Home" and

"Crime Never Sleeps." On the other hand, Jane was careful not to raise opposition to LaVar's "worldview," but only after copious self-medication with handicrafts. Maybe their situation wasn't so unique. Like any good marriage, it was a compromise.

I checked my watch. Four forty-five. Fifteen minutes shy of the magic hour. "That hotel you booked us have a bar?"

Carrie smiled. "You betcha."

The copycat neighborhood gave way to larger lots and older homes, which then gave way to apartments that housed the clean-cut college students who now strolled the sidewalks, many of them still in church clothes. We stopped in front of the Marriott Hotel and got out of the car. The fatigue of the day weighed upon me. One look at Carrie told me she felt the same. An eager bellhop offered to help with our bags. We gladly obliged.

When we entered the shiny new lobby, my first instinct was to look for the watering hole. Thankfully, it existed, complete with a wall of well-stocked shelves and an on-duty bartender polishing the glassware. Outside the bar, however, the lobby looked like the squeaky-clean scene on the street, with much of the wholesome clientele still decked out in white dress shirts, navy suits, and floral prints.

"Ryan?" Carrie stood at the front desk, a cheerful blonde attending to her.

I walked over to receive my key, directions to my room, and information about parking, restaurant hours, and check-out time, all of which I ignored.

Once the young woman had wished us a pleasant stay, I turned to my obviously weary assistant. "How 'bout I park the car and you go to your room for a bit. Meet me in the bar in about an hour?"

Her eyes flooded with relief. "That would be great." She handed me the car key.

Back on the driver's side, I took a moment to adjust the seat backward and turn the mirrors up to accommodate my height. Carrie had done a great job behind the wheel. But now that I had some clue to my surroundings, I figured I'd better step up to the job.

The hotel garage was sparsely occupied. I found a spot near the elevator, which I took to my room on the sixth floor. I slid the card into the lock and pushed the door open to find my roller bag sitting atop an opened luggage rack and my king-sized bed turned down with a mint atop the pillow. The curtains were drawn open to reveal more of the Wasatch Front's snow-capped splendor, this time featuring a giant "Y" fixed into a hillside. I unzipped my roller, found my toiletry kit, and took it to the bathroom for a refresh. Ten minutes later I was riding the elevator down to the lobby. I stopped in the gift shop to buy a map of Utah and then made a beeline for the bar.

My able bartender, whose name turned out to be Tim, possessed the kind of timeless good looks that made it impossible to pin down his age. Maybe as young as thirty; probably not over sixty. He wasted no time in serving up my scotch. Since I was his only customer, he also took the opportunity to demonstrate his gift for small talk.

"Where're you from?"

"Abbottsville, California."

"That near Frisco?"

Cringing inwardly at the dreaded nickname, I put on a smile and said, "San Francisco is about an hour west."

"Interesting place, I hear."

"Indeed." I sipped my drink and then took out my readers. "Utah is turning out to be interesting, too. This is my first visit." Glasses fixed to my nose, I opened my new map on the bar and then refolded it to show the southwestern portion of the state.

"Heading down to Zion National Park?" Tim asked.

"'Fraid not. Got business in Mona and Parowan. Know anyone around those parts?"

Tim frowned and shook his head. "Only go through 'em on my way to Zion. Usually stop for gas in Parowan, though. There's an old geezer who likes to mill around. Always in overalls, spouting off about local history."

"Oh yeah?" I eyed him over my glasses. "Which station?"

He shrugged. "Whatever the big travel center is there. But around here you can find an old geezer at just about any station."

We shared a laugh.

"Staying in the hotel?" he asked me.

"Yup."

"Want me to start a tab and charge it to your room?"

"Read my mind." I pocketed my glasses and tipped my glass in his direction. "I'm in 610."

Tim tapped out an entry on the keyboard behind the bar and then went back to polishing his glassware.

"Are there many bar flies here in Provo?" I asked him.

"Oh, yeah." Tim laughed. "Town this dry makes a lot of folks thirsty."

Carrie climbed onto the stool next to mine. She had changed into an oversized BYU t-shirt, jeans, and pink suede fur-lined slippers. Her hair looked partly damp from the shower, and her unmade-up face, while still attractive, was marked by exhaustion.

"Ready for a martini?"

"You bet." She ordered another Tanqueray, up and dirty, just like the last.

"You two together?" Tim asked.

"She's my co-worker," I explained, somewhat defensive.

He blinked. "Same tab then?"

"Same tab," I replied. Then to Carrie, "You look beat. Do you think you might be coming down with something?"

"Oh, no. It's just been a long day. This place gets to me. The family gets to me."

Tim set a frosted glass in front of Carrie and then garnished the rim with two fat green olives on a pick. He motioned to her shirt. "You go to school here?"

"Believe it or not, I was once a BYU coed." She grabbed her hem and pulled the shirt away from her body. "This is my first time back by campus since my husband graduated."

"Well," he announced, his tone turning ceremonial. "Congratulations on what I suspect to be your first cocktail in Provo, Utah."

Carrie giggled. "Your suspicion is correct."

"You might be surprised by how many people I've said that to." He grinned and then left to resume his bar chores.

She removed the olives to her napkin and, taking care not to spill a drop of the precious contents, took an appreciative sip.

"So how does the first Provo cocktail measure up?" I asked.

"Pretty damned good."

Her rare use of profanity triggered a long burst of stress relieving laughter from both of us. When we finally settled, I sipped my drink.

"Your uncle is very opinionated."

She grimaced. "At least in the old days he sort of kept a lid on it. Now he spends his Sundays terrorizing the poor kid at the gas station and heaven knows who else. Parades around in public with his underwear hanging out." Carrie took another drink.

"From what I understand, he's not unusual around these parts." I smiled. "Tim here just told me there's a guy like your uncle at every gas station."

"Poor Aunt Jane. All that needlework." Desperation crept across her face. "That could have been me."

"Well, it's *not* you."

"Maybe it's because they moved into town." She sipped some more.

"Could be. Some folks really aren't cut out for civilized society."

"Tell me about it." Carrie's voice elevated, evidence that the martini was already working its magic. "You'll be meeting some of those folks when we head south."

I pulled out my glasses and turned back to the map on the bar. "So Mona isn't too far from here?"

Carrie helped herself to one of the olives and then shook her head as she finished chewing. "Only about thirty miles south." She pointed to a spot on I-15. "We can stop by and see Weezie Snow tomorrow, but it has to be early. We have that eleven o'clock appointment in Parowan with Mr. Finlay."

"Finlay's the realtor?"

"Yes, and Parowan is a three-hour drive from here."

"Shouldn't be a problem. Weezie lives on a farm, she's up at dawn."

"Meaning we will be, too." Her voice tinged with resignation, she finished her second olive and then swallowed the last of her drink.

Like clockwork, Tim was again at our disposal. "Like another?"

"I'd better not," she said with a sigh.

"Cash out?" he asked me.

I turned to Carrie, again taking in her exhausted appearance. "You know, I'm pretty sure they've got room service at this hotel."

"We do, indeed," said Tim.

She looked back at me, hopeful. "Do you mind, Ryan?"

"*No,* I do not. I'm fine with eating alone. Go back to your room and order whatever you want. I'll see you in the lobby at eight-thirty tomorrow morning."

"Eight-thirty? That won't even give us enough time to get to the meeting with Mr. Finlay, much less add on a stop in Mona."

I refolded the map. "Finlay's a salesman, sitting on a property that's been on the market for over one hundred years. We're running late; he'll wait for us. Now go and get some rest."

Climbing down from her stool, she bade me a grateful goodnight and then plodded away in her pink slippers.

I turned back to Tim. "Keep the tab open, please, and do you have a dinner menu?"

"Sure thing."

As I slipped the Utah map into my inside jacket pocket, I thought back to Carrie's distress over her uncle and aunt's situation. While she made a joke out of it, I couldn't help but think that the first cocktail in Provo had induced some unsettling memories. Having consumed hundreds of cocktails before I reached the legal age of twenty-one, I obviously couldn't empathize. But after years of lugging around my own unique baggage, I could certainly sympathize. Likewise, I was no stranger to family drama.

That reminded me. I was on the hook for my daughter's open-ended wedding tab, and my girlfriend had just dumped me. Amazing that I'd gone the better part of a day without even thinking about it. "I love my job," I said aloud.

"Then you're one of the lucky ones," Tim remarked as he handed me the menu.

Readers still perched on my nose, I flipped to the entrees. "Sure hope there's a steak on here. Maybe some fries to go with?"

"New York strip and *pomme frites,* coming up. How would you like it cooked?"

"Medium, please." I handed him back the menu and then picked up my glass, only two sips left. "Can you bring me another of these, too?"

Tim hesitated. "I can take your glass away and bring you a fresh one. Or I can wait until you finish this and then serve you another."

I looked back at him, confused.

He grinned. "Sorry, man. Utah liquor laws."

"Oh, right. Give me a sec, then." I winked.

"No problem. I'll have it ready for you."

Sipping and swallowing slowly, I pulled out my phone. Three missed calls and two messages, all from Romano. I hit play and put the phone to my ear. "Ryan, sorry I missed you earlier. Please call back." I hit play again. "Ryan, when you find or recharge your mobile, please call me. It's important." I pocketed my phone, removed my glasses and rubbed my eyes. Then I downed the remains of my drink. So Romano was now eager to talk to me. What a difference a day made.

Tim returned with my refill. "What exactly is this job that you love so much?"

"I'm a private detective."

"So the private eye has a case down in the land of secrets." He raised his eyebrows and sucked in some air. "Good luck with that."

"What do you mean?"

Tim let loose a sigh. "Folks go there to escape the world. They don't much like it when the world comes looking for them."

I gave my scotch a gentle swirl. "Well, I'm not the world. I'm just a guy from out of town looking at a piece of real estate."

Tim's eyes widened. "To buy?"

"Oh, no." I raised both of my hands in protest.

"Good." Tim's gaze softened. "Still, I'd watch my back if I were you. Especially given it's your first visit."

One whiff of my sizzling steak and I realized how hungry I was. I made short work of it, also the fries, which were light and crispy and deserving of the classier title, *pomme frites*. As I ate, more people began to filter in, a few of them still clad in their church clothes, thus confirming Tim's claim about the number of Provo bar flies. I signed the tab, figuring in a healthy tip for Tim, and climbed down from my stool, only to see it immediately appropriated by another thirsty customer.

Back in the room my bedside clock read 7:25. Subtract one hour and it was halfway through dinnertime in California. Unless Romano had managed to rekindle the embers with Davis, odds were she was sitting down to eat alone. Like I would be doing most nights now.

I tossed my key card on the nightstand, shed my sports coat, and sank into the desk chair. Out the window the sun was setting against the mountains, casting the snow-capped peaks in dusty orange. I paused to appreciate the beauty, found my readers, and pulled out my mobile phone. One ring and she picked up.

"I thought you'd died."

"Not dead, Romano. Just in Utah." I returned my glasses to my shirt pocket.

"What are you doing there?"

"Right now I'm admiring waning light cast against the Wasatch Front."

"Well, there must be more to it than that. I've been trying to reach you since this morning."

"Really? This is new. Yesterday you told me I was on my own. Now you can't wait to talk to me."

"Like I said in my message...did you listen to my message?"

"I did."

"I really am sorry I was so hard on you." A clank of silverware and some running water sounded on her end. "I'd like to go back to working together."

"Hmm. Not sure I'm up for that. You go first."

"After you and I exchanged words in front of his campaign office, I went in to speak with candidate Newsome. I had barely started the interview when he was called away abruptly. Not long after that I was also called away, to a new murder scene, one you'd already stumbled onto." The water shut off. "Mr. D. Wendell Flake, shot in the temple like Dr. Christiansen."

"Need me to make a statement?"

"It can wait till you get back."

I crossed the room to snatch the foil-wrapped square of chocolate off my pillow.

"According to his driver's license," she went on, "Mr. Flake is a resident of Mona, Utah, and according to his underwear, he is a Mormon. Say, are you in Mona right now?"

I flicked off the wrapper with my thumbnail. "Nope. You're going first," I reminded her, and then popped the candy in my mouth. It was sweet and rich and satisfying. Nothing like a full-service hotel after a long day.

She described her conversation with Billy Macon, confirmed that he'd "cracked like a bad oyster," and that he suspected I'd lifted the envelope off the motel desk. I did my best to follow along, fatigue creeping up on me. So far, she hadn't told me anything I didn't already know. I crumpled the foil wrapper into a ball and let it dead bounce once and then twice on the desk. I was looking longingly at my suitcase, imagining the pajamas I'd packed, when she let drop that she'd gone to the Mormon church this morning to complete her interview with Newsome.

I straightened in my chair. "Get anything out of him?"

"Yes. For one thing he has a motive. Dr. Christiansen knew about Newsome's affair with his wife. In the doctor's email there was a report from the Hollingsworth Agency. There were pictures of them—"

"Right," I cut her off. More of what I already knew. "Do you have evidence that Christiansen threatened Newsome with exposure?"

"I have Newsome's admission." The whomp of the dishwasher closing punctuated the end of her sentence.

"My goodness, Lieutenant, you've gotten to be one damned good interrogator."

"I had an excellent teacher."

Smiling, I picked up the foil ball and lobbed it toward the can by the desk. Score. "How'd you get him to sing?"

"Showed him the pictures. Evidently Christiansen threatened Newsome but had yet to produce the evidence. Seeing those images for the first time yesterday was obviously a shock to our congressman. They're pretty graphic."

Fighting to keep the visuals of Annie and Newsome from taking shape in my mind, I instead imagined the candidate's face upon his first glance yesterday morning. I couldn't help but snicker. "Just think if those pics went viral on the internet."

"His thoughts exactly, I'm sure. He confessed to the affair and admitted that he'd sent his campaign manager, Jeff Hitchens, over to talk to Dr. Christiansen on the evening before the murder."

"To pressure him?"

"Newsome described it as 'reason' with him."

"Something of an understatement, I suspect."

"Maybe. Anyhow, according to Newsome, Hitchens never spoke to the doctor. There was someone else there, giving Christiansen a piece of his mind. Mr. Hitchens heard them shouting all the way to where he was sitting in his vehicle. He decided to avoid any confrontation and return the next day. Of course, by then it was too late."

I rubbed my eyes. Something about this wasn't adding up. The logical assumption would be that Christiansen's angry guest, if he existed, was Mr. D. Wendell Flake. But that didn't align with what I'd learned so far. According to Flake, the doctor had seemed "jumpy" but otherwise cooperative. He'd left Flake on the porch and then returned with the envelope verifying his purchase of the stone. There was no mention of anger or raised voices.

"OK, but here's where it gets weird," Romano said.

I half laughed. "Go on."

"Right as I was leaving, Newsome asked me where the *stone* and its *documentation* were. Like he might want them himself."

Newsome asked about the Hatcher Stone? Weird, indeed, but probably a dead end. I needed to stay on track. "Can we go back to the guy shouting on Christiansen's doorstep? Did you get a description?"

"After my interview with Newsome, I tracked down Mr. Hitchens. He confirmed that he had gone to Dr. Christiansen's home and said that the man he saw was middle-aged and heavy-set with a receding hairline. The truck parked outside Christiansen's residence had Utah plates and 'Thurgood Automotive' was painted on…"

Suddenly angry, I separated the phone from my ear. That moronic shit Thurgood had lied to me. Said he couldn't travel to California when he'd probably been there all along.

Back on my phone, Romano was still talking. "…caught his truck at a nearby intersection camera around the time of the said confrontation. Ran the plates. Vehicle belongs to a Blair Thurgood of…"

I came back on and cut her off. "I've met Blair Thurgood."

"You *have?*"

"I think it's my turn to share now."

I told her the story about the Hatcher Stone and its original owner, Francis Cannon Snow. Then I explained about Flake, Thurgood, and Gordon Hatcher. I briefly detailed the contents of the envelope and admitted to acquiring it off the desk at the Pine Cone Motel. "I assumed I had the Macon kid's permission," I said.

"Of course, you did," she replied, no doubt with an eyeroll. "What's surprising is the emerging motive for these killings. Could all of this be over a magic rock?"

"It seems a distinct possibility, especially given that both victims were murdered in the same manner as Francis Snow." My mind jumped back to Newsome. "So the congressman was after the stone, too?"

"Seems so. Although, at the time I'd no idea what he was talking about. I did have a fruitful conversation with Mrs. Christiansen this afternoon."

The mention of Annie made my heart race. "Oh, really?"

"Total adjustment on her part," Romano said. "When I spoke to her yesterday at Newsome's condo she was guarded and uncommunicative, said she might want a lawyer. Since she'd obviously kept quite a bit from you, too, I figured I wouldn't get far."

I heaved a sigh. "It's been complicated."

"So I gather. Anyway, I cut things short, left her at Newsome's place, and took the elevator down to the first floor. Knocked on the door of the building supervisor. Um…I'd spoken to him earlier, he's the one who'd buzzed me in the front door."

"OK," I said carefully, anxious about where this narrative might lead.

"Turns out the guy is a nosey parker with time on his hands. He confirmed that Mrs. Christiansen was at the condominium at the time of her husband's murder. He saw her leave and then come back that morning with grocery bags from the local market. I checked with the store manager. His security cameras clear her as a suspect. You can be happy of that."

"Well, she hired me to find her husband's killer, not clear her name. But I'm sure this was welcome news. I assume you've shared this with her this afternoon?"

"Yes. After I left Newsome's campaign manager, I called Mrs. Christiansen. Right off the bat I explained why I no longer considered her a suspect. She immediately relaxed and offered to see me. I jumped in my car and drove back up to the City. We met under the clock at the Saint Francis Hotel. Something I've always wanted to do."

"Check that off your bucket list."

"Indeed." She chuckled. "Mrs. Christiansen and I went up to her room in the tower. She had ordered up a lovely tea service for two. Spectacular view. I'd always wanted to see it from up there."

"Well, check off another one," I said, taken aback by Romano's sudden esteem for my client. Was there no end to Annie's powers of seduction?

"We spoke for maybe forty-five minutes. Evidently Dr. Christiansen confronted his wife about the affair around two weeks ago. He told her he had hard evidence and that, if she decided to proceed with a divorce, he would use that evidence against her in court. He also suggested that he would share this damning information with their son, Sean, who is currently serving a mission in Japan. Presumably Sean might have disowned his mother over such a transgression. Mrs. Christiansen stewed over her decision for a day or two and then finally broke down and sent her son an email. She confessed to the affair, explained why she planned to divorce his father, and expressed her love for him as her son. He wrote back right away, returning his love and support for her. She showed me the correspondence on her laptop and then forwarded it to my email address."

"Good kid." My heart grudgingly went out to his mother as well. She'd been embarrassed when I'd discovered her affair with Newsome. Imagine how difficult it must have been to confess it to her son.

"Also, in the days before the doctor's murder, Newsome called Mrs. Christiansen, insisting that she stay in his San Francisco condo."

"Did he give her a reason?"

"He told her he wanted her away from any potential inquiries from the press."

"Wouldn't their former trysting spot be one of the first places the press would look?"

"That occurred to Mrs. Christiansen, too, and she refused at first. But Newsome kept insisting. Then she got an unexpected visit from Mr. Flake, followed by some hysterical phone calls from her husband. The congressman was due in Washington that week, so she needn't fear any uninvited visits from him. Ultimately, it seemed like the best option."

Leaning back in my chair, I ran a hand over my head and let it rest on the back of my neck. "I suppose that made sense at the time."

"In her mind, yes. But now I'm wondering. If Newsome did want this Hatcher Stone, might he have wanted Mrs. Christiansen out of her house so he could have it searched? Dr. Christiansen might have let slip that he'd stashed it there."

"Good thinking, Romano. But shacking his mistress up in his condo was an awful risk. Would Newsome go to all that trouble to find a magic rock?"

"Not likely, I suppose. Anyhow, Jeff Hitchens paid Mrs. Christiansen a visit at the condo."

"Newsome's campaign manager. Did the nosey parker spot his arrival as well?"

"Sure did. Saw him arrive and then leave within a matter of minutes, just long enough to tell her to keep her mouth shut about the affair and warn her that *some staffers* would be watching. When I was at campaign headquarters yesterday, I saw a couple of big dudes—"

"I know who you mean," I interrupted.

"OK. I saw them again this morning at the Mormon church. They were getting out of a black pickup. Mrs. Christiansen said the two of you were followed by a dark pickup. So, naturally I wondered..." Her voice trailed off.

I gazed out the window. It was dark save for the giant "Y" basking in the reflected light of the moon. "I don't understand."

"Ryan?"

"She didn't tell me any of this." I stood up from my chair and paced to the window, my arm flailing over my head. "She's my client, she's paying me, she appears to be innocent of any crime, except she's hiding crucial evidence from me. Why?"

"I don't know, Ryan. She claimed that when she first told you about her predicament...at the Swizzle Stick, I think?"

I sank down on the bed. "Yes."

"She said she was going to tell you about Newsome but then sensed it best not to. After that it became more and more difficult."

I rubbed my eyes.

"Mrs. Christiansen also said that she was aware of the animosity you and Newsome had for each other," Romano added. "Maybe that figured into her reasoning?"

Now feeling ridiculous, I drew a breath and then huffed a long exhale. "Sorry, Romano. Not your problem, obviously. I'm glad we're working together again."

"So am I, you're still my best teacher, Ryan."

I signed off the call, got up from the bed, and was crossing the room for my pajamas when the hotel room phone rang. Startled, I checked the clock on the nightstand. Eight forty-five. I waited through the second ring and then picked up. "This is Ryan."

"Mr. Ryan, Blair Thurgood."

Well, speak of the devil. "Mr. Thurgood, what can I do for you?"

"I wonder if we could have a chat."

"What's on your mind?" I asked, genuinely curious. Thurgood didn't seem like the chatty type to me.

"I'd rather talk in person. I'm in the lobby here at the Marriott. Tell me your room number and I'll come up."

"How 'bout I come down to you. Meet me in the bar?" I reached for my sportscoat.

"The *bar?*"

The suggestion seemed to make him uncomfortable. Exactly what I was going for. "Be there in a sec," I said, and then hung up before he could respond.

The crowd at the bar had thinned to two men, both of whom were signing their tabs. Tim was still on duty, but there was no sign of Thurgood. I strolled into the lobby and spotted him in a chair near check-in, his face fixed in a pained expression, somewhere between hostility and constipation. I caught his eye, motioned him over with a head nudge, and then went to reclaim my former barstool.

"Another scotch?" Tim asked me.

"You read my mind."

Thurgood crept my way, clearly anxious about his destination. His eyes bounced left-right-left like ping pong balls. He'd lost the tie but still had on the white shirt and shiny too-small suit, his stomach lopping over the waistband.

"Have a seat," I said, and he stiffly obeyed, leaving one empty stool between us.

Tim delivered my scotch and then turned to Thurgood. "Like a drink, sir?"

"Why would you think I want a drink?" Thurgood snapped.

"You're in a bar," Tim replied.

I swallowed a snicker. "How 'bout a ginger ale?"

Thurgood's scowl deepened.

"On me," I added.

He shifted on his stool, his stomach pillowing onto his lap. "Well, all right then," he told Tim. Then to me, "You can't blame me for being uncomfortable about...you know...meeting *here.*"

"I can't?"

Thurgood's gaze darted my way and froze. "I've heard stories about what goes on in bars."

I hadn't the slightest idea what the fuck he was talking about, nor did I care. But I still wanted to know what Meredith had been thinking. She couldn't have found him that good looking, even in his prime, and I didn't buy Carrie's explanation either. This man wouldn't know how to charm the dickens out of anyone. Sipping my scotch, I waited while Tim delivered Thurgood's ginger ale, complete with a tiny straw and cherry.

"How'd you know where to find me?" I asked, once Tim was out of earshot.

"I have my ways." Thurgood's scowl elevated to a smirk.

"Impressive." I rested an elbow atop the bar. "So, why'd you *want* to find me?"

He sucked some ginger ale through the tiny straw, swallowed, and drew a breath. "Mr. Ryan, it is critical that I obtain the Hatcher Stone."

Nodding slowly, I decided it best to give him some slack, easier for him to hang himself. "I could contact the current owner. I can't promise anything, you understand."

His face tensed and his eyes, once frenetic, were now laser focused on mine. "Are you sure the current owner isn't my wife, Meredith?"

"Why do you persist in thinking that?"

"You saw 'em. Her and all those crazy broads wanting to be prophets or some such nonsense." He dunked two pudgy fingers into his drink, pulled out his cherry, and bit it off its stem. "I will not allow *her* to have that stone."

"As I told you earlier, the current owner is not Dr. Meredith Snow."

"Who, then?"

"What does it matter?" I shrugged. "It's not Dr. Snow."

He puffed a sigh. "It wouldn't, ordinarily. But I'm in sort of a pickle right now and I need that stone to get me out of it."

"You think it will bring you some magic?"

"Heck no. Mormons don't believe in that nonsense anymore."

"So I've been told," I said, thinking back to Gordon Hatcher's speech on the subject.

"See, my wife Meredith got her head in a bunch of fool research and wrote a whole paper about some so-called lady prophet who used the Hatcher Stone. Got her in a mess of trouble and then me by association. I'm on the outs at church and losing business left and right."

"Well, that's not fair to you."

"Darned straight." Thurgood aimed a backward thumb at his chest. "I'm the victim here, get it?"

"I'm beginning to. But if the Hatcher Stone isn't magic, why would it benefit you?"

"Because I have a plan." He lumbered off his stool and settled onto the one next to mine, his girth sifting to one side, bringing to mind the old beanbag chair from my first apartment. Then he stole a quick look over his shoulder, and in a loud whisper, said, "I figure if I get the stone, I can donate it to the Church, they can secure it in their vault, and I'm everybody's hero. Maybe even Meredith will come around. Quit all her feminist baloney."

"Aha." Had to admit, this made as much sense as anything so far. Except for the part about Meredith quitting all her feminist baloney. "Perhaps if you and she were to formally part ways—"

"And leave her and that flock of hens to their own devices?"

"Actually, yes. Maybe then your church and your customers will no longer associate—"

"You married, Mr. Ryan?" Thurgood swirled his drink assuredly. A dandy with his snifter of brandy.

"Widowed."

"Sorry to hear that."

"Thank you."

"Girlfriend?" He took another sip and leaned against the bar.

Halfway through his fancy ginger ale and old Thurgood had certainly gotten into the spirit of things. At first anxious, he now seemed at ease with his surroundings. As if he was just a regular guy, having a beer, and shooting the breeze with his buddy. Except he wasn't a regular guy. He was a nutcase who spied on his wife. Also, he was having a Shirley Temple, not a beer, and I certainly wasn't his buddy. "Tell me, Mr.—"

"We can't let the women forget their *place*." Thurgood jabbed his index finger onto the bar.

Tim, who stood counting change at his register, slid an amused look our way. This time my snicker escaped before I could catch it.

"This is no laughing matter," Thurgood hissed. "We need to have control. Otherwise, they're yanking our chains, leading us on, torturing us with that horrible awful silent treatment, and then…tossing us aside."

"Uh-huh." I studied Thurgood's wounded expression. For reasons that passed understanding, the man was still under his wife's spell. It was sad. Pathetic, even. Also embarrassing, given how much of this poor schmuck's situation resembled my own at the moment. "OK, but if you wanted this stone so much, why didn't you come to my office and collect it, given you were in California at the time."

He scoffed. "Who told you that?"

"Police. A witness placed you at Dr. Christiansen's house the night before his murder. Also, that same night, a pole camera caught your truck at a nearby intersection."

"Those pictures are an invasion of my privacy."

This from the man who'd been tapping his wife's phone. "One could argue the cameras impose on an individual's civil liberties," I ventured.

"Darned straight they do. I'm the victim here." Thurgood pointed to his chest again.

I took a measured drink of scotch, pacing myself. "Trade-off is they sometimes help the cops catch a murderer."

Thurgood's posture stiffened and he gripped his glass on the bar, as though for support. "I didn't kill anybody." His eyes were zinging back and forth again. "I swear."

"Then why did you lie and say you weren't in California?"

"Because I wasn't in California. Not at the time I returned your email." His bravado now punctured, he stared into his glass. "I left the morning of Christiansen's murder, drove straight through to Provo."

I took another measured swallow, doing the math in my head. Could be the truth. "You went to Christiansen for the Hatcher Stone?"

"Night before he died." He noisily sucked the rest his ginger ale through his straw, and then tipped what was left of the ice into his mouth and chomped down hard. "I was pretty ticked at him for promising the stone to somebody else."

"Have words?" I asked.

"A few, yeah. But I simmered down when he promised to put me in touch with the new owner. Of course, first he had to find the thing."

Tim set a fresh ginger ale in front of Thurgood. "Free refills," he said with a wink and then pointed at my glass. "I see you're almost finished. Want me to start another one?"

"Not yet, thanks," I said, and then went back to Thurgood. "Christiansen told you he'd lost the Hatcher Stone?"

"More like misplaced." Thurgood pulled out his maraschino cherry and let it dangle over his glass. "He thought it was in his safe. When he couldn't find it there, he said he'd have to go home to get it. Only we were at his house, so I don't know what he meant by that." He demolished his second cherry.

I fixed an unfocused gaze on the jewel-colored bottles against the back wall. I knew what Christiansen had meant. He'd left the stone at 'home' where his estranged wife, Annie, lived. She wasn't there, since he'd warned her out of town. So he'd let himself in with his own key and looked for the stone in her jeweler's bench where he'd hidden it. When he couldn't find it, he'd dumped out the drawers and searched the rest of their former bedroom. That's why Romano couldn't find any prints besides Annie's and Dr. Christiansen's. Because it was the doctor himself who had trashed the place. He was frantic to find it for somebody. But who? Not Flake, obviously, and not Blair Thurgood either. Thurgood was just a bully, and an unconvincing one at that. Nor was Gordon Hatcher a logical candidate, having been happy with just the duplicate stone. Newsome? Or his thugs maybe? I drained my scotch and set down my glass, my eyes still unfocused, until they homed in on the scotch bottle in Tim's hand.

"No thanks, I'm good," I called over to him.

Then I noticed Thurgood, who was staring at me curiously.

"What? You don't believe me?" he asked. "It's the truth, I swear, and I left him right after that."

"You didn't hang around? Try to follow him if he left for this 'home' he referred to?"

"Nope. But I think someone else might've. As I left, I spotted a black truck around the corner. There were a couple of big dudes inside, both of them in sunglasses, even though it was nighttime. No way was I sticking around to see what they wanted. Drove to the lake, stayed in my truck till morning."

Sounded like the congressman's people all right. But why on earth would Newsome want a seer stone? I needed to call Romano, get her to question him again. Then I remembered. She didn't report to me anymore. "When did you hear about the murder?"

Thurgood picked up his glass and slurped ginger ale through the straw, sucking it almost dry. "I went back the next morning."

"To Dr. Christiansen's residence? What time?"

"Just after nine thirty. The place was crawling with police, fire, ambulance. Drew a conclusion when I saw the coroner's van. Never got out. Drove right by and kept on driving clear back here to Provo."

"Police cameras can probably confirm that, too." I motioned to Tim for the tab and fumbled for my readers.

Thurgood's features dissolved into slits, and he set down his glass. "All I wanted was to do a good deed for the Church and get my wife and customers back. End all this nonsense about lady prophets. Be everyone's hero. Now I'm in the middle of a murder investigation."

"Tough break," I said, my mind on the good night's rest I needed ahead of our trip south tomorrow. I calculated another generous tip and then signed the bill. "Thanks, Mr. Thurgood. You've been very helpful."

"What about the stone?"

"Oh, right." I slipped off my stool and buttoned my sportscoat. "I'll get back to you on that."

"Yeah, when?"

"Soon. Just be patient."

"No time to be patient. *I'm* the victim here," he insisted, this time with two thumbs pointing to his chest.

I paused once more to take in the spectacle of Meredith Snow's estranged husband. Jesus, what the fuck had she been thinking? Still, all things considered, I couldn't help but feel a bit sorry for him. Tim did too, evidently, as he was delivering yet another ginger ale to the schmuck, this one with two cherries.

"You're a good man, Timothy." I made a mental note to remember him to management. Then I headed back to my room, leaving Thurgood to cry into his Shirley Temple.

Matt Ryan, Private Investigator
Mona, Utah
Monday, March 29, 2010
9:25 a.m.

C ruising down the slim ribbon of highway, I lowered the window a crack and breathed in the country air, rich with hay and mown grass, and thick enough to bite into. It felt good to be in the driver's seat again.

"Why on earth would Newsome want a seer stone?" Carrie asked, having spent the ride from Provo listening to my recap of the conversations with Romano and Thurgood.

"Beats me. But Romano believes he does. Bottom line, Christiansen was in a position to blackmail Newsome and that gave our congressman a motive for murder."

"But why would Newsome have Christiansen killed in such a bizarre manner?"

"Got me on that one," I admitted.

"And what did Flake have to do with any of this?"

"Got me there, too."

Carrie scowled and lowered her own window. "So, how did Thurgood know where to find you last night?"

I grinned. "By way of his expert detective skills, of course."

"Uh-huh. Speaking of expert detective skills, what are yours telling you about this detour to Utah?"

"That it might be nothing more than a free trip to an exotic locale," I replied, to which she snorted a laugh.

The broad single-story house stood atop a low rise on Highway 91 beneath a colossal snow capped peak. The sky was a solid pane of blue, not a speck of cloud.

"Unbelievable how beautiful this place is," I said as I turned onto the gravel road that led to the front door. A field of dormant shrubs ran alongside my window.

"Unbelievable how strange this client is," Carrie replied. "Do you really want to go on representing Mrs. Christiansen, given how she's hidden so much from you?"

"Not sure." I shifted into park and paused to appreciate the silence. "But we're here on her dime, so we might as well follow through."

We got out of the car and Carrie took in the field, shading her eyes with her hand. "Those aren't sugar beets. What do you suppose they grow here?"

I stepped off the gravel drive, pinched a spiky leaf off a shorn shrub, and held it to my nose. "Lavender."

Carrie let her hand drop to her side. "They make lavender marsh-mallows?"

"Who wants to know?" a female voice called.

We turned to see a woman glaring at us from the top step of the front porch. Her blonde hair was in an elaborate updo, her full cotton skirt fell to her ankles, and her hand clutched a large caliber pistol, inconveniently aimed at my chest. We held up our hands.

"We're not intruders, ma'am," I explained. "We're private detectives from Abbottsville, California."

Her face relaxed, but her gun remained on target.

"Unarmed detectives," I added, cursing myself for leaving the Glock in the glovebox.

She lowered the pistol. "Are you here to tell us about Dell? We know already on account of the deputy sheriff came by last night during supper. Even brought pictures from the California police."

I let my hands drop to my sides, keeping them a safe distance from my pockets. Carrie did the same.

"We're sorry for your loss, ma'am. We're trying to track down his killer and were hoping we could speak with Ms. Louisa Snow."

The woman's eyes narrowed. "She's out in the back field."

"Could you point us in her direction?" I asked.

Her pistol hand twitched the barrel briefly in our direction. "We're a little wary of strangers these days."

I nodded. "I have ID if—"

"I'm actually from Parowan," said Carrie.

"You don't look it," the woman said, her eyes traveling Carrie's tailored jacket and slim black pants.

"My husband and I moved to California after BYU. But I grew up down there. My maiden name is Tanner," she explained, her voice taking on unfamiliar twang. "In fact, we just came from my Aunt Jane and Uncle LaVar's place in Orem. They asked me to give Sister Weezie Snow their best."

"That be Jane and LaVar Shumway?" she asked.

Carrie smiled. "LaVar Shumway is my mother's brother. I'm Carrie Zimmerman—formerly Tanner—and this is Matt Ryan."

Her eyes still fixed on us, the woman's head tilted toward the door. "Crystal, come here."

A child appeared at the screen. She looked to be around five years old. Her blonde hair was pulled back in double braids and her skirt dangled at mid-calf.

"Call Mama Weezie. Tell her some of Sister Jane Shumway's kin are here to see her."

"Yes'm." The child disappeared.

"Thank you." Carrie's smile brightened. "May we ask your name?"

The woman backed up onto the porch, one hand reaching for the door handle, the other still holding the gun. "Weezie'll be here shortly," she said, and then went inside, shut the heavy wooden door, and clicked the deadbolt.

I cast an ominous expression over at Carrie and then back at the house. Little Crystal peeked out the front curtains. Seconds later a toddler's face poked through the slats of some venetian blinds. I thought of the pistol and wondered what else they might be packing in there.

"Best we stay here and mind our p's and q's," I said.

Carrie nodded. "So the deputy sheriff showed them the pictures of their husband's murder scene."

There was that twang again.

"And over dinner. Nice guy," I observed. "Incidentally, you sounded like your Aunt Jane just now."

She stared back at me, her bright blue eyes more terrified than they'd been at the sight of the pistol. "Do you think I've regressed?"

I chuckled. "It's catchy. Own it."

We waited through a slow tick of time until a dusty dark blue pickup rattled up from behind the house and turned onto the gravel drive. It came to a stop just shy of our rental car. Three women hopped out. Thanks to Aunt Jane we had no problem recognizing Weezie Snow. She was literally wearing the pants, overalls actually, and a BYU baseball cap that covered all but an inch of curly red hair. A cellular telephone at her ear, she waved us hello as she signed off her call. The other two wore long skirts and upswept hair. One was short and husky, the other tall and skittish. They lingered behind Weezie, eyeing us cautiously.

Weezie slipped her phone into the bib pocket of her overalls and walked toward us, a broad smile lighting up her round face. "You must be Carrie," she said, giving her hand a shake. "And you're Ryan." Her grip was firm and her gaze exuded confidence. "I'm Weezie, but you already know that."

"How—" I began.

"I just got off the phone with Jane," she explained. "She said you were here on an investigation. Given recent events, I'm assuming it has something to do with Dell."

"You would be correct," I said.

"You called my aunt just now?" asked Carrie.

Weezie's smile faded. "Sorry, honey, but I had to check you out. We've had a bad week."

"We're sorry for your loss," I said.

Weezie tipped her head in thanks while the other two smiled demurely. "Lorinda, honey, go inside and tell Gabby to pour us some lemonade. We'll have it on the lawn by Dell's garden."

Both women scurried inside, making it impossible to determine which one Weezie had just addressed. Then, motioning us to follow, she wound around the side of the house to a scattering of Adirondack chairs. Weezie dragged two of them together, then strode across the grass for a third, her muscular frame maneuvering the heavy thing as if it was a flimsy piece of plastic. "Have a seat," she said.

I settled into the center of the semi-circle, Carrie at my left, Weezie at my right. In front of us a generous patch of upturned soil spread out to roughly the size of my backyard, paling in comparison to the massive field of lavender that lay beyond.

"Is this what you referred to as Dell's garden?" I asked.

Weezie heaved a sigh. "Poor old Dell. He always had some scheme for this property. The latest was sugar beets."

"He promised us a box of his homemade marshmallows," said Carrie.

"Yeah, well, don't hold your breath." Weezie rolled her eyes. "The man hadn't even managed to grow one successful beet. And thank god for that, since the damned fool would have blown himself up in the refining process."

Carrie gazed out at the empty soil, hand shading her face. "Would a plot this size yield enough beets to produce—"

"Not even close," Weezie interrupted. "But it did keep him busy for a spell."

The tone Weezie used when referring to her late husband sounded a lot like Carrie's when she spoke of little Ryan. I forced back a chuckle. Then the woman I now understood to be Gabby appeared, only this time instead of a pistol, she was armed with a serving tray. She bent down for us to take a chilled glass and then retreated, empty tray in hand.

"Thanks, hon," Weezie called after her.

The lemonade was tart and sweet and obviously made from scratch. "Delicious," I said and set the glass on my wide wooden armrest.

"That's our gourmet, Gabby," Weezie said. "Now that Dell's gone, maybe we can turn this plot into a kitchen garden for her."

"You said he had other schemes besides marshmallows?" said Carrie.

"Oh lordy." Weezie removed her baseball cap and ran her hand through her curly mop of red hair. "First it was essential oils. I wouldn't let him near my lavender, of course, so the dang fool tried growing patchouli." She fanned her hat at the bed. "In full sun with practically no water. When that flopped, he tried mint. It took off like a shot, so well it invaded part of that field yonder. Lorinda and I are still finding shoots here and there." She paused and combed her curls with her hand again.

I smiled and took a long drink. Her reference to Lorinda working the field told me she was most likely the husky one.

"Meanwhile the oil Dell extracted wasn't fit for a rusted-out rototiller," Weezie said. "So he moved on to making soap. That was, until Gabby chased him out of the kitchen with her meat cleaver." Weezie's shoulders bounced in silent laughter. "She's a firecracker, that one."

"Yes, we saw," I said.

Weezie went for a long drink that consumed half her glass. "Kind of a shame," she continued. "The lemon verbena he'd planted was a nice addition. But then he switched to chili peppers, thinking he'd go into the hot sauce business."

"Peppers ought to grow here," said Carrie.

"Oh, they did." Weezie tipped her glass in Carrie's direction. "And the hot sauce wasn't half bad either. He even had the good sense to stay out of Gabby's kitchen, moved his laboratory to the workshop."

"So what was the problem?" I asked.

"Problem was he had no market. Folks around here get a dash of vinegar on their tater tots, their eyes tear up and their heads explode."

Carrie giggled. "That's so true. How could he not know that?"

"How not, indeed." Weezie shook her head. "So he set his mind on marshmallows. When his first two sugar beet crops failed the sister wives and I were crossing our fingers he'd give that up too. Then he read online about the Hatcher Stone. Since I'm related to Old Man Hatcher's wife, Francis Snow, Dell thought he could lay claim to it. Harness its magic power." She rolled her eyes. "Damned magic rock. What he needed was a stable soil pH level."

Draining the rest of her glass, she wiped her mouth with the back of her hand. Her expression turned benign, peaceful even. Out of character, I thought, for a woman who'd just lost her husband.

Her pale green eyes shifted sharply in my direction. "Don't misunderstand me, Ryan. I cared deeply for Dell. It's just that I saw this coming. My husband was kind and completely without guile. Just like a lamb. And with all the wolves around here, I always knew he'd end in a slaughter."

I nodded soberly and downed more of my drink, unsettled that yet another woman had seemed to read my mind.

"You folks have your work cut out for you, finding which wolf," she added.

"Gabby told us that the deputy sheriff came by last night with pictures of the crime scene," said Carrie.

"Yup," Weezie said. "Claimed it was for our protection. It was a copycat, you see. Poor old Dell was murdered like the original owner of the Hatcher stone. Same with that doctor Dell was dealing with. But then you probably already know that, too."

"But why show you the gory details?" said Carrie. "He could have just told you."

Weezie sighed. "Deputy Sheriff Ricks is part of the Dawson group."

Carrie caught my eye. "Fundamentalist Mormons," she explained.

"Right," said Weezie. "We were part of them too until Dell took us out of it a couple of years ago. They've been trying to shame us ever since."

"You mean he thought the pictures might scare you back into the fold?" I asked.

Weezie laughed. "Well, I'm sure he knows I don't need the group's protection. But he'll be working on the sister wives. They all will." Her face saddened.

"Think you can keep everyone here on the farm?" said Carrie.

"Try to," Weezie replied. "Lorinda has two sons. If she goes back, she'll have to leave them behind. Dawsons won't take them."

Carrie nodded her understanding while I made a face.

"The group needs women not men," Weezie explained. "In fact, they're in the process of kicking out some of their own boys, leaving them on the side of the road."

"You're kidding," I said.

"It's common practice in these groups," Carrie added. "People refer to them as the 'lost boys.'"

"Of course, Lorinda knows I'll take good care of her sons if she leaves." Weezie laughed quietly. "When we left the Dawsons, Dell looked into acquiring the old Hatcher Farm. Back then I was against it, but now I wonder if it might not have been for the best. Would have put us a good three hours south."

"We're headed there after this," said Carrie.

Weezie's face lit up. "The Hatcher Farm?"

"Yes," Carrie replied. "We're meeting a Mr. Finlay."

"Buck Finlay." Weezie chuckled. "Be warned, that character is a taco shy of a combination plate."

I smiled. "How so?"

"He sounded anxious on the phone," Carrie said and then sipped the last of her lemonade.

Weezie let loose a hearty laugh. "The man's a walking panic attack. You folks might put him out of his misery if you were to buy that farm of his. He's convinced it's haunted."

"Really?" said Carrie. "By the original Hatcher family?"

"By Francis Snow herself." Weezie tipped her leftover ice into her mouth. "When we went to see the place, Buck refused to go past the front gate. Then halfway up the walk Dell got spooked. Left me to go it alone."

"Did you see her?" I asked. "The ghost, I mean."

"Guess I must have spooked her. All I encountered was peeling paint and loose floorboards. A stain that looks like it might have been blood on one of the parlor walls." She shook her head. "The place has a sad history. But it's got good bones. Just needs a lot of TLC. More than I wanted to tackle. I was happy here. Still am." Weezie nodded firmly. "And if I can keep the family together, I hope to do some modernizing."

I was about to ask how when the skittish sister wife appeared carrying a small parcel, her long skirt billowing out in front of her.

"Better hair, new wardrobes, for one," Weezie replied, again reading my mind. Then to the sister wife, "What've you got there, Becca?"

The young woman blinked, and a tear slid down her cheek. "The postman brought it just now." She gingerly handed the box to Weezie.

Sorry recognition crossing her face, Weezie stared at the address and then turned to me. "It's from Dell, postmarked California."

"Sort of thought it might be," I replied.

Frowning, she stared back at the box. "Becca, you go on inside. I'll see to this."

Disappointment showed on Becca's face, but she did as she was told. Then once the girl was out of earshot, Weezie looked up from the box and back at me. "Well, you gonna spill it or let me guess?"

I recounted our dealings with Mr. Flake, explained who our client was and, convinced that Weezie would be on to me anyway, confessed to how and why I had created a fake stone to give to her late husband. When I finished, she stared back at the box again, sighed, and tore it open.

"So this is my final gift from Dell." She held up the fake stone.

I leaned forward in my chair and gazed earnestly into her pale green eyes. "He genuinely believed it was the real thing."

Weezie scoffed. "As far as I'm concerned it's every bit as real as the original."

Carrie giggled and I hung my head and grinned.

"You folks want to borrow it? Protect yourselves against Sister Snow's ghost this afternoon?" she asked.

"No, thanks, you keep it. Protect yourself from the wolves," I said.

Cradling the stone in her palm, she gently rubbed her thumb over its face. "Probably best I hang on to it, seeing how Dell wanted me to have it."

"Speaking of wolves," I said. "Do you think any of your neighbors might have killed Dell? People from the Dawson group maybe?"

"It's possible some wanted to," Weezie replied. "Like I said, women are scarce in the group and some of those men would love to get their hands on the sisters. But killing Dell wouldn't be enough. After that they'd have to deal with me."

"Could be somebody has that in mind," I said. "You be careful, Weezie."

"Oh, don't you worry about me, Ryan." Her pale eyes iced over, like the surface of an alpine lake. "I'm not as sweet as I look."

By the time we hit the road it was a quarter past ten, leaving us only forty-five minutes to make the original appointment with Buck Finlay.

Carrie pulled out her cellphone and dialed. "Mr. Finlay?...Sir, this is Carrie Zimmerman. I'm afraid we've gotten a late start. May we reschedule for today at one o'clock?...Oh...do you think that will be an issue?...I see, well, we're on our way....Thanks, good bye." She closed her cellphone and shot me a bemused look.

"Problem?" I asked.

"He's worried our tardiness might upset *the occupant*."

"Oh boy," I said, laughing. "Sounds like Weezie was right about that missing taco."

"Sounds like."

As we cruised down the interstate, the population thinned along with the vegetation. But the barren landscape was no less stunning, its naked peaks erupting from the tanned earth. Conversation flowed freely, and I was grateful for a traveling companion who was so easy to talk to. We passed by towns with interesting names: Santaquin, Nephi (pronounced with a long "i" according to Carrie), Scipio, and Kanosh. Then, by the time we were thirty miles outside of Parowan, Carrie shifted the discussion to her family.

"You don't have to see them all, just my cousin Jesse, and we can meet him at a restaurant."

"We can't go to his house?"

"Gosh, no. He still lives with his parents, my aunt and uncle, and you definitely don't want to meet them."

"Why not? I met your Uncle LaVar."

"I'm already regretting that."

I let loose a guffaw. "He was fine."

"Jesse's mom is LaVar's sister, my Aunt LaFawn, and she's worse than he is. And don't get me started on his other sister, who also happens to be my mother."

"C'mon, Carrie, I'd love to meet your family."

"That's because you don't know how crazy they are."

"Think I can't handle crazy? I was a San Francisco cop for twenty years."

She shook her head. "We're definitely not in Kansas anymore, Ryan."

"Who said anything about Kansas?"

"Take the next exit." Carrie pulled out her cellphone and dialed. "Mr. Finlay, this is Carrie Zimmerman...yes, sir, we're exiting the freeway now...Great, see you there." She dropped the phone in her handbag. "He's at the property already."

I took the exit ramp, slowed to a stop at the sign, and then looked to Carrie for directions.

"Turn right and keep going until we see it," she said.

"We'll know it when we see it?"

"So he claims."

We'd traveled the two-lane road for several minutes, speeding by flat sand and juniper, an abandoned service station, and a rusted-out pickup truck, when a fuzzy structure appeared on the horizon. As we approached, the image sharpened, revealing a gabled roof, windows, wood siding, and a wide front porch, all of it wrapped in a palpable aura of creepiness. The dwelling now in full view, I instinctively slowed to a stop.

"Oh my god," I whispered. "It's the *Psycho* house."

"Like I said…"

"We're not in Kansas anymore," I repeated along with her, and then accelerated forward to park behind a silver Mercedes S-Class sedan.

We got out of our economy rental car and walked toward the sleek luxury vehicle, so new that the dealer's logo filled the license plate slot, and so shiny one might imagine it hovered over rather than drove along these dusty highways. In spite of what I'd learned this morning, the car told me to expect one of the 007 actors to emerge from its climate-controlled leather interior, impeccably dressed, and exuding sophistication. But when the door swung open and the new car smell wafted my way I was jolted back to reality. Buck Finlay was a classic hayseed, down to the cheap suit, Coke bottle glasses, and Barney Fife hair. An insincere grin was smashed into his face like a wedge of gouda.

"Howdy-doo," he sang. "Welcome to this fine property."

"Matt Ryan." I extended my hand. "And this is Carrie Zimmerman."

His limp paw deflated so sharply under my squeeze it defied the existence of any bone structure. Finlay withdrew his hand, nodded at Carrie, and turned back to me, his smile evaporating. "Where is she?"

I glanced at the house and then back at him. "Excuse me?"

"*Mrs. Christiansen,*" he hissed, his mud-colored eyes made huge behind the glasses.

"She's not here," I said.

"Why *not?*"

"Mr. Finlay," said Carrie, "we're representing Mrs. Christiansen. Isn't that good enough?"

His head wagged to and fro atop his chicken neck, causing his gelled hair to shake loose and then freeze in an awkward position. "No, no, no. I can't risk showing it to just you."

Carrie balked. "What do you mean risk? You just said this was a fine property."

"It is," he replied. "But it's also a very special property, and only she decides who can enter."

"Who is *she?*" I asked, making no effort to hide my impatience.

His eyes expanded to the edges of his Coke bottle frames and he threw up his arms, so violently that his dress shirt yanked from the waist of his snagged polyester pants. "Francis Cannon Snow, that's who."

"Is that what you meant by 'the occupant?'" Carrie asked.

"Oh, yes." His scrawny chest rose and fell in shallow heaves. "I've seen her many times."

I blinked. "You've seen her?"

"Just last month." He nodded at the house. "I was repairing a porch stair after a storm and there she was, hanging over me, with that evil awful glare and...the huge hole in her...in her *head*." Finlay removed his glasses and mopped his face with a handkerchief. "So I grabbed my tools and ran. And then do you know what?"

"What?" Carrie and I said in unison.

"The next day I came back and the stair was repaired."

I huffed a sigh. "This happened last month?"

He put the glasses back on his face. "It did."

"Well," I continued, "maybe now that the weather's improved she's gone on vacation. After all, we've a nice little break before the planting season begins."

Finlay scowled and pocketed his handkerchief. Then he stuffed his shirt back into his pants. The belt he wore was so gnarled it might have doubled as a puppy toy. "You think I'm making this up."

"No, Mr. Finlay," I replied. "I can see that you are entirely serious. But please understand our predicament. We've come over a thousand miles at the expense of our client, Mrs. Christiansen. How can we leave without even looking at the property?"

"If she buys the place won't she want to see it herself first?" he asked.

I nodded. "Eventually."

"Then I strongly suggest you wait for that eventuality." He eyed me gravely, his hair still askew.

"How about this, instead," I said. "You stay here with Carrie, and I'll go in and take a look around."

"You don't want me to go with you?" Carrie asked.

"No use both of us risking it. I have my phone if there's a problem." I looked to Mr. Finlay. "Can you give me the key to the front door?"

He scoffed. "Don't need a key to keep that place locked."

I nodded and started up the dirt path to the front porch.

"Your cellphone won't work in there neither," Finlay shouted.

A chill ran through me and my pace slowed, but I determined myself ahead. After all, Weezie had walked through the place. If she could do it, so could I. The air grew still and quiet. I glanced back at Carrie and Finlay. While only yards behind me, they seemed small and distant. Meanwhile, the house loomed large, its dimensions distorted, like in a fun house mirror. The surrounding silence was eerie but also strangely comforting, awe-inspiring even. I was on hallowed ground. Arriving at the foot of the porch stairs, I spotted a "For Sale" sign planted neatly aside the steps, a tag that read, "Do Not Disturb Occupant," dangling from its base, and to my left, a freshly turned garden bed, as though ready for spring planting. Swallowing hard, I mounted the first step and froze. The wooden tread beneath my feet was brand new, its edge flush with the original riser. Ice trickling into my veins, I climbed the second and then third step, nervously laughing off the suggestion that Francis Snow, gaping hole in her head, had drifted out here with a saw and miter box to perform the repair herself. Had she then dragged out her hoe to till the soil? *Ridiculous*, I told myself. Still, as I mounted the porch, I had the distinct feeling that I was being watched. Then a deafening creak gave me such a start that I jumped, practically tumbling backwards down the stairs. The front door creaked open, leaving just enough space for a person to peek through.

"Hello?" I called into the void.

When no one answered I tilted sideways to see through the opening. Nothing but a swirl of airborne dust and a slice of faded wallpaper, at least to my naked eye. But I felt a presence. There was somebody behind that door. Not a hostile being, necessarily, but dangerous, nonetheless. Like a mother bear guarding her cubs. Pass by on the edge of the clearing and she'll leave you be. Enter the clearing and you're fair game. During my years on the force I'd had a few encounters with the paranormal. While inexplicable, I'd learned to respect them. For that reason, I slowly backed away. Also because I was scared shitless.

My heart pounding, I took the steps down from the porch carefully, fighting off the image of Martin Balsam careening backwards to his death in *Psycho*. Then I strode quickly along the dirt path, breathing a sigh of relief when I reached the street.

"We'll wait for Mrs. Christiansen," I announced, and then noticed I was shivering. Of course I was shivering. I'd just seen a ghost. Almost, anyway.

"Did you see her?" Finlay asked.

"I saw what you meant," I said, my shakes subsiding.

"So next time you'll bring Mrs. Christiansen?"

"Can we have some assurance that our client will be able to enter the premises?"

"Can't assure you of anything," Finlay replied. "But I do know that Francis Snow consistently welcomes her own female heirs. Everyone else is touch and go."

Based on the knowledge that Weezie Snow was allowed entrance, I figured that was a fairly reasonable assurance. "OK. We'll confer with our client and give you a call."

His eyes brightened and the cheesy grin returned. "I'm sure she'll be impressed with this fine property," he said, affecting a casually confident tone that suggested he was plugging a timeshare on Maui.

I re-shook his limp paw and then looked beyond to see another silver S-Class sedan barreling toward us, this one also with dealer plates. It jolted to a halt behind our rental car and the outraged driver jumped out, slamming the door behind him. If it weren't for the gray hair and department store suit, he might have been Finlay's doppelganger.

"Uncle Newt, what brings you out this way?" Finlay asked, his voice climbing an octave.

"My GPS, you blubbering moron. It tracked you here."

"Why Uncle, I was just showing these fine people—"

"Not in one of my cars, you're not," he roared. "From now on you're to stay away from my dealership, and you will return that vehicle immediately."

"Of course. Soon as I bid farewell to Mr. Ryan and—"

"*Now,*" Uncle Newt boomed.

"I'm leaving." Finlay hustled back to the pinched Mercedes. When he got to the door, he cried "Mr. Ryan, you call me as soon as you confer with Mrs. Christiansen." He dove behind the wheel and sped away.

Uncle Newt watched after his vehicle until it disappeared down the highway, then his face relaxed into a smile. "Your name is Ryan?"

"That's correct," I replied.

"Newt Finlay, pleased to meet you." He extended his hand, and I shook it. Not quite as limp as his nephew, but still even on the creep factor. Then he pulled a business card from his breast pocket. "If you're ever in the market for a Mercedes give me a call. We've a fine selection of new and pre-owned vehicles."

I took the card. "Thank you."

He winked, climbed back into the S-Class with dealer plates, and drove off after his nephew.

Slipping the card in my pocket, I exchanged a look with Carrie.

"Welcome to Southern Utah," she said.

Chuckling, I started for our rental car, waving her on ahead of me.

"Did you see a ghost back there, Ryan?" Carrie asked.

"It sure felt like somebody. I know it sounds crazy but—"

"No, it doesn't. I can feel her from here."

I pulled out my readers and checked my phone for a signal. Four bars. "I say we call Mrs. Christiansen and see if she wants to pursue this. If she does, the three of us come back here tomorrow. If she doesn't you and I go home."

Carrie nodded. "You want some privacy while you talk to her?"

This was my first indication that Carrie suspected something less than professional existed between me and our client.

"You can hear whatever I say. In fact, since you know the way, why don't you drive? I'll place the call."

I handed her the key and went around to the passenger side. Once we were rolling, I scrolled my contacts to the number and dialed. She picked up on the first ring.

"Hello?"

"Ryan here, I'm—"

"Ryan, it's you? When I saw the number, I was hoping…but lately I've only heard from Mrs. Z."

I shifted in my seat, simultaneously stirred and annoyed by the sound of her voice. "Carrie is here, too. We're in the car."

"So it's *Carrie* now?"

"I'm putting you on speaker." I hit the icon with my thumb and set the phone in the compartment between our seats. Then I recounted the meeting with Buck Finlay.

"I guess I'd better get out there tomorrow," Annie said, once I'd finished.

"That would involve a lot of money and effort. The farm is four hours south of Salt Lake City, and there's no indication that a personal tour will uncover any useful evidence."

"I'm having strong feelings that it will," Annie replied. "I'll see if I can charter a flight into Provo."

"It's your money."

I signed off the call and stared out at the bleak landscape. A turkey vulture glided across the solid blue sky, tentatively circling, and then diving behind a cluster of brush. "What about you, Carrie? Have any strong feelings at the moment?"

"Only that I no longer believe anything Annie Christiansen says."

"Point taken." So far Annie had been deceitful, fey, and unforthcoming. Also funny, bright, and sexy as hell. And this case was the most exciting thing I'd come across in years. Way outside my comfort zone. "But then, she is a paying client," I observed.

"Touché," Carrie replied. "I'm down with *that*."

I looked away from the window to return her smile.

"So, Ryan, while you were checking out the house, I texted my cousin, Jesse. He should be on his way to meet us. Says he has a new person of interest. For some reason he picked the travel stop."

"Fine. Your aunt's house would also be fine."

"I don't know why we couldn't have gone to the diner." Carrie flipped on the blinker and we exited the highway. "It's family owned and they have good home cooking."

"You mean like your aunt's house?"

There were four semis in the truck parking and a neat row of passenger vehicles in the spots along the storefront. What looked like the obligatory geezer was on a long bench by the door, dressed in overalls. At the other end of the bench sat a glum, sandy-haired young man in jeans and a rumpled blue shirt.

Carrie pulled up next to a white four-wheel drive pickup. "That kid there might be one of those lost boys we were talking about."

"Really?" I gave him a second take. The shirt he was wearing looked homemade, and slept in.

We got out of the car and she pointed to a gray Subaru compact. "Looks like Jesse's here already."

The aging import had a Greenpeace sticker on its left bumper and an Obama/Biden on its right. In a culture that favored pickups, gun racks, and right-wing politics, the car was a standout. I figured the owner might be, too. As I held the door for Carrie, I nodded at the geezer, who smiled, tipped his cowboy hat, and looked as though he was about to speak. As interesting as the old wag's ramblings might be, I sensed they might take me down a rabbit hole. I smiled tightly and kept on walking.

We strolled through the convenience store, past the restrooms and laundry facility, and into the small food court. Jesse was at a table near the Subway counter. He wore a cream button-down shirt. A tan canvas jacket with a tweed collar was draped over the back of his chair. When we approached, he looked up from his laptop with kind, intelligent eyes. Then he stood to embrace his cousin and shake my hand. His grip was firm but not overpowering, his manner genteel, and his face bore a striking resemblance to a young Hugh Grant, so much so I half expected to hear a British accent. Instead, it was a soft, country twang.

He made a sweeping gesture. "Welcome to our fine dining."

"I like Subway," I said. "And I see there's a Taco Bell, too."

"Oh, yeah, we're a diverse demographic. I believe they sell pizza slices over in the convenience store."

Carrie rolled her eyes. "Jesse, why couldn't we meet at the diner?"

He pointed to his computer. "Bud and Wilma don't have WiFi."

She sighed. "Probably just as well. Wilma would call my mom and tell her I'm here."

"She already knows." Jesse returned to his seat. "My mom's cooking up a storm for everyone tonight."

Carrie sank into a chair. "Why?"

"She got wind you were coming. Your parents will be there, also Grandpa Jack, Frank and Minnie, the Kessler cousins, and who knows who else. Maybe even Bud and Wilma. Oh, and you're invited, too, Ryan."

I smiled. "Great."

She shot me a look and turned back to Jesse.

His eyes crinkled in the corners. "C'mon, Carrie, you didn't really think you could sneak in and out of town without the family knowing."

"How did they find out?"

"Aunt Jane, of course."

"I didn't tell Aunt Jane we were coming here. In fact, I specifically—"

"She heard from some lady named Weezie. I think she lives in Mona."

"It's a conspiracy," she half-whispered, seemingly to herself.

"Wow," I said. "These ladies are good. Wish I could afford to hire them."

Carrie glared up at me.

"Anyone up for splitting a sandwich?" I asked.

Jesse shook his head. "Thanks, had lunch already, and we've got that big dinner tonight."

Carrie sighed. "I'm not hungry."

"Well, I'm starved." I went to the counter, ordered a foot-long cold-cut combo, had them slice it in two and wrap the halves separately. She had to be hungry. It was almost half past two and we hadn't eaten all day. When I returned, Carrie was staring at Jesse's computer screen.

"What's up?" I took a seat and slid half of the foot-long across the table to Carrie, then unwrapped my portion and took an eager bite.

"Nothing yet." Carrie looked up from the screen. "Jesse was about to show me his person of interest," she said, then eyeing her half sandwich, she pushed the laptop back to Jesse and also started to eat, her hunger evidently kicking in.

"Good," I mumbled, my mouth still full.

Carrie took another bite, moaning appreciation as she chewed. "This is terrific, Ryan. Thanks."

"Anytime," I said, and we fell silent, she and I too focused on food to talk. Jesse turned back to his computer.

"So, who's this other person of interest?" I asked once I'd inhaled my meal.

"Somebody who calls himself Truth Seeker," Jesse replied.

"Truth Seeker was the author of the original post asking for information about seer stones," Carrie explained.

I pulled a napkin from the holder on our table. "You mean the post that Dr. Christiansen replied to?"

"Yes. I'm just getting up to speed, but it appears Christiansen wrote in under the screen name 'Mormon Doc,'" claiming to own the Hatcher Stone," said Jesse. "Then Flake replied as 'Marshmallow Man,' Thurgood as 'Stripling Warrior,' and Hatcher under his own name, all of them expressing an interest in the stone."

"But Truth Seeker never followed up with any inquiries about acquiring the stone?" Carrie asked.

"Nope," said Jesse. "My stats show him lurking, though, checking out the comments to his original post."

Suddenly thirsty, I reached for my wallet. "Wouldn't you expect him to do that?"

"Sure," Jesse replied, eyes on his laptop. "Which is why I didn't bother with him at first. I figured he was just some history buff collecting stories, like most of the people who visit my site. Then this morning it occurred to me to check him out. I tracked his IP address."

"And?" I fished a ten out of my billfold.

Jesse passed the laptop to Carrie, who smiled and then, gazing over at me, repeated, "Nine twenty-five Windsor Court, Abbottsville, California."

"Congressman Newsome," I half-sighed. Not exactly a surprise, really. Although I still hadn't the faintest idea why our congressman would care about a magic rock. "Anyone like a Coke?"

"Sure," said Jesse.

"Make mine diet," Carrie added.

Back at the counter, I placed my order, mulling over this new discovery. Evidently Newsome had put the query out there and then never followed up on his own thread. But then, if he'd figured out Mormon Doc's identity, he didn't need to reach out to him on the internet, he could confront the man in person.

I bussed the drinks back to our table, poked my straw into the lid of my Coke, and took a long drink. "Was Mormon Doc a frequent poster?"

Jesse paused for his own sip. "I ran a search on him just before you got here. Turns out Mormon Doc posted regularly on my site and dropped plenty of clues about his personal life." His perceptive blue eyes conveyed the same pragmatic sharpness I admired in Carrie. He knew where I was going with this.

"So it wouldn't be difficult for this Truth Seeker, as Newsome called himself, to conclude that Mormon Doc was actually Doctor Christiansen?" I said.

He shook his head no. "Especially given Newsome knew the doctor in real life."

"But why would a guy like Newsome want a seer stone?" Carrie asked.

Jesse shrugged. "He wants to be an LDS bigshot. Maybe he thinks if he donates the thing to the Church, he'll earn a promotion."

I took another drag on my Coke. So Newsome and Thurgood were essentially of the same mind. It wasn't all that far-fetched. Pad an extra hundred or so pounds on Newsome, then stuff him, sausage-like, into a shiny suit, banish him to his wife's basement…

"Maybe Newsome thinks the Brethren will give him a second anointing," Jesse suggested, interrupting my fanciful musings.

"What—" I began, when Carrie cut in.

"He's a United States congressman," she cried.

Jesse let loose a guffaw. "You and I obviously have vastly different takes on the mental acuity of our elected representatives."

"All right." Carrie gave him a playful shove and we allowed ourselves a laugh.

"What's this second anointing?" I asked, finally.

Carrie waved me off. "Long story."

"Aren't you supposed to be my translator?"

"Short version is it's more Parowan craziness," she said.

"Not just Parowan," said Jesse. "The Brethren in Salt Lake are still doing them." He turned to me. "They're the Mormon equivalent of a 'Get Out of Jail Free' card. A special ritual in the temple that ensures highly placed Mormons their salvation is guaranteed no matter how unscrupulous, gluttonous, or slothful they are. Word is Mitt Romney's received one."

I scratched a spot behind my ear, considering what he'd just said. "Well, that would explain the former governor's speeches. He couldn't put more than five seconds of effort into those snooze fests."

Jesse laughed and Carrie scowled.

"That Romney story is just a rumor," she said. "Probably started by a kook from Parowan."

"C'mon, Carrie," Jesse groaned. "You know crazy doesn't stop here at the city limits. There's a whole world of kooks out there." He closed his laptop and slipped his arms into his jacket, pulling its tweed collar up over his shoulders.

"What keeps you in Parowan?" I asked, again taking in his British upper middle-class appearance.

"I'm attached to the history, and I enjoy teaching at our local college extension. But...I found out yesterday I'm moving to the big city this fall."

"You got the job?" said Carrie.

He nodded.

"What's the new job?" I asked.

"I landed a faculty position at Dixie College. It's down the road in St. George. Around here that's the big city."

Carrie beamed. "It is compared to Parowan."

"I haven't told my folks yet," Jesse warned. "So, better not bring it up at dinner tonight."

Her smile collapsed. "How 'bout Ryan and I just skip the dinner entirely?"

"Can't get out of it now, cousin. Mom's roast is already in the oven." He came to his feet. "I'd better go. Got lessons to plan. Also I promised to pick up a can of those French fried onions."

"For the green bean casserole," Carrie repeated, her face going from solemn to tragic.

Doing my best not to laugh at her expression, I stood and fished one and then the other pocket for the rental car keys.

"I have them, Ryan." Carrie pulled them from her handbag.

"Fine, keep them," I said. "You can drive us to that B&B you booked. With any luck they'll have our rooms ready."

"The Rowley House?" asked Jesse.

"Yup," Carrie said. She took one last sip of her Diet Coke, collected our crumpled sandwich wrappers and then walked them to the trash.

Jesse followed after her with his own cup. "You know it's haunted, right?"

"So I hear," she said.

"By whom?" I asked.

"Word is it's Matilda Rowley," Jesse replied. "She and Mr. Rowley built the mansion back in 1870. Then a couple of years later Rowley decided to take on some plural wives. Not long after that, Matilda mysteriously disappeared."

"Matilda was said to be a very outspoken woman," Carrie added. "We outspoken women tend to disappear from these parts…one way or another."

I sampled what was left of my Coke. It was watered down but still had some zap. I decided to hang onto it.

"Seventy-some years later, a family named Cartwright bought the place and turned it into a hotel," Jesse went on. "When they demoed for the elevator shaft, they discovered human bones, approximating a female her size."

I aimed for the door. "Nowadays a crime lab could ID those remains, maybe determine cause of death."

"Unfortunately, her remains have also mysteriously disappeared," Carrie said, following after me. I paused to let her go on ahead.

"But locals insist Matilda's spirit lingers behind, haunting the Rowley House elevator," Jesse said, as we passed through the convenience store.

Good to know. Another female ghost. I wondered if she was acquaintted with Francis Snow. Perhaps they even hung out together, I thought, imagining Matilda Rowley dropping by Snow's house for a round of parlor games with poor Buck Finlay.

Outside, the lost boy was still on the bench, only now devouring a pizza slice, perhaps the gift of a good Samaritan. The geezer was over by the bike rack chatting up a young man in a helmet and bicycle pants. The dazed look on the cyclist's face told me he'd gone down the rabbit hole. I cast a smile in his direction. Then, reaching for the door handle, I turned back to the lost boy on the bench. He was gone.

The Rowley House exuded charm. Decked out in scalloped shingles, gable trim, dormered windows, and pansy-filled planters, it rivaled the Painted Ladies in San Francisco. Collecting our bags from the trunk, I gazed up at the narrow turret atop the building's third story, calculating the dates in my head. According to Jesse, the house was built in 1870 and then renovated some seventy years later, meaning the elevator was installed in 1940, supposedly enduring another seventy years of wear and tear. Not to mention a fabled haunting. But then, the exterior looked well-tended.

"Do you know if the Cartwright family maintains their elevator?" I asked Carrie.

"If Matilda's temperament is anything like Francis's, probably not." She shrugged and climbed the front porch.

I huffed and puffed after her, both bags in hand, weighed down from the strain of traveling. When we pushed through the front door, I gratefully set down the suitcases and let their wheels do the work. My own bag being the heavier of the two, thanks to a quick detour to a state liquor store earlier.

A bespectacled gray-haired woman jumped up from a mahogany and red velvet sofa, her bearing unexpectedly spry. Removing her glasses she forced a smile, and cried, "Why Carrie Tanner, is that you?"

Carrie's face fell. "Hello, Sister Cartwright. So nice of you to remember me."

"Well, of course I remember. How are your parents? I haven't seen them since the ward boundaries changed. Come to think of it, why are you here and not with your folks?"

"This is my employer, Matt Ryan," Carrie went on. "We've booked a reservation—"

"Oh, yes, Mr. Ryan." Sister Cartwright stepped behind an ornate desk, its only visible contents a slim laptop and a large vase of long-stemmed red roses. Glasses back on her nose, she tapped her keyboard and peered at the screen. "Says here you've booked two rooms. Will your second party be arriving later, sir?" she asked.

"The second room is for me," Carrie explained, beating me to the punch.

Sister Cartwright snatched the glasses from her face. "You're not staying with your folks?"

"Mr. Ryan and I are here on business."

"*Business*? What does your mother have to say about this?"

Carrie remained poised. "I imagine I'll find out soon enough. But for now, we'd like to check in, assuming our rooms are ready."

"They're ready, but I'm not sure I am." Cartwright lodged a hand on her hip. "What will I say to your mama when I see her next? How will I explain you stayed here and not with her?"

"You needn't. Anyway, you're in different wards, so ..."

Backing away from their exchange, I took solace in my surroundings. What was now the hotel lobby felt like what the original living room might have been, with its lace curtains and cozy period pieces, a medley of doilies, candles, and ruffled lampshades. One wall was devoted to a quartet of family portraits, each in a carved wood frame with an engraved brass nameplate. I took out my glasses to read the engravings. Three generations of Cartwrights, including a younger version of our current hostess, all formally posed. The fourth frame was the most elaborate and featured a sepia tinted picture of "Rutherford and Matilda Rowley." The young bride's neatly coiffed hair was parted down the middle, and a prim collar rode high along her neck. But there was plenty of mischief in her dark eyes. I couldn't help but smile back at her. Then I turned to see Carrie collecting our room keys.

"Elevator's around the corner," Sister Cartwright told her. "Also Matilda's vase. If you'd like you can purchase a rose for her. They're one dollar apiece."

"We'll take two," I said. "You can put them on our bill."

Carrie pulled a couple of long-stemmed roses from the vase on the desk, and we headed for the elevator.

"I was really hoping Sister Cartwright wouldn't remember me," Carrie whispered once we'd rounded the corner.

"Face it, kid. Your cover's blown."

The elevator appeared to be circa 1940's and, if the width of its door was any judge, barely large enough for the two of us. Aside it a small table held a vase bearing an image of Matilda's face. While large enough for more than a dozen, it currently held only three roses, two of them almost spent. A commemorative plaque on the wall was entitled, "Matilda Rowley." I read the text through my glasses.

Matilda Young Rowley (1849-1872) was the beloved first wife of Rutherford Rowley and the original mistress of Rowley House. She died of natural causes at the age of twenty-two, leaving her grieving husband so bereft, he left a rose in her former sitting room every day until his death. According to legend, her spirit still lovingly watches over this house. Please leave a rose in her honor.

I frowned. "Natural causes at twenty-two?" She was a year younger than Alice.

"And then buried in the walls of this house," Carrie added.

"Seems they've left out that little detail."

"The Cartwrights have whitewashed her history," she said.

Whitewashed was an understatement. No wonder poor Matilda was so pissed off. I looked back at the elevator. One ghost encounter per day was enough. "Maybe we should play it safe and take the stairs?"

"Our rooms are on the third floor."

"OK." I heaved a sigh, took our purchased roses from Carrie, and added them to the vase. "Let's hope these do the trick. Because a woman who's suffered through what Matilda has deserves a lot more than flowers."

The arrow above the elevator swung from three to one and its door flew open. I slid Carrie a droll smile. "I'll be a gentleman and go first."

She giggled and we stepped tentatively inside, the two of us and our bags all but filling the tiny car. The motor engaged and we slowly climbed. The engine was loud but rhythmic, and every clunk of the gears emitted a puff of fragrance, delicate and old-fashioned.

"Apparently Matilda does love roses," Carrie said, her eyes on the air vent.

Roses, of course. Clever gimmick, I told myself, and then breathed in relief when we arrived on our floor and the door opened.

Carrie handed me my key. "At least Matilda's a more welcoming hostess than Francis Snow."

"Let's hope so." I looked at the brass key fob, started for my room and then paused. "What time should we be at your aunt's?"

"Dinner is always at six."

"So…we leave here at—"

"Five minutes to six." She headed down the hall, bag rolling after her.

"Got it. See you in the lobby," I said.

My room was both quaint and efficient, complete with an antique dresser, matching nightstand, and four poster bed. The bath was tiny but squeaky clean, and there was a flat screen TV atop the dresser. A laminated channel guide listed two tiers of cable channels and the clock on the nightstand told me I had a good hour and a half of relaxation ahead of dinner. I intended to make use of it.

I found a luggage rack in the closet, opened my suitcase onto it, and retrieved the scotch bottle, setting it on the dresser for later. I was pleased that the drinking glasses were actual glass, not plastic. All good. I shed my jacket and tossed it atop my suitcase, untied and then kicked off my shoes, and took my shaving bag to the bathroom for a quick refresh. Then I grabbed the remote and cable guide off the dresser and employed my readers just long enough to find CNN in the list. I turned on the set, switched the channel and flopped down on the bed.

Only instead of Wolf Blitzer I was watching a couple of professorial types sitting in leather chairs, a map of Utah territory behind them. Obviously, I'd misread the guide. I was starting for the remote when the one in tweed said, "This brings us to the subject of the Mormon second anointing. The practice began in 1843, correct, Cecil?"

I abandoned the remote and looked back at the screen.

"Joseph and Emma Smith were the first to receive it," said the one in the camel coat. "It guaranteed them their 'calling and election made sure,' or in laymen's terms, the promise of salvation regardless of how they lived their lives going forward."

"They might commit murder, adultery, even apostasy, and still attain celestial glory," said Tweed.

"Eternal sins that could only be redeemed through blood atonement," added Camel Coat.

"Indeed, in Brigham Young's day, punishment for an eternal sin necessitated the spilling of blood," Tweed replied.

I went for the remote again and clicked off the set. Blood atonement. I'd heard that turn of phrase somewhere before but couldn't place it. Maybe a little shuteye would sharpen my memory. Rolling onto my side, I drifted off to sleep.

I awoke to the overpowering essence of roses. Blinking, I checked the bedside clock. Appeared I'd been asleep for an hour, and the TV was on. Curious. I was pretty sure I'd turned it off earlier. My eyes traveled to my open suitcase. The jacket I'd tossed there was gone. Even more curious. I got up from the bed, went to the bathroom, and was splashing my face with cold water when instinct told me to check out the closet. My jacket was on the rod, on a wooden hanger, and wrinkle free, as if it had been professionally steamed. Beneath it were what I had to assume were my shoes. Only they looked different. I picked them up off the closet floor and went to the nightstand for my readers. Turned out my shoes were completely free of road dust and spit-shiny polished. Back on the TV, the same two dudes were still there and still talking about the second anointing. I looked around the room, inhaling the sweetness of rose perfume.

"What are you trying to tell me, Matilda?" I asked aloud.

She didn't reply.

I arrived in the lobby to find Sister Cartwright perched on the red velvet sofa with a paperback. She spied me over the top of her glasses and set the book face down in her lap. "Hello, Mr. Ryan, is your room satisfactory?"

"Very."

"Let us know if you need anything." She picked up her book and then hesitated. "We also offer complimentary shoe-shines."

I glanced at my feet and then back at her. "Thanks."

She smiled and went back to reading.

The grandfather clock in the corner told me Carrie was already two minutes late. I went to cool my heels by the window, eeriness creeping up on me. Had one of the hotel staff entered my room while I slept and tended to my scuffed lace-ups? It was unsettling to think so, but not as unsettling as my earlier assumption, that it was the work of Matilda Rowley's ghost. I looked over at the vase of roses. One dollar a pop. While I couldn't explain my experience on Francis's porch earlier, the "haunting" at Rowley House was obviously a gimmick. Buy Matilda some roses and she'll take you to your room in her elevator and even shine your shoes. I resolved to chain lock my door tonight.

"Sorry I'm late," Carrie said, somewhat out of breath. "I had to take the stairs. The elevator took me down to the second floor and then back up to the third. When I pushed 'one' again it didn't respond."

I refused to be drawn in. No more hocus pocus for me. "It's an old elevator. Probably needs new parts."

"That or Matilda isn't keen on me going to this dinner."

"It's family."

"Yes, but you don't have to go, Ryan. You can bail, right now."

"What? And go hungry?"

"Bud and Wilma's diner is two blocks away."

"I don't know Bud and Wilma." I pouted. "I'd have to eat all by my lonesome."

"Maybe you could ask Matilda to join you," she replied, her voice thinning.

"You want me to eat with a dead person?"

Carrie squeezed her eyes shut. "*Fine*. Let's get this over with." She took off toward the door.

"I don't like eating with dead people," I said, striding after her.

Minutes later we were pulling up in front of another fine old Victorian, Carrie on the driver's side, severe and focused, me tilted back in the passenger seat. A litter of tow-headed boys were romping around the broad front yard, all of them in matching striped t-shirts.

She shifted into park and then pounded the steering wheel. "Jesus Christ on a bike."

I pulled my seatback forward. "Where the hell did you pick up that saying?" When she didn't respond I added, "And what the hell prompted you to use it?"

"My nephews are here. Meaning my sister is, too."

"I didn't know you had a sister." I unbuckled my belt.

"I have three, also two brothers. But Grace is the only one of us who stayed in Utah. Although not around these parts, clear up north in Bountiful."

"Is she older or younger?"

"Older by eleven months. We're Irish twins. Also she's my mother's favorite."

"How so?"

"That would involve a considerable amount of translating." Carrie unhooked her own belt. "The short answer is she goes to church, stays home with her kids, and intends to keep having them. Plus she can build a to-scale model of Disneyland out of popsicle sticks and a glue gun."

"To-scale or not, I think I'd pass on Space Mountain," I joked.

She rested her head on the steering wheel.

Sighing, I gazed out at the boys. There were four, two of them looking like twins, and all of them in matching blue shorts. I wondered if they were home sewn. "Listen, Carrie, forget what I said earlier. Truth is, you really don't have to go through with this. Grown-up kids don't have to mind their parents."

"I know." Carrie leaned back against her seat. "But my aunt's cooked, and I should at least see my dad."

"Are you sure?"

"I am. Could we make it quick though?"

"Absolutely. In fact, I'll be your excuse. We have to leave right after dinner so you can work on all that research I dumped on you last minute."

She smiled over at me. A tragic smile, but at least a smile. "Thanks, Ryan."

We got out of the car and she jogged ahead toward the boys. "Hello, monsters."

"Aunt Carrie," the four hollered and then group tackled her, so roughly I feared they might take her down. She held steady, though, and waved me over.

"May I present my nephews. The twins are Derek and Jimmy. They're both four."

"Four and a half," the one on the right corrected.

"And this is Caleb, and Kirby, he's the oldest. Boys, this is my boss, Mr. Ryan."

"Nice to meet you, Mr. Ryan," Kirby pronounced, an adolescent crack in his voice. We shook hands and he looked me straight in the eye, a sign of good breeding.

"Why is he *Mr.* and not Brother?" Caleb asked.

"Because, *dork*, he's not Mormon," Kirby groaned, weakening the whole good breeding assumption.

"Why aren't you Mormon?" Caleb said.

"Now, boys," Carrie said.

"It's all right." I turned to Caleb. "Because my mom wanted me to be Catholic instead."

"What's that?" said the twin on the left.

Then Caleb again. "Do you like being Catholic?"

"Not much. Didn't work out for me."

Caleb and Kirby nodded, seeming to approve.

The screen door flew open, and a young woman stepped out onto the porch, a yellow-haired baby girl on her hip. First glance and I had a déjà vu of Carrie holding little Ryan. Second glance and I saw that the woman's hair was a shade darker and her waist a tad thicker. But the eyes were the same periwinkle blue.

"Hello, Grace," Carrie said.

"Well, if it isn't my busy and important sister. Come all the way from California," she announced. Then to the boys, "Time to get washed up for dinner."

The nephews barreled into the house, Carrie smiling after them. "This is my boss, Matt Ryan," she said to Grace.

"Hello, Mr. Ryan." Grace stared back at me, just long enough to make me uncomfortable.

"Nice to meet you," I replied, "and please call me Ryan."

"Hi, there, sweetie." Carrie squeezed the baby's foot. "She sure has gotten big."

Grace shifted the child to her other hip. "Well, it's been a while."

"What brings you down from Bountiful?" Carrie asked her.

"Why, you, of course. We never see you now that you've taken a job."

"Speaking of my job. I'm only having dinner. Then I have to work."

"Work? In Parowan?"

"Yes, Grace. That's why my boss is here."

Carrie mounted the steps and Grace and I followed. When we got to the porch, I held the screen door for the ladies.

"You brought the boss, but no kids?" Grace asked.

"I'm on a business trip, Grace," Carrie replied. "The kids are home with Paul."

"You left poor Paul with all three kids?"

Carrie swung around mid-threshold and huffed a sigh at her sister. I pulled back the door as far as it would go.

"Paul's fine," she said. "I just talked to him."

"Nice of you to check in," Grace replied, the child in her arms squirming.

"Did Jordan drive down with you?" Carrie asked as she drifted through the doorway.

Grace shifted the child to her other hip. "Heavens, no. He has to work."

We walked into a roomful of menfolk, all of whom were delighted to see Carrie. I stepped aside to let them congregate around her. Grace, meanwhile, lingered at my side, again with the staring.

"Is something wrong?" I asked.

"You're not what I expected," she said, and then slipped around the corner, leaving me to wonder what the hell she meant by that. Maybe she'd never seen a Catholic before? Then a gentle country twang called out my name.

"Hi Jesse," I said. "Nice to see a familiar face."

"And I'm happy to see a rational one." He laughed. "Welcome to our crazy family."

"We've all got one," I said.

"Yeah, well, you're about to experience Mormon crazy."

"This is a fantastic house," I said, taking in the carved moldings and grand fireplace. It was more impressive than the great room at Rowley House.

"Thanks. It's been in the family since we built it back in 1873."

"Any ghosts?"

"None that I know of. I don't think our ancestors wanted to stick around any longer than they had to."

"Oh, good, you found Jesse," Carrie said. She came toward us, her hand tucked inside the elbow of a tall, slim gentleman. Two matching grins and four bright periwinkle eyes. "Ryan, this is my dad, Max Tanner."

He extended his hand, and I shook it. Right off the bat I liked him. I liked his firm handshake, I liked that he'd raised such a terrific daughter, but even without all that, how could I not like a guy named Max?

"Mr. Ryan, I'm pleased to meet you. I've heard lots of good things about you."

"Likewise, sir. Please call me Ryan."

"I'd better go see what's left to do in the kitchen." Carrie gave her dad's arm a squeeze and then disappeared through the adjoining dining room. It was elegant as well, and currently trafficked by women in a bustle over putting food on the table. A basket of rolls passed by. After that a Jell-O salad. My stomach growled.

The void made by Carrie's absence was filled with an avalanche of introductions. Grandpa Jack calling out, "Company, company, company!" An intense mumbler named Frank. Carrie's Uncle George, who had just advanced to the Silver Level, whatever that was. Given his judgmental posture I assumed it referred to church status. Also two strapping brothers named Kessler—Bo and Kip if I'd heard right—pumping my hand at a full arm's length and then turning away abruptly, as though insulted. It was becoming increasingly clear that I was causing offense, but, other than not being a Mormon, I couldn't figure why. Then the call for dinner drew us reverently to the dining room. A stout buxom woman who introduced herself as "Carrie's Aunt LaFawn" pointed me to a seat at the table.

"We'll put you here, Mr. Ryan, and Jesse across from you. Max, you sit there, next to Mr. Ryan—"

"No, wait, Aunt LaFawn." Carrie hastily set a gravy boat on the table. "I'm sitting next to Ryan. Daddy can sit across from me."

"Now, Carrie." A pale, petite woman in a gingham checked blouse and denim skirt stared her down. "You must be by us so you can hear about Grace's fabulous new calling. She's the new Relief Society Personal Enrichment Leader."

"Ryan," Carrie said. "This is my mom, LaRae Tanner."

Having just taken my seat, I shot up and came around the back of my chair.

LaRae eyed me uneasily. "Mr. Ryan."

"It's nice to meet you, Mrs. Tanner."

I extended my hand. She hesitated before taking it.

"Nice to meet you, too." She yanked her hand back. "My husband and I are pleased that Carrie is enjoying such a diverse circle of friends out there in California."

Since I was as white as she was, I could only conclude by diverse she meant Catholic. "Thank you, ma'am. I just had the pleasure of meeting Mr. Tanner."

"Now, Mom," Carrie said. "Mr. Ryan is my guest, and I'm going to sit next to him." She removed her jacket and draped it over the back of the chair next to mine.

LaRae's lips trembled, and she listed forward a bit. I automatically raised my hands, in order to brace her fall. Instead, she gripped the side of the table and burst into tears. I backed away, stunned. Would it help if I told her I was a lapsed Catholic?

Carrie shut her eyes for a second. "It's my bare shoulders."

I looked askance at her sleeveless blouse. Carrie leaned in and whispered, "She can tell I'm not wearing the angel underwear."

"Don't tell *him*." LaRae fled to the kitchen.

"I'll be right back," Carrie said.

I sank into my chair, lamely studying the table setting. My dinner plate was rimmed with tiny pink and yellow rosebuds. Likewise, the smaller salad plate. Beyond them, the boat of steaming gravy looked rich and brown and delicious, but in the wake of LaRae's outburst, I wondered if I still had the appetite.

Across from me, Jesse and Mr. Tanner settled into their own seats.

"So you've met my Aunt LaRae." Jesse grinned.

"Mr. Tanner, I'm afraid I've done something to upset your wife."

"Please call me Max. And it's not you, Ryan." Max picked up his cloth napkin and delivered it to his lap. "It's between Carrie and her mother. They'll work it out."

Unfolding his own napkin, Jesse raised a skeptical eyebrow at his uncle.

"One thing, though," Max added. "You might want to keep a low profile around LaRae. It's in your best interest."

Jesse snickered.

"What's so funny?" I asked.

He shook his head. "My Uncle Max is right. In fact, except for Carrie, you should probably steer clear of all the women. Just hang with us."

Lips parting, I leaned against the back of my chair.

Carrie returned with a heaping bowl of mashed potatoes. "Here you go, Daddy." She set it in front of Max's plate. He patted his stomach.

Jesse grinned. "You plan on sharing any of those potatoes, Uncle Max?"

"Not sure," Max replied.

"*Share*? No way." Carrie slipped her jacket back on. "But he will be bribed."

She sat down beside me, casting an affectionate gaze on her old man. Next to her the Kessler cousins were going on about chicken feed. Crumbles versus pellets. While across from them, Grandpa Jack leaned sideways to listen to whatever Frank the Mumbler had to say. I was still a bit unnerved by Max and Jesse's warning about the women, not to mention LaRae's meltdown. But I couldn't help but appreciate the cheerful family banter and sumptuous feast before us. Anyway, I needn't fear, as the ladies were all congregated at the opposite end of the table. LaRae had brightened considerably, racing back and forth between her granddaughter's highchair and the kitchen, where I presumed the boys were eating. Her sister, LaFawn, was enjoying a long belly laugh alongside Frank's wife, whom Jesse had called Minnie. Grace was center stage describing her role at some church activity.

"Oh my heck. Can you believe I'm LaRae's daughter and I forgot to bring *the glitter*?" she said, to the ladies' amusement.

I leaned over to Carrie. "What does a Personal Enrichment Leader do, exactly?"

"She teaches the women how to sew, craft, and cook," Carrie whispered, furthering my confusion.

"Why would anyone need to do that?" I asked, taking in the mythic amount of food the women had just served. Clearly these skills were embedded in their DNA.

A clink of a knife against his crystal goblet turned our attention to Carrie's Uncle George. He cleared his throat. "I want to thank LaFawn and LaRae for this amazing meal."

Murmurs of gratitude traveled the room.

"But before we partake, we must ask a blessing on the food." George bowed his head and folded his arms across his chest, the rest of the family following suit. Unfamiliar with this posture of prayer, I did my best to mimic it, while Uncle George asked his Heavenly Father to "bless this food that it might nourish and strengthen our bodies."

Then at the sound of "amen" the bowls and platters began their orbit. I had some of everything. Meat, potatoes and gravy, carrots and green bean casserole, orange Jell-O and some sort of Cool Whip invention, two homemade rolls, and a couple of those little sweet pickles my grandma always put out on her table. Needless to say, it was all delicious, and, despite my somewhat chilly reception, I was grateful to be here with a living breathing family rather than alone at the diner with an invisible dead person. I raised my waterglass and tipped it to the end of the table. "Ladies, this is wonderful, thank you."

LaRae glanced up from slicing carrots onto her granddaughter's highchair, apparently startled, while Aunt LaFawn managed a strained "you're welcome." Then both women looked to Grace, who was now explaining next week's Personal Enrichment activity. Something called "Speed Quilting." I went back to my meal, paying vague attention to the conversation, until Uncle George began boasting to Max about his upgrade to the Silver Level.

I leaned toward Carrie again. "Is the Silver Level that second anointing you and Jesse were talking about?"

She giggled. "My uncle is involved in a multi-level marketing venture. But that reminds me. Jesse, you were going to explain the second anointing to Ryan."

Jesse set down his knife and fork and finished chewing. "Well, I think I've already covered the essentials. It's a secret ceremony offered to elite church members guaranteeing their salvation regardless."

"Elites like Mitt Romney?" I asked, my mind jumping ahead to Dennis Newsome.

"That's just a *ru*-mor," Carrie sang sweetly, ending on a minor note.

"It doesn't seem likely," I admitted. Why would Newsome want such a thing? Why would Romney? They needed votes, not magic.

"It is unlikely," said Max. "But it also wouldn't surprise me." He helped himself to more potatoes.

Carrie balked. "Does that mean *you* have the second anointing, Daddy?"

"Me? I'm just an old coot from Parowan." He chuckled.

"He's not denying it." Jesse winked. "And we'll never know because it's a secret ceremony."

"You mean sacred, not secret," Uncle George declared, clearly annoyed.

"Right, Dad," Jesse said to George, and then to Max, "so, Uncle, come clean about what goes on during those anointings. Is it true they wash everyone's feet?"

"No. Just their brains," he replied.

Carrie, Jesse and I laughed. Max shoved some potatoes in his mouth, and Uncle George glowered at the lot of us. To Carrie's left, the Kessler cousins discussed some girls they'd met at a church dance. Across from them, Grandpa Jack and Frank the Mumbler were intent on cleaning their plates. Meanwhile, down at the other end, Grace had switched from crafts to recipes. Something she called "Family Night Fudge."

Looking back at Max, I caught a glint in his eye and was reminded of my own father, who used to claim that while the rest of us were at Mass, he and God were sitting at the kitchen table reading the funny papers.

"The second anointings from the Brethren are just about status, though, right?" Carrie asked Jesse. "Not the same as the fundamentalist Mormons who take the whole thing literally."

"Oh, sure," he said. "The fundies are a different matter. In the mainstream LDS Church, the pathway to leadership is sort of like that private elevator Romney had at Bain Capital. VIPs only. But in the fringe church, anyone can be a prophet. Just got to have charisma, chutzpah, and some evidence of the Lord's endorsement."

"Evidence like a magic rock?" I asked.

"Exactly," Jesse said, draining his water glass.

"So, how goes this case you're working on?" Max asked.

"Slowly." I volleyed a glance at Carrie, not sure how much of the gory details she'd want me to share with her dad.

"We seem to have hit a dead end here in Utah," she said. "Probably be heading home tomorrow, don't you think, Ryan?"

"Probably." I pushed back from the table, my hunger sated and my mind wandering. I thought of those professors on TV earlier. *They might commit murder, incest, even apostasy, and still attain celestial glory.* Could there be folks out there who actually believed that? In the fringe groups, maybe, like Jesse said. But why would a guy like Newsome go fishing online for the stone? The notion that he wanted to exchange it for this second anointing didn't quite cut it for me. Especially if it was just a status symbol. Newsome already had status.

"We've two kinds of pie. Cherry and rhubarb." Carrie snatched up my empty dinner and salad plates. "Which will it be?"

Rhubarb. I hadn't had that since … my grandma's pickles. But then I loved cherry, too. "Wow. Tough decision."

"Don't make him choose," LaRae scolded as she collected Max and Jesse's plates. "He'll have some of each, and a scoop of homemade vanilla on the side."

"*Homemade* ice cream?" I asked.

"Carrie's sister Grace whipped it up this morning," LaRae replied. "She refuses to serve store-bought."

I caught Carrie's eye. She smiled sweetly.

The women cleared the table with military efficiency, the door to the kitchen swinging to-and-fro. Snippets of chatter drifted into the dining room. Talk of recipes merged with food storage and then moved on to budgeting strategies. Kirby, Caleb, and the twins, still out of sight, contributed their own competing chatter. Meanwhile, Grace's youngest child remained in her high-chair, sucking on her sippy cup, and hopefully content for the time being. Because if the kid did start to fuss, it was doubtful any of the males around this table would have the slightest idea what to do.

"So, Jesse," I said. "Did you say the mainstream church guarantees salvation in their second anointings?"

"I believe so, yes," he replied.

I shifted in my seat. "That's a pretty powerful promise. Even for a casual believer. Might some mainstream Mormons take it beyond the status symbol?"

"Oh, undoubtedly," Jesse said. "There are plenty of kooks within the rank and file. Always have been. Only difference is they've got to keep their crazy to themselves, whereas the fundamentalists can wear it openly."

"So a mainstream Mormon might also want a seer stone for prophetic reasons?"

"No," Uncle George growled.

Jesse ignored him. "Given our history, not to mention our doctrine, it's possible."

"Your great-grandfather had a seer stone," said Max.

"Exactly, Uncle Max. The magical practices don't date that far back. Same with polygamy, they're still part of the doctrine."

"Stop talking about this nonsense," Uncle George barked. "It's heresy."

"It might be heresy," Jesse replied. "But it's not nonsense."

George shot his son a nasty look and then turned kindly to me. "I assure you, Mr. Ryan, we no longer believe in seer stones or polygamy. Today

Mormons are just average, run-of-the-mill Christians."

Nodding politely, I thought again of Gordon Hatcher's assurance. *We're just nice, normal, hard-working folks, like the rest of the world.*

"Average, run-of-the-mill Christians don't dream of having their own planet someday," Jesse observed.

Max choked out a laugh. He covered it with his napkin.

Uncle George pounded the arm of his chair. "You mind your manners, son."

"I'm sorry, Dad," Jesse said quietly, "but facts are facts and history is history."

"Oh, you and your history and facts and highfalutin college degrees," Uncle George went on, his voice escalating. "All they've done is made you prideful."

The table plunged into an uncomfortable silence, all eyes fixed on Jesse and Uncle George. Even the lone female had set down her sippy cup to watch. It was no wonder Jesse was hesitant about announcing his new job in town, what with his dad's attitude toward his profession. I cast a sympathetic glance his way.

Then a fury of ladies' voices drew our attention toward the kitchen. The door swung open, and Carrie blew into the dining room, Grace on her heels. Each had three dessert plates balanced in hand.

"Why would you think, much less say, such a thing?" Carrie plunked pie and ice cream in front of Max, then Jesse, then Uncle George.

"You can't hide it, Carrie," Grace replied, "*Everybody* knows. Except poor Paul, of course." She delivered my dessert. Two generous wedges of rhubarb and cherry with a mound of ice cream on the side. My mouth dropped in amazement.

Carrie rounded the table and braced herself on the back of my chair. "We're leaving as soon as I finish serving the pie," she whispered.

OK, I mouthed and looked back at my plate. Ordinarily I would wait for the hostess before starting. But in the urgency of the moment, my survival instincts kicked in. I downed a healthy forkful of rhubarb. It was tart, juicy, not a bit too sweet, and surrounded by a light, flaky perfection of crust. I audibly moaned.

Max chuckled. "One thing that's always been true about us Mormons. We make good pie." He took his own bite, making me feel less obvious.

"That's for sure." I greedily dug in again, this time to a burst of cherries and an ecstatic floe of creamy vanilla. A combination destined to stalk my dreams for nights to come. I was halfway into another moan when a to-do down the table interrupted my enjoyment.

"Oh my heck. He's *not?*" Kip or Bo Kessler exclaimed.

"Nope." Grace hurried to the kitchen.

I looked over at them, confused.

"Don't worry about it, Ryan," said Jesse.

"Just enjoy your dessert," Max added.

I nodded and then went for another bite. It stalled halfway to my mouth. "I'm sorry. I guess it's the detective in me. But I'd really like to know what's going on."

"They thought you were gay," Max said flatly.

"Why?" I set down my fork.

"Because you used to live in San Francisco," said Jesse. "Hence, my mom and aunt drew that conclusion."

"Who's gay?" asked Uncle George.

"Nobody, Dad," Jesse said, and then back to me, "I'm afraid those of us who knew better didn't bother to correct them."

I shrugged my shoulders. "I don't mind if they think that."

Jesse sighed. "It appears they no longer do."

"So now I'm straight?"

"I'm afraid so," said Max.

A growing volume of female chatter was coming from across the room. This was all very peculiar. Had I inadvertently made a pass at one of the women?

"What made them decide I'm straight?"

"You're not wearing hot pink," Carrie explained, as she sat down to her own dessert. One sliver of cherry pie, sans her sister's homemade ice cream.

"Well." I mustered a laugh. "I don't suppose it matters."

"Ryan, we need to leave," Carrie said under her breath.

I looked longingly at my plate. "Shouldn't we at least finish, you know, out of politeness?"

Carrie put her cloth napkin on the table. "Thank you, Aunt LaFawn, and Mom. It's been lovely. But Ryan and I have to go. We've still lots of work to do."

"*Work.*" Grace honked a laugh. "That's not what I'd call it."

LaRae hung her head, apparently to weep.

"They think we're having an affair," Carrie explained.

I gulped and then paused to process this. "Why?"

"Because you're straight."

"But I'm *not.*"

Jesse shook his head. "They're not buying it."

"No. I mean I'm not…*we're not*…having an affair." I looked down the table. Kip or Bo arched a brow in my direction. I cringed.

"Shall we go?" Carrie started to stand.

"No." I stopped her with a hand on her forearm. "Listen up, everybody. There's something I want to make clear." Carrie whimpered. I carried on. "Carrie is a happily married woman, and I am a happily single straight man. But that's irrelevant because Carrie and I share a professional relationship that has nothing to do with our marital status or sexual orientation."

Confident that I'd put the matter to rest, I picked up my fork and began to cut off a chunk of rhubarb, the surrounding silence seeping in around me. Fork in hand, I looked up slowly and panned my audience, starting with Carrie, who buried her face in her palm. The rest just stared. The men's faces seemed a mix of distaste and envy. But the women were clearly aghast, most notably LaRae, whose hands were covering her granddaughter's ears.

Grace's shrill voice punctured the void. "Oh my heck. This really is how they all talk out in California."

"Indeed." Carrie came to her feet. "It's time we Californians left."

Grace smirked. "In a hurry to get back to the hotel, are we?"

Carrie shoved her chair against the table and stared down her sister. "When are you going to stop judging?"

"When are *you* going stop flaunting your worldliness?" Grace countered.

"That's enough, girls," Max snapped.

Carrie exhaled. "I'm sorry, Daddy. But there's nothing going on between me and my boss, and I really do have research to do tonight." She checked her watch, started to speak, and then checked it again. "Come to think of it, Ryan needs to get back to his own room to watch his future son-in-law's new sitcom."

I set down my fork. *Great.*

The table came back to life. An avalanche of "oh my heck's," "no-kidding's" and "that-so's."

"Is your son-in-law an actor?" Max asked.

"Future son-in-law, and yes, he's trying his hand at acting."

"He's one of the stars of a new show called, *Grown-ups.*" Carrie looked at her watch again. "It starts in five minutes, so we really must—"

"Why not watch here?" Max interrupted. "OK with you, George?"

"You betcha. We've got that new big screen in the family room." George picked up his plate. "Let's take our desserts in there."

"I'll get the boys," said Grace.

"C'mon, Carrie." Max looked at her fondly. "You can spare one more half-hour for the old man, can't you?"

"Sure, Daddy." Carrie leaned down next to my ear. "Ohmygod, I'm so sorry."

"It's OK."

"No, it's not," she whispered.

"Don't worry." I smiled and came to my feet. While I was hardly thrilled at the idea, it was an improvement over the suggestion that Carrie and I were having a fling. Besides, according to Alice, it was on some weird cable channel they probably didn't even have. In the meantime, I could finish my pie. I picked up my plate and motioned Carrie on ahead of me.

The family room was a portmanteau of the original parlor and a converted patio. I settled onto the end of one of two ample leather sofas. Carrie rolled an ottoman alongside me to use as her seat.

Max called to me from the opposite sofa. "What channel, Ryan?" He scooted over to make room for his wife and baby granddaughter.

"I'm not sure," I replied, stuffing down another heaping forkful. "Some obscure cable channel. I don't think many people have it."

"If it's on cable, we have it." Uncle George leaned back in his recliner, wielding a remote large enough for air traffic control. "Given it's family-friendly, of course."

Kirby, Caleb, and one of the twins bounded into the room. Grace followed, holding back the other twin while she wiped his sticky hands. "Didn't you boys mention a new show called *Grown-ups?*"

"Oh yeah." Kirby flopped down in front of the TV. "The trailer looked good."

"There's this dopey guy who keeps saying, 'Duh,'" Caleb said.

I fought the urge to roll my eyes. "I expect that's the one."

Caleb dropped onto the floor aside Kirby while the twins hopped around them singing a chorus of "Duh."

"Quiet, boys," Grace said as she sat down next to me. "It's on the Family First Channel, Uncle George."

Dirk's show was on something called Family First? That suggested a genre shift from his earlier full-length feature, *Bunz*. At least this performance would only be thirty minutes. The television clicked on and Carrie grabbed onto the sofa armrest, bracing herself.

Any hope I'd harbored that my future son-in-law's role in this project might serve to recover his dignity escaped during the opening credits. The montage introducing Dirk's character featured him on a street corner in a pair of floral boxer shorts, at a restaurant with a couple of bread sticks up his nose, and on the toilet.

"Is that your future son-in-law?" Grace asked, while her four boys convulsed in laughter.

"Yes," I replied and then finished off the last of my rhubarb, reminding myself to ask Alice if she intended on taking her husband's name.

The premise was, to say the least, predictable. Three dudes in their twenties shared an apartment. A ladies' man, a techie nerd, and a loveable dimwit. Next door were three single gals. A comely redhead, a ditzy blond, and a wise-cracking brunette. In this first episode, the three dudes moved into their new digs and checked out the neighbors.

But future plots promised the same essentials. The wise-cracking brunette would have all the best lines. The ladies' man would be off a beat in all of his. And the loveable dimwit, played by Dirk, would have barely any lines. Just grunts, groans, and various renderings of "duh." Not that this limited him as an actor. Rather, it afforded him the opportunity to draw on his encyclopedia of goofy facial expressions and gross noises.

"Your son-in-law's a hoot," gushed Aunt LaFawn.

"Handsome, too," LaRae added.

"*Future* son-in-law," I replied, "and yes, isn't he, though."

"He really is pretty funny, Ryan," Carrie said. She'd been stifling snickers for the past five or so minutes.

Finishing off my pie, I turned my attention to the screen. The brunette, having been kept up all night by the dudes' partying, was asking the dimwit if he intended to make that kind of racket every night. Dirk, fully embedded in character, stared into the camera and, with a vapid smile, rolled out a resounding, "DUH," that stretched across several syllables.

The boys heaved on the floor, hysterical. The adults were cracking up, too. Carrie and Grace had set aside their bickering to yuck it up at my future son-in-law. Same with Uncle George, Aunt LaFawn, Jesse, Frank, Minnie, Grandpa Jack, the Kessler Cousins, Max, and LaRae. Even the baby squealed in delight as she bounced on her grandma's knee.

I set my empty plate on the coffee table, rested against the back of the sofa, and smiled in spite of myself. Thanks to my future son-in-law, Carrie and her folks were enjoying thirty minutes of family togetherness. Had to admit, I owed him one.

Back at the hotel, the lobby was empty, an old-fashioned hotel desk bell replacing the laptop on the counter. Alongside it a sign instructed guests to ring for assistance. The elevator delivered us efficiently to our floor, no fuss or drama from Matilda. Not that I still fell for any of that malarky.

"Meet in the lobby around at nine," I suggested. "Maybe scare up some breakfast and then you can show me around. Fill me in on more history and doctrine while we wait on Mrs. Christiansen."

"Bud and Wilma make a mean blueberry pancake," Carrie replied.

"Sounds good," I said, although I doubted I'd want pancakes after tonight's meal.

Back in the room, my bed had been turned down with a mint on the pillow. Management, I told myself. Also the air was thick with rose perfume. Management's schtick, I told myself. But when my eyes rested on the amber filled glass aside the scotch bottle on my dresser, my resolve wavered. Sure, I could see Sister Cartwright turning down my bed. But she didn't seem the type to pour me a drink. Too much to think about after such a long day. I yawned and chain-locked the door. Then, all on its own, the TV set switched on and flipped through channels until it landed on the local news.

My resolve evaporated. "OK, Matilda, what are we watching?" I sank onto the bed, began to take off my shoe, and then froze at the image of Blair Thurgood's face. After that a live shot of Weezie Snow's house, cordoned off by police tape. My shoe hit the floor.

"While the investigation is in its early stages," a reporter on the scene stated, "sources inside local law enforcement confirm that similarities in the crime scene suggest Mr. Thurgood's murder may be tied to some recent homicides in Northern California."

My mobile rang. Carrie.

"Are you watching this?" I asked her.

"Sure am."

"Looks like we're heading back to Mona tomorrow." I pulled off my other shoe. "Better move up our departure time. Say six a.m.?"

"You got it."

I ended the call and reached for my scotch. *Jesus Christ on a bike.*

Part Four

The Lady Prophets

"I do know that there is no cessation to the everlasting whining of many of the women in this Territory."

LDS Prophet Brigham Young, *Journal of Discourses*, v. 4, p. 55

Y esterday a traveler arrived from a place I'm not familiar with. His speech and manners were oddly mannerly. More than a cut above that fool, Finlay, as was the Mormon woman who accompanied him. I detected an intelligence in him, also kindness. He climbed onto my creaking porch to pay me a call. I opened my door, anxious to engage. But he chose a hasty retreat. Alas, this is often my cruel fate. The clever ones never care to tarry.

But I am not discouraged. This foreigner promises to return. He will bring the heirs with him. Also the stone, which will be passed to its rightful owner. The bounty will be restored, and this house will come to life again. My Sisyphean task will be complete.

Only first I must meet my final adversary. The hour is nigh. I can sense his approach, even as I speak. I am anxious for our ultimate encounter, busying myself with preparations. Should I put my domestic skills to use, as I have with other patriarchs? A coat of nettles, maybe? Another stimulating poultice? Perhaps modern times dictate a direct approach. Buckshot in the backside, for example. It's hard to decide. There are just so many options when one lives on a farm!

I must settle on my method soon. Because I will—I must—prevail. Only then, will the truth be revealed. Only then will my soul be at rest.

R omano cruised through the yellow light, pushing the edge of the speed limit. She was booked on the first flight to Salt Lake tomorrow and hadn't even begun to pack. But before she left town to investigate Blair Thurgood's murder, she wanted one more round with Dennis Newsome. Why, exactly, was he so interested in acquiring a magic rock? Why might anyone be? Turning onto Windsor Court, she spotted a weathered Honda Civic parked in the drive of the congressman's McMansion, a faded BYU-Idaho sticker attached to its bumper. Not what she expected.

Romano went to ring the bell and then paused at the sound of giddy female laughter. Also not what she expected. She tilted her head toward the door. It seemed to be coming from deep inside the house. She rang the bell and the giggling stopped. "Police," she called out and rang again. More silence. Growing impatient, she was about to pound on the door when she recognized the sound of approaching footsteps. Romano backed up and took out her badge.

The door opened and a teenaged girl in baby blue footed pajamas stared back at her. "Did you say police?"

Romano smiled and held up her badge. "Yes. My name is Lieutenant Romano and I'm looking for Congressman Dennis Newsome."

"He's not here. They're out of town."

Romano pocketed her badge. "Where?"

"Um…they didn't really say."

"I take it you're a friend of the family?" Three other girls crept into Romano's view, also clad in pj's. "Make that friends of the family?"

"I'm pet-sitting the Newsome's cat," said the one in the baby blue footies. "And these are some other girls from our church."

"Having a little slumber party, are we?" Romano's smile traveled from girl to girl. The two in pink flannel nodded amiably, but the one in gray sweats looked a bit wary. Newsome sure as hell better not be here, Romano thought to herself. "Girls, I wonder if we might have a little chat."

Baby Blue shrugged. "Sure, I guess."

Romano strode purposefully across the threshold and into the marble entryway. She gazed into the elegantly appointed great room. Romano had been here before, again to question Newsome. On that occasion the house had been heady with guests celebrating his daughter's wedding. Today it was like a museum after closing time.

"Would you like to have a seat?" Baby Blue motioned to the living room.

"Maybe somewhere less formal." Romano wound around a grand piano to the dining room. A silver framed photograph stood propped on the shiny mahogany buffet. Congressman Newsome with his wife and daughter. The congressman wore his characteristic smug demeanor. But the women at his side were not diminished by him. Rather, they exuded their own presence, equal to, if not more formidable, than his.

Girls on her heels, Romano pushed through the door to the kitchen to find the large granite island littered with empty pizza boxes and the counters strewn with spent bags and wrappers. A small water bowl in the corner suggested the existence of a cat. She stopped in front of a kitchen wall calendar. "Abbottsville Grill w/Wegmans—6pm" was penciled in today's square, "Book Club" in tomorrow's. No mention of leaving town.

"Was this a last-minute trip?" Romano suggested, to no reply.

She moved on to the family room. A huge flat-screen took up one wall and half-eaten bowls of popcorn and potato chips were atop the ample coffee table. Also some brownies and gummy bears. No beverages. Although a malty aroma mingled with the scent of microwave popcorn. This was a party, all right, but not the sort Newsome would throw.

Romano turned to Baby Blue. "Where is Congressman Newsome?" she asked again.

Baby Blue bit her lip. "I don't know."

"Don't know or won't say?" Romano asked.

"It's just that…Brother Newsome doesn't like things to get back to the press."

"Well, I'm not the press I'm the police." A DVD case caught Romano's eye. She smiled. "*Sex and the City, Season Four.*" She picked up the case. "Looks like we're doing a little binge watching."

"That's not ours," said one of the pink flannels.

"It must belong to the Newsomes," said the other.

"Aha," Romano replied. "So if I opened this I'd find a DVD in here and not over there in the player?"

"You can't do that," the one in gray flannel blurted out.

Romano shot her a sharp look.

Gray Flannel's face caved. "Not without a warrant, right?"

"Probably," Romano replied. "I mean, typically, I would need a warrant to open this case. As I would need a warrant to look in the congressman's DVD player or his refrigerator. Unless, that is, I had reason to believe an illegal activity was occurring and that evidence of it might be destroyed. For example, if I thought I might need to cite you girls for underaged drinking."

Eight eyes fixed on Romano. All of them wide and slightly dilated. She set the DVD case down on the coffee table, right next to the gummy bears. "But I don't want to search Congressman Newsome's house. I just want to know where he is."

"Utah," said Baby Blue.

Romano sighed to herself. Of course. "Any idea where?"

"I assume Salt Lake to see their daughter," she replied.

"Well, then, that's all I'm after." Romano cast her eyes around the family room. Four teenagers with a fancy party house all to themselves and this is the best they could do. The Mormon version of *Risky Business.* "Stay put tonight, girls. No going out joy riding."

"No, ma'am," said Baby Blue.

Romano headed back through the kitchen "Don't worry. I won't be talking to the press. I don't much like things getting back to them either."

"Thank you," a chorus sang as they followed behind her.

When Romano got to the door she stopped and turned back to them. "Season Four. Is that the one where Samantha takes up with the lesbian lover?"

A wisp of a smile crossed Baby Blue's face. "Yes, that's it."

"That Samantha sure is a kick, isn't she?" Romano sailed through the door and then grinned when it shut decidedly behind her.

W e made good time on our trip back to Mona, trading out breakfast at Bud and Wilma's for a spectacular sunrise over the southern Wasatch Front. But the stunning display couldn't distract me from Thurgood's murder, and my unwitting part in it. I'd been so preoccupied with the revelation that Dr. Christiansen had trashed Annie's house, that I'd neglected to properly warn him.

"Don't beat yourself up, Ryan," Carrie said, twice on the ride over and now again as we were approaching our destination. She swatted my shoulder with the back of her hand. "You told him to be patient and wait for you to get back to him."

"Should have made more of an effort." I exited the freeway, Thurgood's voice ringing in my ear. *I'm the victim here.*

We pulled up in front of Weezie Snow's house to find the scene guards taking down the tape.

"So soon?" I shifted into park and turned off the ignition. While I didn't know the details, I felt reasonably certain forensics needed more time to gather evidence after such a violent crime. Twenty-four hours anyway. "Do you think they have a suspect?"

"Either that or they're cleaning things up quick to keep onlookers away, especially the kind with cameras and microphones."

A stiff breeze whipped at the remains of police tape. Carrie wrapped her woolen scarf around her neck. We got out of the car to be met by Deputy Sheriff Ricks, a taciturn stump of a man whose manner was frostier than the morning air. *Yes*, the scene had been thoroughly processed and *no*, he didn't want to collaborate with a private investigator from out of state. End of conversation. Fine by me. I caught a glimpse of Weezie peeking through her front curtains. Figured I'd rather get her take on things. But Carrie wasn't ready to give up on him.

"I'm actually a local," she said, her Utah twang in swing. "I've just come from my Aunt LaFawn and Uncle—"

My phone pulsed. Romano. I took it a few yards up the gravel driveway. "Hear about the murder?" I asked.

"Sure did. I'm in Salt Lake. My plane just landed. What have you learned so far?"

"Mostly what's on the news. Deputy sheriff here is a sphinx. Maybe you'll have better luck with him. But I warn you, he's got his own secrets to guard. Word is he's part of a local polygamist sect called the Dawson Group."

"That might explain why he was so cryptic with me. All I got out of him was a faxed picture of the scene and his insistence that the murderer wasn't *from around these parts,*" she drawled, her voice dropping an octave to mimic his.

"I take it the victim was shot though the temple?"

"Yup, and the scene was in an outbuilding. Looked like a workshop."

I took that to be the place where Dell Flake mixed up his hot sauce. From where I stood, I could see the top of a tall wood-sided structure behind the house. Seemed too big for a shop. More likely a barn. My stomach growling, I chided myself for not paying more attention when I was here yesterday, also for not picking up a truck stop donut this morning.

"I stopped by Newsome's house last night," Romano went on.

"Oh yeah? What did he have to say for himself?" The breeze swept across the dormant field, sending a faint scent of lavender my way.

"He wasn't there. I met his teenaged house sitter. Also three of her church friends. They were having a *wild* party."

Because it was Newsome, part of me wished for an *Animal House* scenario. One the congressman would be cleaning up for weeks, at home and in the press. But I knew better. "Don't tell me," I said, "marijuana brownies."

She let out a hoot of laughter. "You know, I didn't think to check the brownies. I did smell beer, though. Anyway, the house sitter told me Newsome was in Utah, she assumed Salt Lake to see his daughter. But I did some digging. He arrived in Provo yesterday on a chartered flight."

I glanced over at Carrie and Deputy Sheriff Ricks. She'd managed to engage him, all right. He was ostensibly giving her a piece of his mind, jabbing a pudgy finger in her direction. "Hold on a sec," I said, pausing to assess the situation. I didn't like the deputy sheriff's demeanor, but Carrie's serene expression told me she had things under control. I went back to Romano. "So Newsome's not here for a family reunion."

"Apparently not. He's rented a silver Lexus with Arizona plates. Better keep an eye out."

"Thanks, will do." I pocketed the phone and headed back toward the house. The deputy was making for his vehicle, obviously in a huff, and calling after his deputies to do the same. I motioned a quick thumbs up to Carrie.

She grinned and rolled her eyes. "Don't think he likes me much."

"Your Utah gal schtick didn't work on him?"

"A little at first. Then I brought up the subject of seer stones and he flew off the handle. You know, the whole 'Mormons don't do that anymore' business."

"Uh-huh. Like they don't practice polygamy?" I started for Weezie's door.

"Exactly." Carrie strode alongside me. "Probably has his own magic rock, maybe even magic glasses, too."

We climbed the front porch, and I went to ring the bell.

Weezie opened the door before I got to it, wearing a denim shirt, jeans, and a belt with a shiny silver western-style buckle. "Welcome back, you two." She waved us over the threshold, then shut and bolted the door behind. "Gabby's just put on a fresh pot of coffee."

"She has?" I asked and then remembered. The polygamists were allowed coffee in exchange for their sacrifices. Flake had taken his with cream, no sugar.

"I'll go check on it," said Weezie. "Meanwhile, have a seat."

We obliged, Carrie settling onto the mahogany settee and removing the scarf from her neck. I took the antique rocker. Same regional motif. Dark polished wood and velvet upholstery. Only made more accessible by a smattering of homemade throws and embroidered pillows. The current *Farmer's Almanac* was opened upside down on the armrest of a worn chair by the hearth. Beside it, a slim silver laptop rested on an end table. I took that to be Weezie's enclave. But not for company. When entertaining I expected she opted for the wingback opposite the settee and next to my rocker. Precisely where she landed upon return.

"Coffee's coming up," she said. "I'm afraid you'll have to settle for a reheat of yesterday's cinnamon rolls. Things were too hectic for any baking this morning."

My cellphone pulsed an incoming text. I ignored it. "You shouldn't have gone to the trouble."

"Don't be bashful." Weezie grinned. "You missed breakfast this morning. Must be half-starved."

Evidently yesterday's mind-reading ability wasn't just a fluke. I chuckled. "I've learned one thing about Utah. I never have to worry over where my next meal's coming from."

"You've got that right," a young woman said. I looked up to see Gabby walking through the adjoining dining room, laden down with a loaded silver tray. Her hair was drawn back into a wide pink bow and her manner more welcoming than yesterday's armed confrontation in the driveway. Guess Carrie and I had passed the test. Gabby balanced the tray on the edge of the coffee table and removed the coffee pot, creamer, sugar, cups, and steaming plate of cinnamon rolls to the table, the entire service on matching, blue-rimmed china.

"Thanks, Gabby," Weezie said. "Did Lorinda and Becca get breakfast?"

"They had theirs in the kitchen with the children. Now they're up in their rooms," she replied before carrying the empty tray back through the dining room.

"Poor things are traumatized by all this," Weezie said as she poured the coffee. "I'm glad you two showed up when you did. Gives us all an excuse for a little respite ahead of the chaos to come." She picked up the plate of cinnamon rolls and held it out to me. "You'll need your sustenance."

"Thanks. You may be right." I helped myself. First bite was deliciously sweet and light enough to pass for freshly baked. I set the remains on my napkin and licked the glaze off my thumb and index finger, wondering how to proceed.

Carrie beat me to it. "Did you know Blair Thurgood?"

"Nope." Weezie spooned sugar into her coffee. "Never heard of him before he showed up on my doorstep yesterday afternoon. Sure as heck didn't know he was Meredith Snow's husband. Didn't even know she was married." She sipped her coffee. "Should have figured, though. We all are."

"Do you know Dr. Snow?" Carrie asked.

"Only by reputation." Weezie returned her cup to its saucer. "Although I gather we're kin since that controversial paper she wrote says she's in Francis Snow's direct line."

"What was Mr. Thurgood doing here yesterday?" I asked, although I was reasonably sure I knew the answer.

"You already know, Ryan. He was after that fake Hatcher Stone Dell sent me. Even offered to buy it."

Mildly annoyed, I struggled to strip my mind blank. "You sell it to him?"

"Of course not." Weezie started for a cinnamon roll, hesitated, then poured herself more coffee instead. "I'd originally planned on keeping it along with Dell's other belongings."

"For sentimental reasons." I finished off the rest of my cinnamon roll, washing it back with a gulp of coffee.

"Lot of good sentiment does you on a farm. Or magic, for that matter." She mustered a laugh. "I told him it was a fake, but he didn't seem to care. So, I figured, what the heck. Took him out to Dell's workshop where I'd left the thing and was handing it to him when a call came in on my cell. The next farm over. My hens were loose in his pasture. It was getting near sundown, so I had to tend to them right away. Told Thurgood to see himself out."

"Did you rescue all of your hens?" Carrie asked, licking her own fingers.

"I did. Good thing, too, because it was dark by the time I got back to the house. Then I looked out to see Thurgood's truck still in my driveway. Thought he'd be a good twenty miles up the I-15 by then." Weezie paused, her face saddening. "Sent Lorinda out to the shop to see what was keeping him. I'll never forgive myself for that."

"I take it you called the sheriff's office," Carrie said.

"Had no other choice, what with there being a dead body on my hands. That old rascal Ricks played his role to a tee. Towed away Thurgood's truck, did a mock search of the property. Fed the press a load of BS about it being the work of an outsider." Weezie ran a hand though her copper curls. "Of course I don't imagine your California police will settle for his explanation."

"I don't expect they will." I set my coffee cup on the table. "Weezie, would you mind if we wandered out back again? I'd like to see where this workshop is. And the chickens."

"If you're thinking that somebody might have sneaked through the neighbors' property onto ours, let the chickens out as a distraction, and then hid in the barn until he was free to corner Thurgood in the shop, you'd be right. I'm fairly certain that's how it happened."

Right again. That was what I was thinking. Except for the barn. I wasn't exactly sure if there was one. Evidently her ESP had its limits.

"Got any more ideas?" Weezie asked.

I drew a breath. Seemed our hostess wasn't too impressed with our investigation so far. Couldn't say I blamed her. "Did you see any suspicious people or vehicles on or near the premises around the time Thurgood was here?"

"Gabby saw a car. She's an eagle eye, that one. Let me go fetch her."

Weezie excused herself to the kitchen and Carrie poured us each more coffee. "Do you think that's what happened, Ryan?"

Hard to say for sure without another look around the property. I was forming a reply when Weezie plopped back down in her wingback and motioned Gabby to a place on the settee.

Instead, the girl remained standing. She turned to me with a solemn expression. "While Mama Weezie and Brother Thurgood were here in the living room talking, I saw a fancy silver car stop at the top of the driveway and then keep going, kind of slow, until it was out of view. Whoever was in it wore a black cap that covered up his hair."

"Did you see the make of the car, or the license plate?" I asked.

She sighed. "I had a sideways view, so I couldn't see the plates, and I don't know car makes, just that it looked expensive."

I smiled. "That's fine, Gabby, you did good."

"Thank you," she replied primly, and then left.

"Weezie, if you wouldn't mind, I'd still like to look around out back," I said.

"Sure, take your time." Weezie pushed herself out of the wingback. "Meanwhile I'll go check on Lorinda."

"Thank you for seeing us on such short notice," Carrie said, and was wrapping the scarf around her neck when Gabby rushed back into the room.

"A car just arrived," she announced.

"That silver one?" asked Weezie.

"No. A white pickup. I think it's that lady professor from BYU."

Weezie's face lit up. "This is an interesting turn of events."

Just then I remembered the text that had come in earlier. I pulled out my phone. From Annie Christiansen: *Landed in Provo. Heard about new victim. On my way to Mona.* I returned the phone to my jacket pocket. Seemed we were about to experience a Snow family reunion.

Dr. Meredith Snow wore black jeans, a trim white t-shirt, and a denim jacket with a button that read, *A Woman's Place is in the House and in the Senate,* an ensemble that complemented to Weezie's own denim shirt and jeans. Meredith's eyes were concealed by a pair of round sunglasses with metallic lenses. She took off the shades and smiled sadly. "You must be cousin Weezie."

"Pleased to meet you," Weezie replied and the two drew together in a tight hug, as though reunited after a prolonged absence.

They separated and Meredith hooked her glasses through a buttonhole in her jacket.

Weezie frowned. "I'm awful sorry about your husband, Meredith."

"Thank you. But we'd been separated for some time. You've lost yours, too. How are you holding up?"

"The sister wives are kinda blue, but I'm all right." Her smile returned. "Haven't relied on Dell in ages. If ever."

Meredith cast her gaze around the room and then through the window. "This is quite the place you have here."

"I admire that little co-op you've got up there in Orem."

"Thanks, only I wish we had a place of our own, what with our growing circle of sisters."

Weezie ran a hand through her curls. "Maybe you should move out to these parts."

"Maybe so." Meredith sighed. "Especially now that I'm out of a job."

"'Course if you do, you'll have to deal with a lot of potential murderers."

"My specialty." Meredith winked.

Weezie clucked a laugh. "Seems you and I both got Francis Snow's genes, if not her magic rock."

"She didn't need that rock any more than we do."

Carrie and I gravitated to the room's edge, exchanging bemused looks. It was as if the energy between the two was pushing us into outer orbit. Then Meredith turned, said a kindly hello to Carrie, and locked eyes with me. "Well, Ryan, seems your killer is still one step ahead."

No other choice than to concede her point. "I'm afraid so, and I am sorry about your husband."

"Thank you." Her gaze relaxed. "Any leads yet?"

Weezie beat me to the punch. "All we know so far is that somebody sneaked onto my property to commit your estranged husband's murder while I was off chasing my hens."

"Who's that widow that hired you again?" Meredith asked.

"Annie Snow Christiansen," I replied.

"Snow?" Meredith frowned. "Any relation?"

"A direct descendant like yourself," I said.

"I think she may be here now," Carrie said, as she parted the front curtains.

"Another cousin's come calling?" Weezie exclaimed. "Well, then. I must see her in."

Seconds later we heard some lively chatter grow louder on approach. Annie's voice, while recognizable, seemed different. Stronger. Her demeanor had changed, too. She was self-assured, energized even, miles away from the frightened woman I'd met at the Swizzle Stick, much less the one who had succumbed to Newsome. It was as though Weezie had transferred some of her feisty spirit to her newly acquainted California cousin. Hard to believe, but here in this Southern Utah living room, Annie looked even sexier than she had against the view in Newsome's penthouse. Of course, it didn't hurt that she was wearing cute little skinny jeans and a sweater spun from something like that wool I'd taken off of her three nights ago.

"Mrs. Christiansen," I said. "You made it."

She smiled back at me. Polite, but dismissive. "There was another victim last night."

"My husband," said Meredith.

Annie turned to her. "Oh my goodness, I'm so sorry."

"Thank you. But we were separated. I'm Meredith Snow, by the way." She extended her hand and Annie shook it.

"Annie Christiansen."

Meredith nodded over at Weezie. "Our husbands have all been murdered. Probably by the same person."

"What a thing to have in common," said Annie.

Weezie stepped forward with a hand on each of their shoulders. "Not to mention we're cousins."

"Cousins?" Annie looked from Weezie to Meredith. "I mean, my maiden name does happen to be Snow."

"Indeed," said Weezie. "Only we aren't just any old plain Snows. We're the descendants of Francis Cannon Snow."

Annie raised her eyebrows. "Who?"

"Oh my gosh," Meredith exclaimed. "Francis is the reason for all these murders. Didn't Ryan tell you?"

"I haven't had the chance," I said, a tad defensive.

"Ryan hasn't told me anything," Annie went on.

"*I* haven't told *you* anything?" Now I was flat-out defensive.

"Not about this Francis person, anyway." Eyes still on her cousins, Annie held out her hands palms up. "He just asked me to fabricate three seer stones and then flew off to Utah with his assistant."

"You sent us here," I corrected, but they were obviously ignoring me. On second thought, they might not have heard me at all. Wounded, I looked around for Carrie. She had retreated to the dining room. I went to stand next to her.

"Maybe it's time we dropped this client," I said, leaning into her ear.

Carrie slid me a look. "I think that opportunity has passed."

"So, Ryan," Meredith called over to me. "Do you have any suspects?"

"Yes. I have four."

"Actually two," Carrie corrected.

"Right," I repeated. "Make that two."

"Why only two now?" asked Meredith.

Carrie cleared her throat. "Because the other two are now dead."

A heady pause hovered, only to be punctured by Weezie's Utah twang. "Well then, who's left?"

I heaved a sigh. "As Mrs. Christiansen knows, Congressman Dennis Newsome is also suspect."

"Your congressman?" Meredith breathed, obviously skeptical.

Annie winced. "You can't be serious, Ryan."

"I most certainly am serious. Dennis Newsome flew into town yesterday and rented a silver Lexus with Arizona plates."

"So? His daughter lives here." Annie shut her eyes. "Don't tell me you gave one of those fake stones to Dennis."

"No. I only gave out two of the three. One to Mr. Flake..." I began and then reconsidered. Best to drop the subject.

The cousins stared back at me, waiting. When I didn't reply, Weezie again broke the silence.

"That stone Dell had looked like the genuine article. Say, Annie, how'd you manage to get the Hatcher Stone so spot on? Did you have a picture?"

"I did have a picture. But, more importantly, I had this."

Annie reached for the silver chain at her neck and drew out her magical pendant.

"Oh my heck." Weezie reached for it and then drew back.

"It's OK," said Annie. "You can hold it."

"So this is the real deal." Weezie cradled the Hatcher Stone in the palm of her hand. "Maybe magic *can* do some good on a farm."

She passed it to Meredith who accepted it gingerly, careful not to tug the chain about Annie's neck.

"It's so shiny," Meredith murmured.

Annie smiled beatifically. "I polished it in my tumbler."

"It's more than that." Meredith's face brightened, as though reflecting the stone's light.

Carrie leaned toward me. "Are you feeling it, Ryan?"

I shrugged.

She spoke out the side of her mouth. "The chills. Something between divine and creepy."

"I'm with you on creepy," I whispered.

"Now I understand why somebody might want it." Meredith let the stone fall back against Annie's sweater.

"Ryan," Weezie called, "you said you gave fake stones to two people. We know Dell was one. Who was the other?"

I sighed inwardly. With his wealth and prominence in the community, Mr. Hatcher seemed the least likely of candidates. "Someone the three of you will probably also find improbable."

Meredith peered up at me. "Go on."

"Gordon Hatcher."

"Never heard of him." Annie slipped the stone back inside her sweater. "Any relation to the Hatcher Stone?"

"He's a descendant of the Hatcher who was married to Francis Cannon Snow, but—"

Annie cut in. "Never heard of her either. Until today."

I waved her off. "*But—*"

Now Meredith. "We'll fill you in on Francis, Annie."

"But…" I began again, and then waited. When nobody interrupted, I continued. "He claimed he wanted to donate the stone and any of its replicas to the LDS Church."

Meredith's eyes narrowed and she shook a finger at nothing in particular. "He's a Salt Lake developer."

"That's right," I said. "Also a mainstream Mormon who collects artifacts."

"He's a GA wannabe," Carrie added.

"And a lost boy," said Weezie.

We stared back at her.

She nodded solemnly. "The Dawsons kicked him out when he was about twelve or thirteen, old enough to notice the girls."

The Dawsons, I mouthed. That would be the same group Deputy Sheriff Ricks belonged to.

"Not surprised little Gordy Hatcher ended up so successful. He was ambitious, that one. And smart."

"Would a smart kid like Gordy Hatcher grow up to believe in seer stones?" I asked.

"Sure," Weezie replied. "Especially when the said stone belonged to his ancestor. He might think he could use it to restore his family's reputation. Hatcher men always got a bum rap on account of Zedekiah let Francis wear the pants."

My mobile pulsed. Romano. "Excuse me, I have to take this." I put the phone to my ear. A vacuous buzz suggested she was on the road.

"Ryan here," I said as I swung back through the living room and out the front door.

"Hi Ryan. Listen, change of plans."

I buttoned my jacket against the cold. "What's up?"

"We have a new vic."

My heart sank. How many more before I quit flailing around on this case? "Now who?"

"William 'Buck' Finlay of Parowan."

"Don't tell me. He was showing a house."

"Yes. An old place he was trying to sell. How did you know?"

"We met briefly. Same M.O.?"

"Yup. The deputy I spoke with said the vic was shot through the temple aside his vehicle. Actually his uncle's vehicle. Evidently Mr. Finlay had taken the car without permission and the uncle tracked it down. He discovered the body. Are you in Mona?"

"At the moment, yes. Listen, I'm beginning to suspect Gordon Hatcher may be our murderer."

"The developer?"

"Yes. Turns out he was a lost boy."

"What—" Static made the rest of her sentence unintelligible.

"I'll explain later."

"Fine. I'm coming up on Provo. Give me thirty minutes and I'll swing by and get you. You can fill me in on the way to Parowan."

"I'm heading there now."

"Without backup? Not a good idea, Ryan. The killer's still at large."

"The local police are there." I strode back to the house.

"Not so sure you can count on them."

I wasn't so sure either. "Don't worry, Romano. Just get there when you can."

Pocketing my phone, I walked through the front door to find the Snow cousins locked in discussion. Like those three witches in Macbeth, they were cooking up something.

Carrie was still in the dining room. She read my face.

"Ryan, what's wrong?" she asked, prompting the witches to cast their critical eyes my way.

I no longer had patience for their questions. "Ladies, there's another victim. I need to leave to investigate. I'll be back as soon as I can. Meanwhile, stay inside and keep the windows and doors locked. If you see anyone suspicious call the police." I started for the door.

Carrie ran after me. "Wait. I'm going with you."

"Not this time," I told her.

"But we're partners."

"No, we're not." I swung around. "I'm the investigator, Carrie, and you're my assistant, not my partner. This is too dangerous for you. I'm going alone."

Carrie took a step backward, obviously hurt. I didn't have time to repair her feelings. "We'll talk later," I promised, and then walked out.

"At least he's calling you Carrie now," I heard Meredith remark as the door shut behind me.

Outside, the wind had picked up, gusting tumbleweed and swirling sand along the roadside. I turned south again on I-15, my head crowded with competing theories and misdirected leads. Slowly the rhythm of the lonely highway, now absent billboards and big box stores, calmed my inner voice. Free of mental clutter, I spooled through my microfiche of memory, revisiting the impressions I'd taken away from my meeting with Hatcher at the airport taqueria. Custom made suit and black leather lace-ups. Helped himself to a table without ordering food. False friendliness on his face. Claimed he'd never heard of Francis Cannon Snow. Pretty sure that was false, too. Then there was his little speech about the Mormons being normal.

Outsiders like to think we Mormons practice polygamy and blood atonement, put rocks into our hats to see the future…it's been greatly exaggerated…we're just nice, normal, hard-working folks, like the rest of the world.

Blood atonement. That's where I'd first heard that odd turn of phrase. Then again from those BYU professors. Camel Coat and Tweed. What had they said about it? I switched lanes to pass a slow line of trucks. Two carrying oil, the other cattle. No recollection forthcoming.

Time seemed to accelerate the closer I came to my destination, making me edgy over how ill-equipped I was to interpret what I might encounter. Carrie was right. I did need a translator. I thought back to the Swizzle Stick a couple of nights ago. My ex-Mormon assistant sipping her martini, pointing out Francis in the picture, quizzing me on Utah's method of execution. Had to admit, she was damned good at research. Couldn't have gotten this far without her. And why was it that Utah used a firing squad? She'd never gotten around to explaining.

Coming up on the exit, I toyed with the idea of pulling off the road and waiting on Romano. But what could she tell me that I didn't already know? Best I got there ahead of time and learned whatever I could from the locals. Be up to speed when she arrived.

I exited onto the two-lane highway, passing by blowing sand and spikes of juniper, now flattened in the wind. The abandoned service station, the rusted-out pickup truck, more sand and juniper, until at last, the *Psycho* house. A couple of police cruisers and a coroner's van were positioned within a cautious distance from a silver Mercedes S-Class sedan, presumably the one Buck Finlay had "borrowed" from his uncle. Another silver S-Class, this one with dealer plates, sat off to the side. I pulled up next to it, got out, and strolled toward the gathering at the scene, Newt Finlay's department store suit a stand-out among the uniforms. He perked up when he saw me and moseyed over, the wind rearranging his hair into a hasty faux hawk.

"Hey, there, Mr. Ryan. Seems you've picked a bad day to view the property."

"Mr. Finlay, I'm sorry about your nephew." I gave his hand a quick shake, again noting the creep factor, and resumed walking.

"Yes, yes, terrible thing." Uncle Newt bobbed at my side. "But then, this house has a sordid history. I warned the boy to give the place up, stop trying to make any money off of it. Why, I was on his case just yesterday. Remember?"

Rather than respond, I left Uncle Newt to his grief and picked up the pace, wind buffeting my back, and my sights on the man I took for the deputy sheriff. He was tall and slim with salt and pepper hair. When I caught his eye he tossed me a gloomy smile, in the manner of a weathered lawman. Already my opinion of him jumped tenfold over what it had been of Ricks.

"Excuse me, Deputy, my name is Matt Ryan, I'm a private investigator—"

"From Abbottsville, California." He reached out and shook my hand. "I'm Matt, too. Matt Covey."

"Pleased to meet you, Deputy."

"Lieutenant Romano said you were working for the widow of one of the victims. I'll tell you what I've told her. Appreciate it if you could fill in any blanks for us."

"Happy to," I said, and then looked to the sound of crunching tires. The coroner's van was pulling onto the highway while a tow truck slid up to take its place.

"What's this?" Uncle Newt cried.

The wind lifted Covey's cap from his head. He snatched it back and tucked it under his arm. "Sorry, Mr. Finlay, but the car your nephew drove is evidence."

"But it's my dealership's car, not his. And anyhow, he didn't die in it." Uncle Newt waved his arm in a sweeping gesture. "He was shot out here in the dirt."

Deputy Covey maintained an impressive deadpan. "Still, the car is impounded pending examination. At the very least we'll inspect for evidence of anyone who might have been in the passenger seat. Also, there's some blood inside the vehicle that we'll want to analyze."

"Blood *inside*?" Uncle Newt hustled toward his dealership's Mercedes, wind teasing his hair into a fright wig. An officer blocked him. "Is it on the leather?" Newt stood on tiptoe and strained for a glimpse.

I turned back to Covey. "Do you think Buck Finlay's killer might have ridden along with him in the same vehicle?"

"No evidence of that," he replied. "Victim's wife claimed he was meeting a prospective buyer here at the property. The wind's been our enemy, but there are enough scant tire tracks to suggest at least one other vehicle was present, although it's impossible to pin down what make or model. We'll know more after we inspect the Mercedes." Covey twisted backward for a quick pan of our surroundings, holding up a hand to shield against a gust of flying sand. "We did search the immediate area. My guess is Finlay's killer is long gone by now."

"Did you check out the house?" I asked.

"The officers walked through the place. Nobody inside. Would have been surprised if there had been. The house has a curious reputation."

I chuckled. "So I hear. Your officers weren't afraid to enter?"

"Well, they're paid to take risks." Covey smiled self-consciously. "But they did make a point of announcing they were there on police business, not to buy the place."

"Aha."

"Lieutenant Romano said you have a suspect?"

"Gordon Hatcher," I replied, reciting what I'd learned from Weezie, an abbreviated version of what I would be telling Romano since Covey was already familiar with lost boys, seer stones, Francis Cannon Snow, and Zedekiah Hatcher.

"You must think Utah's a pretty nutty place," Covey concluded.

"We've our share of nuts in California."

The deputy laughed. "Well, if it is Gordon Hatcher, he can run but he can't hide. We'll track him down for questioning. I'll keep you and Lieutenant Romano posted."

"Thanks." We turned our attention to the drama playing out a few yards away, as the truck driver deftly maneuvered the Mercedes onto the flatbed of his tow, while an apoplectic Uncle Newt stomped his feet in protest.

The procession of vehicles left the scene, with the deputy sheriff's car bringing up the rear, and then disappeared behind a curtain of windblown sand. I looked to the Hatcher farmhouse. Even from my spot by the road, the place was foreboding. It was probably safe to assume that nobody was lurking inside, also that any potential evidence had been swept away. The tracks of Buck Finlay's Mercedes were disappearing before my eyes, likewise those of the tow. Seemed there was nothing for Romano and me to see here. With Covey now hot on Hatcher's trail, our best option was to return to Mona. I pulled out my cellphone and was scrolling to her number when an image snagged the corner of my eye.

It was sketchy at first, what with the movement of the sand, but as I edged closer, I recognized the faint outline of a heel print between the tracks of the Mercedes and a cluster of wafting juniper branches. I took out my readers, squatted down, and pulled back the branches to expose the full imprint, a left shoe, and its companion to the right. Both pointed away from the car's passenger side. The treads were man-sized and ridged like a hiking boot. A far cry from the fancy lace-ups Mr. Hatcher wore to our meeting in Abbottsville.

But precisely what a former lost boy would choose for a visit to the country. Adrenaline rushed through me. Buck Finlay did have a passenger in that Mercedes, and he was likely still here.

Rising to my feet, I pocketed my phone and readers, and studied the sparse and unforgiving landscape, wind screaming in my ears. Aside from the flattened juniper and occasional tumbleweed, the place was a moonscape. I could only guess what it might be like to grow up in such an environment, and what skills a young man might acquire in the process. Could he have hidden from the police? I looked to the farmhouse, still spooky as ever. It seemed the only option for concealment. Especially if Francis's supposed presence had truncated the officers' search.

I walked back to the rental car. If Hatcher was hiding out there, I'd need Uncle LaVar's Glock. Of course, nothing was going to protect me from Francis. I popped the trunk with my remote, opened it wide, and coughed up a nervous giggle at the sight of the 10-gauge Carrie had borrowed from Uncle LaVar. Then a shock of cold steel pressed against my right temple.

"Something funny, Ryan?"

I shifted my gaze just far enough for his image to register. "Mr. Hatcher."

"We meet again. On my turf this time." He backed off a foot. "Raise your hands and step away from the vehicle."

"Yes, sir." I complied, my eyes dawdling on the Glock 22 as it drifted beyond my reach. "Caught me before I could arm myself."

"Rookie mistake in this part of the country," he said, and then patted me down anyway, tossing my cellphone into the brush. After that, my readers. I wasn't sure which loss distressed me more.

"You are indeed unprepared," he said.

"What should I be prepared for?"

"You know, Ryan, I never wanted to kill you." Hatcher came around in front of me, his gun aimed at my chest. No business suit this time. Just a khaki work shirt, blue jeans, and hiking boots with the ridged tread I'd imagined. But the hair was the same. Despite the howling wind, his impeccable brown coif remained plastered to his skull.

"I still don't want to kill you," he went on. "Not really."

"Well, that's good news." I knew my best option was to slow things down. "Maybe we can strike a deal."

"Only one deal on the table, Ryan. You give me the genuine Hatcher Stone and I don't shoot you."

"I thought you were fine with the decoy."

"Because I figured it would lead me to the real thing. If not from Flake, from Thurgood." He pulled a stone from his pocket. "But this rock I got from them is just as fake as the one I got from you."

"Is that why you killed them? Because you thought they gave you a fake?"

"They were *fallen patriarchs*," he hollered. "Thurgood, Flake, Christian-sen, the lot of them, tied to their wives' apron strings. Only wanted the stone for their women. Even Finlay. Damned fool couldn't even stand up to a ghost."

"O-kay," I drawled. "The women wore the pants, so their men deserved to die?"

He nodded vigorously, hair helmet intact. "It was merciful."

"Merciful? You blew their brains out."

"On account of blood atonement." He rolled his eyes. "But you wouldn't understand and anyway this is a waste of—"

"I think I do understand." My right arm extended its full length, as if teacher might call on me. "The spilling of blood, it's important."

An errant gust dislodged a lock of hair onto his forehead. He brushed it aside. "In case they hadn't received the second anointing. It was essential that their blood be spilled, to atone for their sins."

"That's why you couldn't inject or electrocute them, or even just conk their heads."

"All right—"

"And *that's* why Utah still executes by firing squad." I switched from one foot to the next. "But why bother making them all kneel down and pose? Wouldn't it have been easier to just shoot them in the back?"

"Easier maybe, but not as meaningful."

"Because that's how Brigham Young's men executed Francis Snow."

Hatcher huffed a sigh. "It appears you've done your homework."

"It's really quite fascinating. So, about this second anointing—"

"Enough!" He lowered the gun for a split second, just long enough for me to take a half-step closer. Then he re-aimed, this time at my forehead. "History class is over, Ryan. If you don't want to be shot, injected, electrocuted, or conked on the head, you'll take me to the genuine Hatcher Stone."

"What makes you think that's not it?" I nodded to the rock in his fist.

"It didn't get me in the door." Hatcher tipped his head toward the Bates Motel. "If this stone was genuine, I should have been able to waltz right in and claim the place. Instead, the damned house was buttoned up tighter than my grandmother's bodice."

I couldn't help but grin at his folksy comparison. This was not the savvy businessman I'd met at the airport taqueria.

"Something else funny, Ryan?"

"No, sir. I just find it curious that you couldn't get in the door," I said, still playing for time. Surely Romano would be here soon. "The police didn't have a seer stone, and they searched the entire premises."

"Yeah, I know. First that car dealer arrived, and then the law. Caught me off guard. Luckily I'm pretty good at disappearing in the desert."

Taking in the sparse surroundings, I was wondering where a man his size might disappear to, when another thing occurred to me. "You're also lucky you couldn't get into the house."

"How do you figure?"

"Well, if you had gone inside, the police would have found you."

Hatcher cast his gaze upon the stone, still in his hand and drawing his aim off balance.

I took another half-step forward. "Could it be that the stone *is* the real deal, and that it was actually protecting you?"

His eyes darted back to me. "Seems unlikely."

Swallowing hard, I looked out at the road, searching for a glimpse of Romano, but not finding one. The *Psycho* house was still foreboding, a cyclone of sand swirling about its gabled roof. "But it's worth a shot, don't you think? Why not take the stone back up to the place, and try again?"

Hatcher paused a beat, considering, then he shrugged. "OK. You first."

I drew a long breath. Figured he might suggest that. But what could I do? My options were limited. "Sorry, Francis," I whispered.

Sand blew directly into our faces as we approached the property, a condition that might have worked to my advantage, if Hatcher hadn't been behind me. As it was, my visibility barely extended a foot, and close-range was fuzzy without my readers. When I stumbled into the "For Sale" sign I lingered, again noting the warning not to disturb the occupant.

"You're not afraid of Francis Snow's ghost?" I called back to him.

"Not afraid of any ghosts," he yelled. "Or Snows."

"All right then." I came to a full stop at the base of the front porch and motioned him ahead.

"You go on," he told me. "Stone ought to work from here."

I frowned. Figured he might suggest that, too. I mounted the newly repaired steps to the porch, heart racing, and wind heavy on my back. The front door stood closed.

"Hello," I called. No reply. I gently knocked.

"What the devil are you doing?" Hatcher yelled. "Try the handle."

I jiggled the handle and then pushed on the door. Not an inch of give. "No luck. Shall we try around back?"

"Might as well." Hatcher scowled. "Make it quick."

He gave me a wide berth as I came down from the porch, and then marched me around the side of the house. A spindly stairway led up to the back door, barely wide enough for one person. It occurred to me that if I managed to get in the door, I could lock it behind me before Hatcher could mount the stairs. Of course, once inside I would still be unarmed, vision impaired, and at the mercy of an angry ghost.

I don't believe in ghosts, I told myself, climbing the flight to the tiny landing, wind threatening to knock me off balance. This time the door cracked open. I looked back at Hatcher.

"Well?" he shouted, gun at his side.

I do believe in guns, I reminded myself and, inhaling a gulp of air, tore into the house. The door slammed behind me, and its wooden latch fell in place.

Stay calm. Probably the wind.

Distancing myself from the door, I took in my surroundings. A Victorian kitchen with a woodstove, water pump, oak furnishings, and an enormous stone hearth with a fire smoldering. *Who the hell started that?* I wondered. Then my knees buckled, and my backside dropped onto the seat of a wooden chair. For reasons I couldn't comprehend I felt compelled to stay where I was.

Outside Hatcher was shouting, his cries faint against the wind. I heard thumping. It went on for most of a minute. Then the door unlatched and creaked open again.

Several things happened, and not necessarily in this order. Hatcher stormed inside, gun still in hand. He came to an abrupt halt in front of a tall, thin hutch. On top of the hutch was an earthenware jug. Also, a rolling pin. Also, a conical contraption that looked like it might be used to disembowel a cow. All of them toppled onto his head, knocking him to the floor. His gun broke free of his hand and skidded across the room. And the hutch itself came down, pinning him to the ground. A plume of smoke puffed from the hearth, engulfing the room and momentarily blinding me. I coughed and rubbed my stinging eyes. Then the smoke vanished, as quickly as it had appeared.

There could be rational explanations for all of this. The wind. Gravity. A minor earthquake. An errant spark of flame. Plain old coincidence. But I will never be able to explain the branding iron that had somehow planted itself on Hatcher's rear, searing a red hot "S" through his blue jeans, his angel underwear, and onto his lily-white ass.

"Yeowww!" he screamed. "You wicked bitch from hell."

The door flew open again. I exhaled. *Romano, finally.*

Nope. Even better. Carrie, wielding Uncle LaVar's 10 gauge. "Freeze," she shouted and aimed the barrel at his forehead. The branding iron fell to his side.

I cracked a smile. "He's not going anywhere."

"Don't move," she said anyway.

Hatcher peered up at her, his coiffed hair in a muss, and his eyes unevenly dilated.

"Mr. Gordon Hatcher, meet my assistant, Ms. Carrie Zimmerman." I got up from my chair and crossed the room to collect his pistol. "And, luckily for me, she has been working way above her paygrade."

"Yoo-hoo, anybody home?" Weezie Snow's unmistakable voice sang through the door.

"Come in. Coast is clear," I called, and then to Hatcher. "I believe you're familiar with the Snow cousins."

"Oh, my heck, if it isn't little Gordy Hatcher," Weezie exclaimed. "Ladies, get in here. You've got to see this."

Meredith strolled across the threshold, Annie on her heels.

"Goodness," said Meredith.

"*This* is the GA wannabe?" asked Annie.

Meredith lodged a hand on her hip. "He doesn't look anything like his picture on the Church website."

"Maybe not," said Weezie. "But he looks a lot like he did when I last saw him."

"He killed our husbands so he could get this rock." Annie held up the genuine Hatcher Stone.

Hatcher stared up at the prize, his perfect hair now unkempt, and his face reddened with humiliation. His mouth opened, but no sound escaped, only a ribbon of drool that puddled onto his chin.

"Poor thing." Annie slipped the stone back into her sweater. "I don't think he's GA material."

"Not these days," Meredith observed. "More like inmate material."

Weezie frowned. "Seems he ought to get more than just jail."

"Yes, but no shooting." Meredith held up a cautionary hand to the shotgun. "He doesn't deserve blood atonement."

Carrie lowered her uncle's gun and came to stand by me, leaving the three witches to circle their prey.

"Nice work, Carrie."

She offered up a thin smile. "Not bad for your assistant, hmm?"

"I'm sorry I underestimated you. Won't happen again," I promised, and began to unload Hatcher's pistol.

That's when I saw them.

Blinking in disbelief, I asked Carrie, "Would you mind disarming Hatcher's gun?"

She propped her uncle's shotgun against the woodstove and took the pistol from me. "Sure thing."

"Thanks," I said, eyes on my shirt pocket. I patted it first, for fear I was hallucinating. Then I gingerly pulled them out. My readers. The same pair Hatcher had tossed into the brush. Their plastic frame was scuffed, but the glass looked newly cleaned. *I'll be damned.*

"What's wrong, Ryan?" Carrie asked.

"Nothing," I replied, and swiftly returned them to my pocket.

"Well, lookie here," Weezie announced. She was hovering over Hatcher, Meredith and Annie flanking her sides.

Weezie folded her arms across her chest. "Seems this job is only half done," she declared, and then reached for the handle of the hot iron. "Shall we turn the other cheek?"

The former GA wannabe shut his eyes and whimpered.

Part Five

The Succession

"I have a hard time with historians because they idolize the truth."

LDS Apostle Boyd K. Packer, *Faithful History: Essays on Writing Mormon History,* edited by George D. Smith, April 1992

Ten miles northeast of Parowan, Utah
March 2010

T he intelligent male visitor returned, only without the heirs. Instead, he was led here by the adversary. Perhaps he wasn't all that intelligent after all. But then, he did stay put when told. Proof he possessed some sense.

And the kindness was still there, along with a sadness. The latter probably due to the lack of an attentive woman.

Oh, how revenge is sweet. The mighty patriarch succumbed like all the rest, with barely a gasp. And then the cousins blew in like a storm. I love them all dearly. But my heart swells to see the stone in the hands of the one who will use it to best advantage. Finally, a real family will return to this house, along with the bounteous harvests.

My happiness is so great that a tiny portion of me regrets my departure. Of course, I can always return. I expect I will at some point, to see this land returned to its prior glory. Also to defend it, when yet another rival poses a challenge. Be they warned. I am always watching.

But for now, I bid my dear cousins adieu, with a kiss on their cheeks and joy in my heart. I must rejoin my sisters in our mansion in heaven. They have managed without me for too long

R omano watched the uniformed officers drive off in their squad car, a cloud of dust billowing in their wake. Ryan had been one step ahead. Again. Also Deputy Sheriff Covey, who arrived at the Hatcher place before her, called paramedics to collect the obviously concussed suspect, and instructed his officers to gather what little evidence they could muster. This Covey seemed like one whip-smart lawman, and with no small measure of charm. Romano turned back to the group lingering around the old farmhouse. Covey was leaning against his vehicle, Mrs. Zimmerman at his side. Both seemed engrossed in the conversation between the two Ms. Snows. Weezie shot him a wink and he laughed, a surprise of a smile cheering his otherwise stoical demeanor. Romano ran her tongue across her upper lip. She had to admit, the man was handsome, too.

The witnesses had been cooperative, given what little they could tell her. It seemed the suspect had been apprehended by a self-combusting fire-place, a heroic kitchen cabinet, and a levitating branding iron. Also Mrs. Zimmerman, who charged in with her uncle's shotgun. Not your typical crime scene. Romano had been in Utah less than eight hours, and this trip was already worth the price of her ticket. Although, back home, the chief might not see it that way. She'd have to finesse things. Bottom line, they had a prime suspect who—fingers crossed—was ready to crack like a bad oyster.

But for now, a waiting game. Questioning Mr. Hatcher was postponed until after his medical treatment, making for an empty evening ahead, and in Parowan, Utah, of all places. Romano stole another glance at the deputy, and then scolded herself. *Honestly, the man is probably married, and to a nice Mormon girl.*

"Lieutenant," Mrs. Christiansen called. She and Ryan were kicking back on the front porch steps, their proximity suggesting the ice between them had melted. "How are you finding Utah?"

"Pretty interesting so far." Romano ambled their way, again glancing at Covey.

"Even more interesting if you've got a local to be your guide," she replied.

Romano's eyes ricocheted back to Annie Christiansen.

"He's single," Christiansen added.

"What are you talking about?" Romano asked, her gaze shifting to Ryan.

"My client likes to read minds," Ryan said.

Romano was about to speak when Annie beat her to it.

"Also, he's not a practicing Mormon." Annie grinned. "Go for it. You've been out of the game for too long."

Does she know about my break-up with Davis? Romano's lips parted. *Or do I just look like a woman who needs to get laid?*

Deputy Covey headed their way, Mrs. Zimmerman still at his side. Romano flinched, then smoothed a hand over her hair.

"Well, Lieutenant, it looks like our work here is done," he said.

"And mine is just beginning," Meredith Snow announced.

Covey paused to let her and Weezie catch up. "You really thinking of moving onto this place?"

"Sure am." Meredith smiled up at the gabled roof.

"I imagine Buck Finlay's widow is the one to talk to," he said.

Romano took her own inventory. The old mansion was in surprisingly good repair, given how long it had stood vacant. But it could certainly use a fresh coat of paint. Probably electricity and modern plumbing, too. She shook her head. Even with all that, why would anyone want to live out here on this forgotten patch of dust?

"It does need some work," Meredith said.

Romano turned to see her staring straight at her.

"But this house has a special spirit about it," Meredith went on. "Something more powerful than cable or wi-fi."

The crunch of wheels on gravel drew their attention. A Lexus with Arizona plates.

Ryan pulled himself up from the porch steps and shot Romano a look. "Newsome?" he mouthed.

The car slowed to a stop behind Covey's vehicle, its driver's door opened, and a trim figure in black emerged. Romano shaded her eyes with her hand. *Mrs.* Newsome?

"Renée," Annie exclaimed. "What brings you here?"

"Your late husband." Renée Newsome pulled a *Giants* ball cap from her head, and tossed it through the driver's side window, looking like a local in her black jeans and cowboy boots. "I was in communication with him before he died, about the Hatcher Stone."

Mrs. Zimmerman stepped forward. "You're Truth Seeker."

"How did you know?" Mrs. Newsome strolled our way.

"My cousin Jesse owns the website you posted on. He traced the message to your address. We just assumed it was from the Congressman."

"Oh, Dennis wants the stone, too. Thinks *he* might channel its power." She slowly shook her head.

"But why do you want it, Mrs. Newsome?" Ryan asked.

"Keep it in the family, I guess. You see, my maiden name is Snow. Zedekiah Hatcher's first wife—" she began.

A joyous eruption forced Romano, Ryan, Mrs. Zimmerman, and

Deputy Covey to the side, while the Snow relations celebrated with hugs and laughter. Energy churned around them, something Romano couldn't define, but tangible, nonetheless.

"I'll be darned," said Mrs. Zimmerman.

Deputy Covey cleared his throat. "Strange things tend to happen here. The place has a curious history."

"Does it?" Romano met Covey's gaze. His eyes were an intense blue with rings of gold around the pupils.

"You interested?" Covey asked.

"I am," she replied, and then cheeks burning, returned to the Snow cousins. The four women were staring up at the Hatcher farmhouse, their chatter quieting.

"You know," said Weezie, "I can almost feel her presence."

"Well, then, we must pay our respects." Meredith waved them forward. The front door cracked open, seemingly on its own, and the four Snows disappeared across the threshold.

"Should they be going inside?" Romano asked. "I mean, it is still a crime scene."

"Probably not," Covey admitted. "But the officers didn't find much in the way of evidence." He grinned. "Anyway, are you gonna stop 'em?"

"Nope." She shook her head. Those four made a powerful team, and that house was a force in and of itself. Ice trickled Romano's spine. The wind, once brisk, had gone still, and an uneasy anticipation hung in the air. "But I don't feel good about this."

"Don't worry," Ryan told her. "Francis must like them. She doesn't open up to just anyone."

Romano smirked. "Since when do you believe in ghosts?"

Ryan looked to his shirt pocket, reached for his glasses, but then left them be. "Since one pushed me into her chair today," he said.

"Looks like she's already chasing them out," Carrie Zimmerman said, nodding to the house.

Mrs. Newsome, Weezie, and Mrs. Christiansen breezed through the door. When they got to the base of the stairs, Annie pulled them into conversation.

"That was fast," Ryan observed. "But they don't appear to be spooked."

Meredith emerged onto the porch and the three other cousins parted to include her. Romano, Ryan, Covey, and Carrie inched toward them, still a respectful distance, but close enough to hear.

"Still set on moving in?" Weezie asked Meredith.

She nodded assuredly. "The sisters and I will be happy here, and I believe I have Francis's approval."

"She's as much as said so," said Mrs. Newsome.

"Then there's only one thing left to seal the deal." Annie Christiansen drew the seer stone out from inside of her sweater, pulled the chain over her head, and held it out to Meredith. "We think you should have this."

"Oh my heck," Meredith gasped. "No, Annie, I couldn't."

"But you must," Renée Newsome insisted.

"Not that you need it, mind you," said Weezie.

"No, you don't need it," Annie agreed. "But while the magic exists with or without it, the Hatcher Stone—"

"You mean the Snow Stone," Mrs. Newsome corrected.

"Right," Annie went on. "The Snow Stone belongs here, with Meredith Snow and her sisters, in the Snow House." She took a step toward Meredith, who smiled shyly and leaned forward just enough for Annie to slip the chain over her head.

A reverent silence settled upon them as the stone shimmered around Meredith's neck. The gem indeed seemed magical, reflecting the late afternoon sunshine like a tiny planet. In the thickness of the moment, Romano felt the hairs stand up on the back of her neck. Then an errant gust swirled toward them, picking up soil, and temporarily blinding Romano. Shielding her face from the wind, she opened her eyes to see a fanciful dust devil skipping across the sand, and the four Snow cousins watching after it, each with a hand to her cheek.

Romano looked to Covey.

He grinned. "Like I said, strange things tend to happen here."

She turned back to the desert, now windless and quiet as a pin. *He has that right.*

With that they all scattered. The Snows caravanned down to Mona, for an impromptu reunion at Weezie's house. Ryan and Carrie left for the Provo Marriott, intent on a drink at the bar. That left Romano and Covey, or so she hoped. Annie Christiansen was right. She'd been out of the game for too long. But was Annie also right about Covey being available? *Hmm, might as well go for it.*

"Say, Deputy, do you happen to know a good place for dinner here in town?"

His expression remained nonplussed, but those blue eyes of his grinned back at her. "Sure, there's a nice little diner. Also a not-so-nice watering hole that I've been known to frequent."

"Hope your bishop doesn't catch you there."

"Actually, I've caught him there a couple of times." He winked. "Like many around these parts, I was raised in the faith but long since quit practicing."

"So…no wives back at home?"

"No ma'am. Not even one." Covey removed his hat. A curl of salt and pepper hair fell charmingly across his forehead. "Follow me back to the station so I can drop off the patrol vehicle and change back to street clothes? We can go on together in my car."

"Sure."

Romano let him show her ahead, feeling all girlish and giggly. She wished she'd packed more than just lip gloss for this trip. When they reached her car, he paused and gave her a quick up and down. Not the wolfish kind, but it made her tingle, even so.

"On second thought, maybe I should meet you at the bar later."

Her shoulders drooped. *Had he looked her over and changed his mind?* "Oh?"

That surprise of a smile cheered his face again. "I didn't bring my best clothes to the station, also the showers are on the fritz. Thought I'd better run home and make myself more presentable."

Oh my goodness. Why can't we grow gentlemen like this in California? "Don't be silly. You'll be fine as you are." She beamed up at him. "Besides, I'm anxious to hear more about Parowan's curious history."

His smile widened. "Yes, ma'am."

Romano climbed behind the wheel and then paused to appreciate the sight of Covey walking away to his vehicle. She blew out a sigh. *Best we save that shower for later.*

A lice never looked more beautiful, all wrapped up in cream silk and frothy lace, her warm brown eyes shining up at me. Her mother's gown. Her mother's eyes. And in my arms for a dance at her wedding. The band played a song I didn't recognize. But I knew it would be in my heart forever, as would the memory of this moment.

"What's on your mind, Daddy?"

"Happiness."

"So, you're finally glad I'm with Dirk?"

"Well, of course I am." And I was happy for her. Even this morning at the Hollywood Burbank Airport when I spotted a guy in a shirt with Dirk's goofy face plastered across the front, captioned with the inevitable: *DUH.*

But then, I was buoyed by my choice of traveling companions. I gazed over at Annie Christiansen. She was on the sidelines chatting up Dirk and two of his fellow castmates, none of whom resembled the parts that they played. The "techie nerd" looked vaguely bohemian while the "comely redhead," an actual brunette, sported a pair of wire-framed glasses. As for Dirk, he was decked out in a custom blue suit and tie, looking the picture of a respectable, clean-cut, all-American boy. Someone any man would be proud to call, "Son."

"Annie seems really interesting," said Alice.

"Indeed," I replied, my eyes still cast her way.

"Is it serious?"

"No." I turned back to Alice. "No more serious girlfriends for me. I'm afraid your mother spoiled me for that."

She stroked my cheek. "I guess you ended things with Angie."

"Yes."

"I hope it went smoothly."

"Oh sure. I invited her over. We had a nice talk." That was almost true. I'd surprised Angie on the porch when she was trying to surreptitiously drop off the stuff I'd left at her condo. But while, yes, I'd invited her, she had firmly declined to come inside. Moreover, I would hardly call what we had nice. Or even a talk.

"And you parted friends?"

"Sure." I nodded, hoping that in the joy of the moment Alice would look past my obvious bullshit. Truth was I'd never seen Angie so angry, so unyielding, and admittedly, so powerful and appealing. Naturally everything she said rang true. That was the silver lining to this storm cloud. Angie was moving forward without me. And was already better for it.

"So, Daddy, I have some news."

"Oh yeah? Good news?"

"The *best.*"

I gulped. "You're pregnant?"

"No!" Alice cried, pushing me away.

"Sorry. Bad call." I pulled her back to me. "What then?"

"I got the internship."

"That's fantastic." I scooped my arm around her waist and swung her around. My little girl was coming home. Almost, anyway. "When do you move up to San Francisco?"

"Well, I didn't get that one."

My steps slowed. "Oh? Where, then?"

She braced a hand on both my shoulders and beamed. "New York."

New York? I stopped dancing entirely. *Three thousand miles away New York?*

"C'mon, Daddy. Did you think I'd be moving back into my old room?"

"No…it's an office now." I forced a smile and resumed swaying to the music. "Congratulations, honey."

"Thanks."

"Won't that be a bit hard on you and Dirk, being clear across country from each other?"

The song ended and Alice linked her arm in mine, leading me off the dance floor. "Dirk only needs to be here during filming. In fact, he just landed a part in a limited run on Broadway. Shakespeare."

"Dirk is doing Shakespeare?" I half laughed, not realizing the kid was less than three feet away.

"Can you believe it?" Dirk grinned.

"What I meant—" I began.

"It's *Hamlet,*" He interrupted. "I play the fool."

I blinked. "Good for you."

"I'm kidding," he replied.

"Of course," I began, and then rolling my eyes added, "well…*duh.*"

He smiled back in that easy way of his, the way he had of winning so many people over, including me.

Alice let go of my arm and took her husband's. "Dirk has the part of Don Pedro in *Much Ado About Nothing.*"

"Does he now?" I replied. "That's a big part."

"I know, right?" Dirk drawled. "And with my limited range. But it's Shakespeare. I figure he can take it."

Now I laughed outright. "Don't be silly. You'll blow the doors off the house." I ran a hand over my head. "Think you could scare me up a ticket?"

"You bet," said Dirk.

"Daddy, do come visit." Alice squeezed her husband's arm. "We'll see

Dirk's play and the Empire State Building and the Statue of Liberty and what-ever else you like."

"I'd love to," I replied, pausing to regard the two of them. Young, in love, and utterly clueless. Their happiness was almost blinding. "Go on, now. You're missing the fun."

Alice kissed me on the cheek. "Thanks for everything, Daddy," she murmured, her mother's honeysuckle perfume teasing.

Then she grabbed Dirk's hand and was gone, disappeared into the crowd of celebrants. His old frat brothers and dates, her former flat mates and dates, even Mr. and Mrs. Z were out there, kicking up their heels. The whole lot of them dancing on my dime. Not that I objected, mind you. There was absolutely nothing I regretted about this magical evening. Not the three courses with wine pairings. Not the phonebooth sized cake. Not the band. Not even the open bar. Speaking of which…

"Nice couple." Annie slipped her hand into the crook of my arm. "You did good, Dad."

"Why, thank you, Mrs. Christiansen."

She performed a theatrical sigh. "*When* will you ever stop calling me that?"

I slid a glance her way. The case was officially closed. Hatcher had coughed up his confession, I was paid in full, and the seer stone was safe and sound. I'd even gotten over that whole business of Annie and Newsome, for the most part, anyway. But where would we go from here? Not back to the congressman's flat, obviously. But I wasn't keen on revisiting her home in Abbottsville either, with its remnants of the stale routine she shared with her husband.

The band started into a new set. *The Eagles.* Finally, something I recog-nized. "C'mon, let's dance." I tugged her onto the floor.

"Guess what?" Annie said, once we'd relaxed into a slow dance.

"What?"

"Dirk offered me a ticket to his new Broadway show."

"Really?" I tensed. Yes, I'd invited Annie to my daughter's wedding, but with the clear understanding we were just buddies. Well, make that buddies who spend the night in the same hotel room. But in the southern portion of the state where we both live. Was I ready for a king-sized bed all the way in New York? Visiting my daughter? Wouldn't that make us a couple?

She wrapped both arms around my neck. "No worries. We don't have to sit together."

"I'm not worried about—"

"Yes, you are."

There she went, reading my mind again.

"Look, Ryan." She leveled her clear green eyes at me. "I know your wife has spoiled you for other women. But we're in the same boat."

"Are we?"

"Sure. My husband's spoiled me for other men." She winked. "For different reasons, obviously."

"Obviously."

Annie nodded. "Here's what I propose. We meet up in New York this fall, just friends."

"Go on."

"We see Dirk's show—"

"Seats next to each other?"

"That's to be determined. But from there I thought we'd go on to Paris."

"*Paris?*"

"Just friends."

"Same hotel room?"

"Well, of course the same hotel room." She frowned a beat and then brightened. "Should be lovely that time of year."

"Maybe," I mumbled. *Up and run off to Paris?*

"Oh dear," said Annie. "Would that make you think of your late wife?"

I grinned. "Annie, nothing about you makes me think of my late wife."

"Is that good or bad?" Her smile wavered.

"What? You can't read my mind?"

"Not always," she replied quietly.

For a second I was reminded of that vulnerable widow at the Swizzle Stick, on the night that she walked back into my life, so long ago. "It's good, Annie," I said, and pulled her to me, humming along to "Peaceful Easy Feeling."

Paris this fall might be just the ticket. But then, that was months away. Who knew where we'd be then? For now, it seemed best to relax and enjoy the moment.

I danced Annie through the remainder of the Eagles set, and then made it halfway through a hip hop number before collapsing into a seat on the sidelines. Annie was still out there, gyrating alongside that bohemian looking kid who plays the nerd. He appeared to be teaching her some new steps. A few feet away, Alice and Dirk were moving to their own beat, with eyes only for each other.

"Sir, would you like some champagne?" A cheerful bowtie held a tray of flutes.

"Thank you, yes."

The waiter obliged, setting the glass atop the linen coated table, it's fancy cloth evidence of the very expensive dinner that had been consumed here earlier. I sipped slowly, aware of the effect the fizzy stuff had on me, and then studied the glass, my eyes zigging from one bubble to the next.

"Ryan, guess what?"

"Carrie," I replied, still observing my glass. "Where's Mr. Z…I mean Paul?"

She dropped into the seat next to mine. "He's caught up in some pub game with Dirk's frat brothers."

"Aha." I leaned back in my chair. "Seems like the perfect opportunity for you to take advantage of the open bar. I made sure it was well stocked with Tanqueray."

"Later. I just checked your voicemail."

"Why, Ms. Carrie Tanner Zimmerman, are you telling me that you checked the office voicemail during a party?"

She winced. "I know. It's a sickness."

"Remind me on Monday to look into some good health insurance plans." I sipped my drink. "Also to sign you up for class."

"What class?"

"If you want to be more than an assistant, you'll at least need an Associate's Degree in police science or criminal law. A mentor at the department will also be a plus. Romano's already volunteered."

"Oh my gosh. That's amazing. Thank you."

I held up my hand. "Don't thank me. If there's one thing I've learned from this crazy case, it's that I need more powerful women in my life." I caught a glimpse of Annie on the dance floor. Her young partner was starting to fade, but she was still going strong. "Can't get enough of 'em," I concluded, turning back to Carrie.

"Good." Carrie put on a Cheshire Cat smile. "Because that voicemail was from Mrs. Newsome."

"You're kidding."

"She wants to hire you."

"To do what?"

"Dunno. But she said you're the perfect man for the job."

I stared back at my champagne flute and swallowed hard. *Jesus Christ on a bike.*

www.ingramcontent.com/pod-product-compliance
Lightning Source LLC
Chambersburg PA
CBHW051241250626
47155CB00009B/3116